PENGUIN BOOKS

Thorne Princess

L.J. Shen is a *Wall Street Journal*, *USA Today*, *Washington Post*, and #1 Amazon bestselling author of contemporary, new adult and young adult romance. Her books have been translated in over twenty different countries, and she hopes to visit all of them.

She lives in Florida with her husband, three rowdy sons and even rowdier pets. She enjoys good wine, bad reality TV shows and reading to her heart's content.

T0333010

ALSO BY
L.J. SHEN

Thorne Princess

USA TODAY BESTSELLING AUTHOR

L. J. SHEN

PENGUIN BOOKS

PENGUIN BOOKS

UK | USA | Canada | Ireland | Australia
India | New Zealand | South Africa

Penguin Books is part of the Penguin Random House group of companies
whose addresses can be found at global.penguinrandomhouse.com

First published in the United States of America by L.J. Shen 2023
First published in Great Britain by Penguin Books 2023
002

Copyright © L.J. Shen, 2023

The moral right of the author has been asserted

Printed and bound in Great Britain by Clays Ltd, Elcograf S.p.A.

The authorized representative in the EEA is Penguin Random House Ireland, Morrison
Chambers, 32 Nassau Street, Dublin D02 YH68

A CIP catalogue record for this book is available from the British Library

ISBN: 978-1-405-95956-8

www.greenpenguin.co.uk

"Hell sent us the most evil disease and we humans called it love."
—**Conny Cernik**

For Pang, who asked for this book. And for all the people who didn't ask for it, but need it.

Trigger warning:
This book contains sexual assault and dubious consent.

Prologue

HALLION THORNE CAUGHT IN THE ACT!

By Anna Brooks, *Yellow Vault* Contributor

She's kept a high profile since the controversy surrounding her latest boyfriend, baller Kieran Edwards, suddenly coming out of the closet two months ago. Now, Hallie Thorne is letting it all hang loose on a night out on the town. That's right, my little Vaulters! You're seeing correctly. Here is Hallie Thorne showing off her nipple. And with none other than cable TV's most beloved hunk on her arm.

Next station? Has-been Celeb Rehab, if you ask me.

She may be a hit with Hollywood's men, but whispers on the street are saying Daddy Dearest cannot stand her.

Hallie

O kay. Wait a minute. Pause. Don't make a judgment.
I know it looks really bad. Not my nipple—my boobs are awesome, they're probably my best feature—but I swear I can explain all the other stuff.

So, this is the story of my downfall.

Of how every household in America got to see my nipple.

Go back to a year ago when my nip-slip picture was plastered all over internet websites, magazines, tabloids, and social media accounts. At some point, I wondered if I should get it an agent and a tiny pair of dark film-noir sunglasses. That's how crazy things got.

Not that I had anything to hide. I was, as the media pointed out, *curvylicious*. With wide hips, D-cup breasts, and a butt worthy of every one of Lil Wayne's heart-wrenching poems.

The problem was…my nipple wasn't just a nipple.

It was the nipple of the first White House baby. I was the First Daughter on a few levels.

America was obsessed with the fact that I, Hallie Margaret Thorne, the first child to be born to a sitting president, was also a royal fuck-up.

The tattoos, cherry-red hair, thick eyeliner, and community college I'd dropped out of one semester into my studies provided a certain easy-to-hate optic…

Everyone thought I *had* it easy. All I had to do was literally not screw up. But I did. Constantly.

And this last time? I'd taken it one step too far.

Yellow Vault wasn't lying. My parents *had* had enough of me. Desperate times called for desperate measures for their pretty, loose cannon in need of protection, a mental slap in the face, and a wake-up call.

Enter Ransom Lockwood.

Formidable, forbidding, frightening, and…excuse me, but *fuckable* to a fault. My new bodyguard.

Sorry, *close protection officer*.

The devil who blew up my life and annihilated whatever was left of my self-esteem.

The ornery protector who stole my heart, smashed it into pieces, then handed me back the broken shards with a lopsided smirk.

They called him *The Robot*, but I didn't think that's what he was.

He had a heart, somewhere under all those layers. Dusty and scarred, but still beating.

So all you need to know is that in some ways, that nip slip *did* destroy my life. But it also saved me. Or at least, one part of me.

The part that was worth saving.

The part that survived.

When Princesses Fall

My corseted little black dress was a mistake.

I knew as soon as I slipped into the back seat of my driver's Cadillac, my upper face covered by a sequined, red masquerade mask.

My best friend Keller was already perched on the opposite side of the seat, rearranging a stray hair in his perfect blond mane, his phone's camera serving as a mirror. He had a beautiful, golden Roman mask on.

"Hey, Den! The Chateau Marmont," I instructed my driver, rearranging the underwire of my dress.

Keller tucked his phone into the pocket of his Prada suit, throwing me a glance. "Honey, the corset looks like it's about to launch itself out of the Milky Way. What size is this dress?"

Sitting upright, I shot him an offended look. This garment

was the kind of claustrophobically tight that would later need to be surgically removed.

"Balmain only makes stuff up to size twelve," I mumbled defensively.

"Well, the zipper is probably one hors d'oeuvre away from filing a restraining order against you, so I suggest you go back and change." Keller smoothed an invisible wrinkle on his cigar pants.

Dennis glanced in the rearview mirror to see if he should turn around and drive back to my house. I shook my head. Absolutely not. I *was* a size twelve. Sometimes I was even a size ten (though definitely not between Thanksgiving and Christmas. Or Easter. Or while PMSing).

The problem with designer numbers was that they were made exclusively for trim people. I *loved* my body. Every curve and hard-earned cellulite cell. I knew, logically, designers rarely made true-to-size garments. Their ten was an eight, their twelve was a ten, and their fourteen was…well, *nonexistent*. But I never bought anything off the rack. To keep it eco-friendly, I always shopped in secondhand stores for gowns, but that limited my options pretty significantly.

"The dress stays," I announced.

"Not for long, if your tits have anything to say about it," Keller muttered.

"You're just bitter because your eyes are baggy."

"My eyes are baggy?" Keller thundered, ripping his gaze from his phone.

Grinning, I shrugged. "No, but now you know what it feels like to be dissed by your best friend. Doesn't feel too good, does it?"

Twenty minutes later, Dennis stopped by The Chateau. I squeezed my driver's shoulder from behind, squishing my cheek against his. "Thanks, Den! You can take tonight off. I'll Uber it home."

"I think I'll stay," sixty-five-year-old Dennis said wearily. "Your parents aren't gonna like the Uber idea." He'd been my driver since I was eight, and knew my parents better than I.

Mr. and Mrs. Thorne did not like it when I left the house—not because they *so* enjoyed my company. My mere and flawed existence caused them embarrassment by proxy. The nicest thing my mother had ever said about me in an interview was that I added texture to the family. *Texture.* Like I was a decorative wallpaper. And so, I didn't particularly care what they'd approve of.

I waved Dennis off. "Keller is going to be right here with me. He'll keep me out of trouble. Right, Kel?"

"As much as one can." Keller slipped out of the Cadillac, eyeing the arched entryway eagerly. "Unless whoever attacks you is armed. You know I just *cannot* with blood. Or if I get hit on by someone hot. But I'm talking Zac Efron as Ted Bundy hot. If it's just Zac Efron in *High School Musical* level, I've got your back, girl."

"If you find your Zac Efron in *High School Musical*, I won't be bailing you out for lewd acts with a minor," I fired back.

Keller raised his thumb. "I'm sure this conversation is totally reassuring to Dennis. He now trusts you not to get into trouble."

I brought my mini smartphone to my lips. "Siri, remind me to make a voodoo doll of my best friend and use it as a pincushion tomorrow morning."

"*Event added to calendar,*" Siri replied primly.

Hopping out of the vehicle, I flashed Dennis an angelic, *I'll-be-good* smile and pressed my palms together. "Seriously, Den. I'll behave. Go home. I'm sure Ethel is waiting with her special gingerbread cookies."

He stroked his chin. "She did say she's making a fresh batch this morning..."

In a lot of ways, Dennis and Ethel were more of a family to me than Mom and Dad. I'd spent more holidays with them, they took care of me when I was sick, and showed up for my parent-teacher conferences whenever Mom and Dad had been busy at a climate change summit or grilling a tech bro in Congress.

Dennis swung his gaze from my forced smile to the open jaws of The Chateau. He'd taken me here enough times to know I was bound to get drunk, rack up a bill, and end the night vomiting champagne more expensive than his suit into his back seat.

He didn't want to deal with me. Who could blame him? *I* could barely tolerate myself. Which was why I planned to drown myself in alcohol tonight.

He sighed, rubbing at his temple. "Just be careful, all right? And go home early."

"You're the best, Den. Send Ethel my love!"

He tilted his cloth hat downward. "How 'bout you pay her a visit sometime soon and tell her yourself?"

Dennis and Ethel only languished in Los Angeles because of me. They longed to go back to the East Coast, to their family. I hated that I was a part of their misery, which was why I never dragged myself to their Encino bungalow and endured weak tea and *Jeopardy!* on loop while Ethel took out her photo albums to show me pictures of the grandchildren they weren't able to see…because of me. Too depressing. I hadn't found a liquor strong enough to counter *that* guilt. Yet.

"Will do, Den."

He drove off, leaving us in a cloud of exhaust smoke. *Ugh*. We had to talk about switching to a Tesla.

Keller laced his arm in mine, gazing at the infamous white stack of bricks with twinkling eyes. "At last, we're in our natural habitat."

The masquerade ball was hosted as a fundraiser by a plastic surgery clinic in the valley for veterans who'd suffered burn scars. Keller and I had both put 5k in our envelopes, but neither of us showed up for the pre-ball dinner. Keller didn't like eating in public (true story) and I didn't like being bombarded with questions and requests about my family.

"You know…" I flipped my dyed burgundy tresses as we made our way to the bar, bypassing masked up bellboys, concierges, and maître d's. "The Chateau Marmont is known for being populated by people either on their way up or on their way down. Which category do you think we fall into?"

"Neither." Keller led me to the oaky, red bar of the hotel, with the familiar maroon stools and matching overhead chandeliers. "We're just beautiful spawns-of. Born into high society and low expectations. We're going nowhere."

Keller was the son of Asa Nelson, front man of the band She Wolf and the biggest rock n' roll legend still alive. Both our last names opened doors—not all good.

We settled at the bar. Wordlessly, the bartender Frederik, slid a Marmont Mule cocktail my way, fixing Keller his regular, Bleu Velvet. Frederik wore an all-white rabbit mask that highlighted his piercing blue eyes.

"I should take him home," Keller muttered, elbowing me.

"He seems like a bad idea."

"My favorite type," my best friend retorted. "Yours, too."

I didn't acknowledge that last part. It wasn't Keller's fault he thought I slept with everything with a pulse—a common general vibe I gave people. But it never felt good to be reminded that I was lying to my best friend.

Before we even made it to our first sip, we were surrounded by two wannabe actresses, one reality TV star, and a life coach I was certain also moonlit as a waitress at The Ivy. Everyone stood around, preening, while trying to convince the people they mingled with that their big break was just around the corner. This was how Keller and I spent our nights. Every single one of them. Partying, drinking, mingling, pretending like the world was a big, fat piñata, ready to burst and rain fat fashion contracts, *Vogue* covers, and Oscars over our heads.

We were socialites. Young, rich, and bored.

We answered to no one and were sought after by everyone.

Technically, Keller and I both had jobs.

At twenty-seven, Keller was the owner of Main Squeeze, an upscale juicery in West Hollywood known for its detox bundle, favored by Victoria's Secret models and Real Housewives.

I was an Instagram persona, meaning I got paid in luxury products and compliments, advertising products to my eight hundred thousand followers. Anything from clothes and handbags to tampons. My so-called "work" took two hours a week, but I was oddly protective of it. Maybe because I knew it was the only piece of me no one was allowed to invade or shape. It was all mine. My doing, my responsibility, my little, small win in this world.

"Isn't it funny," I mused aloud, swirling the swizzle stick in my drink. "How we can pretend like we're productive members of society and the tabloids just run with it?"

The two actresses, reality star, and the life coach evaporated from our place at the bar the minute they spotted a Netflix star who'd entered the room wearing a medieval plague doctor mask.

That was the catch about L.A. It was a great place to accumulate people, as long as it wasn't true friendship you were after.

Keller shot me a frown. "Speak for yourself. I *do* have a job. I own a juicery. I source all the ingredients myself."

"Oh, Keller." I patted his hand on the bar and held up my drink. "I'm 'sourcing local ingredients' right now. Don't get me wrong, it's an amazing hobby, but neither of us needs the money."

We never spoke of it, but I'd always assumed Keller, too, got a hefty sum of allowance each month from his dad.

"No, Hal, you don't understand. I *have* a job." He frowned, rearing his head back. "With people on my payroll, quarterly meetings with my CPA, budgets, the entire shebang. If I don't do things, they don't get done."

He was deep in denial. We were both counting on our parents to pay our rent, car leases, and life expenses. At least I had the dignity to admit it.

I took a sip of my drink, struggling to breathe in the tight dress. "I mean, sure. What I meant was, we have really fun jobs, so they don't *feel* like jobs."

Keller rolled his eyes. "That's not what you meant."

He was right. It wasn't. But I was too exhausted from my deep-cleanse facial earlier to pick a fight.

"I just noticed Perry Cowen's here." Keller tilted his head behind my shoulder. "Her new balayage is fierce."

I didn't turn around to look. "Not sure a good balayage is going to fix the ugly that's her soul."

"Aww. When God made you pretty, he forgot the R." Keller hopped off his stool. "I'm gonna go say hi."

"But she is *so* basic, Kel." I scrunched my nose.

"Behave while I'm gone." Keller's eyes flicked toward his own reflection dancing along a stainless-steel wine bowl before he headed toward his target.

Perry Cowen was an up-and-coming fashion designer and a woman I didn't like. Mainly because she was designing my sister Hera's rehearsal dinner dress. And anyone who was a friend of my sister's was an enemy to me.

Perry had also sold a story about me to *The Mail*, after an unfortunate incident involving me, a bridesmaid dress, and an unexpectedly spicy pizza sauce. I knew it was her, because no one else in the room would leak it. My mother was horrified we were even related, Dad wasn't an ass, and Hera…well, she hated how I always made headlines for the wrong reasons.

I flagged Frederik, ordering two more cocktails and a shot. I needed some liquid courage to get through the night. Even though I was in a room full of people, I felt desperately alone.

Perry was a reminder that a flight away from me, in Dallas, lived the most perfect First Daughter to ever grace the face of the earth.

My twenty-nine-year-old sister.

An androgynous, sylphlike creature. The type you see on the cover of *Vogue* magazine. Put-together, quick-witted, and impeccably mannered.

Hera finished med school at Stanford University with her fiancé and high school sweetheart Craig, and was currently planning their upcoming wedding while slaying an internship at Baylor University Medical Center.

Hera's whole life was meticulously planned.

I couldn't even control my breasts (which were still wrestling the chiffon of the corset, trying to break free).

I downed the two cocktails and the shot, then snuck a look at Keller and Perry, standing in the corner of the room, laughing. Perry swatted his chest. Around me, masked people swirled and danced. Some kissed in darkened corners of the room. This was my life. Stilettos and overpriced drinks. An empty mansion, full bank account, and blank dance card. There was a hole in my chest that kept on growing, taking more space, until it felt like that hole was real and visible and see-through.

I signaled Frederik for another shot. My drink arrived promptly. Unfortunately, so did Wes Morgan, celebrity trainer extraordinaire.

Wes was the co-host of *Big Fat Loser*, a TV show as horrible as its name. He "helped" celebrities lose weight, normally by yelling at them while running shirtless by their side, as they keeled over and vomited mid-exercise. He'd tried to recruit me to season three of his show, promising to get me to a size four within two months. I hung up the phone on him, but not before keeping him on the line for fifteen seconds, while I alternated between laughing and munching loudly on a sleeve of Thin Mints.

Apparently, our last interaction had left him craving more.

"Howdy, Hallion." He braced his elbow on the bar, next to my drink, flashing me a blindingly white smile. Hallion was the nickname the tabloids gave me for my antics. "Did I ever tell you I'm a fellow Texan, too?"

He had enough wax in his hair to sculpt a Madame Tussaud figure. I wasn't talking young Dakota Fanning, either. More like Dwayne Johnson.

"You don't have a mask," I commented blandly.

"Don't need one." He shrugged, grinning wider, still. "You're looking at a man who just donated 10k to help a veteran get his surgery."

I examined the paint job on the ceiling, waiting for him to go away.

"D'you hear what I said?"

"Yes." I scooped a cherry from my empty cocktail glass, sucking it clean of alcohol. "You said it a second ago."

"I meant about both of us being Texans."

"I'm not a Texan," I said flatly, tying the cherry's stem in my mouth and dropping it back into my hand.

"Oh, yeah?" He leaned closer, so I could truly appreciate the eye-watering scent of the five gallons of cologne he'd bathed in. "Coulda swore President Thorne was—"

"From Dallas, yes. But I was born in D.C. and spent the first eight years of my life there. Then my parents tossed me into a boarding school in New York, Swiss summer camps, British winter camps, and French soirees. Texan, I am not. A cultural mogul, however…"

I could tell from Wes' vacant stare that I'd lost him at 'culture'. Perhaps even 'soirees'.

I'd spent some time in Texas over the years, never by choice. My parents would beg, bargain, and drag me "home," encouraging me to attend local schools, stay close to the family. I always dodged their efforts. Texas was too hot, too wholesome. All in all, I considered myself a Texan no more than I considered myself a neurosurgeon. And besides, I knew why they wanted me around— it was better optics for them. Showed they at least tried to rein in their wild child.

"*Tsk.*" Wes clucked his tongue, his megawatt smile intact. His teeth couldn't be real. In fact, I'd wager his biceps weren't, either. "I'd be happy to give you a tour sometime. Though I was born and bred in Houston, I sure know Dallas inside out."

"I'm not planning any trips there." I stared at the bottom of my empty cocktail glass.

"Then maybe we can meet here, in L.A." His elbow touched mine. I jerked back immediately.

"Busy schedule, eating all those pies."

"Don't be so touchy, Hallion. Business is business, yeah?" He ran a hand through his hair, but that thing was stiffer than concrete. "I thought you'd make a great contestant."

"You'd make a great taxidermy," I drawled.

"Tell you what. I'll work around your schedule. I really think we could benefit each other."

He was just another person who saw me as a walking, talking meal ticket. He was just another user, and possibly an abuser. People like Wes reminded me why I'd sworn off men. They all wanted something, and that something was never to have an actual relationship with me. I was their leg-up. Their key to unlock an opportunity.

My stomach churned.

I want to go home.

Tragically, I didn't have one. The mansion was a stack of expensive bricks and nothing more.

"I'll have my PA contact yours." I hopped off the stool.

"I don't have a PA," he said, confused.

Neither do I. That's the whole exercise, Einstein.

I signaled Frederik for the check. Screw Keller. I was tapping out. He could mingle with Perry, who did, in fact, sport great new highlights that complemented her cheekbones. I tossed them one last look. Perry's friends were now asking Keller all kinds of questions about his juicery. He was basking in it. Was I the only one who was upfront about his fake job?

I paid, tipped Frederik forty percent, and made my way out, weaving through people who tried to stop me for a chat. Wes followed me eagerly. He'd officially graduated from a pain in the neck to a stalker.

"Wait, where are you going?" He tried to put his hand on my shoulder. I hissed, shaking him off almost violently.

Don't touch me. Do not touch me. Never touch me.

"Home." I quickened my steps. My heels slapped the dark floor.

I loathed myself for forgetting to grab a jacket on my way out of the house. I could use something to cover my boobs with, ensure my breasts weren't peeking out of the corset. Though now that I thought about it, said boobs weren't feeling so constrained anymore. Just oddly cold. I looked down and realized why—my right breast had torn through the fabric. It was literally hanging out. Flapping in the wind like a half-mast flag just as I was about to exit the hotel and call myself an Uber.

Gasping, I frantically tried to tuck it back into my dress.

"Man, oh man." Wes chuckled, leaning against a nearby wall. "Looks like the ladies came out to get some fresh air."

"Shut up."

I made a beeline to the hotel reception to see if I could borrow someone's jacket. There were so many people. *Everywhere*. And the mask made it impossible to see anything. I ripped it off my face and dumped it on the floor. Panting, I looked around me.

Jacket. I needed a jacket. But this was L.A. People hardly walked around in layers.

A voice beside me soothed, "Don't be so angry, Hallion. Let me drive you home."

"No, thanks." I folded my arms over my chest and strode faster. I was almost at the reception.

"If you ask the concierge for a jacket, they'll know what happened and sell the story."

I stopped cold in the middle of the lobby. Wes knew he had my attention.

"Do you really want to be humiliated again? Especially after the pizza stain story *Page Six* published about you." His voice slithered behind me, sinking into my skin like claws.

He was right. If I admitted my dress had burst, it could be leaked. Hera would have a fit, and my parents… God knew what they were going to do. Cut off my allowance. Force me to move to Texas.

I had no actual life skills, other than peeling tangerines in one long piece. Which was impressive, but not exactly the kind of stuff you put on your résumé.

I whipped around, sizing Wes up, still protecting my modesty by resting my arms over my chest.

"I don't trust you." I squinted.

He raised his palms up. "You should. You're President Thorne's daughter. A national hero. I'd never hurt you. Do you think I'm that dumb?"

The answer, unfortunately for Wes, was yes. But since he gave himself more credit, maybe I should do the same. Just for tonight.

Every bone in my body told me it was a bad idea, but I wasn't exactly swimming in options.

"Promise me no funny business."

"Promise me a photo-op, and you've got yourself a deal. I need to get back on the headlines before season five premieres."

I closed my eyes, breathed hard. I was furious.

"Wouldn't it be counterproductive to be seen with a curvy girl when your job is to make people thin?" I opened my eyes, smiling innocently.

"So, about that." Wes let out an exaggerated sigh. "I might've gotten a rep as a fat phobic after one of my episodes went viral. Can you believe this woke bullshit?"

Great. So I was officially his "some-of-my-best-friends-are" token. I wanted to scream.

"One coffee on Rodeo Drive." I raised my finger in warning. "That's all you're getting."

"Fine, but you can't look like you're revolted by me," he bargained. "People need to think you're having a good time."

"If I had those kind of acting chops, I'd be winning Oscars, not advertising acne creams on Instagram." I let out a sarcastic laugh.

"C'mon now, Hallie."

I sighed. "I'll be ordering a pastry."

"I'll tell the valet to get my car." He winked and pointed at me. I, in return, flipped him the bird.

Wes ambled out of the lobby, swaggering like he owned the place. Minutes later, he returned to where I was standing tucked in a discreet alcove not too far from the entrance. It was a fairly secluded spot. My heart was racing, threatening to tear through my skin.

No one could know about my wardrobe malfunction.

"Goddamn, how much longer is it gonna take?" Wes craned

his neck to see if his car had arrived. "My Tinder date is waiting down the street."

My phone started buzzing in my fist. Keller, undoubtedly. I couldn't answer, because I was firmly covering my breasts with my arms, and also because I was still riding the petty train of anger from him talking to Perry Cowen all the way to Beefville.

It was taking a long time—longer than it should—for Wes' car to arrive. Every time he tried to start a conversation, I blocked it with, "Can we not?"

Finally, Wes announced that his car was waiting for us outside. He grabbed me by the elbow, ushering me to the entryway.

"Don't touch me!" I whimpered, hating my voice, how lousy and whiny it sounded in my ears.

It all happened so fast from the moment we stepped out in the open. I let go of my boob, slapping his hand away. The flashes of the cameras hit me all at once. Instinctively, I raised my hand as a visor for my eyes. My right boob swung in the air and said hi to the dozen or so paparazzi photographers Wes had clearly invited here to catch us leaving together.

Oh, fuck.

I was so going to get shit about it from the forty-ninth president of the United States.

AKA, Dad.

Anthony John Thorne.

Chapter One

Ransom

"I have something I need to ask you, and you can't say no."
Tom barreled into my office, tossing a glossy magazine onto my desk. The type you see in the waiting room of a B-grade dentist.

"No," I drawled, not bothering to look up from my Apple screen.

Chuckling, my business partner fell into the seat across from me, loosening his collared shirt.

"Did I invite you to sit down?" I asked, still typing.

"It's important," he said mildly. Everything about the fucker was mild—his nature, his looks, his tone. I found his averageness appalling. Less so than the general population, but still annoying enough that I didn't want his company unless I specifically asked for it. Which happened never.

This begged the question—why the fuck was he here?

"Out." I crushed the end of my pen with my teeth.

"Not before we talk."

"Talking is overrated. Silence is golden." I spat the pen out onto my desk. It rolled and fell in Tom's lap.

He probably wanted to invite me to a family dinner, or worse, golfing. For reasons beyond my grasp, my business partner did not understand the fact I gave zero fucks about socializing, and minus fifteen fucks about his beloved geriatric sport. My hobbies included CrossFit, pussy, and red meat. Above all—being left alone. I didn't have a family, and I liked it that way. Trying to rope me into his didn't win him any brownie points.

His insistence on validating our shared past only encouraged me to spend *less* time with him. We'd already spent our youth together. And neither of us enjoyed it.

"It's work." He grabbed a stress ball from my desk, crushing it in his palm.

I tore my gaze from the screen reluctantly, taking a break from emailing a client to notify him that he was three seconds away from getting violently robbed if he continued flaunting his Rolex collection on Instagram.

I was the co-owner of Lockwood and Whitfield Protection Group. As such, I spent my day explaining to dumb, rich people why they needed to stop doing dumb, stupid shit that could land them in danger. In this case, the heir in question was not complying with my company's contract. The agent I'd appointed to protect him complained that Vasily informed his 2.3 million followers in which New York hotel he was staying, including what floor.

The man did not deserve his wealth, not to mention the oxygen he consumed.

Babysitting rich morons wasn't a dream come true. It paid well, though, and it sure beat everything else a man of my skill could do for employment. The other option was a hitman. Although I disliked humans, I did not particularly yearn for prison time.

Tom dumped the magazine onto the desk between us.

"What am I looking at?" I grabbed the tabloid. A shit-faced young woman with hair like a Disney mermaid was staring back at me. Her tit was spilling out of her torn dress. Her nipple was covered with a tiny yellow star. The headline read: *Hallion in Trouble! Party Girl Suffers a Nip Slip.*

"Never mind." I threw the magazine back in Tom's lap. "I got my answer—a fucking mess."

"A *hot* fucking mess," Tom corrected, grinning. "Uncensored pictures appear inside."

"Great news for my thirteen-year-old self. Grown up me wants to know what she has to do with us?"

"Hallie Thorne." Tom boomeranged the magazine back into my hands. "Ring a bell?"

"Should it?" I sat back, already bored with the conversation. I never watched TV. It was full of people, and as established before, I hated them. Television also reminded me other people had shit I didn't—friends, family, hobbies. This woman looked like the type to give someone a mediocre makeover on a cable show.

"President Anthony Thorne's daughter."

I spared the magazine another disinterested look. "Must've taken after the pool boy."

She looked nothing like her father. Then again, her father didn't look like an OnlyFans pin-up girl.

"Anyway," Tom continued, "I just got off the phone with Thorne's former chief security officer, Robert McAfee. He knows me from a hole in the wall. Thorne wants to hire security for her after this incident."

"You mean public indecency."

"Tomayto, to-ma-to." He laughed. "McAfee recommended us based on our experience with oligarchs, actors, and political personas. Thorne seems interested, provided we sign all the paperwork to ensure confidentiality."

"Couldn't he pull a few strings to get her someone from D.C.?" I frowned.

Technically, only living former presidents and their spouses were entitled to a lifetime of security from the government. But ways around it existed. For instance, if this Thorne chick lived at home, which she must, since she looked seventeen, she could "borrow" her parents' security while they were in their premises.

Also, showing your tits in public did not put you at security risk, which told me that Daddy Thorne mainly needed someone to nanny his troubled child.

I wasn't in the diaper-changing business.

"He seems hell-bent on going the private sector route. He wants to be real discreet about it," Tom explained.

"Good luck with making this woman do anything discreetly." I ran a hand over my hair. It was growing out too long. I probably should've already cut it.

"McAfee is still the chief security officer at the White House." Tom stroked his chin.

"His medal's on its way." I popped two mint gums into my mouth.

"They're serious, Ran. This is an immediate post. For the princely sum of 250k a month."

"It's a babysitting gig," I retorted.

"Exactly. Zero work. All the glory."

I understood why Tom had a hard-on for this assignment. If we played our cards right with Anthony Thorne and Robert McAfee, it could earn us D.C. clientele, and *that* was an interesting prospect.

Though both Tom and I were former counterintelligence officers, it was near impossible to get a foot in the federal door. Washington didn't like to outsource security. They preferred to train their own, then put them on a government payroll, the cheap bastards. But once you found your way in, you were looking at fat salaries, ongoing contracts, and a lot of prestige, all from the comfort of running your own business.

Not to mention, Tom and I were about to launch a cybersecurity department next year. We could use governmental ties.

"She in Texas?" I remembered President Thorne's Dallas drawl, which had won him the suburban housewife vote and flipped a few purple states during his reelection.

Tom shook his head. "Los Angeles."

The place I loathed the most. How fitting.

"Fine. Process it." I shrugged. "Put Max on the case. His family's from Oceanside. The pale fucker could use a tan."

Max looked like every designated emo kid in coming-of-age shows. I was also fairly sure a guy like him wouldn't touch this pile of designer skirts and Daddy issues with a ten-foot pole. He would be a good influence on her.

Tom rubbed the back of his neck, shifting uncomfortably.

"Max is good, but he's a rookie. He can be the standby officer. He'll need to be paired with someone with more flight time hours. This is our big breakthrough. Make this girl presentable and get all the connections. It's only for six months."

"Get Jose on the day shift."

"Jose is still in Scotland, remember?"

Of course I hadn't remembered. What was I, his mother?

"What about Kent?" I growled.

Tom shook his head. "Paternity leave."

"They let him *father* something?" I scowled. Kent had a sadistic streak a mile long and five kilometers wide. He'd once punched a paparazzi photographer in the face for asking him for the time.

"Not something, someone. We went to his son's bris together."

I saw where this was going, and I didn't like it. Three weeks ago I'd finished my last job in the field—a British royal—and told Tom I wasn't going back to tailing famous ass.

I would probably miss the international pussy—certainly the private jets—but nothing was worth putting up with someone else's bullshit twenty-four seven. Especially the young women.

They were always the worst.

Plus, I was the one in charge of vetting our cybersecurity staff, and that was two jobs and a half.

Plus, what the fuck was Tom thinking, sending me to Los Angeles? Last time I was there, some nasty shit went down. Stuff even I couldn't stomach.

But then you never told Tom the whole story. How could he possibly know what drove you to quit and go private?

By the puppy dog eyes Tom was giving me, my guess was he wanted me to be the one to personally ensure Titty McFlash wasn't going to show the world any more of her privates.

"You're high," I said decisively.

"You mean practical." Tom stood up, ready for an argument.

I sniffed the air. "Smell that?"

"Smell what?"

"That fart scent all your gaslighting is causing."

He chuckled. "Look, I know it's not what we discussed—"

"What about the cybersecurity unit?" I darted up to my feet, ready to wring his neck. "Who's going to open it? We made verbal commitments to clients. You can't even make a PowerPoint presentation."

I'd seen this guy wrestling with his phone to find the poop emoji.

"It can wait until we're done with this job. We need clients on the Hill when we launch," Tom argued.

"Putting the cart before the horse, are we?" I unbuttoned my cufflinks, rolling my sleeves up my elbows. "We didn't get the job yet, not to mention the connections."

"Thorne wants us. *You*, specifically. Ransom Lockwood. The Robot. No heart, no sentiments, no strings. He knows you've dealt with some top secret shit. Knows you saved Prince Pierre several times from life-or-death situations. You have a flawless track record, and you won't be tempted to screw his daughter's brains out."

"You can say that again."

Ordinary sex bored and frustrated me, and most women were…well, *ordinary*. I liked it rough, unconventional, and with people who were willing to sign a long dos and don'ts contract. My taste ran on the dark side of the spectrum. Specifically, CNC. Consensual Non-Consent. Rape fantasies, if you would.

My sexual partners liked to be taken by force—and I enjoyed forcing. This type of kind—primal play—was about strength. To be clear, I did not want to *rape* anybody. I liked the thrill of the chase, the anticipation that came with the danger of pushing our limits and boundaries. All of my partners were consenting, intelligent, and powerful women who shared the same kink.

I enjoyed the sophisticated. The sharp-edged women who, like me, enjoyed playing with their demons.

No part of me craved putting my dick into a vanilla, attention-seeking teenager.

"Thorne will open doors for us." Tom pressed his lips into a thin line.

"No," I said flatly.

"You have no choice!" Tom banged his open palm over the table.

"News to me." I arched an eyebrow. "Watch me leave this conversation, right now."

I grabbed my phone from my desk and sauntered to the door. Tom snatched my sleeve. "Ran, *please.*"

Turning around to face him, I drawled, "I said no more teenyboppers. The last one tried to tie me to the bed in the middle of the night and rape me."

I'd had to break the headboard to loosen the leather belts she'd used. The only reason I hadn't pressed charges was because her father was the third richest man on planet Earth and I was paid handsomely for my silence.

Tom laughed nervously. "Being handsome is one occupational hazard I wouldn't mind dealing with."

"Have you forgotten what happened last time I was in L.A.?" I ground my molars to a point of dust. He didn't know the entire story, but he knew enough to guess the place wasn't on my to-visit list.

"A lot of shit went down." Tom cleared his throat. "But it's been years. You cannot avoid the city forever."

Of course I could. Los Angeles had nothing to offer me but pollution, bad Hollywood movies, and overpriced gourmet food.

"You do it." I stabbed a finger in Tom's chest.

"I would. In a heartbeat. But I'm starting an assignment with Mayor Ferns next week."

He got a local post with the mayor of Chicago.

"Unless you want to play a game of switcheroo? I'll go to L.A. Pack Lisa and the kids and go live in a McMansion."

I gave it a brief thought. Mayor Ferns had enough enemies to sell out Wrigley Field, but that wasn't what concerned me.

The fact that I'd screwed both of her daughters—simultaneously—not even two months ago did. In my defense—not that I needed one—I'd had no knowledge of their pedigree when one was sucking my balls while the other bent over a bar for me, letting me shove my fingers inside her.

We parted ways amicably, but I knew better than to play with Lady Luck. Putting myself in a situation with both of them again wasn't asking for trouble—it was begging for it.

At least there was no danger of my getting frisky with the Thorne girl.

I did not fuck the ward. That was the rule.

Besides, she was not my type.

Besides, she was…what? Seventeen?

Besides, Tom was right. I was giving Los Angeles power over me that it didn't deserve. It was just a city. An ugly, filthy, expensive one, but a city, nonetheless.

I didn't want to work for an airheaded bimbo, didn't want to move to Los Angeles, and didn't want to talk to people unless I absolutely had to.

But I'd never met a challenge I didn't annihilate, and this kid wasn't about to set a precedent.

Tom blinked at me expectedly, waiting for an answer.

"What are we dealing with here?" I leaned a shoulder against the wall.

He sagged in relief, letting go of my sleeve.

"It's a low-risk job. She's very active on social media. Informs people of her whereabouts often. But at the end of the day, she's just somebody's daughter, you know. Not that high profile, separate from her father. The main concerns Thorne has for her in terms of safety are assault and robbery. She seems like an especially easy target after looking so drunk and out of it, getting groped by the meathead from that reality show."

I drew a breath, digging my fingers into my eye sockets. This kid better not tie me to a bed with leather belts.

"I want a direct line to Thorne if I do this."

"He's already agreed to that," Tom surprised me by saying.

Well, *shit*.

Anthony Thorne really wasn't pleased with his airheaded teenybopper.

"And a meeting about launching our cyber unit, with this McAfee guy after the post is over. He'll have to make some commitments."

"Way ahead of you, Ran. I already told him." Tom nodded enthusiastically.

"This is my last field assignment," I hissed.

"Pinky promise." Tom offered me his pinky. I snatched and bent it, to the point of almost breaking it as I pulled him close to me. His chest bumped mine.

"*Last. Fucking. Time.*" I watched him squirm in pain.

"Aw."

I let go of his finger. Brushing my shoulder against his, I stalked out of my office.

"Where are you going?" he yelled after me.

"To stab myself in the neck."

Chapter Two

Ransom

I did not stab myself in the neck.

A travesty, I realized twenty-four hours after my conversation with Tom, as I made my way through an overcrowded, filthy LAX.

The last time I'd been here, some years ago as a counterintelligence agent, a lot of blood had been shed. I'm talking *Squid Game* level shit. It was one of the reasons I left. It became clear to me I was at risk of losing the very little humanity I had left in me if I didn't quit.

I didn't give much of a damn about being humane. The main incentive was not to snap into a machete-yielding killer who'd end up going on a rampage.

Prison life seemed uninspiring, and I heard the food there left a lot to be desired.

It also helped that as a CI agent, the money wasn't half that of going private. A no-brainer.

Speaking of no brains, I had to get to that Hallie person's house before she decided to document her trip to the gynecologist on TikTok. Since I'd been advised by McAfee that the brat had no less than four cars in her Hollywood Hills' mansion's six-car garage, *and* a driver, I cabbed it.

Glaring out the window with my duffel bag perched in my lap, I again marveled at how stunningly ugly Los Angeles was. Rundown buildings, grungy bodegas, littered streets, graffiti-filled bridges, and more shopping carts on the street than inside Costco.

To top all of this, the air was so polluted, that living in this shithole was akin to smoking two packs a day. You had to be seriously stupid to move here voluntarily.

Coincidentally, I had very few expectations for Hallie Thorne.

Though I'd never had a proper home, I did consider Chicago to be my sort of base. Chicago was where I worked, where I played, where I fucked, and where I lived in a maximum-security building, in a three-million-dollar penthouse.

Me, a boy who'd once had to eat scraps from the garbage can behind grocery stores.

"That's you." The cab driver killed the engine in front of a hideous mansion that looked like origami put together by a child with ten thumbs. An architectural phallic gesture if I ever saw one. A black square on top of a white square, which were the stories of the house, with numerous floor-to-ceiling windows revealing the "promising" inside:

Vintage wallpaper, tasteless art, and a huge, tacky chandelier.

I tipped the driver and slammed the passenger door behind me.

Since McAfee had warned me that the Thorne child was difficult and unruly, I didn't bother milling around after hitting the doorbell twice. I took out my trip wire, tampered with the keyhole, and saw myself inside.

She had a state-of-the-art security system, but just as I suspected, she didn't bother using it.

The house, like its renter, was a mess. An array of masquerade masks were strewn across the living room furniture, along with fabrics—gowns. Piles of unopened goodie bags and gift boxes, labels still intact. The TV was on. A Korean drama full of sulky, young people in school uniforms. A canvas print of the Thorne princess took up an entire wall in the living room. Sprawled over a windowsill in black and white, overlooking Manhattan's skyline, wearing nothing but knee-high black socks, and a black birdcage veil over her eyes.

I looked away (she was seventeen, maybe eighteen), ambling toward the bookshelves in the living room, in no hurry to meet my new client. You could tell a lot about a person from the books in their library.

The shelves were aggressively up-to-date with all the Oprah and Reese book club staples. I plucked one out and sifted through it. The pages were crisp, with the same ink and woody scent lingering from the bookstore. They still clung to one another, the stiffness of the spines revealing more than titles:

These were props. The little princess didn't read a lick of the books she possessed.

After a quick inspection of the place, I leisurely ascended the stairway. No sign of the Thorne girl on the second floor either. The only hint of her was a trail of clothes leading from the hallway to the master bedroom.

The last item—a pink, lacy bra—was tossed by the double doors to the balcony. Where the girl I'd seen on the cover of that magazine lay on a lounger, naked as the day she was born, a towel flung over her face.

Is she allergic to clothes?

Not stopping to check out the goods, I made my way toward her. She was twenty-one, I'd learned on my flight here. As I suspected—a child, especially to my twenty-nine-year-old self. Not to mention, stealing a look was in bad taste. I was a professional—and didn't need to creep on sleeping women. One kink was enough.

I stood directly above her, blocking the sun. Her skin prickled, turning into goosebumps as I provided her some shade and cool. Motionless, I waited to be acknowledged without touching her. As a general rule, I did not touch my clients.

I did not touch anybody, if I could help it.

Unless, of course, it was part of a well-plotted fantasy controlled for all variables.

She tossed the towel from her face, stretching her limbs.

"Keller? Did you bring me kombucha? I'm *so* dehydrated. I'm still mad…"

The last words died in her throat. Her eyes widened as she took me in for the first time.

An impersonal smirk touched my lips. "Hello, Hallie."

In response, the little shit grabbed the closest thing to her from the floor—a San Pellegrino bottle—smashed it against the edge of the lounger and tried to stab the side of my thigh with it. She came a few inches shy of my knee when I caught her wrist easily, twisting it. Not enough to break it, but enough to indicate I wasn't ruling the option out if she acted up.

"*I'm not here to hurt you, but I will if you don't let. Go.*"

The broken bottle dropped on the floor. I kicked it to the other side of the balcony. She gasped, her big, blue eyes—innocent as a doe's first glance at its mother—clung to my face desperately.

"I—I—I…" she stuttered. "Please. I…I'll give you money. Jewelry. Anything you need."

Anything that wouldn't require her to answer to anyone. Typical brat, after all. Her parents must've warned her I wouldn't put up with her antics.

"I don't want anything you have to offer," I said quietly. Understatement of the century.

"I'll fight." She tried to pull her wrist away, wiggling in her spot. "I'll scream and I'll bite you."

Don't threaten me with a good time.

I loosened my grip on her wrist. "Let's pump the brakes a little. Do you—"

Hallie started screaming. Deafening, desperate wails for help. I had no choice but to shut her up by plastering my palm over her mouth. She tried to bite me as she kicked her legs frantically in the air, trying to break free. Jesus, if she was making a stink this big with me, how had she reacted with her father when he told her she was getting a new bodyguard?

Her nails dug into my hand, breaking the skin, until my blood trickled over her chin. I had to look away. It reminded me too much of my extracurricular activities.

"You can fight all you want. You'll tire out before I do," I said, my voice flat and bored. My muscles barely flexed as I pinned her to the lounger. "This is a done deal, Miss Thorne."

Then she started crying.

The first out of many dramatic fits, no doubt. Did she *want* to get robbed and killed? Not all of my clients' spawn wanted close protection, but none tried to actively attack me thus far.

She was lucky I had a hard-on for the Anthony Thorne connection or I'd have left her house right then and there.

Her tears raced down the back of my hand, disappearing into my blazer.

"Cut it out." I avoided touching anything but her face and shoulders. Or looking anywhere but the neck up. "This is for your own good."

Through the muffled sobs against my palm, I heard her hiccup, "Please don't rape me."

My blood turned cold. Bile hit the back of my throat.

Rape her?

When I unglued my hand from her mouth, stepping back, she took advantage of not being held anymore, and jumped up from the lounger, stumbling on the parquet toward her bedroom.

I wouldn't touch her with a ten-foot pole if the future of this planet depended on it. Polar bears and rainforests be damned. "Did you just say *rape*?"

I accidentally got a good look at her ass as she crawled across the floor like a D-list actress in a scary movie. I now fully understood why President Thorne wanted to put security on that ass. It invited trouble. Round and smooth, with an ivy tattoo crawling up her leg, lacing around her inner thigh. A lesser man would wonder what it felt like to knead it as he bent her against one of her ridiculous designer credenzas and plunged into her mercilessly while she begged him to stop.

A lesser one, but not me.

Leisurely, I followed her as she crashed into furniture, patting her nightstands and linens desperately. She was sobbing too hard to speak.

"Is this what you're looking for?" I held her phone in my palm, raising it in the air. The little color on her face had drained completely. She looked so genuinely scared, I was beginning to actively hate the situation we were both in.

"Next time don't leave your phone on the first floor. Now that I've got your attention, let me be clear—I am not going to touch you, not going to harass you, and I'm sure as hell not going to rape you. Put something on and meet me downstairs, Miss Thorne. We are going to have a little chat. *Fully clothed.*"

With that, I exited the room and went downstairs to roam her kitchen. I hadn't eaten since breakfast. Nothing seemed to be remotely edible. It was all clean juices, pre-packed salads, and organic bars that could moonlight as horse feed.

Hallie joined me in the kitchen twenty minutes later. She was dressed in some kind of crocheted dress and was wide-eyed and shaking. Her nose was pink. She'd cried a lot before coming down here.

What was her angle with the histrionics? Had this alone been enough to make weaker guards run from the job?

I took a sip of my Nespresso, the one good thing about this house thus far.

"Sit down," I ordered, leaning against her dark green granite island.

She did, her eyes hard on mine, like it was a hostage situation instead of an adult conversation.

"I just want you to know…" She took a ragged breath as she closed her eyes.

I raised an eyebrow. "That's not a complete sentence, Miss Thorne. Think you can put me out of my misery and finish it?"

It was critical to ensure that I had the upper hand in our dynamic, albeit despite my unorthodox strategies.

She was going to give me trouble and put me through bullshit to see how far she could take it before she outlasted me. I'd seen this movie many times before. Better to establish clearly now, that my patience was not to be tested.

Or in existence, for that matter.

Anthony Thorne himself had given me the green light to use tough love and set clear boundaries to force her back on the straight and narrow when we spoke on the phone. Worked for me—I don't do kiddie gloves.

"Look, Lockwood, I know why they call you The Robot. They said you're pragmatic. Get the job done with minimal mistakes, never let your emotions rule you. I need her to learn to be more like you. My daughter, bless her heart, is a good kid. But she's reckless, and I don't want her next mistake to cost her more than just her dignity."

Reckless Princess over here was now glaring at me, eyes red with fury, not acceptance.

"I want you to know that I used my laptop upstairs before coming down here." Her voice quivered. "I messaged the police. They're on their way. And my dad's security detail—they know, too. I don't know how you found your way in, but this is your last chance to run away and never come back."

My phone started blowing up in my pocket, signaling that she indeed called for help. And I noticed when she came downstairs that she had a Swiss Army knife tucked into her waistband.

Then it hit me. All at once.

The one thing I hadn't even considered.

She'd had no idea.

She *had* no idea.

No idea I was her new protector.

She thought I broke into her house.

President Thorne, you flaming bag of sh—

"Everyone knows. Time's out. Just leave," she pierced my thoughts.

He hadn't bothered to tell her. My guess was because he was scared of her. Parenthood was a debilitating affliction. The man had led the free world for eight years, and couldn't get his daughter to keep her tits in her tops.

Smiling cordially, I said, "I'm glad to hear that you did the smart thing."

"Excuse me?" She tilted her head sideways.

"I'm glad you told your father's security detail I arrived, since they were *my* next call. He was the one who hired me."

Her mouth hung open. She was speechless.

Finally, she blinked. "But I...I...I don't need a bodyguard."

"I'm not a bodyguard." I dumped the coffee cup into the sink, flinging her fridge open. "The term is close protection officer. Bodyguards are the brainless meatheads who carry your girlfriends' Gucci bags for them while their photos are being taken."

Truth was, I didn't give one crap about my title. I simply wanted to establish I wasn't one of the Chihuahua holding gym-rats she was used to for security. Testing my patience wasn't going to end the same way. Then again, this debacle didn't seem like a typical start for her either.

The fridge was stacked to the max with leafy greens, organic, gluten-free pizzas, and colorful cupcakes.

"Where's the real food around here?" I asked.

"Define real food." She massaged her temples, still processing.

"Something that was once alive, or a product of it. Something not made of useless carbs."

"I'm vegetarian," she announced.

Of course she is.

"Of course you are."

"Meat is murder," she said with conviction. Even though she still looked like she wanted to kill me, her shoulders slumped. She relaxed visibly, registering that, at the very least, I wasn't there to murder her.

"It is also delicious. I'll stock up the house tomorrow."

I plucked a healthy grain bowl that looked suspiciously like something you'd give your pet parrot and stepped back.

She folded her arms over her chest, tilting her chin up defiantly. "You'll stock up on nothing, which brings me back to our original conversation—I don't need a bod…*close protection whatever*. Leave."

"Tough luck Daddy thinks otherwise and he's paying for all of this nonsense." I kicked the fridge shut, motioning around us with a fork.

"You can't do this." She bared her teeth at me, ready for round two. I already knew she was ready to brawl if it came down to it.

"I can, and I am," I said around a mouthful of a quinoa and chickpea salad.

"This is a breach of my privacy!" She slapped the granite kitchen island between us.

I shoveled more food onto the fork. "No offense, kiddo, but you couldn't find your privacy if it were hand-delivered to you by Amazon. And for the record," I paused to swallow my bite, "I don't want to be here anymore than you want me to be. But your father offered me a six-month post, and I'm not going to let him down."

"This is bullshit." She flung her arms in the air.

"It's what happens when you decide to show the world your tits," I countered.

"*One* tit," she corrected.

"Let's aim for none for the next half a year. Now, deal with the consequences of your behavior and suck it up. You'll have to change your ways, or your father is going to extend the contract and I'll unleash my colleague Kent on you. Fair warning: if you think I'm a teddy bear, wait till you meet this grizzly."

"*You* are the most horrific person I've ever met." She bolted up from her seat. "And I want you out of my house."

"I don't work for you. I work for your father."

"This is not how any of this works. It's the twenty-first century!" She got in my face, so close I could smell her breath—peaches—and noticed that her eyes were an interesting shade of turquoise.

Silver dots swirled around her irises. There was something rather innocent about her. Something that told me she wasn't fully-baked. That the world had not tarnished her completely.

"It's the twenty-first century, and people are still inheritably bad, and want to harm and/or use loved ones of influential people. Which is why I'm here to help," I reminded her calmly, finishing the bird food bowl and tossing it into one of the fucking *five* trashcans. This woman did not mess around when it came to recycling.

"You used the wrong can!" She nearly football-tackled me on her way to the trash, picking up the bowl and throwing it into the black bin, not the green one. "Next time, rinse and dry it, *then* you can put it in the green one."

"What the—"

She swaggered back to her spot behind the island, now that humanity was no longer in danger from my lack of recycling. "I thought you were going to rape me."

She still had the Swiss knife tucked close. If nothing else, I appreciated her resourcefulness.

"Rest assured, I have no intention of ever touching you."

I started making my way to my duffel bag at the entrance. A lot was riding on this Hallie Thorne post. I'd earned a meeting with Anthony Thorne himself from this. He said he'd meet Tom and me to discuss our company if he was satisfied with my work.

And while it was true I hadn't left Los Angeles with sweet and fuzzy memories, Tom was right. It had been years, and I needed to get over what happened, even if it kept me up at night, every night.

I grabbed my duffel bag, about to head upstairs to unpack. A knock on the door stopped me. Hallie launched herself at it, tossing it open, revealing two LAPD officers on the threshold.

She practically pulled them inside by their uniforms.

"This is the guy!" She pointed at me with a shaky finger. "He's trespassing. I don't want him here. He saw me naked!"

"Who hasn't?" I glimpsed at my watch.

The officers chuckled. Hallie's face fell further as one of them squinted my way.

"Lockwood, that you?"

He didn't look familiar.

"Mike." He pointed at himself, laughing. "Mike Slayton. We went to training camp together in Huntsville?"

"Mike." I faked a smile. I still had no clue who the guy was. "Long time no see."

Twenty-nine years to be exact, and I haven't the faintest clue who you are.

He walked right past her. So did his colleague. We all shook hands. Hallie looked between us, her surprised, blow-up doll face on full display.

"What are you doing here? Are you still with...?" Mike left the question hanging.

I shook my head. "Private sector now. Tom Whitfield and I went solo."

"Whitfield!" Mike snapped his fingers. "That son of a gun. He's always been talented. Tell me, did he end up marrying what's her name? Laney? Lila?"

"Lisa. They have twins now. Boys." Fuck if I even remembered their names right now. Something with an S, I was forty percent sure.

"Well, I'll be damned." He rearranged his belt around his thick waist. "What brings you to our neck of the woods?"

"He is forcing himself on me!" the brat roared, slipping between him and me. She was doing the weird dance thing again, where she waved her arms and jumped from side to side. I had to hand it to her—she was persistent. I'd dealt with the spawn of rich people before, and normally, they didn't put up this much fight.

"Miss." He swiped his eyes over her cleavage, licking his lips. "Sexual harassment is a serious allegation."

"You might want to tell that to my face. My bra doesn't speak English." Her hands balled into tight fists, and I had a feeling my first assignment was to keep her from stabbing him.

"Shame." I yawned, sauntering back to the kitchen and picking an apple from the fruit bowl. "Maybe it could've told you the other night to put it back in, and spare both of us this unfortunate situation."

She whipped her head around, pinning me with a death glare. "I've known you for all of ten minutes and you've already assaulted me in my own home and insulted me like my father."

I took a bite of the juicy apple. "Her father, former President Thorne and current owner of this residence, hired me as her close protection officer. I can call him to confirm this."

Because I had his number on speed-dial now. Which reinforced my original point—I wasn't going anywhere, no matter what the Thorne Princess wanted.

"No need." Mike hiked up his belt over his belly. "This seems like a simple misunderstanding that got cleared up. Right, miss?"

"Are you kidding me?" the brat screamed. "I understand the situation perfectly. Someone is squatting in my house, and you're taking his word he has a right to be here! Why the hell aren't you *doing* something? I'm not a child making a prank call, I'm twenty-one!"

"And living off your parents' dime." I finished the rest of the apple. "Which brings me to my original point: abide by my rules, or lose every privilege you have."

"That all?" Mike asked. The guy beside him was staring at the artistic nude painting of Hallie in the living room. An urge to drive my fist into his jaw slammed into me. I did not like it when women were objectified.

"Know what? I'll deal with it myself. Thanks for nothing." She stormed upstairs.

"You're welcome, honey." Evidently, Mike was not well-versed in sarcasm. He turned back to me. "So? Drinks this afternoon? I finish my shift at three o'clock."

I opened my mouth to tell him there was no way in hell I'd intentionally spend time with him, when he got another call. He took it, sighed, then frowned.

"Looks like there was a robbery two streets down. So, drinks?"

With a cold smile, I answered, "Raincheck."

I closed the door behind the officers and let Brat sulk in her room for a while. If this was what being a parent felt like—I was glad I'd opted out of having children.

In the meantime, I went upstairs and unpacked my bag in a burgundy-walled freak show of a guestroom, complete with neon pink lamps. The place looked like it had been decorated by a blind brothel Madame. I wondered if Anthony Thorne had ever set foot in this wasteful, five hundred-room mansion. My gut told me the answer was no.

My gut was never wrong.

Question was—was it his choice to avoid this place, or Brat's?

I proceeded downstairs and started making some calls. Max was supposed to arrive tomorrow. Miss Thorne required around-the-clock supervision so we had to take shifts. I also called a local CrossFit place. I normally liked to get my workouts out in the open, but the only pieces of green Los Angeles had to offer were the golf courses.

I sifted through emails, checked my Kink app for appealing like-minded people in the area, and then got back to sorting through résumés for the cybersecurity unit.

An hour after her dramatic departure, Brat reemerged downstairs, swathed in black from head-to-toe and dark sunglasses, holding a designer suitcase. She sloped her chin up.

She looked like an especially bad actress on a soap opera.

"I'm leaving," she declared from her place by the door.

I didn't answer.

"There's nothing you can do to stop me."

Wanna bet?

"I'm just taking my keys." She let go of her suitcase and advanced to the kitchen, then came back, red-faced, to the dining table where I sat.

"Where are all my keys?" she demanded. "This is *theft*."

"In my pocket." I kept typing an email as I spoke. "And those cars are technically under your mother's name. She confirmed I could confiscate them as I deemed fit for safety purposes."

"You—"

"So much for being an environmentalist." I continued typing on my laptop. "Owning four cars."

"They're all hybrids."

"You're one person," I reminded her. I had a feeling math wasn't her strong suit.

"That's because I like supporting green companies."

"Sure, on your father's dime."

"I'll call my driver," she mumbled, more to herself than to me.

"Mr. Drischoll is on an overdue paid leave," I announced flatly. "He's spending some time across the country with his family."

"Dennis!" She gasped, slapping a hand over her chest. "He never had a vacation before."

"My point exactly."

"Well, I'll get an Uber," she shot back.

"Would they let you pay in pearls of wisdom?" I inquired dryly.

"What?"

I stopped typing. "Your credit cards have been canceled. Couldn't risk you running into trouble while I wasn't looking."

"You're kidding me."

"Oh, I should warn you in advance—I have no sense of humor. No joking in this household for the next six months." I double-clicked one of the résumés waiting in my email.

"I'm going to get revenge."

I yawned, wondering if all one-dimensional creatures of excess in L.A. talked in poorly scripted *Riverdale* dialogue.

"Revenge's an admission of pain. Tuck your feelings back in. Everyone can see them, and what they can see—they can exploit."

"I'm going to find a way out of this." She was pacing back and forth now, peering at the walls like they were closing in on her. She was coming to terms with her new reality. *Good.*

I opened another Chrome tab of résumés. A bachelor's degree in information security, UC Berkeley cybersecurity boot camp graduate, five years' experience in NESSUS, SPLUNK, and APP Detective, blah, blah, blah.

Not good enough. *Next.*

"I am!" She stomped her foot. "Just watch me."

My eyes snapped up to meet hers.

"I'll watch you, all right, because Daddy Dearest pays me a hefty sum to do so. Your ass is under my supervision for the next six months, Miss Thorne, whether you like it or not. Forget about everything you knew to be your former life. Gone are your days of stumbling out of bars and clubs naked and drunk. From now on, you will have to prove to me that you are responsible enough to operate your social media accounts, to have a credit card, and to socialize with other adults. You will be abstinent, sober—those are your parents' demands, and on your best behavior—the latter is mine. And by the end of my stay," this was where I got to the cherry on the shitcake, "you will be gainfully employed, too."

"Abstinent!" she shouted to the sky, outraged. I could kind of understand where she was coming from. Being sexually active had nothing to do with good behavior. But I didn't make the rules—I simply enforced them. "Will *you* be abstinent?"

Wouldn't put money on it.

I could go without for weeks, sometimes months. Finding the right partner for my flavor of kink was not easy—fortunately my self-control was second only to my stamina. But the Brat and I weren't playing the same game.

"What I do with my personal time is my business," I clipped out.

"Yeah, thought so." She laughed mirthlessly. "And sober? I don't even drink that much."

"Then giving it up shouldn't pose an issue."

She glanced around, looking for creative ways to get out of the situation. Clearly, the Thornes had allowed her to grow as wild and free as a weed until she was not in the habit of answering to anyone.

"I'll make your life a living hell," she said matter-of-factly.

"Kiddo." I flashed her an impatient smile. "I was forged in hell. I'll feel right at home. You, however, are in for a challenging few months."

"This is not over," she warned, wiggling a finger in my face, an explosion of colors and attitude. "In fact, I'm going to walk out of here right now and sell this story about how you walked in on a naked, sleeping woman to—"

Not interested in hearing the rest of this sentence, or anything else to come out of that smart mouth, I stood up, picked her up, and locked her upstairs, in her room.

It was the first time I'd physically—unprofessionally touched a client.

But it was time Brat got some discipline.

Better late than never.

Chapter Three

Hallie

I was going to kill a man. Violently.

I didn't know how yet. After all, this guy—what was his name, anyway? Bastard never introduced himself—was at least six foot three, if not taller. And buff. Not in the way Wes Morgan was buff, with enough visible veins to look like a roadmap. Nameless Asshole had a toned body without looking like he lived at the gym. He appeared almost indecently masculine. Like those ultra-athletes who survived in the woods for years at a time.

Complete with jade-hued eyes, soot-colored hair, sculpted cheekbones…*okay, since when do you notice men? Specifically, men who barge into your life, while you're naked?*

Anyway, without getting into minutiae, the jerk deserved to die.

Luckily, I still had my laptop in my room. He could take my phone, but he could never take my fight.

My first move was to try to call my parents through a questionable app I downloaded, and in the process, probably installed fifteen viruses on my computer.

I got my mother's voicemail—twice—while Dad was on another call.

The coward. My father was great about sending me money and gifts, and horrible at being available for me physically or emotionally. He called me frequently, but conversation was always so boring, so stilted, I'd wish he hadn't even tried.

My mother was a different story. She openly resented me. According to her, *I* wasn't making an effort. She criticized me often, but through the harsh words, I could always pick up the undertone of a wounded woman. It brought me sick pleasure. Knowing she hated our relationship as much as I did.

Leaving a voicemail was out of the question. They didn't listen to those. So I resorted to calling their respective secretaries and leaving messages with them, like a cold caller trying to offer a solar panel installation deal.

It made my blood bubble to think Nameless Asshole, who was currently occupying my dining room, had access to my dad and could call him at any time, while I had to go through his administrative team.

"Hi, Daphne, it's Hallie. Can you please do me a favor and ask Mom to call me back? It's important. Yes. Very important. No. It's not about Chanel raising their prices and my needing to stock up on bags. I actually find it super triggering to suggest that I buy new products. It is so not eco-friendly. Plus, there are steals at secondhand stores. Steals, I tell you."

"Heyyy, Tyrese How are you? How's your wife? Oh, really? Two years ago? I'm so sorry. Anywho, is Dad around? Any chance I could leave a message for him? Yeah. Tell him it's urgent. Super urgent. What? No, I didn't accidentally make the ATM machine swallow my credit card! That you would even suggest that…no wonder Beverly left you."

Once I was done thoroughly humiliating myself with my parents' staff, I paced my room. I considered calling Hera, then quickly thought better of it. First of all, she was probably not going to answer. She worked twenty-six hour shifts at the hospital. Also, I was her least favorite person in the world. And in the unlikely event that she *did* answer, she'd spend the duration of the call telling me how irresponsible I was, and how I deserved an abusive, cold bodyguard to straighten me up. Hera had an uncanny gift for making me feel like shit. So even though I knew she could get Mom and Dad on the phone in a second, I didn't want to call her.

Freezing in my spot, an actual good idea assaulted my brain. *Keller.*

Keller would know what to do in this situation. He'd driven countless nannies away when he was a kid. After his mother passed away from an overdose when he was nine, his dad took sole custody of him. Every time his father would put someone in charge of him, Keller found a way to either get the nanny fired or to run away screaming. He was a master at making people quit.

Sure, I'd been kind of at odds with my best friend since he'd abandoned me to mingle with Perry Cowen. I hadn't taken any of his calls after the nip-slip debacle.

No matter. It was time to suck it up and play nice.

I FaceTimed Keller. He picked up immediately, in the middle of a jog, the camera bouncing between his beautiful face and the cloudless blue skies.

"Finally descended from the tree you climbed, I see," he greeted me warmly.

"Only because the bough's about to break into a rocky river," I murmured, remembering the big, surly predator occupying my dining room downstairs.

"Down will come baby. Cradle and all. Am I still in the doghouse?" He rounded the corner of his street.

"That depends on whether you can help me or not."

"Ultimatums and emotional blackmail. You speak my love language." He sighed. "Let's hear it."

I took a deep breath, then told him about my last few hours. How I spent the morning innocently working on my tan. How Nameless Asshole barged into my house, stole my phone and my car keys, and canceled my credit cards. How he sent Dennis—*our* Dennis—on paid leave, and scared away the police officers (I may have tweaked some details to fit the overall narrative).

I explained that my parents were not answering me, probably

scared of my reaction, and I simply couldn't live with this heathen of a man for six months. Or six days. *Or* even six seconds.

When I got to the part where Nameless Asshole picked me up as if I weighed no more than a cardigan and locked me in my room, Keller gasped.

"Horrible, isn't it." I sniffed.

"Monstrous." There was a pause. "And hot. Is he…?"

"*Keller*! What an inappropriate question."

When he continued staring at me expectantly, I rolled my eyes. "I guess he is attractive, if you consider Jason Momoa and David Gandy's hypothetical lovechild handsome. But that doesn't matter. The man is literally ruining my life. Being hot is not everything in this world, you know."

"You are right, and I apologize." My best friend cleared his throat. Finally, he stopped by his front door, collapsing on the welcome mat of his building. "So how do I loop in?"

"I need you to help me scare him away. You scared off all of your former nannies. No one is as good at being unbearable as you."

"Actually, honey, you give me a run for my money." Keller laughed. "Besides, my nannies weren't menacing, alpha-males with probable military background."

"Not helping!" I moaned, burying my face in my hands.

"All right, let's make a game plan. Your parents are trying to show you that you're theirs to mold and reshape. Failure is not an option. You are a strong, independent woman."

I nodded, taking it all in. I wanted to show my parents they couldn't spring something on me like this, without consulting me. I hadn't spoken to them since the nip slip. They'd tried to call dozens of times, but I didn't pick up. I was scared, and embarrassed, and—okay—feeling a little guilty.

I knew they saw me as a ditzy, silly girl, who shared nothing but DNA with them. They'd viewed me this way for so long, even I'd started to believe it.

"What do I need to make this mission successful?" I asked.

"Guts, motivation, and a working Amazon account."

"I have at least two out of the three." Motivation wasn't my middle name, but I was fired up about the entire situation.

Keller laughed. "Good enough. Grab a pen and paper, and start writing this down."

I was going to fight back against Nameless Asshole.

And win.

Chapter Four

Hallie

I didn't go downstairs for dinner.

I couldn't stomach anything, was too scared to see him again, and didn't have an appetite.

Oh, and also, my door was still *locked* from the outside, though I had no idea what magician-slash-bodyguard trick he used to make that happen.

I was a prisoner in my own home. Simple as that.

That night, sleep did not come. I kept thinking about the plan Keller and I had come up with to get rid of Sergeant Scumbag. It seemed juvenile, half-baked. I wasn't sure it was going to work. But doing something felt better than doing nothing.

Sunrises had always been my best friend. My constant companion in the lonely existence of being Hallie Thorne. They reminded me that every day was new, fresh, and held endless opportunities.

But when the sun rose the day after Nameless Asshole stormed into my life, all I felt was dread and anger.

Hours crawled in succession. I remained completely motionless in my bed processing, plotting, overthinking. Then, for the first time in my life, I heard the telltale signs of another human in the house.

Despite growing up in boarding schools, I'd always lived on

my own. I'd never had any roommates. Mom and Dad forbade it. They'd said that confidentiality was key for people like us. That other kids would kill to have their own room, and I should be thankful for the privacy.

They didn't care that I wanted company, friends, actual relationships.

Relationships were off-limits for me. They posed a security risk. A political risk.

Each year, my parents would email me a curated list of people with whom I could socialize from my class. Every year, the choices not only consisted of, but were limited to, girls who wanted nothing to do with me.

The Brainiacs, the overachievers, found me lacking. Not smart enough, not interesting enough, not motivated enough. They snubbed me, making the task of living a pseudo-normal life impossible.

I never went to the movies with friends, never attended parties, never slurped neon slushies with a classmate. Nobody wanted to hang out with the weird Thorne girl.

I had also suspected what I now knew to be true—my parents hadn't isolated me from others for my own benefit. They didn't want me to have confidantes. People I could share my life and secrets with. They didn't want a scandalous headline on their hands in case I put my faith in the wrong person. Anthony and Julianne Thorne *still* didn't care about my mental health as much as they did their precious reputation.

They wanted me to come back home so they could monitor me.

I always refused. I'd had a taste of what it felt like to be with them during holidays. They fawned over Hera, their perfect child, while berating me for the way I looked and behaved, the second-best grades I brought home.

After I graduated from high school, friendless as a junk food wrapper on a bench, I went to a community college in Los Angeles. Mom and Dad were horrified. They'd wanted me to go to Harvard or Yale. At the very least Dartmouth. But I liked the idea of "slumming it with the plebs" they "protected" me from. Thought maybe, just maybe, I'd finally find my crowd in people who didn't have a trust fund and shadow yachts.

My parents had rented me this Hollywood Hills mansion. The terms were clear—they were happy to pay whatever the owner was asking, as long as nobody else lived here.

No boyfriend, no roommate, no BFF.

I cried and begged, reasoned and bargained, but nothing worked.

And so, pathetically, today marked the first time I'd heard the noises of someone else living under the same roof as me. And for it to be someone as hostile as *him* stole a treasured hope. My heart coiled into itself painfully, the vines around it twisting. My chest hurt.

I heard a door on the second floor whining open—probably of the bedroom the bastard had now claimed as his own—followed by footsteps descending the curved stairway. The Nespresso machine coming to life. The drapes were pushed open. A speakerphone call between Nameless Asshole and a man I assumed was his business partner ensued.

"How's L.A.?" the other person asked. He sounded wide awake, so I guessed Asshole was either from the East Coast or Midwest.

"Filthy. Ugly. Plastic." Asshole opened the screen door leading to the backyard. The casualness in which he used my house as his own made my blood boil.

"Having fun, I see." The other man laughed. "Is she…?"

"Bearable?" Nameless Asshole completed. "No. As likeable as an ingrown toenail."

You're no ball of sunshine, yourself.

"Have you sat her down in front of our contract?" the other man asked.

There was a *contract*.

"Not yet. Locked her in her room overnight to tire her out."

"Ransom!" the man chided, chuckling.

Ransom? Really? What a bad-ass name for a world-class prick. Couldn't he be Earl or Norman?

"You can't take a page out of Moruzzi's book. You ain't in Kansas anymore."

Who was Moruzzi?

"She tried to stab me with a bottle. Then called the police."

"On herself?"

"On *me*. Brat doesn't have two gray brain cells to rub together."

My scalp stung, as if the insult had been poured over me.

Not much offended me at this stage in my life—I'd been called everything under the sun by the press, and by my own sister, too. But it always hurt when people called me stupid.

Maybe because I believed them. I felt so lost, so in over my head.

The other person laughed a hearty, good laugh. He sounded like a genuinely nice person, which surprised me, because he was in business with a sociopath. "You're getting your fair share of female drama for the first time in your life, and I'm here for it, Ran."

"I'll bring the bitch to heel," Ransom clipped out.

"I'll make some popcorn in the meantime."

"She'll be defanged, declawed, and wearing a collar long before the microwave pings."

The air got stuck in my throat. I couldn't breathe. The man was so cruel, so unbearably callous. I'd dealt with bodyguards before. But only for decorative purposes. *He'd* been right about them—they existed solely for the clout and as stand-in photographers for random Instagram opportunities.

This man actually had power over my life. A frightening amount of it. And it sounded like he couldn't wait to abuse it.

After he was done making fun of me, I heard Ransom's footsteps ascending the floating stairway. I held my breath. He unlocked the door from the outside. He shoved it open halfway, but stayed firmly outside, knowing he wasn't invited. I froze into clay. Even after he'd explained that he was my so-called protector, everything about him made the hair on my arms stand on end.

"Are you decent?" he asked gruffly.

"Why? It hasn't stopped you before," I spat out, before sighing. "Yeah, I am."

"That's refreshing." He pushed the door open, propping a shoulder against its frame.

I decided to greet him by clutching the first thing I could grab on my nightstand and hurling it across the room at him with force. Ransom caught it effortlessly, an inch before it hit his nose. He tilted my Magic Wand—*unwashed*—here and there. A cocky sneer smeared across his haunting face.

"Not my first choice for a weapon, but it beats the banana in *Scary Movie*."

I huffed to cover the embarrassment. Pain and shame swirled in the pit of my stomach like eels. "Give it back to me. That was a mistake."

He must have thought I was a sex maniac. Just another rumor I'd never bothered to correct. According to the tabloids, I'd gone to bed with more than twenty Hollywood heartthrobs. No one, not even Keller, knew the truth.

That I was still a virgin.

That I'd never even gone on a *date*.

Not a real one, anyway.

Ransom tossed my vibrator behind his shoulder, ignoring my request. "Make sure you charge it often, because like I said, no boys under this roof while I'm here. Sleep well?" He moved along my room like a demon, seeming to hover over the floor. He flung open all the curtains. Natural light spilled into the room.

Not a vampire, then.

"None of your business."

He *tsked*. "Where are your manners, princess?"

I was about to tell him they were hiding in whatever hole his decency had crawled up into, when he raised a manila file in the air, boomeranging it my way.

"My company's contract. Read it."

I tossed it on my nightstand, unblinking. "Sorry, my literary taste runs more sophisticated."

"I wouldn't believe that even if there wasn't a copy of the *National Enquirer* on your nightstand."

Touché. I'd only bought it because they'd published a nip-slip picture of mine that looked altered. No matter how bad it seemed, though, one thing was for sure—Ransom looked like a predator, but not the kind who wanted to eat me whole. The way he looked at me, with such disinterest, told me there was no way he was going to try to touch me in a sexual way.

I examined my fingernails with boredom. "I might skim it in my spare time if you play your cards right."

"You'll read it now." His glacial steeliness made my skin pebble. "*Aloud*. We need to discuss the details."

My heart stopped inside my chest. I felt like I was about to throw up. I couldn't read it aloud. I also couldn't tell him that. What kind of kick would he get from knowing the truth about me? Had Dad even made him sign an NDA? Of course he had. He would never risk having the truth about his daughter come out.

Drawing a shaky breath, I grinned. "Know what? I changed my mind about skimming. I don't feel like reading your stupid manual after all. Not now. Not ever."

He leaned a shoulder against the wall, looking morbidly bored. I wondered if anything in the world could fluster him. He seemed so heartless, so robotic. There was no way this man had a partner. No one could deal with this kind of impassive demeanor.

"What?" I barked defensively.

My face was unbearably hot. Sweat pooled under my armpits. I was so sickeningly close to danger that the metallic taste of humiliation exploded on my tongue.

He produced something from the back pocket of his jeans and raised it in the air. My phone. The screen was popping with messages and notifications.

The battery was so low, the line was red.

A grin found his sculpted lips. "Read the contract, agree to the terms and conditions, and you can have your phone back. How does that sound?"

Divine.

But that didn't change the fact that I couldn't…

Not without sufficient time and a clear head…

"I'm not for sale," I said detachedly. "And I'm not reading your stupid contract."

"You want to play?" His smile widened, and it was so mean, so full of venom, I could feel it in my bones. "Let's play."

He turned around and walked away, leaving me to cry into my pillow.

Stupid, stupid Hallie.

Two hours and a mental pep talk later, I mustered the courage to traipse out of my room, descend the stairs, and venture into the kitchen. I found Ransom sporting a sweat-soaked wifebeater and gray sweatpants, making himself an egg white and spinach omelet on my stovetop.

His muscles glistened. Every inch of him was long and lithe. My eyes lingered on his veiny forearms. On the outline of his abs, as they appeared through the thin fabric of his shirt.

The perfection of him—so acute, so mouthwatering—depressed me. I knew, despite his horrible personality, that he was probably considered a godsend to women.

What surprised me, though, was the realization I did not disagree with said women. I did find him attractive. And I never found *anyone* attractive.

Dragging my feet toward the Nespresso machine, I poured myself a cup.

"I'll have one, too." Ransom flipped his omelet expertly.

"Do I look like a Starbucks?" I bit out.

He paused with the spatula in his hand, frowning. "Expensive, overrated, with an obsequious, post-liberal belief system. Now that you mention it…"

"The only beverage I'm willing to serve you is poison." I slammed my cup on the granite, coffee sloshing everywhere.

"Bad news for your phone, which is currently still in one piece, but I understand."

"Did anyone ever tell you you're a tyrant?" I could swear smoke was coming out of my nostrils.

"Yes, often. Your point?"

He slid the airy, fluffy omelet onto his plate. Despite his flat, husky tenor, I recognized something in his face I hadn't seen before. It was confusion, or maybe mild surprise. I had a feeling this guy was not used to people standing up to him. I caught him off-guard. He'd expected me to acclimate to my new situation after he locked me in my room for a whole night.

Recognizing this was an opportunity, I changed my tune.

"Know what? Fine." I poured coffee into a second cup. Sneakily, while he wasn't looking, I slipped the pink Himalayan salt from behind him and poured a generous amount into his cup. At least five teaspoons.

I handed him the cup just as he was taking his omelet to the kitchen island.

He perched on a stool and began digging in. "Read the contract yet?"

I leaned against my counter, holding the steamy coffee to my nose. "Nope."

"It's a five-minute read."

"Still more time than this *bitch* is willing to waste on you." I examined my red-tipped fingernails, letting him know I'd heard his conversation with his business partner.

He took a sip of his coffee. I watched him intently. At first, his eyes flared. Then they met mine. Something zinged inside them. A touch of darkness.

Spit it out, I thought desperately. *Show weakness, goddammit.*

He swallowed. My knees went weak.

How did he do that?

"How is your cup of joe?" I batted my eyelashes innocently.

He shook his head, pounding the rest of the drink without flinching. "A little bland, but I wouldn't expect anything else from you."

I coughed out a chuckle. "Bland and I don't know each other."

"Why? Because of your funky hair dye and 'edgy' tattoos?"

"Why are you so mean?" I knew the answer. Why were people mean, in general? Because they weren't happy with their lives.

In his case, I wouldn't put it past my parents to tell him to be extra harsh on me.

"Because someone needs to teach you a lesson, and unfortunately for both of us, that someone is me."

He'd drained the entire coffee cup. Even though it had more salt than the Dead Sea. Who was I dealing with here? Now I wasn't only terrified but also worried he wasn't entirely human.

Quickly, and before I could chicken out, I grabbed my cup of coffee and plopped in front of him. "Listen, I need my phone back. It's for work."

"You don't work," he reminded me, finishing his breakfast in two bites. He took his plate and coffee cup and washed them in the sink.

I shifted around in my seat. "I do, actually. I'm an Instagram influencer, for your information."

"That's a hobby, not a job." He made his way upstairs. I darted up, running after him.

"Of course, it's a job. Actually, I've made a commitment to appear at someone's new bakery on Rodeo Drive with my friends for brunch today."

I wouldn't call NeNe and Tara friends, exactly, but they were people I saw on the reg. Besides, I shouldn't have to justify my life to this guy.

Ransom went up the stairs with me on his heels.

"Fun-fucking-tastic," he said dryly. "Read the contract, accept the terms, and we can attend your obligation, after I scope out the destination and figure out how and when you'll make your appearance. Your new budget is a hundred bucks a day, by the way. Use it wisely."

My *what*?

Ransom tugged his sweaty wifebeater off by gripping the back, and letting it slap the wall with a *thwack*! before entering his room. Desperately, I followed him there, too. He was about to get naked. This was the part where I ran for the hills, but again, this man wouldn't take me against my will. He was too prideful for that.

He turned around, popping an eyebrow. "What are you doing?"

"Negotiating?" I winced.

"Get out."

I dug my heels deeper into the floor. "Give me my phone first."

"Read the contract *first*," he quipped back.

I closed my eyes. Took a deep breath. Was I really going to share my biggest insecurity to this monster? No. There was no way I was talking to him about something so intimate, so humiliating.

"I…" I licked my lips. "I'm…"

"You are not too busy. Don't even pretend with me."

Ugh. "That's not it."

"Is this an autonomy flex, or an influencer thing about how you're too important to bother reading your own emails?" His mocking tone seared through me.

"No!"

The words felt like bullets, piercing through my chest. The air felt hot and charged in my lungs.

"Forget it. I'm not moving an inch until you give me my phone back."

"Very well."

With that, he lowered the waistband of his gray sweatpants. I caught a glimpse of the sharp V bracketing his abs. The golden, smooth skin of him, and the trail of hair rolling down from his belly button to…

"Jesus!" I looked away, coughing to conceal my embarrassment. "What are you doing?"

"Making you run away. Or, alternatively, setting the ground for a nice, cushioned settlement agreement after the sexual harassment lawsuit I'm going to file against you."

I squeezed my eyes shut. He was playing chicken with me. And winning. How was I going to survive him for six months?

You're not. You're going to have to make him quit.

"Well?" he asked. With my eyes closed, I could feel his warm breath fanning the side of my neck. Shivers trailed down my spine. "Your move, Brat."

He saw this as a chess game, as nothing but entertainment. This was my *life*.

"I'll read the damn thing," I heard myself say. I opened my eyes. Fortunately, his pants were still on. Unfortunately, so was a condescending smirk.

"If you come across any big, intimidating words, let me know."

"Fuck you, Random." The words came out shaky, and I hated myself for it.

"It's Ransom," he corrected.

"Random suits you better."

He paused, scanning me through hooded, ominous eyes that reminded me he was a man who fought—protected?—for a living. My lower lip trembled. He looked like a heartless prince, distant and untouchable.

Whatever he saw in my eyes made him realize I was too easy a prey. His locked jaw loosened, and his expression turned from murderous to done-with-my-shit.

"I'm hopping in the shower. When I get out, you better be ready to sign, having understood the contract." He flung a towel over his shoulder and exited the room.

I went to my bedroom and perched on my mattress, my fingers clutching the wad of papers. My eyes roamed the pages.

The words all bled together, as if the paper were wet. I tried to take it one word at a time, but I was too upset to concentrate. After a few minutes of trying, I stood up and opened the balcony doors to try to get enough air.

You can do it. You've done this before. All you need to do is focus.

By the time a knock sounded on my door, I'd only made it to the second paragraph. Something about personal liability.

Ransom waltzed inside, wearing a dashing Prada suit and shiny loafers, looking like he was attending the Oscars. He buttoned his cufflinks. I leaned a shoulder against the doorjamb of the balcony, pretending not to want to hurl myself over.

"Well?"

"Boring and uninspiring. One out of five stars. Would not recommend."

I walked over to one of my nightstands, taking a pen from a drawer. I signed the dotted line at the bottom of the contract, even though I hadn't actually any idea what it entailed. I handed the file back to Ransom, flashing him my femme fatale smirk.

"So. You are capable of making a good decision after all." He plucked the contract from between my fingers.

I expected a pat on the head, he was so demeaning, but of course, I wasn't good enough for Ransom's touch.

"Your father owes me a hundred bucks," he said, matter-of-factly.

They'd *bet* on it? I wouldn't put it past my father. He always viewed me as his little, simpleton, adorable Sugar Pie. With the big eyes and the small brain.

Maybe Dad had told him about my…*issues*. Maybe Ransom knew I hadn't read the contract. And how sad was it that this complete and utter stranger who didn't even like me had more faith in me than my own pops?

Tears filled my eyes, and I felt my throat clogging up with a scream.

"Look at me now, Brat."

Brat. It was so patronizing, so belittling…and there was nothing I could do about it. My parents wouldn't even take my calls.

Why hadn't I answered them when I still could? When it was still up for discussion?

I turned my head, giving him a hate-filled look, squaring my shoulders.

"I fulfilled my side of the bargain. Now give me my phone, jerk."

"Ask nicely."

"*Please*, jerk."

Chuckling darkly, he produced my phone from the inner pocket of his jacket and handed it to me. I reached to take it. He raised the phone in the air, not letting me touch it just yet. He was so tall the phone brushed the ceiling. In that moment, I could tell liquid gold ran through his veins, not blood. He was no mortal. Nor was he a god. He was, quite simply, something else entirely.

"Remember the rules: no telling anyone your whereabouts. You are only allowed to post pictures of a place after you've left it, and once it's been cleared with either Max or me."

Max? Who the hell was Max? I supposed the manual/contract covered it.

Ransom continued. "No check-ins. No telling anyone about your schedule. And absolutely no showing off your cars and their license plates. Capiche?"

I nodded, feeling like a punished child, loathing him more and more each second that passed, but he hadn't said I couldn't post pictures after leaving said locations, which felt more practical while being restrictive. Still, I didn't have an optimistic glow about the rest of the contract's mysterious contents.

"I would just like to make one thing clear, though." I tilted my chin up.

He stared at me with his signature, would-rather-be-anywhere-else expression intact, waiting for me to continue.

"I *do* have a real job, and it is important to me. Contrary to what you believe, I'm not some scatterbrained heiress with entitled teenybopper friends. Got it?"

He slipped the contract into a briefcase and ignored my words, which I supposed was better than laughing in my face.

Waltzing through the vast hallways of my mansion, he vanished, like a ghost in the stories my mom told me not to read after dark.

"So where do y'all think Sundance will be held this year?" Nectarine, or NeNe, wondered aloud when we sat at Bakersfield, a new bakery on Rodeo Drive. She flung her lavender hair to one side, popping an orange pill bottle open and sliding a Xanax down her throat.

Ransom was sitting at a table next to us outside by the curb, working on his laptop and looking like he wanted to murder everyone on the premises. I was hyperaware of his presence, so I noticed when his fingers stilled over the keyboard. He'd definitely heard the verbal fart NeNe had just let loose.

"Where it is held every year," I said woodenly. "In Sundance."

NeNe pouted, swirling the straw inside her iced coffee without drinking it. "I thought it was like the Olympics."

"It would make sense if the Olympics were only held in Greece," my other companion, Tara, said. She tugged at her ash-blonde chignon, making it purposefully asunder.

Tara was a leggy supermodel. I could safely say we three had never shared an enlightening or intellectual conversation, but we found ourselves hanging out together more often than not. Advertisers liked our combined market pull. Tara brought the fashion-obsessed audience, Nectarine the makeup buffs, and my specialty was Midwestern women between the ages of eighteen and twenty-four.

Despite that, I couldn't call Tara and NeNe my friends. They knew very little about my life. Not that there was much to know. All I did when we were together was hang out with Keller and post stories of my freebies on Instagram.

Ransom's nostrils flared as he kept working on his laptop. It was obvious he thought the three of us were a waste of space.

"What else is new with you guys?" I redirected the conversation, taking a sip of my dairy-free cappuccino. I needed to stir the subject to safer territory.

"Well, I think I'm going to stop with the eyelash extensions. I saw this documentary—" NeNe started.

"Oh my gosh, me too!" Tara cut in. "It was so sad. That girl is never going to be able to even put mascara on again."

"You know what would've worked to unglue the eyelashes?" NeNe jumped in passionately. "Acetone. That shit removes anything!"

"Including your eyesight…" I muttered under my breath.

I shot another disgruntled look at Ransom, who glanced at his expensive timepiece. I'd never felt embarrassed about keeping company with Tara and Nectarine before. I did now. I hated that his mere presence was like calling me on my bullshit. Suddenly, my empty existence had a context. I didn't like it.

All this while, a photographer we'd invited from a medium-sized gossip website had been taking pictures of us enjoying our time at Bakersfield. Or at least pretending to.

"A bit of subtlety, Hal-Pal," Tara mewed. "We can all see you checking out Mr. Hot Shot at three o'clock."

She was talking about Ransom. My stomach churned. It was time to fess up. They were going to find out sooner or later.

"Actually." I cleared my throat. "That's my bodyguard."

"Shut the fuck up." NeNe slapped her chest, like this was national news.

"Gladly." I sighed. "Everything I say is used against me with this guy."

I sneaked a peek to see if he found my barb funny. His expression remained blank.

"He is *gorgeous*," NeNe gushed. "Where'd you find him? Ford Agency?"

"Is he single?" Tara demanded. "Is he rich? His Rolex says yes, but his job description says no."

He was listening to the entire exchange. My so-called friends were so used to discussing their staff when they were in the room, they forgot that people could actually hear them. Or that that should matter. My cheeks stung. It was like he'd put a mirror in front of my face, and suddenly I'd realized I was no beauty. I was a beastly creature.

"I don't know his financial situation, and frankly, I don't care," I said, pushing through despite the metallic taste in my mouth. "We're not exactly thick as thieves. We don't discuss our finances."

"Hey! *Yoo-hoo!* Bodyguard dude!" NeNe leaned over her straw chair, waving at him frantically. She wore a very tiny, very flowery dress and a hot pink smile. "You got a name, or what?"

Ransom completely ignored her. He just continued working on his laptop, refusing to acknowledge our table. *What a toolbag.*

"Is he deaf?" NeNe turned to me, twisting her mouth.

"He can't be deaf, stupid." Tara rolled her eyes. "How would he be able to hear if someone attacks her? He's just trained. Like… you know, guard dogs."

I closed my eyes, dropping my face into my palms.

The owner of the bakery, a former reality star who'd made it to the semi-finals of a baking show, trudged out, snapping off her apron. "Can y'all look a smidge less interested in the hottie at table five and be more focused on my pastries?" She pointed at the mouthwatering basket she'd put in front of us, still untouched. "What am I even paying you for?"

"Question of the fucking millennium," Ransom muttered under his breath, continuing to type.

"I like this guy." Tara grinned, jerking her finger in his direction. "He's got sass. Do you have a girlfriend? A boyfriend?"

"Irrelevant," he said, not tearing his gaze from his screen. "I have *standards*."

"Rude." Tara wrinkled her nose.

"Honest," he shot back.

"How can you even let him talk to us like this?" NeNe gasped in my direction, offended on Tara's behalf.

"Technically, you were completely ignored before you interrupted me, so you're not in a position to complain." Ransom slapped his laptop shut, stood up, and turned to me. His look sent a chill down my spine. "Playdate's over. Wrap it up."

Anger simmered in my blood. He couldn't tell me what to do with my time. He was my bodyguard, not my nanny. Plus, as I'd said—I was *working*.

"Sorry, you want me to leave because...?" I crossed my arms, sprawling on in my seat.

"You've been here for longer than an hour, which means you've completed your professional obligation, and that people probably know your whereabouts by now."

His explanation made sense. Unfortunately for both of us, sense was currently overruled by my need to rebel against this guy. What can I say? Women didn't burn their bras in the sixties just so I could take orders from some jerk with an inflated sense of importance.

"Nah. I think I'm going to stick around."

"As history taught us, your thinking has never led to anything good." He *tsked*. He produced his phone from his pocket and began texting someone. My spine stiffened. He'd managed to screw up my life plenty in less than twenty-four hours, and it didn't look like he was running out of ideas.

Despite my best efforts to look unaffected in front of my so-called friends, I caved.

"What are you doing?" I asked him finally.

"Canceling all of your professional obligations for the week. I gave myself access to your Google calendar yesterday when you were busy screaming into your pillow." He didn't look up from his screen.

Tara cupped her mouth. NeNe keeled over, pretending to gag.

"You can't do that." I shot up to my feet, balling my fists beside my body.

"Already did." He tucked his phone into his front pocket. "Ladies." He nodded toward them. "It was a displeasure, if not a complete nightmare."

Tara and NeNe did not produce a sound. I couldn't think of a single occasion where they might have encountered someone as rude and as unimpressed with their existence as Ransom.

Rather than stand there and convince me to come with him,

he began making his way to my Nissan LEAF. This reminded me that he had my car keys—he had insisted on driving here himself because, quote, "I don't trust you with a Q-tip, let alone a vehicle."

He was *leaving* me there to fend for myself. After canceling my credit cards and putting Dennis on paid leave.

I glanced around me, and saw that Tara and Nectarine were staring at me with a mixture of shock and horror.

"I…I have to go." I followed Ransom, who was already rounding the street corner and walking into the parking lot. I put my hand on his arm to try to slow him down, but he was fast.

"What's your problem?" I roared.

His face was stone-cold, his jaw tense as he answered. "Some abandonment issues with a dash of anger management, and inherent impatience. All self-diagnosed. Your turn."

"My problem is you!" I panted, trying to keep up with his steps.

"Shame." Mild amusement colored his tone. "Your opinion means so much to me."

"Did you really cancel all my obligations for this week?" I demanded.

"Yes." He unlocked my black Nissan LEAF, sliding into the driver's seat. "You overstayed at the café, breaking your contractual obligation, not even two hours after signing it. If you can't play by the rules—you won't be playing at all."

He revved up the engine before I got inside. I had to jump in quickly from fear he'd leave me there.

Shit. If only I'd read the stupid contract, I'd know what on earth he was talking about. What else I'd signed up for.

"You're a sadist," I remarked.

He backed out of the parking space and bolted out of the lot like a professional racecar driver. "Thank you."

"That wasn't a compliment."

"It was, coming from someone with the rhetorical prowess of a nursery schooler. Nice job you got there. Cool friends, too."

NeNe and Tara weren't really my friends, but I didn't want to wash my hands of them just because this man was the most condescending creature on planet Earth.

"My friends aren't idiots. They're just…" I tried to think of a flattering way to describe Tara and Nectarine.

"Morons?" Ransom suggested unhelpfully.

"*Sheltered*."

"From what? Libraries?" he spat out. "Your friends are a reflection of who you are. And right now it's looking pretty damn shallow, Brat. You're aiming too low."

"We conduct business together. That doesn't make us soulmates," I said shortly.

"Those girls couldn't even spell the word *business* if they put both their heads together." He weaved through the condensed Los Angeles traffic. It was so hot the palm trees looked like they were trying to hunch down to avoid the sun.

"I've never met someone more judgmental than you!" I flung my arms in the air.

"Try leaving L.A. The world is full of people who actually appreciate substance."

No point in going back and forth with this guy. We spent the rest of the drive in tense silence. I didn't dare imagine what Tara and NeNe must have been saying behind my back right now. The scene with Ransom was beyond humiliating. I couldn't afford to be seen bickering with him in public. He was going to ruin what little respect I'd gained for myself in Tinseltown.

But caving to his tyrannical ways was not an option, either. I had to get rid of him, fast.

When we got back to the house, Ransom informed me he was going out to run errands. He did so in his signature, obnoxious fashion. Flinging open my bedroom door without knocking, and giving me his wouldn't-burn-you-with-my-last-match expression.

Despite his crudeness, I was ecstatic. Finally, I was going to have some alone time to execute my get-rid-of-Ransom plan.

"I'll try not to miss you too much." I jumped up from my bed, about to slam the door in his face. I was on my phone, calling people he'd canceled on that week—party promoters, PR managers, and even Keller—and apologizing for the last-minute bailout.

"Max'll keep you company, so don't get any ideas." Ransom scowled.

Yes. Of course. Max. If only I had the faintest idea who the man was.

"Remind me about Max?" I twirled a lock of my burgundy hair around my finger.

"Your second close protection officer."

"Oh, right." I laughed airily. "Is he all sunshine like you?"

He walked away, done with the conversation. Ten minutes later, I heard the front door open. Ransom was talking to this Max guy, who arrived at four in the afternoon sharp. I loitered in my room, listening closely to their conversation in hopes to gain some intel on what was going on. It felt like my house wasn't mine anymore, with all these strangers coming and going.

When Ransom left, I tried desperately to call my parents. They didn't answer. When I called their secretaries, I got the same runaround—they were too busy, unable to deal with me right now.

Dejected, I dragged my feet downstairs to introduce myself to Max. No point in making two enemies under this roof.

When I got to my living room, I found a lean, jarringly young-looking man sitting on my couch, flipping through a thick fantasy book. Boyish and unassuming, Max looked like your best friend's older brother in a '90s chick flick. He didn't look threatening like his boss. Better yet—he didn't stir in me the same discomfort most men caused.

"Oh. Hi." He stood up awkwardly as soon as I came into view. He put down the book on the couch, wiping his hands over his pants. He offered me his hand. I decided, against my usual judgment, to take it.

My shoulders loosened some. He didn't look like a bodyguard at all. Not that Ransom did. Ransom looked like a stunning, wealthy heir who found it unbearable to share a planet with average folks.

"I didn't want to interrupt you upstairs," Max explained.

Now, *that's* the kind of bodyguard I was down with.

"Thanks, I was just working." The lie rolled smoothly over my tongue. "I'm Hallie."

"Max."

We both smiled. He looked so young, for a moment I wondered if he was my age.

"I'm twenty-five," he said, as if reading my mind. He ducked his head, his cheeks pinking. "It's just that everyone asks, because I look kinda young. I'm a former SEAL. You're in good hands."

"Oh, uhm, I wasn't doubting your abilities." I shifted my weight from one foot to the other. "Are you gonna live here, too?" I blurted out, making my way to the kitchen to make both of us smoothies.

Maybe if Max and I got along well, Ransom would take the back seat and give him more shifts and I could have some of my freedom back.

He shook his head in my periphery. "Ran will be with you most of the time. I'm just going to be on standby. But I'll be on call no matter what."

My heart sank.

Max sat on a stool in front of me, watching as I shoved a banana, kiwi, strawberries, crushed ice, and coconut milk into my smoothie machine. I poured the finished product into tall glasses and glided one his way across the kitchen island.

He raised his glass in a toast. "Been a second since I've had one of these."

"A smoothie?" I asked.

He nodded. "I used to live in Oceanside. Jamba Juice was like my second home during high school. Quit the healthy habit when I got deployed, though."

I smiled in understanding. "I'm like that, too. I change my habits, depending on where I live. When I was in New York, I was all about the Sicilian pizza and cosmos."

"Sicilian pizza is a *sin*. Pizza dough needs to be like a condom—thin, airy, without any unnecessary extras," Max said.

"Well, sin is *delicious*." I shrugged, laughing.

"So is your smoothie. Thanks for that." Max grinned around the reusable straw I'd put in his drink.

There was a beat of silence as we both took a breath.

"You're really different, you know," he said finally. His smile immediately dropped.

I knew what he meant. Ransom had painted him a different picture of me. Difficult, unruly, and rude. I didn't know how anyone could take Ransom's word at anything. He seemed to have such a cynical, gloomy outlook on life.

"How so?" I asked gently. I didn't want to scare Max away. He had the potential to become an ally.

He took a sip from his smoothie to buy time. I waited patiently.

"I don't know. I just imagined…"

"Someone unbearable?" I quirked an eyebrow, propping my elbows on the surface between us.

"Pretty much." His ears turned tomato-red.

"Did Ransom have anything to do with this image by any chance?" I tilted my head sideways. I knew I was treading dangerous waters. Ransom was his boss. The security company they worked for had his last name. But I needed to feel validated.

Max frowned, looking genuinely confused.

"What do you mean?"

"Did Ransom tell you that I'm a nightmare?"

"No. Ransom only discusses the technical stuff. That's why they call him The Robot." Max's entire body went into rigor mortis, stiffening. He knew he shouldn't have said that. My ears perked.

"They call him The Robot?" I asked.

"Well…yeah."

"Who's they?"

"Just about everyone in the industry."

"Why?"

"Because he's never made an illogical, heat-of-the-moment decision—ever. He's the most pragmatic creature on the planet. Almost like he's been wired a certain way. He's a…you know."

"Robot," I finished, satisfied with the fact that at the very least, Ransom's lack of interest in me wasn't personal.

Max nodded. "Anyhow. I thought you'd be unbearable because, uhm, I googled you and you seemed kind of high maintenance. Ransom doesn't talk about clients. Like, at all. He's insanely professional like that, so don't worry."

I wanted to tell him that this insanely professional man had canceled my credit cards, stole my phone, and caused a scene in front of my friends, but by the glint in Max's eyes when he talked about his boss, I wasn't going to succeed at convincing him Ransom was out of bounds.

Instead, we sipped our smoothies and Max told me about the time he'd had to smuggle a pop star out of a hotel room in a service trolley.

Max was nice, funny, and engaging. By the time the clock hit ten, I'd grown to like him and wished he'd have more shifts with me.

I still had the war with Ransom to think about, and time was not on my side. Sometime after ten, I stretched my arms and pretended to yawn. "I think I'm going to take a shower and hit the sheets."

"All right, I'll be downstairs if you need me."

"When will Ransom be back?" I asked, standing up. I wanted to know how much time I had to execute my plan.

And another, smaller part of me, wondered where the hell he was, and why it was taking him so long to return.

Max worried his lower lip, thinking about it. "Probably not until the middle of the night. Maybe the morning. I'm set to stay here until nine a.m. But don't worry, I don't plan on falling asleep on duty."

So Ransom was getting some action tonight. Hypocrite. I wondered what kind of women he went for. Tall and leggy? Smart and sharp? Geniuses? Probably all of the above. My sister, Hera, could surpass all of them. Now I was thinking about Hera and Ransom dating, and a shiver ran down my spine.

Weirdly enough, the thought of my bodyguard showering

another woman with attention—*positive* attention, no less—made me feel irritated and uneasy. Though I doubted an asshole like him would take the time to seriously woo a girl.

"All right. I'll just grab dinner to eat in my bedroom." I smiled sweetly, flinging the fridge door open and taking out one of the huge raw steaks Ransom had stocked up in my fridge.

It infuriated me that he did not take into consideration the fact that I was a vegetarian on moral grounds. Putting what I considered to be an animal corpse in my fridge was a huge middle finger to everything I believed in.

Covering the steak with another plate, I made my way upstairs, where I stopped by one of the bathrooms to get scissors, before entering Ransom's room.

It was the first time I'd been in this room since he'd moved in, if I didn't consider the show-down that happened earlier today, in which I hadn't had a good chance to take a look at it. I glanced around me, hungrily taking in every detail and filing it to memory. One of the most important strategies of war was to know your enemy.

Unsurprisingly, the room was extremely organized and neat. In fact, almost nothing had changed in its appearance, save for the fact that all the decorative pillows which were previously on the bed were now gone, probably stuffed into one of the closets.

It felt weird, to sniff around a room that was a part of my house. Ransom's scent clung to the sheets, woodsy and leathery and rich. I opened one of the drawers and found a watch and belt collection. The belts were looped around themselves tidily. The watches were at least 50k a pop. Ransom was *minted*.

I opened another drawer and found his socks, cufflinks, and underwear. They were all black, all designer, and all brand new.

Next to it lay a gracefully pleated rope. Sorry...*what*?

Why did the man need a *rope*?

Trying to convince myself that it was normal, that maybe he needed it for his job (but *how*?) I shoved the drawer shut. There had to be an explanation. Ransom was an asshole, but he hadn't given me creeper vibes. And I could pick up creeper vibes pretty well. Experience and all.

Moving to the closet, I found his suits and dress shirts. Snapping the scissors in the air, I got to work. I cut the steak into tiny pieces, then hid them in darkened and discreet places in his closet, where he'd never be able find them. If he loved his meat so much—it was only fair that he smelled like it, too.

I'd never done something so conniving in my life, and I was beginning to feel twinges of regret when the last of the steak pieces was tucked into a corner of the carpeted walk-in closet.

This was stupid. The man was actively ruining my life, and all I'd done was a harmless prank to make his clothes smell bad. It was infantilizing.

I advanced toward his laptop, which was sitting on his night-stand, and flipped it open. It needed both a fingerprint and a password to allow access. *Dammit.* I put the laptop back on the nightstand, wondering if Ransom was having sex with another woman right at this moment, and flipped open his briefcase. There—*voila*—I finally found something interesting. Paperwork. About *me*.

I skimmed the pages, gulping as much information as I could— within reason. It listed Ransom's weekly salary—*wow*—and the job description, including my father's specific requests for him. My heart beat loudly in my chest. I could barely make out the words before I felt dizzy and clammy. I was about to shove the papers back into the briefcase when a steely, husky voice ricocheted over the walls like a bullet, piercing a gaping, painful hole in my back.

"Big mistake."

Whirling around, I clutched the scissors in my fist and tried to duck beneath his arm to dash into my room. He caught me by the waist, scooping me like I was a toddler and positioning me back in front of him. I looked up at his face. His green eyes narrowed into dangerous slits. His lips became flat with anger. His façade of perfection remained in place, but his hair was tousled and his neck flushed.

Where were you?

What did you do?

Why do you look so glowy?

Best question of all—why do I care?

I fisted the scissors by the finger holes, aiming the blades for his thigh. He quickly caught the shears between his fingers, his gaze never leaving mine.

Shaking his head, he sighed. "We're past this, surely."

He pried the scissors from my hand, tossing them onto his nightstand behind me. I caught a glimpse of his palm. It was bloodied. I'd made him *bleed*. Somehow, I didn't feel horrible about it. It was good to know he was flesh and blood after all.

"What are you doing in my room, Brat?"

I gulped, feeling my throat bob with a swallow. His face was close. Too close. Close enough that I could taste the whiskey on his tongue and the hint of cherry. My lips curled in revulsion and I shook all over. I wanted to spit in his face. He was giving me all this grief for *my* behavior and was hooking up with someone who used flavored lip gloss?

And he'd told Tara he had standards!

"Snooping, Random. What else?" I smiled casually, smoothing the fabric of his already ironed shirt. "I wanted to find out things about my new *roomie*."

"And did you?" He swatted my hand away, his eyes dead and cold.

His body was flush with mine. My thighs brushed his knees. I felt his heat engulfing me. It shot a thrill through my spine. Never had I felt someone else's warmth against my own like this.

For the first time in my life, I didn't want to run away from a man. It made no sense at all. I hated men. Men, in general, were a threat to me. And this one had already proven he was capable of hurting me. But something about Ransom was unfamiliar. Maybe even a little surprising. Weirdly, I kind of got off on our hatred toward one another.

Inside the avalanche of chaos he brought into my life lived a measurement of safety. I knew he would never raise a hand to me. Conversely, he'd protect me from whatever harm might come my way.

"Yes." I licked my lips, not moving an inch back, not cowering or showing him that he scared me. "I learned, for instance, that you're hooking up with a twelve-year-old."

"*Dafuq*?" he boomed. He looked disgusted...but also a little alarmed? Like I was onto him.

Dear God, please don't make my bodyguard a pedo. I'd have to kill him, and I really don't want that on my conscience.

I flicked my hair. "Who else would wear cherry-flavored lip gloss? C'mon, Random. Don't make me alert the authorities."

With that, I winked and tried to make my way out of his room. He caught my wrist, spinning me in place, baring his teeth ferally. It was the first time I'd seen him angry. Up until now, all he'd given me was his bored and disinterested version—even when he'd thrown me over his shoulder and tossed me in my room... I did *not* like angry Ransom.

"Listen here, Brat. This room is off-limits for you until our time's up. Am I understood?"

"Will this be reciprocated?" I demanded.

"Will what be reciprocated?" he asked shortly.

"Will you stay away from my room, too?"

"I'm your fucking security!"

Oh, boy. He *never* dropped the F-bomb. I'd really hit a nerve tonight.

"You can secure me that closely *outside* of my safe haven," I answered smartly. "I want some privacy here."

"And I want a bearable client. Tough luck. I will enter your room whenever I feel it's necessary, Princess. But let it be known—if you come in here uninvited, you'll leave through the goddamn window."

Threatening me with violence. That was pretty counterproductive to his role in my life. But I had a feeling he already knew that. He was full of bullshit. He'd never hurt me. I didn't know how I knew. I just knew.

"Aw, too bad. I pegged you for someone with a little more self-control than that."

Ransom bent down, his lips almost touching mine when he spoke. "Get out of here before I tell your father you tried to seduce your close protection officer."

That got my attention.

My mouth dropped in shock. "That's a lie!"

He shrugged. "Your constant presence in my room raises red flags. If it's not your intention—stop wandering in here. Either way, my conscience is clear. I never use it. Now *leave*."

I did. In a flurry of tears and feverish panic, slamming my bedroom door behind me dramatically. As soon as I was alone, in the dark, I picked up my phone and called Hera. I'd been hoping to avoid it, but my parents were obviously not going to call me back and I was out of options. I couldn't continue living under the same roof with this man. Hell, I needed to sage the whole neighborhood to get rid of his demonic vibes.

Hera picked up on the fourth ring. She sounded sleepy, in comparison to my hysterical panting and sobbing.

"Hallie?" She yawned. Her voice alone felt like a slap in my face. "Are you okay? Are you *safe*?"

Yes? No? How was I to even answer this question?

"Hera. I need—need—need your help!" I howled, burying my face inside my pillow. This douchehole was manipulating me, controlling every aspect of my life…he wasn't a protector. He was an abuser.

"Are you okay?" She sounded alert now.

"Physically, I guess." I huffed. "But mentally—"

"If this is about the bodyguard, there's nothing I can do for you." The concern in her voice morphed into annoyance. I heard her sit upright, the bedsprings squeaking under her slight body.

"You don't understand!" I said desperately. "He is a nightmare, he—"

"You showed your tits to the entire world, Hallie. Do you really think what you need right now is *more* independence? He's been hired to help sort things out. Let him help."

"He is threatening me. Manipulating me. Not to mention he confiscates my belongings."

"Yeah, well, let's admit it, if you still act like a teenager, maybe it's high time someone confiscated your things." She let out another yawn.

I closed my eyes, gritting every single word out of my mouth like they were made out of glass. "Hera, Mom and Dad won't answer me. I know they'll listen to you. You're their favorite."

She *loved* hearing that.

"Mom and Dad don't play favorites," she countered primly. "I don't think you stand a chance at getting through to them, regardless. They're really upset. They've tried so hard for you. I can't even start counting the ways you've broken their hearts. They *are*, however, asking that guy they sent to babysit you for updates, so maybe if you finally come to your senses and start behaving like a grownup, he'll tell them to call you back."

"Hera! I—"

"No, Hallie. I'm sorry. You need to deal with this on your own. I have to catch up on sleep. I have a shift in two hours."

With that, she hung up, leaving me in a darkened sea of satin sheets and misery.

Chapter Five

Ransom

Then.

T he first rule was to never develop feelings.
Not for the toys.
Not for the food that was served.
Certainly not for people.

When Mr. Moruzzi adopted us, it all looked so promising. He had a big house and a wife who was a therapist, and had a nice, airy room with a lot of plants and framed inspirational quotes by notable people.

When I was dropped there, many months ago—I couldn't count because I was still too young—I'd thought it would be a game-changer. I was going to have a warm room, with toys, and clothes, and food.

And for the first month, that's exactly what happened. I wasn't the only kid. There was Tom, too. He was three years older than me. And Lawrence—or Law, to his friends. He was two years older than me.

Their lives seemed different from mine. They weren't there when I got home from school. They came in the evenings, looking dirty and beaten up. Mr. Moruzzi would let them eat a huge plate of whatever Mrs. Moruzzi made that day—mainly pasta or lasagna or pizza.

Then the kids would go to bed. I didn't know if I should envy or pity Tom and Law for their lives. They seemed much closer to Mr. Moruzzi than I was—but I soon learned it came with a hefty price.

A month after I got there, Mr. Moruzzi came to sit on the edge of my bed. It was nighttime. I was already half-asleep.

"Tomorrow, after you finish school, Tom'll wait for you. He'll teach you how to do the work."

"Work?" I asked groggily.

Six-year-olds weren't supposed to work. Even I knew that.

"You'll see. The Moruzzi family has a business. A very profitable one."

Mafia, Tom would explain to me later on. Mr. Moruzzi was the ringleader of a small Italian mafia that had a century-long beef with the Russians.

"Disappoint me, and you won't get your toys, your meals, your nice, comfy bed. Tell CPS—and you'll be back in the system, where nothing good ever happens."

The next day, Tom waited for me after my first class.

"I'm Tom."

"Ransom." I didn't shake the hand he offered me, though. It seemed weird. We were supposed to be foster brothers or whatever.

"Cool name."

I didn't answer that.

"Did they pick that out for you, or did your parents call you that?"

"Don't have any parents," I answered dryly, my stomach clenching painfully. "You here to talk or to teach me?" I wanted to get it over with.

Tom smirked, pleased. "Ever pickpocketed?"

"No?" I wasn't even sure what it meant.

"Well, you're about to learn from the best."

I downed an entire bottle of water before raising my head from the pillow, slam-dunking the bottle into the trashcan on the other side of my brothel-themed bedroom. I'd noticed that Brat sneaked into my room to sift through my trash, but I'd soon realized it was more to do with her recycling obsession than to try to get intel about me.

Last night's encounter had gone fine. Better than fine. *Good.* With my brand of kink, anything short of disaster was a godsend. But it didn't take the edge off. I was still feeling restless. Uncertain. I knew I was treating Brat like crap, but I didn't know how else to rein her in.

I'd lied to her. Said I didn't have a conscience. Truth was, I wasn't feeling too hot about how I'd treated this kid. But what other option did I have? The only way I knew how to play was to cheat the game.

And breaking her spirit was the easiest, fastest way to get to my goal and deliver the goods to President Thorne.

She's just a kid, and you're treating her inhumanely.

But she pushed back every step of the way, making it impossible to give her breathing room.

Anyway, I was now paying for drinking my weight in whiskey last night at a random hole in the wall. My hangover was hell. At least Max told me she'd behaved throughout the evening.

Scraping my miserable ass off the bed, I hopped into the shower, brushed my teeth for ten minutes (when Brat had said I smelled of cherry lipstick, I almost vomited in her pretty little face), then hit the kitchen for some coffee, eggs, and bacon.

Brat was probably still admiring her perfect pout in her bedroom mirror. If yesterday proved one thing, it was that the Thorne Princess wasn't aiming high for herself. Those friends of hers had the combined IQ of a pickle. And she knew it.

Not that Brat had a Stephen Hawkins-level brilliant mind, but at least a decent education and cut-glass vowels made sure she didn't sound as dumb as a brick.

I scowled out the kitchen window, calculating how many shifts I could transfer to Max without making him Hallie Thorne's primary nanny, when an armored, bright green Lamborghini pulled to a screeching stop in front of the entryway, knocking over an exotic plant in the driveway.

The driver flung the door open. I put my coffee cup down by the kitchen sink. What in the ever-loving shit was happening?

"What's going on?" Brat echoed my thoughts, tornadoing down the stairs in a pink kimono dress. She wasn't wearing a bra, and her nipples were straining against the thin fabric. My dick nodded her good morning. The rest of me wanted to file a restraining order against it. Stupidity was an unfortunate side effect of desire. Yet the interesting part was that my body responded to her at *all*. Normally, physical traits didn't do anything for me. I was more turned on by situations. The more salacious—the better.

"Who's the asshole in the Lamborghini?" she demanded.

The doorbell chimed on cue. Rather than answering her, I opened the front door.

Tom stood on the other side, wearing a checked suit and his good guy smile. A smile only I and one other person in the world knew was disingenuous.

Behind him, I spotted Lisa and the kids in the car, all waving at me. I scowled, as if he'd dumped a bag of flaming shit between us on the threshold.

"What are you doing here, Whitfield?"

"Why, howdy, partner!" Tom clapped my shoulder cheerily, winking at Brat, who stood behind me.

"Wifey and I were in the neighborhood and I thought I'd pop in and check on how y'all are doing before I start my new post in Chicago."

He lived five states away. The 'in the neighborhood' excuse was as believable as a Vegas stripper's tits. He obviously wanted to check and ensure my new client was still in a favorable mental state. Side note: the world would be a slightly better place if men would stop calling their spouses *wifey*.

"Are you the Whitfield in Lockwood and Whitfield?" Princess Thorne inquired behind my back.

"Yes, ma'am. And you must be Hallie!"

"The one and only." Brat shouldered past me, prancing about in her ridiculous robe to shake his hand. Tom took her palm in his and squeezed firmly. I waited for them to get it over with so I could slam the door in his face.

"You know your car was voted Most Polluting by most car magazines last year? Your Lamborghini burns a gallon of gasoline for every eighteen miles traveled. And it can't be family-friendly."

Tom shot me a look. I shook my head. "She's a tree hugger."

"The Lamborghini is a rental." He turned to her.

"Promise to return it to the agency and get a Tesla and I'll welcome you in."

"You got yourself a deal." Tom laughed.

Brat opened the door invitingly, offering him a little bow. "My kingdom is yours then, Mr. Whitfield."

His laugh intensified. What the hell was happening?

"Actually, I'm with the family. We're just passing by, see. I promised my kids I'd take them to Disneyland."

Disney World was closer to Chicago.

"Traffic to Anaheim is insane this time of the day. Your car will singlehandedly cause a volcano to erupt. Come on in, all of you." Brat opened the door wider, ignoring me. "We've got pastries. I'll make smoothies for the kids. It'll be fun."

"Don't mind if I do." Tom turned around and signaled Lisa to get out and bring the two terrors with her.

"Uncle Ramb-son!" one exclaimed. One of them was named Silas, the other Saint.

I'd never heard more white bread names in my life.

The twins ran, tackling my legs and hugging them firmly. I had no idea why. I'd never made any effort to be nice to them. I didn't actively scowl when they came around—a refreshing change from my usual behavior toward humans—but that was the extent of my relationship with them. I did buy them birthday presents. Mainly because they were born on April Fool's, so it was easy to remember the date.

I could see Brat was looking at me with a fresh expression, one full of curiosity and delight. I imagined she was having a *Beauty and the Beast* moment, where the ugly-ass beast feeds the birds in the snow. Little did she know, if I had birds in my palm, they'd be rotisserie chicken before the stupid song was over.

"Ransom, it is good to see you again." Lisa rose on her toes to kiss both my cheeks.

Lisa was a decent woman. But she also constantly tried to coerce me into family dinners, blind dates, and other social functions.

I turned around to face Tom. "What the hell are you doing here?"

He bumped his shoulder against mine, dropping his voice. "We need to take a little trip."

I rolled my shoulders. He'd kept it vague for a reason. "I'll grab my stuff."

"Grab your kit, too. I've a feeling we're dealing with some serious shit."

I went upstairs to get my gun (I always carried, and it was always hot), cell phone, and bag. When I got back down, I found Brat handing the little monsters two pink smoothies while having a heated conversation with Lisa about curling irons. I'd always detested the human need to fill silence with mundane small talk, but I especially hated how the Thorne Princess was seemingly winning over the small handful of people in my life.

"…and so," Brat concluded to Lisa, who stared at her, eyes like two full moons, "the real secret to perfect waves is to curl each section in the opposite direction. Like—" She lifted her hands and took pieces of Lisa's blonde hair to demonstrate. "If I curl this part inward, I'll curl the one next to it outward. And you have to keep them tight until you're completely done, then set them with hairspray before gently brushing. Do you have, like, twenty minutes? I can show you."

"She does," I said grimly, motioning to Tom to get his ass up from the stool and join me at the door. "We're leaving. Lisa will keep an eye on you."

"Leaving? Really?" Brat perked up. The sparkle in her eyes was telling. She loathed me.

I smirked cruelly. "Don't look so sad. It's only for a couple hours."

"A girl can dream."

"Can she? Creativity is not your strong suit," I volleyed back.

"And you know this conclusively about me from what, an impression based on these last couple days?" She parked a hand over her waist, cocking up an eyebrow.

"I know because you can't seem to read anything over two paragraphs long if the text isn't accompanied by pictures."

All this while Tom and Lisa's eyes ping-ponged between us.

The last jab seemed to do the trick, because Brat looked thoroughly wounded. She didn't like to be told she was stupid. I made a mental note not to do it anymore. No part of me wanted to see her banged up emotionally. I just wanted to survive this damn assignment.

"Uncle Ran-wrom said a potty word!" One of the twins—the smaller one—raised his head from his smoothie, his face smeared with pink.

"Very true. Uncle Ransom will now have to give each of you one dollar as an apology," Tom said primly, like he didn't grow up like me, in the guts of Chicago's whorehouses and drug dens.

Huffing, I took out my wallet and slapped a fifty-dollar bill in front of each twin. "Here," I groaned. "Since I know I'm about to rack up a bill here."

Finally, Tom and I left in his Lamborghini. I wasn't feeling completely confident in Brat's ability not to screw it up while I was gone, but Lisa was levelheaded, and I had every reason to believe she'd call us if Brat did something stupid, like flash the neighbors or invite domestic terrorists for a pool party.

"Where are we headed?" I asked, checking my Ruger LC9 to make sure it was fully loaded. I had zero trust in people. But I did trust my weapon to always function when I needed it. It was a good rule of thumb, and one I'd adopted the hard way.

"Huntington Beach."

"I'm going to need more than that."

By my calculations, Tom was supposed to start his work with Mayor Ferns on Monday. It was unlike him to make a trip to the West Coast so close to an assignment. We both had that poor boy complex, where we were eager to prove we were worth our salt.

"Ian's not been answering me."

"Ian Holmes?" I asked, removing invisible lint from my dress pants. Holmes was a fellow counterintelligence agent from our previous lives. He was much older than us and worked as a chief operating officer by the time we'd left. Which basically meant he ran the show and was our boss the last two years of our employment. Tom kept in touch with him.

"Yeah. Haven't heard from him in a week."

"So? Are you two having an affair?" My eyebrows shot up. "Why would you be talking to this random ass person more than you talk to your mom?"

"I don't have a mom, and you damn well know that," Tom muttered. "Ian and I talk pretty regularly. He's got a lot of insight. Has been in this business for decades. Speaking of affairs..." Tom scrubbed the stubble on the front of his throat, grinning. "Nice banter you had there with Miss Thorne."

"Don't go there," I warned. The image of her smoothing my dress shirt last night with that lopsided, siren smirk assaulted my memory every half hour or so.

"I'm not suggesting you're having an affair with her," Tom explained. "But...if she wasn't business, would you?"

"Absolutely not."

Tom had no idea about my sexual life, how depraved it was. But even if he had, he seemed to think even the biggest fuck-up could be reformed. He said he was living proof of that. He was wrong. I was ten times more damaged.

"She's not your type," Tom mused, unimpressed by the death glare I was sending him.

"Naturally." I rolled my window down. "My favorite type is without a pulse."

"Bet that sounded more warped than you intended it to." Tom tapped the steering wheel, flashing a shit-eating smile at nobody at all as we passed by palm trees and half-naked people. "You usually go for women you wouldn't ever bring home for a family dinner or a double date with Lisa and me. Which begs the question, do you still use call girls?"

"Jesus. No," I murmured, scowling at the view. That was so far back in our past. And not something I'd done by choice. I had no way of avoiding it. Avoiding *them*. Why would he bring it up now? "In case you haven't noticed, the girl's an airhead."

"Nah." Tom shrugged, and I could see in my periphery that his smile was widening. "She just has a big attitude, and it's all L.A. But once you strip that down…well, I think there is someone interesting behind the persona. She just called me out on my ride… pretty impressive."

"You mean rude." I flicked my Aviators on. "Good thing I'm the one vetting personnel in our company. You are always off when it comes to reading people."

The rest of the drive, Tom caught me up to speed about Ian Holmes. Apparently, Ian and he had been real close the past couple years, ever since Ian had been diagnosed with prostate cancer.

"It's just not like him not to answer," Tom explained. "Usually, if he's busy, he'd text back."

He pulled in front of a white, Spanish villa in a sleepy cul-de-sac in Huntington Beach, a stone's throw from the ocean. "He has a pretty strict routine, especially since his wife passed away."

We both got out of the car and made our way to Ian's front door. Only two more immaculately taken care of houses lined the cul-de-sac. Upscale neighborhood, for sure.

Ian's front door had three days' worth of rolled up newspapers in front of it. The first telltale of trouble.

Tom frowned and picked one of them up. "Not a good sign."

"Does he have any living relatives?" I peered around, craning my neck past his garden's gate.

"One daughter. She lives in Modesto, up north. She calls him once a week. Rarely visits. Some daughter she is."

Tom didn't always have a judgmental attitude, but fatherhood did that to him.

"Hey. Some parents don't deserve the respect. Maybe he went to visit her?"

He shook his head. "He'd have gotten one of his neighbors to take care of the newspapers. He's no rookie."

I checked my watch. I did not like the idea of leaving Brat without proper supervision. Even though my main job was to scare her off from pulling any stupid shit, I still took it seriously. For all I knew she could be filming a sex tape right this second.

With whom, ass-face? Lisa?

"Problem is, we can't just break into the place," Tom murmured somewhere to my right.

Couldn't we? Why not? If anything, we'd be helping the old man. He was obviously not doing too hot if he hadn't picked up his newspaper in three days. Elderly people—especially sick ones—told people when they left town. Ian never did.

I took out a bobby pin from my lockpicking kit and bent it to a ninety-degree angle, tampering with the door lock. I pushed it open in less than twelve seconds.

"Problem solved, I guess," Tom deadpanned. "You like skirting the edges of right and wrong, don't you?"

I shot him a look, shouldering past him inside. I wanted to get this over with as soon as possible.

We saw no obvious break-in signs. The house looked relatively neat—considering it belonged to a retiree widower, anyway—and it didn't appear ransacked—as if someone had been looking for something to steal. The place was modestly decorated, but even the belongings worth a dime or two were intact. Vases, paintings, an especially hideous decorative golden bowl. Nothing was out of place.

I ran a finger over the fireplace. No dust. "Been cleaned recently."

Tom threw the fridge door open. "That may be, but half the food in here is expired. I'm going upstairs to the bedrooms."

I nodded. "I'll check the garage and backyard."

Tom took the stairs while I opened the garage. An old school black Jeep was parked inside. Wherever Ian went, he hadn't taken his car.

I strolled along the garage, which was jam-packed with hardware, including weapons. Everything appeared untouched. This was not your run-of-the-mill burglary case. If someone hurt or took this man, they didn't want anything that belonged to him, just the guy himself.

"Coast is clear upstairs. All the rooms are empty," Tom shouted from the second floor.

I ambled from the garage to the balcony doors. I stopped cold when I noticed what should have stood out to me from the beginning—a slight gap in the glass door. It was open. Rather than using the handle and fucking up potential fingerprints, I curled the fabric of my sleeve over my fingers as I pushed the door gently open. The garden's layout was simple. It was a square space with a patch of grass and some outdoor furniture arranged randomly on one side.

And smack in the middle of the garden, arms and feet poked out of the ground.

I repeat—human feet.

Well, shit.

"Tom," I barked, "Don't come out here. And don't touch anything on your way down."

He knew the drill and it was unlikely that he would, but I wanted to err on the safe side. I flicked my phone, about to call 911. And Tom, who never was very good at taking orders, stood beside me five seconds later, his face screwed in repulsion and agony as the horror show in front of us became clear to him.

"I told you not to come here," I hissed out. No part of me desired to see him emotionally destroyed by this.

"And you thought I'd listen? I wanted to see wha... Oh, shit."

"My thoughts exactly."

There was a long beat in which he digested what had happened.

"They half-assed the burial." He swallowed.

"Or deliberately botched it."

Tom took his phone out and called 911, and our local FBI friend, Chris. This was definitely retaliation.

The arms and legs were purple and blue—and unmistakably those of an elderly male. Ian had been this way for over twenty-four hours.

"Feds and the police are on their way," Tom announced, turning around and bracing his hands on his knees. He sounded faraway. Deep in thought. I imagined it was hard for him. I liked Ian, too. But it was never a difficulty for me to say goodbye to people. I'd done it more times than I could count. Moving between foster homes, institutes, units. Death, specifically, did not faze me in the least. It was just another station in life. The last one, to be exact.

Tom could still make connections. Even friendships.

"Are you thinking what I'm thinking?" Tom asked. I felt his shoulder brush against mine as he joined me near the shallow grave. He seemed to be alternating between wanting to throw up to wanting to do something about what we'd just discovered.

"Too soon to tell," I ground out, shoving my hands into my front pockets. "But the initial signs are there. The burial method is haphazard. Whoever did this wanted to send a message, not conceal a body. And unless we find strangulation or bullet wounds... well, he could've been buried alive."

Chechen burial.

Parts of the body were visible for all to see—on purpose. The person was normally buried alive, for extra torture. This was something I was familiar with, as I had worked in the Los Angeles area with Ian himself before retiring, and the local Bratva was fond of getting rid of people that way.

I also knew this from my days in Chicago, when the Italians and Russians tried to slaughter one another on a weekly basis.

"This is bullshit," I gritted out. "I'm sorry. I know you were close."

I *was* sorry. I just wasn't sure what that meant.

"You want to tell me it stirs nothing in you?" Tom pushed my chest suddenly, baring his teeth. He was angry. He needed to redirect that anger at someone. And right now, that someone was me.

I didn't know what else there was to be said. I had not wished death upon Ian Holmes. I didn't wish death upon most people, despite my misanthropic tendencies.

"That's it?" Tom spat out.

I stared at him levelly. "I wasn't the one who killed him, all right? Lay off."

He pushed at my chest again, harder this time. I let myself stumble a couple of steps.

"You don't give two shits, do you? He was our boss. He mentored us. We worked together. He treated you like a son."

"I'm no one's son," I replied tersely.

"Yes, and you are just so fucking eager to never forget it!" Tom barked out a bitter laugh. "You really love the whole tortured screw-up persona. Makes you feel important, doesn't it?"

I was getting tired of getting bitched about for something I hadn't done. Sure, Holmes was one of ours, but I did not consider anyone family. Not even Tom himself. Family was a liability other people had. I had acquaintances.

"Look, this is not constructive." I sighed.

"You know what's not constructive?" Tom balled my collar in his fist. "The fact that you don't have a damn heart."

"No heart is better than too big a heart. Remember where you came from. Life ain't pretty."

He let me go suddenly, and I had the good grace to pretend to stumble back from the impact.

Two minutes later, a few police cars and a black sedan pulled in front of Ian's front door. We gave them our statements, then our business cards. We weighed in with what we thought had happened. Who we thought could be behind this.

"Kozlov," we kept saying. "His name is Kozlov."

Like they didn't know. Like they weren't busting their asses trying to catch him this very minute. That is, if they weren't in his pocket and under his payroll.

They sent us on our way and asked us to give them a call if we remembered anything more. Standard protocol.

During the drive back to Brat's house, I considered telling Tom I was sorry for his loss, but then remembered he would just use it as a way to club me for not feeling as shitty as he did.

Tom was the first to break the silence. It happened when we glided onto Interstate 5 and got stuck in one of the longest traffic jams known to mankind.

"You know it's the Russians." His jaw ticked. He wore sunglasses, so I couldn't see his expression, but I had a feeling he was misty-eyed.

"Logic dictates."

"They're ruthless," he said animatedly.

"Most people are. But they're also fearless. Not a good combo."

Shortly before I'd handed in my resignation and went private, I was involved in a bloody operation against the Bratva in Los Angeles. These were tough-as-nails criminals who came here after the Soviet Union fell and muscled the Italian mafia out of Los Angeles in less than three years, leaving rivers of blood in their wake. The FBI would probably have been perfectly content with letting the two gangs kill each other off, but during my service, the Russians had gotten sloppy—power drunk—and often claimed civilian casualties.

Mistaken identities, assassinations gone wrong, gun fights in broad daylight forced us to step in. And in we stepped. Only we didn't deal with amateurs. Soon, these people had our names, our addresses, a list of our loved ones. Tom and I, especially, were on their shit list. They knew about us from their friends in Chicago. How we worked with the Italians. Kozlov'd had a bullet with my name on it before I'd even known of his existence.

The Russians fought back. In the end, we'd managed to throw some of them in the can, but not nearly as many as we wanted to.

And not the main villain—Vasily Kozlov.

Ian Holmes had been in charge of that operation. He was no doubt a target for them. And what do you know? They'd decided his time was up.

"They're clapping back." Tom stroked his jawline. "Years later."

"Technically, didn't Holmes retire last year?" I asked. "He'd been on their case for a lot longer than we were. And they don't exactly play nice."

"Now, here is where it gets sticky for me." Tom cleared his throat, shooting me an uncertain look. "You're here, in Los Angeles. They have your name, your affiliation to Moruzzi. That makes you a target."

I'd been trying to tell him as much back when he asked me to take the post.

"I can take care of myself," I said flatly.

"I don't doubt that. But then, you'd be putting Hallie at risk, too."

He wasn't wrong, but I also wasn't going to let a bunch of low-lifes mess with my plans, my aspirations, my career.

"I would like to see them try to get to her."

"I'm not kidding," Tom said, looking gloomy as shit.

He'd really taken Ian Holmes' death hard. I imagined he was going to call the daughter next, maybe help arrange for his service. That was the kind of man Tom was. Broken, but glued together, somehow, into something whole.

"You're going to be putting her at risk instead of eliminating risks that could put her in danger."

"I'm well aware, all right?" I barked, staring out the window. "If anything, it would add some spice to this job. All this woman does is shop and take pictures with her friends."

"You can't be serious right now."

I was, in fact, being serious. I wasn't going to let a bunch of assholes run my life. For starters, I had no reason to believe they knew I was in Los Angeles. For another, I left here years ago. Tom was making a mountain out of a goddamn molehill.

"All I'm saying is—"

"You wanted me here, and now I am. I'll keep an eye out for the Bratva."

Tom let out a short breath. "How do I tell Lisa that Ian is dead?" he asked finally. "She's going to be devastated."

Grief was something I had no concept of, so I kept my mouth shut for the remainder of the ride.

Chapter Six

Hallie

The rest of the day was a cluster.

As soon as Ransom came back, he kicked Lisa, Tom, and the kids out and dragged me to my room.

"You're staying in today, Princess," he said, no particular tone to his voice as he threw me in there without so much as an explanation.

Something had definitely gone wrong for him while he'd been out with Tom. I doubted it had anything to do with me. I'd been here all along, getting to know Tom's family. Lisa was a cool chick for sure. She collected Toulouse-Lautrec prints and had one of the most extensive collections outside France. And she was big on sustainable, green living, just like me. We even exchanged numbers and emails. I could only imagine what kind of hell Ransom would have put me through had he suspected I was forming connections with people from his real life.

"I'm not your prisoner." I kicked around haphazardly as he carried me to my room, more curious than upset, really. I dragged my feet over the stairs to make it hard for him. Unfortunately, he seemed completely unfazed by my weight and tucked me under his arm like I was no more a burden than the morning newspaper.

"Agreed," he said, surprising me. "But I need to sort out some shit today. I'll call Max to keep an eye on you. He'll let you out of the room, but you have to stay home for the time being."

"Why?" I demanded breathlessly, after he put me down on the floor in my room. "Did something happen?"

"Nothing that concerns you."

"But something did. Are you doing side hustles now?" I flat-eyed him, desperate to make him feel as small as he made me feel. If he got himself into trouble, and I wasn't a part of it, it pretty much meant he was dragging me down with him.

He gave me a pitiful look. "Stop talking."

"Stop breathing."

"Your parents will be disappointed to learn you've made no progress in the shrew-taming department."

"Good. Means I'm wearing you down. Maybe you'll decide to quit soon. Or better yet—have a heart attack."

He slammed the door in my face, then locked it. I found myself wishing he were dead. The heat and rage with which I hated him stunned me.

Which reminded me—today, I found a voice message from my mother on my phone. She was careful to leave it at four in the morning Pacific Time, when she knew I wasn't going to pick up.

"*I hope you are doing okay, and that you understand we only did what we had to do. We worry about you, Hallie. We'll talk when you calm down.*"

But when I called back, she didn't pick up. Hera wasn't kidding. They really had decided to cease all communication with me and get reports from Ransom.

Well, if the mountain won't come to Mohammad...

It was time to pay the Thorne family a visit.

As if reading my mind, my sister's name appeared on the phone screen in my hand. I felt slightly alarmed. Hera did not call me all that often. Maybe once a month to tell me how big of a screw-up I was. My existence seemed to embarrass her, but not enough to warrant an interaction with me. Sometimes I wondered, if my parents had known what kind of woman I'd grow up to be—would my mother still have chosen to keep her pregnancy with me?

I swept a finger over the screen and put my sister on speaker.

"Hey," I said, trying to sound neutral, but fully preparing myself for a verbal whiplash.

"Hey, are you feeling better?"

"No."

"Great. That must mean you're making progress. When are you coming here?" She sounded disinterested and a little annoyed. Like I somehow should have predicted she wanted to talk to me and called her myself to save her fingers the stress of dialing.

"Never, if it's up to Mom and Dad," I joked. Flinging myself onto my bed, I began browsing through online catalogs on my phone. I could never just speak on the phone without doing something else. It seemed like such a waste of time.

"Yeah, well, the rehearsal dinner is in a few weeks, and you're invited. So." She left her sentence hanging.

I liked how she said I was invited. Like your sister has to be invited to your wedding. I knew, in fact, there had been discussion of leaving me out. And though it didn't surprise me, it hurt me a lot. Craig, her fiancé, and I didn't exactly get along.

"We still have weeks until then."

"You need to come for the dress measurements," she countered flatly. "Plus, it's been a long time since you paid Mom and Dad a visit."

"Well, when do you want me in Dallas?"

"Next week."

"Next week?" I felt my hands becoming clammy, and my feet going cold.

"Yes," Hera said impatiently. "There's a lot to discuss. Just book a ticket, will you?"

"I—I can't," I stuttered.

"You never miss measurements for a premiere or a new club opening," Hera drawled.

Actually, I recycled dresses like crazy, but when had Hera ever taken the time to get to know me?

"Random—I mean, the bodyguard—took my credit cards. I don't have a way to book tickets."

"Oh." The surprise in her voice gave me a glimmer of hope. Maybe she'd step in and tell Mom and Dad how horrible he'd been to me. "I'll give you my credit card details."

Her spurt of altruism surprised me to a point I almost felt touched, which I hated myself for. I lived on those crumbs of small gestures from my family.

"But don't go crazy. Just buy what you need, or I'll tell Mom and Dad."

"Okay. Thank you." I had no idea what else to say with some level of dignity.

"And please pack some respectable clothes, if you have any."

By the chatter around her, about polish colors and different foot treatments, I could guess she was getting her manicure. Hera always got the same thing—a short, natural, gelled French manicure. "I mean, I know you'll never cover those horrid tattoos, and I can't make a silk purse out of a sow's ear. But can you at least wear something that doesn't scream dominatrix in a sex club?"

Sex club. Sometimes I suspected my twenty-nine-year-old sister was actually ninety-two.

"I serve at your pleasure," I joked. "Consider it done. And I—"

I started to tell her that I was excited for her, but she'd already hung up on me, as I was midway through spewing sentimental words at her.

I used her card to purchase a plane ticket to Dallas, and booked myself a nice suite in the Fleetwood Mansions of Tortoise Creek. A cool one grand a night, but surely, my only sister would not want me sleeping in a dumpster while I visited my family.

Hera knew as well as I did that I refused to stay at my parents' house. I didn't feel welcome there, and for a good reason. My parents always berated me—about my clothes, my manners, my walk, my grades. But even if they hadn't, I simply couldn't feel safe. Not after what happened there the first time.

Or the second time.

Or the third.

Anyway. So here we were.

I heard Max walk through the door and exchange some words with Ransom and felt a deep sense of relief. I'd been feeling like a caged animal these last few days. Claustrophobia closed in on me.

I wondered if the meat in Ransom's closet had already started decomposing. I hoped so. Maybe it would remind him of his rotten soul.

A few minutes after I heard one of my cars drive off—Ransom felt very comfortable using my things—the door to my room was unlocked.

"Decent?" he called *and* knocked.

"Sure."

Max appeared in front of me. He tipped an imaginary hat down, all chivalry and sugar.

"Cinderella."

"Prince Charming." I stood taller, my tone several notches colder. Nice or not, Max was still a man and I needed to remember that. "You're late, as always."

"Want me to accompany you anywhere?" He leaned one shoulder against the doorframe. Clearly, he was happy to see me, and it made me feel uneasy. I was not used to people genuinely liking me.

"Didn't you hear?" I grimaced. "The tyrant forbade me to leave the house today."

"That true?" He rubbed his upper lip. He was blushing. Again.

"Didn't he say?" A lesser woman would exploit Max's obvious disorientation next to her to her advantage.

"Must've forgotten. Man, I dropped the ball on that one."

Rolling my eyes, I fell back into a heap of silky sheets. "I'm so over your boss."

"He means well." Max winced. "How 'bout a movie? I'm not supposed to be doing recreational stuff on duty, but…"

"Only if I get to choose."

"You're going to choose something super girly, huh?" He rubbed his chin.

"Hello. Hi. It's me. Duh."

But once we settled in the living room, we opted for the new James Bond installment. Max wanted to see the action and pretty women, and I wanted to see Daniel Craig existing, just in general. We shared a popcorn bowl and two cans of diet soda. I convinced myself to take a deep breath and enjoy the moment. Forget about Ransom. Which could have been easier, had Ransom not burst into the house an hour after the movie started, sweaty and *shirtless*.

The shirtless part was really tragic, because he looked so incomparably hot next to Daniel Craig. Long and lithe and muscular. The ridges of his six-pack were glistening with his sweat. He must've been running. I stared at him, open-mouthed. I didn't even care that I was gawking. Surely, he was used to it.

"What're you doing?" he demanded, parking his hands on his narrow waist. Even his *fingernails* were perfect. Square and clean and...*focus, Hal. Focus.*

"Staring at the worst human alive, willing him to burst into flames on the spot?" I batted my lashes angelically.

"I wasn't talking to you," Ransom barked.

Oh.

Max stood up. His face looked like it was about to explode. "Sir."

"Don't sir me," Ransom clipped. "You're not supposed to shoot the shit with the ward."

"I know," Max hurried to say. "I know. I'm sorry, it's just that she said she was not permitted to leave the house—"

"She isn't," Ransom cut in dryly. "You were briefed about this."

"Yes," Max said gravely. "Yes, I was. My apologies. I just think she's still adapting to the new situation and wanted to keep her company. I figured if I could keep an eye on her while..."

"Also keeping an eye on a Bond girl?" Ransom finished the sentence for him. "I should demote you to the office stapler for this."

"Oh, for Pete's sake." I threw my hands in the air. "Stop being such a huge baby, Ransom. Half the time you don't even look at me, too busy on your computer. Don't lecture others about professionalism."

The men whipped their heads to stare at me. Both looked shocked. Neither looked happy. I'd just dropped a truth bomb squarely on its target.

"Max," Ransom said, his intense, darkened gaze set firmly on me. "Get out. I'll talk to you this evening."

"Yes, sir."

Max scurried away, but not before saying goodbye to me. I liked that he stayed sweet and apologetic, even when Ransom was on his ass. I tried to stand a little taller, extending my spine as much as I could and tilting my chin up. I wasn't going to cower in front of this bully.

He got in my face, scowling. His eyes were a peculiar shade of green today. Like an eternal forest. A sick thought entered my mind. How proud and cocky Mrs. Lockwood must be to have a son as gorgeous and accomplished as Ransom. I wondered how many girls he'd dated. How many he brought home. How many he took in the back of his beat-up truck I spontaneously decided that he'd owned as a teenager.

"Your phone's ringing," he said, making me break our stare-off to look down at the coffee table, where my phone was sitting.

"It's Wes Morgan." I cringed, remembering that awful night that led to Ransom becoming a part of my life for the next six months. "I promised him a photo-op if he gave me a ride home."

It sounded supremely stupid, now that I listened to it with my own ears. It seemed a million years away from where I was today, from this new reality of mine.

"Chivalry isn't dead," he deadpanned.

"It wasn't completely his fault—"

"It was. He called the paps."

"Anyway, I don't want to handle it." I sighed.

"I will, then."

Ransom studied me quietly, waiting for an okay. I felt triggered by how hot he was. How was I supposed to stand my ground when he looked like a book boyfriend?

Still staring at me with a death glare, Ransom swiped the phone from the granite coffee table between us and put the call on speaker.

Oh, God.

Oh, no.

Oh, why.

"Heyyyy, gorgeous." Wes popped his gum loudly on the other line. "How about that photo-op? Feel like a trip to the zoo together? We can kiss by the bird cages."

"The only trip you'll be making is to the cemetery if you ever call this number again."

Ransom was so stoic, so collected, his tone sent a chill up my spine. I had no doubt he meant those words. I also had no doubt Wes was dumb enough not to understand the graveness of the situation.

A brief pause on the other line was followed by Wes' demands. "Who's this? Do you know who I am?"

"Unfortunately," Ransom said conversationally, leaning a hip against the credenza. "A meathead with a receding hairline and a reality show. Got a whole dossier on your ass. A hundred and thirty pages long, if you feel like a quick summer read. That's how I also know you cannot possibly let your reality gig die while you owe 250k in unpaid plastic surgery."

I knew those biceps weren't real!

"Holy shit!" Wes exclaimed. "H—h—how? I mean, who—"

"Now, and let me introduce myself," Ransom continued. "I'm your biggest nightmare. I eat men like you for breakfast. And I've been appointed to help Miss Thorne rehabilitate her reputation—a reputation which you tarnished—meaning she'll be staying far away from you. You are not to contact her ever again, understand?"

God save the girl who was going to become this man's daughter. Might as well tattoo the word UNDATABLE on her forehead.

In other news: I was impressed by Ransom's research on Wes.

"Geez, man. Okay. Okay," Wes whined. "Can I at least—"

"No." Ransom hung up, handing me my phone back. "Case dismissed."

I took it, staring at him in pure horror. "I noticed. You should try your hand at politics. Such finesse."

He turned around, about to go up the stairs, probably to take a shower. I cleared my throat, bracing myself for the conversation we were about to have.

"I'm traveling to Texas." I dropped the bomb, making him stop in place, his back to me.

He turned around slowly, looking at me with mild curiosity. Was it just me or did he actually look *relieved*? Whatever was on his face, it was an emotion. The Robot had an emotion. And it wasn't a bad one, either.

"We are?" he asked laconically.

"*I* am," I corrected him. "There's some stuff ahead of my sister's wedding I need to tend to. She'd rip my head off if I missed the dress fitting. I already booked a ticket and a hotel and everything."

"With what credit card?"

"Hers."

His eyes darkened. The man wasn't used to being outsmarted.

"I'll need the dates and flight arrangements. We're going to be rooming together. Separate beds."

"Over my dead body!"

He shrugged. "Not my favorite sleeping arrangement, but whatever works for you."

He took the stairs up. I trailed behind him, pleading my case.

"Random, you can't be serious."

"Deadass, as you influencers say."

"People will talk." I went for the weakest excuse possible.

"People aren't that interested in you," he countered.

"Are you kidding? The media is *obsessed* with me. I'm a hot mess. I swear, it'll be all over the news, and super counterproductive to us trying to clean up my act."

He gave me a *what of it* glance.

"You'll never be able to show your face in public again!" I squirmed, attempting to snatch the hem of his running shorts.

"Never cared too much about the public."

"But don't you care—"

"No."

"Random—"

"It's Mr. Lockwood to you." He stopped at the top of the stairs, whirling toward me like a storm. "Listen carefully here, Brat. My job is to protect you. I cannot do that from two doors down the hallway in a hotel. This trip is going to have maximum security. I am going to get hooked with local agents who'll sweep the hotel, prepare exit routes, and install cameras and motion sensors, which will be wired to an operation room in a neighboring suite. You're under my supervision, under my care, which means that you'll be operating under my sole jurisdiction. Not sharing a room together is not an option."

"*Random*," I insisted. He'd called me *Brat*. "Am I in any kind of danger? This all seems so…excessive."

"Possibly," he said, and for the first time, he sounded honest. "You're the daughter of one of the most prominent presidents in American history. And thanks to your social media antics, every single idiot with an electronic device knows where you live."

"All right." I sighed. "If you think it's necessary."

"I do."

We stayed frozen on the spot, a step away from the second floor.

Ransom frowned. "What's the catch? It's not like you to follow simple instructions without kicking and screaming."

"There isn't one," I said, bypassing him and making my way to my home gym at the end of the hallway.

Maybe I *was* in danger. If I was, I definitely didn't want to get hurt just because I was trying to prove a point to this jerk. Plus, it had to be said—watching Ransom in various stages of undress while sharing a suite with him would not be the worst of punishments. How had Ransom's rampant sexiness been able to stir a little reaction in me?

I'd been dormant for so long…what if I could *really* get turned on?

Was it him, or timing? Was I ready to meet someone, date…? If I wasn't horrible to him, maybe he'd actually let me live my life and I could get out there and see if I had chemistry with someone else. He didn't seem to be anywhere closer to quitting this job early. Perhaps learning how to live with this beast for six months wasn't the end of the world, after all.

"If you're up to something…" He narrowed his eyes.

I waved him off. "So skeptical. People are capable of altruism, you know?"

"Highly debatable."

"Well, debate yourself because I'm going to hit the gym and blow off some steam."

I disappeared into my home gym, bypassed the elliptical, treadmill, and weight rack, and went straight to the mini fridge, where I kept a supply of bottled water and my favorite gelato. I took out a Kit Kat flavored ice cream and a spoon. Some situations required more than a smoothie.

And living with the grumpiest ghoul in middle earth was one of them.

I was deep into my ice cream eating session when I decided to FaceTime Keller since he was away. Every quarter, Keller Airbnb'd a place in Palm Springs to work on his tan and try variations of new green juices that would later be introduced as Main Squeeze's seasonal Boost Camp drinks.

Keller was just telling me about his surprising new combination of celery, kale, turmeric, and spearmint, when Ransom stormed into the gym. This time—escalation—he was only wearing a towel. A flimsy little thing, hanging from his waist teasingly. His dark hair was wet and tousled to messy perfection. Steam radiated from his body. This was the part where I would normally scream and try to stab him with a random object. Oddly, though, I was not scared.

I wasn't the only one who caught sight of that.

"Bodyguard with benefits? Really?" Keller cooed from my phone screen, his eyes almost bulging out. "Me likey. And a little jelly."

I gagged loudly enough for the Pope to hear in the Vatican. "It's close protection officer. He gets touchy when you call him a bodyguard."

"Close protection officer? Makes him sound like a condom," Keller laughed.

At this point, Ransom decided he'd had enough of this conversation, grabbed my phone, and tossed it to the other side of the room. It fell on my lululemon yoga mattress.

Turning to face him, I made sure my expression was as blank as possible. "Care to tell me what crawled up your ass? Whatever it is, please do not try to make me pull it out of you."

Silently, Ransom lifted his hand to reveal a piece of meat between his fingers. It looked darker than when I'd left it in his closet, and had two maggots hanging out of it, squirming, about to fall to the floor.

I cupped my mouth, fighting my gag reflex for real now.

"What the hell, Random?" I jumped up from my spot and ran out of the room and along the corridor to escape the smell. He charged after me, his stride long and purposeful. I took the stairs down. So did he.

"Get away from me!" I yelped, ignoring the fact that I had, in fact, tarnished his entire designer wardrobe with rotten meat just to get back at him. He'd had it coming. He had been horrible to me. I didn't have many principles. But vegetarianism was one of them.

"Not until you clean up the mess you've created."

Unlike the salt incident, this time he reacted to my prank. I'd finally pushed him over the edge. He was insane if he thought I was going to clean that up.

"In your dreams." I used the kitchen island as a barrier.

"Well, my dreams are about to become your reality." He tossed the piece of meat between us, on the marbled surface. It was missing the two worms, and now I couldn't help but think they were somewhere in the house. *Shudder*.

"No." I braced the kitchen island, splaying my fingers over it, my stance ready to pounce and get into a fistfight with him. "What are you going to do about it? *Hit* me?"

"Touching you is not on my agenda, so stop worrying about something that'd never happen."

It was good news. Very good news.

So why was I slightly disappointed when he said that? Oh, that's right. Because I did know what his hands felt like on me. And they felt good. More than good. *Great*. And that was when he simply carried me from place to place.

"I will report back to your parents," he said without missing a beat. "*And*, as expected, your phone must be confiscated once again. That didn't take long. I'll go grab it."

He turned around and went upstairs, not giving me a chance to cool off, to explain nicely that I couldn't touch meat. It made me vomit. And that it wasn't just about murdering innocent animals, but also about the environment.

I couldn't believe he was taking my phone again. I also couldn't believe I was dumb enough to follow Keller's plan without considering the consequences. That biting feeling of aloneness slammed into me again.

It was then, in a complete moment of madness and desperation, that I decided to do the undoable. To run away. I didn't have a plan. Nor did I have car keys. Or a phone. But I'd had *enough*. Ransom was pushing me too far, barging into my life, taking my credit cards, my cars, demanding things I didn't know how to give him. I wasn't even sure what it was he wanted from me. My entire existence seemed to aggravate him.

Jamming my feet into my sliders, I swung the entryway door open and trudged outside. To freedom. To independence. To… what the hell was that, sticking to the bottom of my shoe?

I bent down to pick it up. *Ugh*. It looked like an unsolicited leaflet or something. Seriously, did anyone actually fall for these things? Their only purpose seemed to unnecessarily kill trees.

Crumpling it in my fist, I started making my way out of my gated neighborhood. A rush of adrenaline coursed through my veins. With it, came fear. I had no idea what to do. A part of me assumed I was just going to give Ransom a little scare, sit in the park for a few hours, then come back and renegotiate the terms of my imprisonment with him. I also needed to find a trashcan to throw away the leaflet. I couldn't believe that this was my life now. A week ago, I was hanging on the rooftop of a skyscraper, drinking vintage champagne with movie stars.

I was about a hundred feet away from the gate surrounding my neighborhood when my Nissan LEAF appeared in my periphery, zipping past sprawling villas and eye-popping pools. Ransom had gotten dressed, and even managed a close shave before coming to pick me up.

"Get in." He slowed the car to match my stride.

I stared ahead, determined not to give him what he wanted.

"I already told you, you're not allowed to leave the house without supervision. I can't protect you without your cooperation."

"Cooperation!" I exploded, coming to a halt. I turned around to face him, feeling my eyes wildly dancing in their sockets. "Are you kidding me? You take everything I have and own, everything that represents me, you treat me like a spoiled child, you call me *Brat*, and also a bitch once—yes, I heard your conversation with Tom—and you don't even tell me what kind of so-called danger I'm in. And you want my cooperation? I'm completely in the dark." I flung my arms sideways. "I have no idea what's going on, and you don't seem to care. You're doing a miserable job."

He stopped the car. Got out. Rounded the car. I stayed rooted in place. He couldn't kidnap me in broad daylight, could he? I supposed technically, he could. There was not a soul in sight.

But he didn't. Instead, he stopped a few feet from me.

"You're right."

"No! Don't give me that. I am entitled to my…wait, what did you just say?" My face twisted in confusion.

"I said you're right. I could have given you more context to what was happening, and I chose not to. We can still rectify that. *Privately*. In your house."

This was my time to bargain. I needed to pick my battles smartly.

"First things first, I do not want meat in my fridge." I raised my hand. "This is absolutely non-negotiable. It makes me physically sick to see."

His jaw ticked, but he didn't answer, which I took as confirmation that he heard and intended to comply.

The air between us stilled, as if the world was holding its breath to hear the verdict.

"I will not put meat in your fridge," he said finally.

"Thank you." I wrung my fingers together. The paper dropped from my hand.

"What's that?" Ransom asked, already bending down to pick it up.

"Some leaflet I was about to throw in the recycling can."

He smoothed the white paper—who knew? Maybe Ransom was one of the suckers who could be convinced to join a sauna Zumba class?—but when I noticed the color drain from his face, I realized this was no ordinary leaflet.

"We have to go. *Now*." Ransom grabbed my hand, tugging me to the car.

It scared me. I'd never seen him express emotions other than boredom or anger. I climbed into the passenger's seat of my car. He drove us up the road, back to my house, glancing at the rearview mirror. A lot. Like he was expecting to see someone.

"What was in the leaflet? An ad for penis enlargement? Are you all geared up to book a consultation meeting?" Naturally, I thought this would be a good time to break the ice with a terrible joke.

Ransom did not look amused. He *did*, however, look like he was going to break the steering wheel, the way he held it in a chokehold.

Finally, he spoke.

"Your parents hired me to monitor your whereabouts and to ensure your safety. This was their chief goal. However, there is a side goal, and that is to bring you to relative independence and teach you the value of money. They would also like to see you taking more responsibility over your life, and find a profession that requires more commitment than posting pictures on TikTok."

"Instagram," I corrected him. "I *wish* I could break into TikTok."

"Whatever." He slid the vehicle into my garage.

"So, basically, you're my parole officer."

He killed the engine, got out of the car, rounded it, and opened the door for me. I had a feeling it was a safety measure, not a statement of gallantry.

"Correct."

Ransom turned, making his way to the house, the crumpled leaflet still in his hand.

"And what happens if I fail?" I trailed behind him, fascinated. He seemed to have had a very long conversation with my parents, something I couldn't say for myself in the last three years.

I was experiencing a moment of epiphany. Or maybe—God forbid—self-awareness. What if my family had been avoiding me in a bid to make me do better? Should I try? I mean, Hera *did* invite me to her rehearsal. And paid for everything. I should be trying, too, shouldn't I?

"Not my problem, not my fight. I guess they'll find another, less expensive way to make your life miserable until they bend you into shape."

"They don't seriously expect me to work, do they? An actual real job, I mean."

"Is your blood too blue for manual work?" His pointed expression was a punctuation mark.

"No," I weighed my words carefully, "but I'm useless. I'm not good at anything." I couldn't believe I'd let these words get out of my mouth. I was usually so private about my shortcomings.

"Most people aren't," he said. "Averageness is humanity's greatest common ground. You'll find your way."

"Great pep talk, dude. You should be a motivational speaker."

"What, and neglect my new aspiration to become a politician?" he quipped.

When we got back inside, he double-locked all the doors, checked the windows, and splayed an impressive (and terrifying) collection of guns on my counter, which he began to clean.

Without lifting his eyes from the guns, he said, "Pack up, Princess. We're going to be in Texas for a while."

Chapter Seven

Ransom

Calm. Stay calm. You're The Robot. The impenetrable every VIP would love to have. You're…

Fuuuuuuuuuuck.

And a few more times for the people in the back—fuck, fuck, fuckity fuck.

When I accepted the Hallie Thorne gig, I imagined the most challenging aspect would be putting up with her mind-numbing chatter. Now, less than a week into the post, I'd received a letter from the Bratva informing me that they knew my whereabouts and did not appreciate my presence in SoCal again.

Good to have you back.

Looking forward to carving new memories with you.

—K

Luckily, Brat's shopping interest seemed to vanish with her credit card. I doubted she'd even read the contract I'd given her. Maybe her interest had vanished with her purchasing power.

Now, if I were flying solo, I would take the news as a personal invitation to rip Kozlov a new one. The issue was—I was on a job. And right now, the only threat to Brat's life was being associated with my ass.

Logic dictated I call Tom to let him know about this, then make the next call to Anthony Thorne, informing him of my immediate resignation, my reason for it, and referring him to another security company.

Logic, however, could suck it. Now that I'd started this assignment, I had my eye on the prize. I was getting that meeting with the former president and milking the connections I got out of it to the max.

By the time I was done with Brat, she was going to be enrolled in an Ivy League school, working full time, and volunteering at a shelter.

All I needed was to ensure that Brat was far away from her natural habitat.

Los Angeles.

Hallie

The next few days passed in a daze.

Ransom did not leave my side. Barely even gave me privacy when I went to the bathroom. I counted down the days, the minutes, the hours until we flew to Dallas. He was obsessed with keeping me safe, and it obviously got to his psyche, because after four days, he called Max and asked him to bring a backup to my house.

"Make sure you patrol the place and don't leave her alone for one minute," Ransom ordered. "I have to get some fresh air."

Oh, did *he* now? Funny how it never occurred to him I might be needing a breather, too.

Max was too wrapped up in his job to be nice to me. He seemed relieved when, shortly after Ransom disappeared, I went upstairs and roamed the lonely rooms of my mansion, trying to find something to do.

I never quite understood how lonely I was until Ransom got

here. His imposed lockdown made me realize that without my nighttime outings, I barely even left the house at all.

Like a ghost, I wandered the rooms on the second floor, until Ransom's was the only one left.

Don't go in there. Don't ask for trouble.

But trouble was a great cure for boredom, as any ditzy heiress could tell you, and I wanted to stir the pot a little. Besides—what else did I have to do? Max was anxiously sitting downstairs, checking the windows and doors every half hour like war was upon us.

I sauntered inside Ransom's room, closing my eyes and inhaling him.

I liked that I was attracted to him. It felt safe, because I knew he would never try anything with me.

A scribbled note on his desk drew my attention. Was that the same note he took from me? The leaflet that made him change his behavior and become so protective of me?

I made my way to the note and picked it up. It didn't look like the paper I found in the doorway the other day. No. This looked unmistakably like Ransom's bold, long-stroked handwriting. An address. In downtown Los Angeles.

Let's look for trouble.

For a long time now, I wanted to find out something interesting and intimate about my bodyguard.

He knew so much about me. It was only fair I had some information on him, right?

Shoving the note into my pocket, I grabbed my bag and denim jacket. Max was downstairs, and I knew two more men were patrolling the neighborhood. The so-called backup.

The security app on Ransom and Max's phone was on, so if a door opened in the house—even a window—they'd know about it.

But they wouldn't know about my bedroom balcony.

My bedroom balcony did not have a camera installed, which made it a blind spot. It had one, when I first moved in three years ago, but it fell a couple years ago, and I never got around to fixing it.

I'd done it before. Slipped out via my own balcony. A couple times when I accidentally locked myself inside the house, and another time when Keller was here and made me promise him I wouldn't break my promise not to eat ice cream after midnight.

My hands and feet shook. Despite that, I slid down easily. Hopping over the balcony, firmly placing one foot over the gutter, then lowering myself until I was leaning against a garden statue.

I hopped down, cleaning mud and grass from my hands and knees. I peered into the house. Max was there, looking out the opposite window, his back to me.

Turning around, I slipped into my second favorite car, the Prius. It was parked outside the garage from the time NeNe had borrowed it to stealth from a Botox treatment undetected, so no app was going to ping.

The entire drive downtown, I kept staring at the note with the address. What could Ransom possibly be looking for in this part of town? It wasn't seedy per se, but it wasn't swanky, either.

Forty minutes later, I was at my destination. I parked in front of the address on the note. It was a Mexican bar. Small, loud, bursting with colors and music. The front patio was teeming with people drinking and laughing.

He'd gone drinking?

Slowly, grasping my clutch to my hip, I began moving through the thick crowd on the patio searching for his face. What was I expecting to see? Ransom on a date? How stupid. I didn't even know the guy and I knew he wasn't the dating type.

He wasn't in the bar. He wasn't in the seating area, either. It occurred to me that he may have tricked me, to see if I'd take the bait and follow him here.

I made my way out of the bar, the music shaking the ground beneath my feet. The street was still alive and buzzing. I decided to take a quick walk. Maybe he went somewhere nearby instead?

I knew I was getting myself into trouble. Worse still, I knew I was getting Max into hot water, too. He was supposed to be keeping an eye on me. But I'd wanted to see what Ransom was up to when he wasn't at the house.

Passing by an alleyway full of industrial trashcans, I heard a noise.

"*Aww.*"

I stopped in my tracks, my ears perking, straining to hear more.

The muffled moans—like a small child crying—grew louder and more desperate. They were coming from the passageway.

When I was in college (for one semester, mind you), the sorority house director once told us if we found ourselves getting physically harassed or attacked, to scream "fire" instead of "rape". Because fire was a collective problem, and people were more likely to rush to help you, while rape was something people didn't want to witness or get involved in. And now hearing these voices…I couldn't just turn around and risk the chance of not helping someone in need.

Well, I wasn't one of those people.

I opened my small clutch, taking out the taser Keller got me for Christmas, and stepped deeper into the alleyway.

Immediately, two darkened silhouettes came into view. The woman was pressed against a red-bricked wall. Her cocktail dress was pushed up, her panties shoved down haphazardly to her knees. Her face glistened with tears. The man behind her pounded into her mercilessly. His fingers were shoved deep into her mouth, making her gag. His form was big, strong, wired with muscles.

I clutched the taser in my hand, getting ready to aim it at him as I gingerly stepped closer.

"Don't try to fight it, sweetheart. You'll just make it worse for yourself," he taunted viciously into her ear.

My legs froze.

Ransom.

It was Ransom.

I'd recognize that deep, callous voice anywhere.

"What the fuck!" I was shaking so bad I almost dropped the damn taser I aimed at him.

Both Ransom and his *victim!* turned their heads toward me. The bastard had the decency to remove his hand from her mouth and wipe it over her dress. The woman looked more shocked than relieved to see me, but I couldn't exactly blame her, considering the circumstances.

"I cannot believe you!" I felt tears, hot and fat, streaming freely down my cheeks. My mouth was coated with sour bile. "I cannot believe what you just did."

"What're you doing here?" His voice was inscrutable. Void of emotions. Well, of course it was. He was a goddamn psychopath. "Where the hell is Max?"

That's the conversation he wanted to be having right now? Desperate gaslighting if I ever saw it.

"I'm calling the police." I fished for my phone out of my clutch, before remembering the bastard confiscated it.

"Please don't!" the woman next to him cried out. She stepped into the light, under a lamppost, tugging her dress down. She appeared to be in her early forties. "Don't ruin this."

Cocking my head to the side, I waited for an explanation for her bizarre request. "Honey…*what*?"

"Because we're role-playing." Ransom stepped beside her protectively. She looked sideways at him, giving him an I-cannot-believe-this-is-happening look. I wanted to bury myself in the ground.

A role play?

Like… *rape* fantasy?

I'd been exposed to a lot of different kinds of porn online, but not this. What kind of people did that?

It was sick. No, worse than sick, it was degrading and harmful.

You shouldn't be shaming people for their sexual preferences, a voice inside me countered.

"Just…don't say anything," the woman warned, her tone implying it wasn't the first time she'd fired orders at people. "Please,

Please, I have two kids at home and an ex-husband who respects me."

"She's not gonna say a word," Ransom soothed. "I give you my word."

"Thank you." She turned to Ransom, putting a hand over his chest. "I think I'll head home."

He nodded curtly. "My apologies for the disruption. I'll take care of this."

"You sure?" She grimaced.

"Positive."

He sounded sincere and polite and…almost warm. The first time I'd seen him exhibiting this kind of behavior.

She gave him a brief kiss on the cheek and wiggled past me, rushing off into the night.

I was so confused I thought my head was about to blow up.

Standing rooted to the ground, I stared at him. He tucked his shirt in, and looked presentable enough, but I still couldn't wrap my head around anything.

He'd been…

Or at least, he'd been pretending to…

Was there even a difference, if she was in distress? Yes, for fuck's sake, there was a difference when she had chosen that situation, made it happen because she wanted it. Universes apart difference. And she'd chosen Ransom to be the one to give her such a shocking experience?

And…oh, no. Why did it feel like my thighs were sticking together? I couldn't be turned on by *this*. I couldn't. No. After all these years, *this* is what turns me on? I mean, really?

"I'm…uh…" I glanced around me.

"In trouble," he finished for me, rearranging his dress shirt. "Where's Max?"

"Home." I cleared my throat.

"Very professional."

"It's not his fault. I'm sneaky. You left a note on your dresser with this address. I wanted to know what you were up to."

"Why?" he shot out.

"Because you're hiding a lot of secrets, and we share a roof."

Surprisingly, he wasn't outraged by my answer.

"So...this is what you do at night?" I gulped. My heart was still racing. Did I want it to be his first time trying this or his fiftieth? I couldn't catch my breath.

"I'm a nocturnal creature."

"You're a monster, is what you are." The allegation came out as a desperate bark. My whole body was caked in cold sweat and goosebumps.

His laugh, raw and rough, rang out through the starless night. A thin wire fence separated us from the industrial, funky part of Los Angeles people used as an outdoor sex spot. "Labeling something you're afraid of as monstrous is the easy part. Understanding how they got that way is what takes true courage."

"W—w—what you did there was—"

"Having sex with another consenting adult who shares the same fantasies and kinks as me. Nothing wrong with that. She was into it, so was I."

More than anything else, I hated that *I* was into it. When I first thought I saw what he was doing to her...when I imagined him doing it to *me*...I didn't hate it. I was scared, but I didn't hate it. And that was awful to admit, even to myself.

"What got you into...uh...these fantasies?" I didn't think I'd actually get a straight answer, but it was worth trying.

Ransom began making his way out of the alley, certain I would follow him. I did. He shoved his hands into his front pockets.

"Initially, just the sensation of it all. You don't have to suffer trauma or abuse to enjoy kink, as long as you're owning your and your consenting partner's way."

"And still?" I asked, knowing there was more.

He shrugged. "Childhood trauma, mainly. The idea of using violence freely, unabashedly. There's safeness in this scenario. It requires trust and a level of protection. In a way, acting out a date-gone-horribly wrong is much safer than engaging in a real, random, Tinder hookup. It's about the safety of the expectation. Here, we have rules. We have dos and don'ts. We have limits we do not cross. I find it much more respectful than screwing a random person without knowing what they're into. What their boundaries are, their background."

Without meaning to, he was kind of selling the idea for me. The prospect of telling someone in advance what I wanted and didn't want, what I would and wouldn't do… what they could and couldn't do… I liked it. I liked it a lot. It didn't seem so crazy when he explained it to me.

"Were you hurting her?" I gulped.

We were strolling toward the Nissan. It went without saying that he was my ride home. We would pick up the Prius tomorrow.

"Only the ways she wanted me to, but in terms of actually hurting her? Not really, no. Maybe a few light bruises here and there if she decided to 'struggle harder' to make it feel real."

"Is she your…?"

"I do not have a BDSM partner. I prefer more casual hookups."

"How often do you…?" I trailed off.

"That depends." He scratched his chin. "But not often. You need to choose your partners carefully for this kind of thing. Mutual friends, people you know and trust."

"Do you ever have like, just, regular…?"

I couldn't believe he was answering all these questions. I had a hunch it had more to do with the fact that he didn't want me to tell my parents and less about wanting to be open with me.

Or maybe it was because he could see my heart beating in my throat and he (thankfully) mistakenly thought I was still scared instead of sort of terrifyingly exhilarated.

"No," he said flatly. "This is the only form of sexual relationship I'm seeking. I trust this stays between us."

"Yeah," I said finally. "Don't worry about it."

He unlocked the car automatically, jerking his chin forward for me to get into the passenger seat. "Good, because this discussion is over, and I'm about to rip Max a new one."

Ransom

The next couple days were spent in Los Angeles, preparing for the Dallas trip. I touched base with my contacts, while trailing after Brat. Even though she did not have her phone—not only because I was the one who ended up eradicating the wormed meat, but also because that phone was a bad influence—I allowed her to attend some social engagements, as long as they were indoors and I was around.

What could I say? Now that she knew about the darkest side of my life, she had some leverage on me.

She kept her old patterns, desperately clinging on to a reality that was no longer a part of her life. Goodie bags. Designer dresses. Cameras flashing. Brat didn't even look like she was having fun. I wasn't sure why she was doing this to herself. What I *was* sure of was that I didn't care enough to ask. The lines between employee and employer had been blurred enough after her little snooping stint.

Generally speaking, I'd done my best to talk to her as little as humanly possible after she caught me mid-act. I'd watched as she squirmed, trying to make ends meet with her flimsy daily budget, which I'd cut in half from the original sum Anthony Thorne had named. Last night, Brat had to resort to making her own acai bowl, because she didn't have enough to DoorDash and leave a twenty-five percent tip.

"Subhuman," she had complained to the vast, ugly space she called home as she sliced a banana into thin pieces. "That's what I've become."

To Brat's credit, she, too, seemed wildly uninterested in me. That was refreshing. Usually, straight, unmarried women I worked for wanted to climb me like a tree. But she seemed so disoriented, so uneasy in her doodled skin, sex didn't seem high on her agenda.

A week after the note from Kozlov had arrived, Brat and I boarded a plane to Dallas. First class. Not as good as flying private, but I was relieved to leave Los Angeles behind.

We settled into our respective reclinable pods, which faced

each other. I didn't need to look at her more than absolutely necessary. Brat made a show of snapping open a glossy magazine and crossing her legs in her head-to-toe pink Juicy Couture sweats. She frowned in concentration during takeoff, but her eyes were not moving along the text.

I answered emails and reveled in the fact that in a few short hours, I would get to meet a former president. Anthony Thorne hadn't exactly left a lasting impression on me during his administration—I wasn't even in middle school during that time—but he was well-loved enough.

After takeoff came an endless stream of snacks and alcohol. I refused everything the flight attendant offered. Something about eating during flights unnerved me. Brat said yes and even asked for seconds. She loved snacks, and the little pillows they gave you, and chitchatting with the staff. In fact, I was pretty sure the only extraneous object she didn't like in her vicinity was yours truly.

Deciding it was time she got a perk after everything she'd been through, I allowed her to have a drink during the flight.

She polished off three glasses of wine—the first time she'd drunk alcohol since I'd arrived in the picture—before smacking her lips and announcing, "I'm going to the restroom. Be right back."

I stood up before she did, cracking my knuckles.

She tilted her head up in confusion. "I'm not the queen. You don't have to stand up when I do."

"I'm tagging along."

Was it absolutely necessary? Probably not. But it wasn't superfluous, either. I didn't know what I was dealing with when it came to Kozlov. I didn't know how much he knew about our whereabouts. And I didn't want to take any chances.

"No, you're not," she said firmly, standing up and taking a step sideways. I rounded my pod, blocking her way to the bathroom.

"What if you use drugs?"

Of course, I was fucking with her.

Tilting a thick eyebrow, she said, "Then at least one of us would be in a good mood. Move out of the way, assface."

I didn't budge.

She stared at me, wide-eyed and exasperated. The plane hummed as it charged through the sky. People around us napped or worked on their laptops.

"Random," she said slowly, *again with this stupid nickname*. "I need to go number two."

She let the words settle between us and I decided I was going with her to the bathroom, after all. I did not believe her for half a second. Not even a quarter. And I'd force her to call my bluff.

"I cannot afford to take my eyes off you," I said shortly.

"Wow. That's the most romantic thing anyone has ever told me, and it's coming from a guy I would likely stab if I could guarantee there wouldn't be any criminal repercussions," she bristled.

I almost let loose a smile. *Almost*. I had to admit, even though she was a royal pain in the ass, and likely the most self-centered person I'd ever met, she was mildly entertaining.

"Move it, or your bladder will burst with all that wine," I barked.

She rolled her eyes but charged forward, muttering profanities all the way there. She didn't put up a fight, and in doing so I knew she was planning something that would piss me off.

We both entered the tiny lavatory (why were they always the size of a matchbox?) and Brat got to business immediately, pulling her pink, studded sweatpants down and squatting in an angle toward the toilet seat, without actually touching it with her thighs.

I turned around to give her some privacy. I was an asshole, not a creeper.

"So, tell me," she started, a solid stream of pee as our musical background. "Do men pay less attention when they pee in public places? Like, do you care less about aiming when you're on an airplane?"

"I've always been a good shot." Both with my dick and pistol.

She groaned behind my back, "Unsung American hero. The Pulitzer Prize is on its way."

"I'll hold my breath."

"Now there's an idea I could get behind."

"I pity women," I drawled, in the mood to throw her off-kilter. "You have to crouch like a constipated frog to keep from touching the toilet seat for fear you get an STI or pregnant."

"Don't pity us. We outlive you, have stronger immune systems, and scientifically, have way better memories. I'll take doing a few squats over being a man any day."

"You seem to know a lot about this. Don't tell me you opened a book," I concentrated on the door, and not on the reflection of her in the mirror.

"God forbid. It was on the back of a tampon box."

I allowed myself a small grin, listening as she flushed the toilet. The sound shook the walls. She washed her hands, squirting a generous amount of soap.

"I do apologize," she said.

Here we go.

"What did you do now?" I demanded. If she'd peed on my black Italian wingtips, I was going to punch a hole through this goddamn wall.

"Nothing...*yet.*" She leaned forward in front of the mirror, applying lip gloss and smacking her lips. "But I'm about to."

She pocketed the lipstick, turned around, then leaned close to my ear. Being a true dom, I could read her body language, anticipating what she was about to do before she did it. Her mouth fell in an O-shape.

She was about to scream.

I acted quickly, pushing her against the sink, covering her entire body with mine. My palm squeezed flat against her mouth, sealing all of it.

"Are you crazy?" I hissed in her face with a snarl. "Do you think this is funny?"

She attempted a smart-ass answer, from the look in her eyes. Her words were muffled by my hand.

"That was a rhetorical question. You're as crazy as a soup sandwich. You've gone a step too far now, Brat."

In response, she sank her teeth into my palm, then started

grinding her jaws like a Chihuahua. My skin broke, creating a slow, scarlet trail of blood that ran down her chin and along her pretty little throat. The little shit *bit* me.

And that turned me on. Because when I got bitten…my instinct was to bite back even *harder*.

I pressed my hand more forcefully against her mouth, feeling aroused and annoyed and *fuck*, I should have chosen the Mayor Ferns post. My blood was the exact shade as her hair. Another turn-on.

"Stop this. I already told you, I won't touch you in an inappropriate way. You have my word. Why do you think I'd try anything with you? It's like hetero assholes naturally assuming gay people will come on to them."

She said something animatedly, but again, it was muffled by my palm. Brat reached at my face, trying to claw my eyes out. She *wanted* an altercation, and I wasn't sure why.

She was feral, unruly, and a goddamn pain. She was also the first client to make me bleed, which didn't disturb me as much as it should have.

"You aren't going to stop, are you?" I asked.

She shook her head wildly, looking at me with a crazy twinkle in her eye. I recognized that abandon. It appeared whenever I hooked up with a woman who liked to be roughed up. But it couldn't be. Brat wasn't that kind of person. She was used to Hollywood pretty boys who probably fucked like they were starring in French art films. Making looooooooove.

My blood had disappeared into her cleavage. We both watched as it trickled between the valley of her breasts. My cock throbbed, thick and pulsating against my jeans.

"Don't hold back." She hooked her fingers inside my front pockets, tugging me closer. "Grind against me."

"What do you want?" I shifted uncomfortably, unsure how to get out of this bathroom without cooperation. It sounded more like a plea than a question.

She began moving her lips. Reluctantly, I pulled my hand away to let her speak.

"My phone back. Permanently, Skipper the Creeper."

She licked her lips, looking up at me like a little vampire. Forbidden and fey. I wondered about the men she'd been with—or had they been pretty boys, unable to deliver what she needed? What was Hallie Thorne like with each of them? How many? A good amount, no doubt. Although interestingly enough, when I sifted through her text messages and call logs, I couldn't find any evidence of hookups. She had a Tinder account on her phone, but obviously hadn't been using it since meeting me—and there had been no new notifications. Maybe she was going through a self-inflicted dry spell.

A greasy beef-head like Wes Morgan could trigger celibacy, even in nymphomaniacs.

"And you think acting like a child is going to achieve your goal?" I snarled. We were crowded together in the tiny space, my body flush with hers. Someone shook the lavatory door from the outside, groaning in protest when they realized it was locked.

"I think we both need to learn how to compromise if we want to make this work."

"Compromise," I repeated, bracing the sink on both sides around her, my nose very nearly brushing hers. Her entire body was humming with charged, pent-up…something. Desire? Hate? Disdain? I couldn't tell. Parts of her personality made me suspect she was a grade-A sex kitten, and others hinted she could give the Virgin Mary a run for her money. "Fine. Let's bargain. Tell me why I should give you your phone back."

"Because in return, I'll give you my cooperation." She smiled winningly.

"Nice try."

"Well, what do you want?" Her eyebrows pulled together like two perfect checkmarks.

That was easy. Not get a stiffy every time she decided to get a rise out of me. Could she make that happen? Doubt it.

"I want you to make a promise and keep it."

She stared at me, wide-eyed, like a child listening to a story, waiting eagerly for more.

Was I really letting her off with a bit of homework? Yes. It was too soon for her to find an actual job. If she got one now, she'd be fired before she even showed up to work. Besides, I could follow her around the mansion all I wanted, there was no way an employer would accept me scaring away the customers.

"You may have your phone back if you promise to use the time in Texas to think about what you want to do with your future. I'm talking about getting a real job, Brat. Not one you can do from your phone while taking a dump. Once we get back to Los Angeles, you'll be making some changes to your lifestyle. Am I clear?"

Hatred stared back at me through those baby blues. She really didn't want to get a job. Why? Thousands of jobs, in Los Angeles alone, required minimum intelligence and even less commitment. She could be a stylist. Or a reporter for one of those cable channels. The very thought of putting herself out there seemed to paralyze her.

"I still don't understand why I can't just continue as an influencer."

"Well, that's because your annual income is currently $3,392."

"How do you know that?" she demanded.

The lavatory door shook again, reminding us that outside, someone waiting now believed we were either fucking or taking the longest shit known to mankind.

"It's my job to know everything about you."

Her shoulders sagged, and she closed her eyes. "Fine. Whatever. I'll think of something."

"And no more pranks. No steak in my closet, salt in my coffee, screaming in public. I apologize that you had to witness what you did the other night, but it was a sexual relationship between two consenting adults."

Now that I'd listed all of her little stunts, I had to admit, she'd crammed a lot into a short period of time. The door shook more prominently now. I banged my palm against it. "Go away."

"All right." She pouted. "Guess it's only fair, since I don't seem to be able to get you to quit. Truce?" She raised her pinky finger, offering it to me.

I unlocked the lavatory and stalked out, passing by a man in a suit with a white moustache. Assumingly the shit who'd tried to rush us out of the restroom.

"Congratulations on joining the Mile High Club, boy, but some of us have to drop the kids at the pool."

Chapter Eight

Hallie

Home.

A pleasant tingle ran up my spine, and my heart filled with unabashed, explosive warmth. I ran hesitant, shaky fingers along the smooth surface, shivering again in pleasure. I imagined this was how people who reunited with their loved ones after war had felt.

My phone.

My precious, wonderful phone was back in my hands again.

Immediately, I took the internet package the airline had to offer and read through my messages. I plugged in my earbuds and listened to the dictated version of them, angling my phone so he couldn't snoop over my shoulder.

Keller: Please show signs of life. I really don't want to call 911. The person who answers always gives me SO much anxiety. No pleasantries.

Keller: Or maybe he just took your phone again. Merp.

NeNe: How's your hot bodyguard doing?

***Natasha PR Manager: Hi Hallie! Hope you are doing well**

and keeping safe. We were wondering if you would give us the utmost PLEASURE and grace us with your presence tonight. We are launching a super exciting product. It's called Totes for Toddlers. Did you know an increasing number of toddlers in the world feel anxiety at the prospect of not bringing their beloved toys and attachment objects with them when they travel? These are DESIGNER tote bags, all handmade and from organic material. I can send a taxi if you are interested? ☺

Wes Morgan: Your new bfrnd is a syco.

Wes Morgan: *sycho

Wes Morgan: Psycho?

Wes Morgan: Anyway, that's what he is. And forget about the zoo. I already got what I wanted from you.

Hera: Please, for the love of God, don't forget to pack something semi-respectable to wear. Have a safe flight.—H.

Tara: Do you think I can pull off ankle boots? You know my cankles are, like, my worst feature. But idk. They're just so in right now.

I pressed my phone to my chest, closing my eyes. I finally felt connected to the outside world. Even if that world kind of sucked.

When the plane landed, a private chauffeur was waiting for us on the tarmac, Ransom's doing, probably. Normally, my parents sent their driver to bring me home. The entire trip to the hotel, I tried to focus on my surroundings and not on the fact that earlier in the lavatory, when Ransom pressed against me, I didn't feel the usual fear and dread that accompanied being close to a man. No. I'd wanted him. I'd craved him. When his blood trickled between my breasts, I knew the slightest touch between my legs would have made me come.

It's probably just the wine. It had to be the wine. And the altitude.

Melancholy always fluttered through me whenever I came face-to-face with my family's hometown. Perhaps because I was not a part of it. The skyline was beautiful, dotted with skyscrapers and washed by the pink hues that signaled the beginning of another Texan morning.

I redirected my thoughts to my deal with Ransom. I had to think about what I wanted to do for a living. My options were limited, considering I didn't even possess basic skills. Was there a job out there that didn't require literacy and basic knowledge of Microsoft Anything?

I guess I could sweep floors. Sweeping floors didn't sound too bad. Maybe even therapeutic. But I knew my family wouldn't allow just any job. No. It had to be something they deemed respectable and Thorne-worthy. Something with a long title and vague job description. Problem was, I wasn't Hera. I wasn't capable and brilliant. I didn't get 1250 on my SAT.

Besides, getting a job was risky. If I got fired, it would be the final nail in my confidence coffin. And that sarcophagus was already hermetically sealed.

We arrived at Tortoise Creek Mansion. The palatial hotel, once a private estate, boasted sixty-five rooms, a Michelin-starred restaurant, and a world-famous spa. It also housed one of the best bars in Dallas. Since a sober sighting of me rarely happened in Texas, a good, well-equipped bar was an amenity I cared about deeply.

Rather than drive toward the main entrance through the golden cobbled road, our driver used a back alley leading to the underground parking.

Two bellhops who wore exclusively dark suits and grave expressions carried our suitcases to the master suite. I quietly admired the weathered barnwood of the walls, the exotic plants bracketing each door, and the industrial, brand-new scent of a luxurious hotel as the security men spoke to Ransom, ignoring me completely.

"We wired the suite nice and good," one of them said. "Sixteen devices. All of them linked to the room next door."

"And that room will be manned around the clock," Ransom reminded them. "Two at a time."

"Correct. I can give you the shift schedule, so you can get to know the team."

"Email it to me."

A dollop of anxiety hit the bottom of my belly. What if Ransom and I spoke about something intimate and they heard? (Unlikely). Or what if I said something on the phone that I didn't want them to hear? (*Much* more likely).

"Stay here, Brat. I'm going to check the suite first," Ransom instructed, using the electronic key to enter the room. I stayed in the hallway, smiling at the two mammoth men he'd spoken to a minute ago.

"Having a good day, ma'am?" one of them offered in a friendly Texan drawl.

"Everything's a peach," I cooed.

"Ya know," one of them sighed, "it is a travesty to me that a Thorne child ain't living in her home state. Rankles my sensibilities."

"Oh, please don't take it personally. I love Texas."

Or I would, if I knew it.

The Lone Star State had some small pleasures that I found celestial. The vastness of the sky. How it stretched above your head like loving arms. The endless iced tea refills. The bluebonnets. The way people were friendly as a way of life, and not because they wanted to be invited to Heidi Klum's next Halloween party.

"Thank fuck for open carry states." Ransom strode out the door of our suite, tucking his gun into his waistband.

Ransom stopped, scowling at me. "There's steam coming out of your ears. Don't think too hard, Brat."

"Are you insinuating I'm stupid?" I crossed my arms over my chest.

"It was more of an open statement." His mouth quirked to one side mockingly. "Ready to roll?"

No, but my stomach was. It churned violently, warning me that making an unannounced trip to my parents' house was not a good idea. Ransom, however, acted as if nothing had happened between us on the plane. Probably because to him—nothing had.

"I don't think we're expected at my parents' right now."

Normally, I only arrived at their mansion when I was summoned. When they couldn't take it anymore and threatened me with sanctions if I didn't show myself. The majority of my time in Dallas, I usually spent drinking in my room or working on mockups of my next tattoo. Sometimes I'd catch a movie.

Dallas reminded me of some of my loneliest times. Of the family-shaped hole in my heart. Of memories I never made, and moments I never experienced. Of the fact that my entire being was a pappus—an individual piece of a seeded dandelion—floating in the universe.

Not so coincidentally, I'd inked a dandelion blowing away across the back of my left shoulder. Only those who squinted really hard could tell that each individual pappus was made out of the letters T, E, X, A, and S.

"Who cares?" He spun car keys over his finger, advancing toward the elevators. I followed him. "They're your goddamn parents. They'll find time for you."

A nervous laugh bubbled from my throat. "They're important people, you know. With busy schedules."

The elevator pinged and the doors slid open. We walked inside. Ransom chose a parking lot floor. I guess he'd rented a car. An armored one, no doubt.

"They're not currently in office, which means whatever shit they have can wait. Your dad isn't in a position to start or cease a war anymore. You only see them, what...a few times a year?"

I swallowed hard, uncomfortable at the casual stripping away of my historical excuses as to why their distancing shouldn't hurt. "Yeah. Something like that."

Once in the underground garage, we slid into a Ford Explorer that looked missile-proof. I wasn't a fan of fuel-run cars, but decided to pick my battles.

Ransom drove, not bothering with a map app, like he grew up

in this place. I was on edge the entire drive, as if I was on my way to face a firing squad. It was bad enough that my parents treated me like an embarrassment, but now we were going to have an audience in the form of Ransom Lockwood, hottest and scariest man alive.

Again, I wondered about him. About his family life. His background. I knew so little about the person who was sharing a house with me. Even the basics were cloaked in an enigmatic veil. Where was he born? Was he married? What had he done before he opened his security company?

I'd performed a cursory social media hunt on him as soon as I'd been able. Unsurprisingly, there wasn't a trace of this man ever being alive. I couldn't even be sure Ransom Lockwood was his real name.

"I can tell you want to say something." Ransom's eyes were hard on the road. "Just go ahead and say it."

It then occurred to me that I was staring at him.

"Is Ransom Lockwood your real name?"

"Why wouldn't it be?"

"Are you capable of answering one question without evading it?"

"I don't know, am I?" he asked smartly, then sighed. "Yes, it's my real name."

"Aww, I feel like we grew super close in one sentence," I teased. He didn't say anything.

"So…were you a SEAL, like Max?" I munched on my lower lip as we zipped past the glitzy midtown area, which was sparkly and new.

"No," Ransom said shortly. Then, when he realized I was squirming in my seat, desperate for a distraction, he added, "Counterintelligence."

"Look at you, Mr. FancyPants."

"It's a long word for a very broad department. Anything you have to break in your head into two separate words to write is considered extravagant."

Well, I couldn't write it if you gave me five hours and three dictionaries.

"Must've been dangerous." I watched him intently. Not a muscle in his face moved. Treading carefully, I added, "Your family must've been worried for you."

"I suppose they would have."

"What do you mean?"

"I don't have a family."

"You mean you don't talk to them." And I thought *I* had a flair for dramatics. Everyone had a family, came from somewhere.

"I mean they are not in *existence*." A flicker of irritation passed on his face, but his tone remained flat and calm.

"So how did you come to be?" I arched a skeptic eyebrow. "Test tube baby?"

"Obviously, biologically, I was created by Jane and John Doe. But I have no clue who they are. One of them left me in a shoebox at the door of some church in rural Illinois. I was two hours old and still had an umbilical cord dangling from the cardboard. People who passed by thought I was a lost kitten, because I could barely cry anymore, my voice was so hoarse. At least it had been tied off, so I hadn't bled out."

"You're kidding me." I sucked in a breath.

"My humor's not much, but it's better than *that*."

I'd never met anyone with such a tragic life story. I felt physically ill with sorrow for him. I also wondered what the heck had come over him, to make him open up to me like that. Then I remembered I probably looked white as a sheet and nervous from my impending showdown with the people who'd created *me*.

And perhaps also this teeny, tiny mishap about me catching him acting out a semi-public, semi-violent sexual fantasy.

Ransom needed to win some humanity points with me right now, and, the robot that he was, this was how he chose to do it.

"Wow." I let out a breath. "I must really look like I need a distraction, if you decided to share *this* with me."

"Not a pile." He flicked the indicator. "Maybe a small mound."

"Oh, God. I'm so sorry, Ransom. What an awful beginning to your life."

"I survived."

"Were you adopted?" I swallowed.

"Yes," he hesitated, as if contemplating whether to tell me more. "The family's name was Moruzzi. They were well-off. Lived by Lincoln Park. Jack Moruzzi adopted three of us. All boys. But… well, let's just say it wasn't a childhood full of Scouts and summer camps."

"Did he ever…?" I sucked in a breath. Were his fantasies prompted by being abused before? He'd said he'd experienced trauma. I didn't know. All I knew was that I wanted to try what Ransom was offering by opening up.

But by the way he bristled, flooring the accelerator, I gathered the conversation was over.

"Point is, stop feeling sorry for yourself, Brat. We all have a story, and it's rarely a fairy tale."

The way he cut me off, so abruptly, made me want to strike back.

"Does Max have a story?"

Ransom's face hardened, his eyes narrowing over the road. "Do I look like his biographer? Ask him yourself. He's supposed to arrive on a later flight tonight and will be covering for me whenever I'll be away."

"Why would you be away?" Did he know anyone in Texas? He seemed to know his way around these roads.

"My business."

"More *playdates*?" I was pushing it, and I knew it.

"This conversation is over."

"I really do feel like we've had a breakthrough today, though." I crossed my legs, realizing for the first time that I was still wearing my tacky sweatpants and hoodie from the flight, and that my parents would probably vomit on impact when they saw me. "Now that we've opened up about our insecurities, it will be easier to address them and try to be nice to one another. Who knows? Maybe it's the beginning of a friendship. The way you opened up to me—"

"Brat," he cut me off.

"Hmm?"

"Shut up."

An hour later, the Ford Explorer pulled in front of an all-white Mediterranean-style mansion. The manicured lawn was precisely cut, as if the landscaper had used a ruler. There were grand fountains, dramatic columns, and all the status symbols required of a wealthy Dallas family.

Before Ransom turned off the ignition, an unfamiliar man in uniform greeted us from my side of the car. I rolled the window down.

He looked to be in his mid-forties, with a sweaty face and hard-earned wrinkles. "Sorry, folks, this is a private property."

"I know. I'm the daughter of the people who own it." I arched my eyebrows meaningfully, the international signal for back-the-hell-off.

His demeanor did not change. In fact, he looked even more suspicious.

"You're not Hera." The accusation cut through his tone like a blade.

"No," I agreed. "I'm their youngest, Hallie."

He seemed momentarily confused. Finally, he turned around and pressed a walkie-talkie to his mouth. Static noise followed, along with an answer to his question. He began pacing in front of the car. A cold shiver rolled along my skin. I hadn't visited for so long. I felt like an intruder. For a moment, I even doubted my own legitimacy. Was I truly Anthony and Julianne's daughter, or had they disinherited me?

"Relax," Ransom rasped. "We're getting inside if I have to run this asshole over."

A warm rush passed through me. It was odd, and almost felt like I had a stomachache. No one had ever stood up for me before.

Finally, the man approached the car again. I took a quick breath, bracing myself for the worst. I hadn't spoken to my parents since the nip slip.

"Park at the end of the street, then follow me." He looked grim and uninviting.

Ransom and I exchanged looks. Ransom did as he was told. When we both got out, I crooned, "I think I finally found someone who gives you a run for your money in the personality department."

The man, who never bothered introducing himself, guided us through the familiar, melodramatic black and white checkered two-story foyer. The house was vast and empty, the clicks of our shoes ricocheting through the walls with a depressing echo. Maids in blue ironed uniforms hurried along the hallway, keeping their gazes down and posture straight. The sound of a piano lesson in session drifted from one of the drawing rooms. My parents often welcomed gifted kids from low-income families for piano lessons. It was good PR, and my mother was a classical music enthusiast.

I never knew what to think about my parents' charitable gesture toward children. On one hand, it was undoubtedly cool to give back to the community. On the other—shouldn't they start by being kind to their own child?

The man led us to what my parents referred to as the guest living room. A preppy, all-white space with a pale bricked fireplace and matching brown leather couches. The entire space was littered with family photos of Mom, Dad, and Hera. Sometimes Craig and the family dogs, Bubs and Bamboo, were also featured. Not a single picture included me. Mainly because I'd refused to show up to any of the functions in which these photos were taken. The one holiday I did tag along for—a ski trip—I refused to be a part of the picture. I didn't want to give my parents the pleasure of pretending we were one, big, happy family.

My palms began to sweat as I took a seat on a lonely stool. I couldn't stomach sitting on real leather. I prayed that Ransom did not notice how absent I was from the family memorabilia, but doubted it. He had a sharp eye.

An assistant wearing a black swanky suit trotted inside on high heels. *Daphne*. Mom's right hand.

"Hello, Hallie. Hello, Ransom. How wonderful that you've finally decided to grace us with your presence." Her subtle but pointed dig was aimed at me. "Mr. and Mrs. Thorne are so excited to have you despite not being given any prior notice." She smiled broadly, her gaze halting on Ransom for a moment too long as she took him in fully. "Understandably, they are currently tied up in prior engagements, but they should be with you shortly. Anything to drink?" Her scarlet smile stretched. Her platinum hair was slicked back. I hated that I was wearing rags. And I hated even more that I didn't have anything to change into here. Leaving anything here would be like recognizing this house was a part of my life.

"Coffee for me. No sugar, no milk." Ransom stood up and walked over to one of the windows overlooking my mother's lush garden.

"Water for me," I added. "Tap, please."

"Your mother told me the environment is your new passion." She smiled. "Better than designer bags, right?"

I was shocked to discover my mother remembered anything about me, let alone talked about me to someone from her staff. Too bad my "sudden" passion with the environment started when I was five and left unattended to watch a pretty grim global warming documentary that sent me into meltdown mode.

Twenty minutes passed before our beverages arrived. Another ten before Ransom took out his laptop and started working in the corner of the room. We rounded an entire hour without being seen.

This was my punishment. For not taking their calls. For refusing to be a part of their family.

An hour turned into two.

By the third hour, I began pacing, sweating, making excuses for them to cover for my embarrassment.

"It's probably something urgent. I've never had to wait this long."

Ransom did not acknowledge my words. He kept working on his laptop, which he now plugged into the socket. This was for the best, since his answer would probably be: *How long do you usually have to wait to see them?*

"I think maybe we should go and come back later. I don't want to be a burden." I tried in vain to smooth out the wrinkles in my sweatpants.

"You're already a burden," he drawled.

"Not to you, to them."

"I'm sure they share my sentiment," he deadpanned.

"Better to be a burden than to be an asshole." I made quick steps to one of the windows, opening it and looking outside to keep myself distracted.

"Debatable." His condescending tone rose from the other side of the room.

Something caught my eye in the corner of the garden. Right behind the red yucca bushes and sage. It was my mother, sitting on one of the stone benches, clad in one of her cashmere sweaters and a sensible, ankle-length skirt, leisurely swinging a ball launcher and throwing a ball as far as she could. Bubs and Bamboo, her two Pomeranians, ran toward it excitedly, pink tongues flapping.

"Bubs! Run faster, bunny. You're getting a bit chubby," she fussed as the little dog wobbled toward her, the ball in his mouth.

This was why I was left waiting? So that my mother could play with her stupid dogs? I was losing to four-legged creatures? That *lived* with her on the reg?

I stepped away from the window, turning to Ransom. "I would like to leave now."

"You and I both." He didn't lift his eyes from his screen. "But we're already here, and I'm not making this trip twice today. Dallas' traffic is a bitch."

"So am I, when I don't get my way. I don't want to be here." I raised my voice, aware that I sounded like a brat from hell, exactly what he'd been accusing me of.

"Tough luck." He typed furiously on his laptop. "No one cares what you want."

The words slammed into me, physically making me keel over. He was right. No one cared about what I wanted. The cards had been laid like this ever since I could remember. And today was a prime reminder of it.

I stormed toward my bodyguard, slapping his computer screen shut. It snapped over his fingers, but all I drew was a passive, *what-now?* look.

Leaning down so our faces were aligned, I snarled, "I said I want to leave, and since you are my hired assistant, the person whose job it is to fulfill my orders, you will grab your keys right now and do as I say."

It was a low blow. Especially since he'd opened up to me earlier today. But what could I do? I was so hurt, so wounded, so nauseous with rejection, I had no other choice than to flex what power I had *hard*. This visit hadn't even started and I already felt unwelcome. Hell knew what awaited me once I met my parents. Hera. Craig.

I was hurting so bad all I wanted was to hurt someone else. Cutting Ransom open might ease the pain. Or at least provide a distraction.

Ransom held my gaze, not a muscle moving in his face. He looked calm, collected, but alert. Desperation seeped from my skin. He could smell it. His eyes darkened.

My face was only a few inches from his. My skin prickled with an awareness I'd never felt before. I breathed him in. Exhaled the anxiety out.

"Be a good boy and follow orders, or I'll have no choice but to make sure your life is miserable for the next few months," I hissed out.

Still, he said nothing. Almost like he was giving me the opportunity to ride out the tantrum by myself. I felt like a child, like an idiot, and above all—dispensable. Unimportant. An afterthought.

"All righty, here we are. Hello, hello. Apologies for the delay," a voice boomed from the doorway leading to the hall, low and southern. I didn't turn around to meet my father's eyes.

"Sugar Pie? Everything all right over there?"

It took everything in me to inhale, swivel on my sneakers, and plaster a smile on my face. Ransom remained seated behind me. Nothing in his body language betrayed he was meeting a former president.

Dad wore cigar pants, a navy sweater, and his favorite slippers. His silver-bluish hair was parted on the side, and he was impeccably shaved, sporting a relaxed, almost teasing smile and round, vintage reading glasses.

"Hi, Dad." I pushed the imagery of Mom playing with the dogs to a back drawer in my mind.

I didn't really have a choice but to be nice to him. He was the person who bankrolled me.

"Sugar Pie, my dearest." He approached, kissing both my cheeks, squeezing my shoulders with affection. "I was worried about you."

"Sure had an interesting way of showing it." I smiled sunnily.

He ignored the barb. "I see you've added to your tattoo collection since last we met."

Two years ago, I hadn't had the semicolon tattoo on my wrist (symbolizing my story hadn't ended yet), the flowered Zen circle on my collarbone (to find the strength within myself), and the cloud spreading across my inner arm (because even though reality sucked—my dreams could always carry me to exciting, beautiful places).

"Oh, you know how it is when you have too much spare time." I didn't know if I was being sarcastic or berating myself.

"Don't give yourself a hard time." He patted my arm. "Nothing wrong with self-expression."

Dad swung his blue eyes from me to Ransom and disentangled from our embrace, turning in his direction. "The man of the hour, eh? McAfee spoke highly of you."

Ransom stood up, tucking his hands into his front pockets. "Sir."

"Sorry you were kept waiting," Dad apologized, keeping his gaze firmly on my bodyguard.

"So am I."

Did Ransom just hand the former president of the United States his ass? Even I, Anthony Thorne's flesh and blood, didn't dare show discontent with his behavior.

"How've you been settling into the job?" Dad clapped his shoulder, chuckling at my protector's sour nature. I wondered if I was invisible. If I was in some sort of a teen fantasy flick and had to find a magic potion to gain back my visibility. I imagined gulping the potion down, my legs appearing first, like in cartoons, before the rest of my body. Then the collective cries of delight and relief from my family.

"There she is!"

"We haven't lost her!"

"Oh, Sugar Pie, don't leave us ever again!"

Meanwhile, in reality, Ransom drawled, "Without a hitch."

"She's not easy to tame," Dad said, as if I were a wild raccoon.

"I'm not easy to cross," Ransom replied blandly.

I wasn't surprised he wasn't tongue-tied in front of my father, but must he treat him with the same attitude he would jock itch?

"This is great. Follow me, Ransom. I need a word. Sugar Pie, I will see you in a minute. We have much to discuss, and I'm sure you have questions for me."

My father always said life was about priorities. Right now, he made it clear he would rather talk to the man he hired to kick some sense into me than find out what I'd been up to these past couple years. Although, one could argue, he didn't need to ask. It was all splayed on my Instagram page and in the tabloids.

Left alone in the grand room, I ambled back to the window, hoping to catch a glimpse of my mother again. I liked to feel the delicious pain as it pierced through layers of my skin until it reached my heart. The ache was bittersweet. It felt like getting a new tattoo. It made me remember that I was alive. That I could still feel.

But the bench was empty, and the dogs were gone. Bees swarmed around fat flowers, and birds continued to chirp. The world went around its day, oblivious to my heartache.

Ransom's meeting with Dad barely took thirty minutes. Ransom returned on his own, his face not betraying a word that'd been said during his visit to my father's office. He collected his laptop and slipped it into a leather case.

I watched him, filled with sudden, urgent rage.

So what if this man had been through a lot? He chose to channel his anger toward being an unbearable, mean-spirited man. And his ire was directed at me. He wasn't here to protect me. He was here to ensure I didn't screw up publicly. I was his paycheck. His *fat* paycheck. And he'd probably spent the last thirty minutes telling my father how much of a bother I was, so he would give him a bonus.

"Was it everything you hoped for and more?" I cooed mockingly, pretending to study the view outside.

"Your parents are ready to see you. Make it short. I want to go."

Did he, now? Well, I wanted things, too. I wanted to talk to my parents. I wanted respect. I wanted to stop being looked at as an unruly child.

"Actually, I decided to spend the night here." I turned to face him. "Don't wait up."

Slinging his laptop bag over his shoulder, Ransom said levelly, "Go see your parents. I'll wait here. We're leaving in an hour."

"You're not listening." I adopted the same tone my teachers used in private school for impact. "I want you to leave. I'm sleeping here tonight. There's security here. Plenty of it. You're dismissed."

I didn't know what I was doing. I certainly didn't know if I was welcome to stay here. I just knew I couldn't deal with Ransom after this...this...ongoing *nightmare*. To be absent from all the family photos, left for three hours to wait like a salesperson, and above all, to be discarded for *him*, after my parents hadn't seen me in so long...

Ransom's parents may have given up on him when he was a baby, but it was probably because they didn't have the means to keep him. My parents had all the means in the world and zero will. They knew exactly who I grew up to be. They chose to opt out after trying the finished product.

"Leave!" I stomped, exasperated. "Go away."

He stayed put, seemingly taller and wider and more intimidating than he was a second ago.

With a feral growl, I ran toward him, pushing at his chest. He didn't move. My throat produced something between a roar and a whimper. I shoved at him once again, this time harder. I clawed at his torso, my nails scraping through the skin under his dress shirt, trying to make him bleed.

Nothing.

"Fuck!" I balled my fists, raining them down on his chest.

"Leave." Thump.

"Me." Thump.

"Alone!" Thump.

"That's quite enough." The voice, like an ice-cube, ran down my back, making me freeze in my spot. Suddenly I didn't want to stay anymore. I didn't turn around, knowing who it belonged to.

"Step away from the man, Bunny. Heaven knows you were raised better than that. Mr. Lockwood, our daughter will be staying with us tonight. You may take the rest of the day off."

The voice grew louder, closer behind my back. My mother had entered the room. The delicate clicks of her heels rang gracefully, like champagne glasses clinking together.

"Turn around, Bunny."

I did, feeling the air *whooshing* out of my lungs in one go. Oftentimes, I found myself disappointed and dissatisfied with my relationship with my father. But when it came to my mother, I was downright frightened.

She controlled Dad with an iron fist and was the main cause for every sanction against me. I always had the feeling my father's disappointment with how I turned out was lighthearted. He'd accepted early on that nothing would become of me, and treated me with the same, offhanded sympathy he would to an old, farty family pet. An adorable discomfort, if you would. My mother's displeasure, however, hit differently. More personal. She viewed me as a failure. An unfinished project. I was a chink in her otherwise flawless list of accomplishments. The house. The husband. The career. The perfect, doctor daughter. Even the stupid dogs won awards. She had trained the entire Thorne household to jump through hoops. Everyone except me.

"Hello, Mother." My right eye twitched with annoyance. Sometime during this whole ordeal, Ransom must've found his way out, because I couldn't see him. At least he wasn't here to witness *that*.

She strolled toward me, hands clasped behind her back. Circled my frame, taking inventory. I tipped my chin up and stood up straighter, trying to swallow a lump in my throat.

"You hadn't been answering our calls." Disdain dripped from her voice. "Before we hired your security detail."

"You haven't been giving me a good reason to," I countered.

"We're your parents."

You don't act like it, I wanted to scream. *I drifted away, and you let me. I opted out, and the door was wide open for me to walk through. You never wanted me.*

"Well, I'm your daughter, and you haven't been taking my calls, either."

"You know exactly why." Her mouth twitched in annoyance. "Don't you, Bunny?"

To that, I said nothing.

"You've added a few tattoos." *Nice to see where our money is spent,* she didn't add.

"Someone needs to give you something to talk about at the dinner table, and God knows Hera and Craig are perfectly boring." I shrugged.

"Actions have consequences. You're going to live with these tattoos for the rest of your life."

"My *whole* life?" I widened my eyes, slapping a hand over my chest. "Oh, my. That's why they don't come off in the shower."

She made a face. I couldn't tell if she was disappointed, exasperated, or both. "When your father gets h—"

"I'm here." The devil we spoke of walked into the room. "Step back, Jules. Let the kid breathe. Y'all look like you're about to get in a fistfight."

Mom stepped back, looking lost and confused all of a sudden.

"Let's take it to my office, shall we?" Dad smiled good-naturedly.

Following them silently to Dad's office on the second floor, I remembered I didn't have anything here with me. No deodorant, no creams, no underwear, no PJs. I would have to make a Target run. The problem was, that would require my parents' security. One of them would have to accompany me, too.

Mom and Dad conducted a short and efficient discussion about their winter vacation plans on the way upstairs.

"Why must you insist on skiing every year? You know Craig absolutely loathes it. He is no good at it. No good at all." My mother pleaded my sister's fiancé's case.

"So, because Craig isn't a fan, I shouldn't do what I want with my limited free time?" Dad huffed. "Craig and Hera are welcome to stay at his parents' for Christmas if they're so inclined to. Sugar Pie, you'll come, right?"

"Christmas..." I murmured behind his back, thinking of a good excuse. "Yeah, I don't know about that. I'm involved in a lot of charities back home."

"Don't be dreadful," my mother chided, playing with the pearls on her neck as she hurried her steps. "Hera finds them stunningly tedious, and their house is far too crowded for a young couple. Four children. My word, have they not heard of contraception?"

Or overpopulation. Although, here in this house we pretended overpopulation was not a part of global warming. Dad had run on the ticket that he was both an environmentalist and a devout Catholic. Don't ask me when the last time was he went to church when there were no cameras around.

"In that case, Craig'll have to toughen up and bear the burden of skiing,"

Dad said.

Finally, we reached the oaky, double doors of his office. Dad pushed one of them open, and the three of us walked inside. He settled behind his desk. My mother and I took the seats in front of him. I felt like I was heading for a life-or-death trial.

"Hallie, my love, how have you been?" my father finally asked, a staggering four hours after I set foot in his house.

I squared my shoulders. I had to plea my case, even if I knew I stood no chance. *Here goes nothing.*

"Been better."

"What is it, Sugar Pie?" Dad demanded, his brows creasing worriedly. "Tell us."

"Well, let me preface this by saying I know I screwed up. Bad. I know that, okay? I've absolutely no excuse, and take full responsibility for it. I was drunk, and wore too snug a dress—"

"I have a feeling I know where this is going." My mother crossed her legs, folding her hands over her knee. Daphne walked into the room, asking if we needed any refreshments.

"Not now, Daph!" Mother barked. "Read the room, for Pete's sake."

Daphne scurried away with her tail between her legs.

You and I both, girl.

"You were saying?" Mother turned to face me, squinting accusingly.

"I know I didn't win any Daughter of the Year awards the night I left the Chateau. But I've learned my lesson. I haven't drunk a drop of alcohol since." (Other than the three glasses of wine Ransom let me have on the plane here, but that was a one-off, just because I caught him banging someone publicly.) "And I've been on my best behavior since then. I don't think having Mr. Lockwood follow me around is necessary."

"You are contradicting yourself." Mom uncrossed her legs, lounging back in her seat. "You just told us you haven't drunk a

drop of alcohol and have been on your best behavior since his arrival. We haven't seen this kind of behavior from you in *years*. The
tabloids haven't mentioned you once since he arrived. What would
inspire us to get rid of Mr. Lockwood when obviously he is the one
who should be credited for this improvement?"

I stared at her, ticked off. "If anyone deserves credit for my
being on my best behavior, it would be *me*." I stabbed my chest
with my finger.

"I'm sorry, Sugar Pie, but your mother isn't wrong." Dad tugged
at the collar of his cashmere sweater, smiling apologetically. "We've
been avoiding your calls because we knew you'd try to dodge the
arrangement. But the truth of the matter is…sweetheart, you *need*
this. For whatever reason, you want nothing to do with us. You've
been lost for far too long and you need to be found."

*You never made an honest attempt to get to know me. To help
me. You never reassured me that I wasn't a complete waste of space.
You always planned things without me—vacations, moves, travel—
inviting me to tag along like I was a family friend. Worst of all—you
failed to protect me.*

"He's a jerk and a half," I said instead. There was no point pleading my case to Mom and Dad. I'd tried a few times when I was a
teen. They never got it.

"Oh, Bunny." Mom clucked her tongue. "Tough love is exactly
what the doctor has ordered."

My cheeks were on fire. "There's no love in his behavior toward
me. He calls me Brat."

My father chuckled. "I've been called everything under the
sun. Words are just that—words."

"Dad." I closed my eyes, feeling my soul sagging with defeat. I
was tired. So tired of my constant battle with my family. "He makes
me really unhappy. Doesn't that count for anything?"

It wasn't the truth. Not in its entirety, anyway. Ransom fascinated and scared me. Worst of all, he attracted me, and I couldn't
allow for that to happen. Men were dangerous.

A thick blanket of silence fell over the room. For a brief

moment, no one spoke. I studied my father intently. The way his fingers drummed over the desk. He was considering his answer. One of his best traits was to think before he spoke. *Really* think. Even if it left the person in front of him waiting.

My mother, by comparison, was a quick shooter. "If I'm allowed to be frank, Hallie, you've been causing us a lot of heartache and bad press. You had been utterly unmanageable, and with your sister's wedding coming up, we simply cannot afford any slip-ups."

Ah, this was about Hera. I should've known. Everything always boiled down to creating the perfect life for Hera and Craig. My lower lip curled around my upper one to stop myself from screaming.

"Mr. Lockwood is the highest rated bodyguard in North America. We wanted the very best for you." Mother's voice floated over my head, like a poisonous cloud of smoke. "I pray that when his post is over, you consider spending some time with us in Texas to mend our relationship. For now, you're going to have to make do with him."

I looked up, feeling my eyes burning with unshed tears. I spoke through gritted teeth. "You don't love me, you tolerate me. Don't think I don't see the difference."

My mother stood up. In this light, I could see every wrinkle in her face. She wore her age with pride. Deemed women who hid behind fillers and Botox tacky and uncultured.

"Don't be ridiculous, of course we love you." She brushed dog hair from her clothes, her words hollow and empty. "We're crazy about you. You are our child, Bunny."

"Your mother is right. Also, you can use one of the guestrooms." My father stood up, on cue, to join my mother. "Dinner is at six, and we'll be having company."

He stared pointedly at my clothes. *Fix yourself up, Sugar Pie. Please. For me.*

At the door, my mother paused, her hand fluttering over the frame. "It's good to have you back. I don't always understand where you are coming from, but you always light up the room when you're here."

They left, leaving the door open. I could hear them picking up the conversation they'd left off before we entered the office. Skiing versus a sunny Christmas getaway. I couldn't muster the energy to move an inch. I slacked there for a few moments, my gaze gliding over the walls. Pictures of my father hugging and shaking hands with other world leaders glared back at me.

I couldn't stay here. Or maybe I could. Maybe I simply didn't want to. Since no one gave two shits about what I wanted, it was time to do something for myself.

But I couldn't even call an Uber. Ransom had canceled my credit card, which was attached to it. I fumbled for my phone in my pocket, about to call him. Then I stopped myself. *No.* Telling him I was coming back was admitting defeat. Better if I just showed up and told him I had a change of plans. Bonus points: he'd know I traveled unaccompanied, and possibly—*hopefully*—would have a heart attack as a result.

I picked up my phone and called Keller.

"Howdy partner," he said in his most mocking Texan drawl impression. "How's home treating you?"

"Terrible, as per usual." I darted up from my chair, pacing. Dragging a hand over my forehead confirmed that, yes, I was sweating buckets. Maybe I was coming down with something. "I need you to call me an Uber. I'll pay you back."

"You want an Uber from Texas to California?" he asked, confused. "Ever seen the US map, sweetie?"

"No!" I flung my arms. "From my parents' house outside of Dallas back to my hotel."

"But…" I heard him hesitate. "Why can't you do it?"

"Because, didn't I tell you, Ransom Lockwood canceled my credit cards!"

"The bastard!" Keller sounded outraged. "And he left you to fend for yourself, ride-less?"

Not exactly. He'd insisted he stay here, until my mother sent him away. He'd probably predicted I didn't have the stomach to spend an entire night here.

"It's an absolute nightmare." I put a hand to my collarbone, dodging his question. "I need your help."

"All right. Send me the deets. Help's on the way."

I did just that, then stomped my way out of Dad's office, down to the second floor, and outside, completely uninterrupted. No one noticed I'd walked right out of the mansion. This was the perk to being invisible, I supposed. I could slip under people's radars.

The Uber arrived ten minutes later, and as a midnight blue evening fell across the sky, I started my journey to the hotel.

The entire drive into Dallas, I felt like a giant ball of puke was stuck inside my throat. It was ten past six when my phone started blowing up with calls from my parents. I hadn't shown up to their dinner. My heart raced in my chest. Ransom was going to lose his shit when I showed up at the hotel. As it happened, bickering with him was my new favorite pastime.

My thighs clenched when I thought about him pressing against me. When the memory of his blood in my mouth seeped into my brain. He was so messed up for getting off on kinks like that. Then again…apparently, so was I.

When the Uber pulled up at Tortoise Creek Mansion, I stumbled out, making my way toward the nearest trashcan, and vomited the little I'd eaten in the past forty-eight hours. Cold shivers rolled through my arms as I swayed onto the premises.

Somehow, I found one of Ransom's men milling around the reception area, probably making sure nothing seemed suspicious. I could tell them apart from the crowd, because they were all over six foot four and dressed exclusively in black.

I tapped one of them on the shoulder to get his attention. He turned around. "Take me to my room."

He recognized me instantly. His face paled. I couldn't blame him. He was about to deliver his boss a very distressed looking, unaccompanied client.

"We need to tell Ransom."

"No. You work for me, not him." I started for the elevator. He followed me.

"I don't think it's a good idea for you to go up there right now." His thick throat dipped with a swallow.

Of course not. Ransom was going to make a huge stink about it.

"I don't think I asked for your goddamn opinion!"

"Miss Thorne—"

"No, you listen here." I wagged my finger in his face, unbothered by the fact the lobby was jam-packed with people in evening gowns and suits, sitting around the bar and listening to a pianist playing an unpolished version of "Hungarian Rhapsody". "You're going to be in a world of pain if you don't let me into *my* suite right now. Lockwood may be your point of contact, but don't forget who's signing that paycheck."

"Ma'am—"

"I want to go to my room. Now."

The man ushered me into the elevator, where he swiped a card over the access control panel, before pressing a button leading to the top, private floor.

I glanced at my reflection in the mirror. My eyes were bloodshot and my hair was a mess. My lips were dry and cracked. My sweatpants were stained. I looked as bad as I felt. And I felt like garbage. I wanted to stumble into bed and forget today had ever happened.

The elevator pinged open. Muscle Man got out first, glancing left and right before motioning for me with his head to join him. He stopped in front of my suite's door, his hand hovering over the card reader.

"Do it," I bit out. "And leave."

If Ransom took the bigger bedroom, I was going to strangle him in his sleep.

Reluctantly, Muscle Man followed my directions, bowing his

head before slinking back into the open elevator. Running away from the scene.

As the door clicked shut, my skin prickled with awareness.

Danger crawled over me like spider legs.

There were sounds coming from the second bedroom of the suite. Alarming sounds. Like someone was sobbing uncontrollably.

Not again…

I made my way to the open bedroom door, clutching the phone in my fist just in case.

The image in front of me unfolded all at once.

The sight of Ransom fucking a complete stranger against the floor-to-ceiling window overlooking the hotel restaurant, sliding in and out of her, his muscled ass cheeks contracting each time he pressed home.

He was fully dressed, his smart pants barely tugged down, not a hair on his head out of place. She was naked as the day she was born, wearing only red-tipped heels, which were wrapped around his waist, her ankles knotted together, pulling him closer. Her hair, shimmering gold, was blown out to perfection. She was the quintessential Texan beauty. Her breasts looked red and raw, like they'd been slapped and tugged painfully.

You didn't waste any time, did you?

"That's it. Take it all, and don't forget—if you ever tell anyone, I'm going to make it very painful for you," he growled into her face.

I stumbled back, choking on my saliva. An imaginary sword slid through my gut. At first I felt the burn—then the pain.

Deep. Wild. Curling over my throat like talons.

Not because I was disturbed.

But because this time, I wasn't just turned on. I was *jealous*.

I didn't get it. This delicious, breathless ache that spread through me like wildfire. I hated him. He was a disgusting pig. But I couldn't look away. Couldn't rip my eyes off the sight of Ransom driving into another woman while she moaned, pretending to protest while her heels urged him for more.

The woman slapped him.

He laughed roughly, pinned her arms above her head against the glass, and thrust harder.

"You'll never get away with it." But as she spoke, she met him thrust for thrust.

He pinned her harder, thrusting faster. "You just watch me."

The woman's eyes climbed from his face, and she noticed me. "We've got company."

Oh, shit.

"She can watch. That's all the action this little brat is allowed."

Burn in hell.

"Unless you're not into that?" He stopped thrusting, rubbing blood back into her wrists, searching her face now. He was being considerate and nice. Both qualities I didn't recognize in him.

She shook her head slowly. "I'm having too much fun to stop."

"Good." He shoved her hands back above her head and continued thrusting, ignoring me completely, this time not even trying to apologize to me.

I'd been caught. The Peeping Tom in the room. No. Worse. *Horny Hallie.* Watching shamelessly as my bodyguard got his rocks off with another woman.

"You like to watch me fuck a stranger, don't you, Brat?" he purred.

His gaze was on me as he drove into her. She spun her head the opposite way, so I couldn't see her face. She was participating in being his prop! A part of his twisted, elaborate game between two, very unwell people.

"That's right. See this shit through. Own your kink."

I was mortified. Mainly because, as he was studying me, I was fixated on the sliver of space between his body and hers. Where I could see his cock through the glistering condom, engorged, thick and dark, draw back then disappear inside of her.

My belly dipped with shame. I felt my pulse thumping between my legs each time he drove into her, my thighs slickening. I wanted to be her. I wanted to be fucked. Disrespectfully. To be used by this heartless man. To be submissive, and docile. To stop fighting. Once.

What was wrong with me?

Everything, I thought. *You don't need a bodyguard; you need a therapist.*

But I didn't believe in therapists anymore. I'd had sixteen of them throughout the years, and not one could fix me.

"Do you like when I do this?" His white teeth twinkled in the dark. He snaked his arm behind the woman, fisting her hair in a death grip, angling her face down to watch how he was fucking her, deeper, more furiously now. Whimpers of happiness escaped her.

I didn't say anything. I didn't trust myself right now. Not my words. Not my actions.

"Or maybe you're into this?" He pulled out of her suddenly, snapped the condom off, and brought her down to her knees, shoving his cock into her mouth. She gasped before taking him in eagerly, sucking and gagging as she wrapped a fist around the base, zero doubt she was as willing a participant in this depravity as I wanted to be.

As that other woman the other night had been. He was sexy and safe and within reach.

There was so much saliva in my mouth. I wanted to touch myself. The unbearable craving blurred my vision. I didn't have to touch myself, as it turned out. Because my body came alive on its own, my creative limbs stretching, using invisible brushes to paint myself where the blonde woman was, on her knees on the carpet. I imagined I was her. And that was enough to make my knees weak and my nipples pucker. To feel an earthquake shivering through my spine, like a long crack in the ground as it split open.

I climaxed on nothing, the orgasm making my entire body arch and tense at the same time.

He came in her mouth. She came, too. Came from sucking him off.

She gulped. He tucked himself back in, finally sliding his gaze off of me.

He removed his watch from his wrist. "Thank you, Marla. It's been a pleasure."

"Same. You have my number." She winked at him, wiping at her mouth.

He put his Rolex in its case, leaning over to kiss her cheek like a perfect gentleman. "I called you a cab. Take as long as you need to get ready. He'll wait."

It was a part of Ransom I didn't know. A part of him I wanted for myself. I realized I didn't only want the shameful, unrestricted, violent sex. I also wanted the way he snapped out of his role and became someone else. Someone *soft*.

Pulled back from my unexpected orgasm, I finally managed to see beyond the thick tendrils of desire. What he'd done was horrible toward both her and me. It was… I didn't even know what to call it.

Degrading. Sick. Punishing.

She got dressed and slipped away from the room, avoiding eye contact with me. Her shoulder brushed mine on her way out, and I caught a whiff of Ransom's scent on her, which made my blood boil again.

Not good. Not good at all. I couldn't be possessive of this man. He hated me, he was here for only a few months, and beyond all that—he was simply unbearable.

Ransom and I stood in front of one another, like two cowboys, waiting to see who was going to draw first.

Me, I decided. I was feeling trigger-happy today.

I leaned a shoulder against the doorjamb, just as the sound of the front door slamming echoed between us.

"Your after-hours activities should remain outside my safe space, Mr. Lockwood."

"If safety meant jack-shit to you, you wouldn't be running around in an Uber taken directly from your parents' house like a moron."

He tugged the back of his shirt, removing it and discarding it on the floor. His shoes, socks, and pants followed suit. He walked out of them on his way to the en suite bathroom. I followed him. I'd seen his secret now. *Literally*. I wasn't going to be intimidated by a little nudity.

"So you know about the Uber." I stayed at the door to his bathroom as he pushed his briefs down. I took a moment to appreciate his ass again. The hollows on each side of his cheeks. The prominent Dimples of Venus I wished I had for myself.

He entered the shower *before* turning it on and waiting for the hot water. The psychopath.

"I know about everything you do." He brushed his wet hair back from his face. A cloud of steam formed over the glass, blocking the view. "And you're going to be grounded for that little stint. One month, minimum."

"I don't think you understand the situation here." I adopted Hera's tenor. Prim with a touch of oh-you-little-peasant-you. "This whole place is wired, remember? Tapped. And you just made a big boo-boo."

"Not my room," he said indifferently.

Shoot. I believed him. It made sense, since no one was counting on me spending time in this room.

"And what I made, was two women come. One of them I didn't even touch."

He knew he'd made me climax. I didn't confirm it. Although my red-hot ears, I suppose, did.

"You just forcibly made me watch you have sex with another woman," I reminded him. "This is the second time I watched you be inside someone else. I have huge leverage on you."

How could he not know that?

"Really? Forced, you say?" He used a soap bar to shampoo his hair. And as a shower gel, too.

"You didn't stop when I walked in."

"Into *my* room. Please tell me how I forced you to watch me fuck someone else, rather than, oh, let's see—you walking in on me, in *my* room, during *my* time off, having sex with a woman, and kept staring at us like…how did you call it? *Skipper the Creeper.*"

My mouth fell open. He was such a cunning…manipulating…

"You're not going to get away with this," I hissed.

Of course, he was getting away with it. He already had. My

parents were firmly on his side—or at least they weren't on mine. I had no way to negotiate myself out of this nightmare situation.

"Stop sounding like every badly-written superhero." He turned off the water and walked out completely naked. He was a vision, and he knew it. I looked away, not giving him the satisfaction of being openly admired.

"This isn't over."

He grabbed a towel, patting himself dry. "Are you done?"

"No. You're a pervert."

"Yes," he surprised me by saying. "But so are you."

"I'm not—"

"Go back to your room. I'll think of your punishment tomorrow."

"I'll run away before bending to your will."

He secured the towel over his narrow hips, grabbing his shaving foam and razor. "Better get some comfortable shoes then."

Not wanting to keep this awful exchange going, but desperate for some destruction points, I settled for grabbing the expensive cologne by his sink and hurling it against the wall. It shattered noisily, cologne everywhere. I turned around and marched toward my room, realizing one of the glass shards had lodged in my foot.

"Shit!" I roared but kept marching. Now I needed to take the glass out.

I heard him laugh behind my back.

Bastard.

Chapter Nine

Ransom

Poor Brat.

Poor, poor Brat. Couldn't catch a break if said break was sitting still right in front of her, with a Post-it note reading, **CATCH ME.**

I didn't feel bad about last night. The fact that she'd decided to stop and enjoy the show was unexpected, but definitely not unwelcome.

I wasn't much of an exhibitionist, but I liked having Hallie's eyes on me when I fucked Marla, a flight attendant I'd known from years back and was in Dallas for a layover.

Brat had a dark side, and I had to remember she was off-limits, because nothing turned me on like darkness.

I did feel sorry for her. Her parents were two pieces of work. The shit show yesterday was very telling. A quick scan of the Thorne estate had confirmed zero mentions or sights of anything Hallie-related. Though I'd seen plenty of photos of her horsey sister along with her fiancé, who looked like a piece of bread soaked in water.

The time her parents made her wait conveyed the message that she wasn't important to them. Then her father had invited me for a talk, in which her mother was present, and I realized these people didn't know their own daughter as well as I did. They thought she had an alcohol problem, something I'd have picked up on if it were true.

They thought she had multiple sexual partners—in practice, I'd wager she was seeing very little non battery-operated action between the sheets.

And they thought she was as dumb as a rock. But I was starting to suspect there was more to their daughter than meets the eye.

I woke up with a headache. It was six in the morning. Brat was fast asleep. I hit the hotel gym, but not before giving the security company I'd hired a piece of my mind about letting Brat get into the room without calling me first last night.

I hit the shower back in the suite. Brat's soft snores were still rising from the master bedroom. I wondered what kind of plan she had waiting for me today. Brat was always in the mood for retaliation whenever I messed with her. And yesterday I'd made her come in her studded pink sweatpants just from watching.

I found her fight amusing. Now that I knew her background was comprised of such a shitty family, her unreasonable behavior almost made sense.

The Princess woke up at ten in the morning and found me in the kitchen, working. She was extra pouty. She was also dressed—thank God—though I couldn't exactly describe what she was wearing. It looked like an old gingham curtain that had suffered a midlife crisis and decided to become a '50s-style dress.

She put her ruby hair up into a high ponytail, letting tendrils spill across both her shoulders. I had to admit—she was beautiful in broad daylight. Fragile, elegant, and succulent, all at the same time.

"Coffee?" I asked, my idea of giving her an inch of a white flag. A white stamp, if you would.

She shook her head, sitting directly in front of me at the table. I shut my laptop screen. I had a feeling she wasn't used to having people give her their full attention unless she was naked.

She stared at me. I raised my eyebrows, in a *what-the-fuck?* gesture. No doubt, she wanted to clear the air after yesterday.

"My parents…" She licked her lips.

Her parents? Did not see that one coming.

"They thought I was staying at their house, and I left without saying goodbye. Did they call you?"

"Yes," I said evenly.

"Am I in trouble?"

"Also yes."

Her expression collapsed to something full of annoyance.

"Stop fighting everything and everyone. Accept the situation. These are the cards you've been dealt. Me. Your parents. This life. It's not the worst."

"I'm not going back there today." She folded her arms over her chest.

"We have to," I said dispassionately, taking one last sip of my espresso and standing up to dump the cup into the sink. "They invited us for dinner."

"I don't want to." Her eyes were glassy, and I hated that I had to make her. Catering to assholes who didn't deserve your time was something I knew a lot about.

But I had to play nice with Anthony Thorne because he was a key figure in what I was trying to achieve for my business.

"Maybe we can tell them I'm sick." She snapped her fingers, her eyes lighting up. The way she had forgotten about yesterday, about the charged chemistry between us, about climaxing at the same time, like it hadn't happened, surprised and confused me. Usually, I was on the receiving end of sexual propositions. Yesterday, I'd been minutes away from kissing the shit out of her in the bathroom.

Maybe she didn't want to broach the subject when the place was wired. A car ride alone would change that.

"No." I picked up my phone and scrolled through my messages. "You're used to people letting you off the hook. Time to change that. We're going."

"I hate you," she murmured.

"I understand," I said blandly, but I didn't believe her.

"Well, then." She stood up. I did not check out her ass. Okay, fine, I did. *Fuck*, she had Jessica Rabbit's proportions. And hair. "I have an appointment to get to, if you want to join."

"Want is not the operative word here." But I was glad for the distraction. "Where to? I need to check out the place in advance."

She gave me the address of a small tattoo shop in downtown Dallas. I sent the team to sniff around while she got ready. Hallie took approximately five-and-a-half years to make herself presentable.

"What tattoo are you getting?" I asked as I drove her down to the shop. Downtown Dallas was awash with shoppers, joggers, and people walking their dogs.

"Promise not to laugh." But she didn't look concerned about my opinion. Also, she *still* didn't say jack-shit about last night.

"Don't give yourself too much credit. I'm a hard man to entertain."

She produced a piece of paper from her secondhand Gucci bag, handing it over to me. It was a drawing of an anatomically correct heart, made out of a diamond. It looked morbid, real, and surprisingly compelling, even though tattoos weren't my jam. I handed it back to her.

"Where?"

"Hipbone."

"Does it represent something?"

"Sometimes I feel like my heart is as hard as a diamond. Or should be, to survive my life."

This was the part where I mocked her for her hardship, while balancing a 3k bag in her lap. But baiting her was getting old, not to mention all of her shit was secondhand. In fact, I didn't know a lot of women who rummaged through trash the way she did to take care of the environment. No. Hallie's lack of employment and direction didn't come from laziness.

Instead, I asked, "Did you draw this yourself?"

It was surprising both because I didn't normally show that I gave a damn and because I didn't realize she had any talents other than pissing me off.

"Yes."

"You're not terrible."

"Lofty praise coming from you."

I let her lay in the puddle of her own thoughts for a while, knowing she was incapable of keeping her mouth shut for more than five minutes.

Sure enough, two seconds later, she sighed audibly and said, "Sometimes I worry."

"About?"

"That I'm too numb. I think I love tattoos not only because it's easy to hide behind them, but because...well, the pain gives me an excuse to feel."

"Pain's not a feeling," I corrected her. "This is why you keep getting inked. You're searching for a feeling, but you're not getting it."

"What do you mean? Of course pain is a feeling." She turned to face me, and I swear the temperature in my body rose a couple degrees. Goddammit. I had to bang a Hallie lookalike and get rid of my stupid fixation with her. This was ridiculous. And dangerous. And putting a strain on my cock, which wasn't used to being erect nineteen hours a day.

"No. It's a sensation. There's a difference."

"What's the difference?" Her eyes were two sapphire saucers, directed at me.

"A feeling is an emotional state. A sensation speaks to your nervous system."

"How do I fix this?" she demanded.

"You don't."

"I *must*," she insisted. "Tell me how."

"Do I look like a shrink?" I snapped.

"No, but you charge more than one, so you should go the extra mile."

I didn't answer that. Getting life advice from my ass was as good as celibacy tips from a whore.

"And what about you?" she redirected. "Do you have feelings or sensations?"

"Neither." I pushed my sunglasses up my nose. "And thank fuck for that."

I parked at the back of the tattoo shop so as not to draw attention, but when we rounded the alleyway, spilling onto Main Street, Brat pointed out we'd have to enter through the front, anyway.

As soon as we appeared on the corner of the street, next to a Starbucks, dozens of paparazzi photographers swarmed us like raptors, aiming their cameras at us, crouching to try to catch an up-skirt money shot.

Hallie stopped, smiled, and blew kisses to the cameras. She waved at all of them, practically glowing. She was giving them old Hallie. The person they wanted to mock. The one who drew bad press.

"It's good to be in Texas again, y'all."

This was her little payback for last night. Inviting the paps and making me look like I didn't have control over her ass.

"Hallie! Are you here for your sister's wedding?"

"When's your turn?"

"Is it true that Wes Morgan dumped you because you're having an affair with your bodyguard?"

"Are you pregnant?!"

I grabbed her wrist and ushered her inside.

"Did you hear?" she purred. "We're having an affair and I might be pregnant. Should I tell them your favorite flavor is unwilling?"

"We both know that's not true."

"I'm sure the tabloids will listen to reason instead of capitalizing on a juicy detail."

Never have I wanted to murder and kiss someone more. Simultaneously.

I pushed the door open. We both entered a tiny space with checkered flooring and posters of skulls and zombies on the coral-hued walls. Very refined.

"Oh, come on. You couldn't expect me to just let you get away with what you did yesterday." She laughed, her throaty voice filling the small space, drowning out "Young Folks" by Peter Bjorn and John.

Now she wanted to talk about last night. In front of a three-hundred-pound tattoo artist with a bushy beard and enough bodily piercings to moonlight as a sieve.

"You wanted to watch," I snarled.

Case in point: she'd stood there and stared at my cock like it was a Broadway show.

"I was shocked, is all."

"Bullshit. You're curious."

"And if I am?" She twirled a piece of hair around her index finger. "What does it mean for us?"

It meant my cock was about to fall off for wanting her so badly, but I was never going to act on it.

I turned around, giving her my back.

"Just get your shit done."

While Brat was getting inked, I hopped on the phone with Tom. He was back in Chicago, shadowing Mayor Ferns, and sounded bored out of his ass.

I didn't call him to hear about his day-to-day life. I called about Ian Holmes and the soap opera we'd left in L.A.

"The feds are taking their time," he complained. I heard him unbuckling his belt, taking a piss. "And the LAPD is so overworked and underpaid, my guess is they'll try to bone up some bullshit info just to get someone to trial, but it doesn't look great. Mainly, there's not enough evidence against Kozlov."

"They aren't digging deep enough," I insisted.

"If Ian couldn't stop them with his resources, ya think they'll want to stitch up a case against these career criminals? This is not the eighties, Ran. These people have lawyers on retainer. The type who charge four figures an hour."

"Are you saying they're scared to touch the Bratva?" I asked.

"I'm not saying they aren't, is all."

This meant I had to drag out Brat's stay here in Texas until I had a better idea of how to protect her in Los Angeles. If the Russians had impunity, and didn't fear getting caught, I was certainly the next one in line to get offed.

The best course of action was to tell Anthony Thorne there was a threat to Hallie's life in L.A. She wasn't going to be happy about it, but sparing her feelings wasn't as important as keeping her safe.

Brat was done three hours later. She wobbled out of the back room toward the register, wincing with each step she took. The artist slipped behind the desk and checked her out. With a faux smile on her face, she snapped her fingers in my direction, like I was her butler. "Pay the man, Lockwood."

"My apologies, ma'am. I forgot my checkbook in the suite, along with my servant uniform and, apparently, your sanity." I smiled cordially.

What made her think I'd pay for this shit?

"Cash'll do. So will a credit card." She didn't spare me a look.

"Nonetheless, I'm still not reaching for my wallet."

"I haven't received my daily allowance in days," she reminded me. "Go on. Pay up. That should cover the tattoo and the tip."

"I'm not paying for this."

"Well, someone is," the man behind the desk said, popping the buttons of his leather vest open. "And I ain't got all day, pals."

"Gee, I understand," she sassed, draping herself over his desk seductively. "The last thing we need is a headline, sir. *Anthony Thorne's Daughter Leaves Local Tattoo Shop without Paying Bill.*"

Yeah. Hallie Thorne wasn't dumb. She simply channeled every cell in her brain being a manipulative little minx.

Reminding myself that I was about to keep her in Texas for a long time, and that was retaliation enough, I took out my wallet and handed him my card.

Brat twirled her way out of the shop, all sunshine and rainbows. "See? That wasn't so bad."

After a quick stop at a bridal shop to get her measurements for the maid of honor dress, we drove to her parents' house in silence. My favorite soundtrack.

About halfway through our journey, she let out a little sigh, and that was when I knew my luck had run out and she was about to start talking.

"I think I might be a horrible person."

"Finally, a statement we can both get behind." Was she expecting a pep talk? We were in the midst of a cold war.

"I mean it, Random. I think I am."

I didn't want to get to know her better right now. I didn't want to hear about her woes. In fact, I regretted the moment I made the error of telling her about *my* humble beginning, but at the time, she'd looked about ready to off herself and a dead client would've looked really bad on my résumé.

She stared out her window with a slight pout. I thought I saw a tear sliding down her cheek.

I guess self-realization was part of the 'grow the fuck up' itinerary I'd thrust upon her. Sighing, I said, "Why do you think you're a horrible person?"

"I just realized yesterday that I have no real friends. No real connections. My relationship with my family is in shambles. My life is keeping up appearances. It's an empty shell."

I said nothing. If this was her having a breakthrough, it was better she come to the conclusion herself.

"And all those Instagram friends…NeNe and Tara…" She frowned, shaking her head. "They haven't even called me once since I got here. No one but Keller—he's the closest, but… Don't you think it's weird?"

"No. It is very possible NeNe and Tara don't know how to operate a phone."

"I just feel like I'm wasting my life away."

"You are," I confirmed. It was the first crack in her tabloid princess persona, and I was going to break the rest of it apart and pull out whatever was hiding underneath.

"What should I do?"

"Get a job. Do something meaningful with your life. Contribute. It's not like you're a stranger to altruism," I gritted out. "You care. Put your good intentions to use."

"I always thought work was a means to an end. A way to pay for the pleasures of life."

She looked mesmerized by the idea that doing something with herself was an option, rather than a bad joke.

"Why do you think people who retire deteriorate fast? Humans need to be on the move. Fight or die."

"But I feel like everyone would love to see me fail." She bit at her lower lip.

"Prove them wrong."

"What if I can't?"

"Then die trying."

"What's the point of trying if you fail?"

I smiled grimly. "You look at yourself in the mirror differently. Have you given any thought to what you want to do with your life?"

She inclined her head. No surprises there. To me, the answer was obvious. But she had to realize it herself. It was no good if I handed her the idea. It had to come from her. And, she deserved to choose that for herself, at least. Not like she'd had much say over the rest of her life, not with the family she'd been born into.

"Better come up with something." I drummed the steering wheel. "It's part of our process."

"Okay." She rolled her shoulders back, sitting straight. "Do you think I'm a decent person?"

We were still on that subject? Jesus.

"I think it doesn't matter," I said, and when she opened her mouth to speak again, added, "This conversation is over, Brat."

The way dinner had gone, I was pleasantly surprised by Brat's resilience. Her loyalty. She had every reason to write these people off, but she still kept it civilized.

"This is an informal supper. Please, feel at home," Julianne Thorne urged, snug in her Alexander McQueen red satin jacket.

We followed the Thornes across the foyer, with Brat staring down at her feet, looking much younger than her twenty-one years.

"Good to see you again, Sugar Pie." Anthony eyed his daughter. He glossed-over the fact his daughter ran away from their house yesterday without so much as a goodbye.

Hallie, stiff and uninterested, sported the facial expression of a prisoner of war. "The pleasure is all mine," Hallie deadpanned.

"We were so shocked when you left without saying a word," Julianne whined to her daughter.

"Oh, yeah? I was shocked you thought I'd stay after our conversation in Dad's office."

The girl had an admirable amount of fight in her.

We sat down at the "informal" table in the kitchen, not the fancy one in the dining room, while three chefs in absurd white hats produced sweet potato and buttermilk pies from an AGA. Accompanied by chicken fried steak, a hearty stew, and sweet tea.

Very casual, you see.

"So. Ransom." Julianne kept patting the corners of her mouth with a napkin, even though she didn't consume any food. "Please tell us all about your company. We're eager to get to know you."

I provided them minimal information about Lockwood and Whitfield Protection Group, occasionally glancing at Brat, who seemed to have shrunk into herself until she was the size of a toddler.

I told myself it was not my monkey, not my circus. But it took them forty minutes to remember she was there while they grilled me about my life, my upbringing, my career, and my business partner.

"Oh, Bunny, I forgot to tell you. Remember Felicity Hawthorne?" Julianne gave her daughter a frosty look, taking a sip of her red wine. "She went to school with Hera. She's the director of a think tank now, in Los Angeles. She said she'd love it if you sent her your résumé!"

"I don't have a résumé, but I *do* have an allergy to nepotism." Hallie smiled, and that was when I noticed her plate was empty. Which, of course, made sense, since almost everything on the table contained meat. She must have been starving—no wonder she was hangry.

"Oh, I'm trying, Hallie. Could you at least throw me a bone? Sarcasm is beneath us, Bunny." Julianne's face fell.

"Good thing I'm not a part of 'us' then, right, *Mommy*?" Brat tapped her pointy nails along the table, a habit she'd developed five seconds ago to get on her mother's nerves.

"This conversation is redundant." Anthony tossed his napkin onto his plate. "You don't need to get a job right away. There's still time for that. We haven't seen you in so long, Hallie. Let's focus on catching up."

"Let's." Hallie perked. "Do you have a month or two? I have a *lot* of news from the last twenty-one years."

"You're a product of a generation that has too much, and of whom is required too little." Julianne wasn't in the mood to de-escalate the atmosphere.

"Whatever, *Ma*." Brat rolled her nails along the tattoos on her arms, making her mother's eyes stop and examine them. "Personal responsibility is a foreign concept to you."

"That is rich." Julianne smiled. "Coming from someone who hasn't worked a day in her life."

"Dessert's almost here!" one of the staffers in the room cried desperately, leaning between Hallie and me to clear our plates.

"Good," Julianne said. "I'm in the mood for something sweet

and comforting, since I obviously cannot get any affection from my own daughter."

I was starting to see the pros of not having a family.

"So what did you want to talk about, son?" Anthony referred the question to me, pouring more iced tea into my glass. I wasn't his son, and I found the endearment denigrating.

"I understand that the rehearsal dinner is tomorrow." I didn't spare Brat a look. I was about to deliver a knockout.

"Correct." Anthony nodded. "My security team was instructed to send you all the details."

"They did." I took a sip of my iced tea. "And the wedding's in two weeks."

"Yes." Julianne touched her tinted cheeks. She obviously took pride in her other daughter. "That's exactly right."

"I would like to bridge it out and stay in Texas," I said, not looking at Brat, who stiffened beside me. "Other than saving everyone the logistical headache, it would also ensure Hallie is protected in her hotel suite, where she already has a security team working around the clock."

"Sounds like a solid plan to me."

"No way." Brat stood up, slapping her palm against the table. Her face looked ashen, yet she was animated enough to safely assume she was close to stabbing someone with her steak knife. "I'm not spending two-and-a-half weeks in Texas. I'm allergic to this place."

"Dearie me." Julianne swirled her red wine in tiny circles. All good manners and bad intentions. "Are we not glamorous enough for you, Bunny?"

Hallie's gaze was fixed on her father, the lesser evil. "I want to be where I belong."

"You belong in Texas." Anthony's face softened. "With us."

"You belong nowhere," I interjected. "You have three friends in L.A. Two of which probably cannot spell your name. It is too big, too crowded, and the paps would love to have your head on a platter. Texas may not suit your lifestyle, but it'll keep you away from temptations and potential news coverage. You'll be staying here, doing some volunteer work, getting to know the area. I've already set it up."

"Thank you, Ransom." Anthony winked. "Now, this is what I call money well spent."

Brat stared me down. Though words didn't pass her lips, her eyes screamed volumes.

I wasn't letting her put herself in danger in Los Angeles. Even if I was the one responsible for this unfortunate predicament.

"I'm not staying here a minute past the rehearsal dinner," she announced.

"Careful now, Miss Thorne, or your parents won't be able to see the staggering progress you've made." I smirked at her.

Our plates cleared out. Servants came out of the kitchen with Bananarchy, ice cream sandwiches, and an unholy amount of cake, lining shiny silver spoons on fresh napkins.

"Random, please." I saw the exact moment when she lost her fight and tried to appeal to my conscience, knowing damn well mine was working only ten percent of the time. "Just once, let me have my way."

I swallowed. Amazingly, my feelings were not as flatlined as they usually were. I hated doing this to her. And I hated she didn't deserve this.

"I'm sorry," I said quietly, meaning it. "It's settled."

She hung her head low between her shoulders.

We left shortly after dessert.

Chapter Ten

Hallie

My face was buried in my pillow the next morning when I heard the door to my room click open. Heavy, confident footsteps pressed along my carpeted floor.

"You lucked out."

Even without seeing him, I could envision him, draped like a mythological deity against a heavy piece of furniture, his destructive beauty almost baiting me to pick a fight.

I burrowed deeper into my pillow, wondering if I could suffocate this way. Surely, I wasn't that lucky. Besides, I knew other ways to take my life. Less painful ones. A bullet to the skull, maybe. Though honestly, I didn't trust my aim. Maybe Ransom could do it? Ha. He would save me just to spite me. The bastard.

I didn't want to see Craig and Hera today. I really, *really* didn't want to see them.

"Earth to Brat, you listening?" I heard Ransom push off whatever he was leaning against and walk toward me. "I said I've some good news."

"Deliver it and be gone," I murmured into my pillow.

"The rehearsal dinner is postponed. Your sister's fiancé's

grandfather is in the ICU. They're shelving the dinner to just before the wedding."

I rolled over onto my back, staring at the ceiling. The relief I
was expecting didn't come. Instead, dread gathered in the pit of
my stomach, like debris.

It was like prolonging an open-heart surgery. Sans the anesthesia.

"Is he going to die?" A voice croaked, and I realized, belatedly,
that it was coming from me.

"Who?" Ransom asked, sitting on the edge of my bed. "Actually,
never mind. The answer is yes, either way. If you mean the grandpa,
then probably in the next few days. If you mean the fiancé, I'd give
the guy a few more decades before he kicks the bucket."

"Shame."

"You don't like him?" He peered into my face. I was too le-
thargic to look back.

"He's literally perfect."

"Sounds appalling," Ransom offered.

"My family loves him. They treat him like their son."

He raised his hand. He was holding a stack of papers. That's
when my eyes shifted from the ceiling, studying him with a mixture of dread and curiosity.

"What now? My parents want to sign me out of the will?"

"Don't think they'll need your permission to do that. But they
did send your bridesmaid's speech for you to memorize." He flung
it in my lap. I didn't touch it. I turned my head toward the window, watching two birds landing on a tree branch at the same time,
tweeting at each other.

I want to be you.

"Shouldn't I be the one to write it?" I sulked.

"Good morning. The year is 2026 and your family is overbearing. Also, Michael Jackson is dead, and we still haven't found
a cure for cancer."

"They don't trust me with anything." I tossed my arm over my
eyes. An acute pain clawed into my chest. The prospect of drawing
a breath felt unbearable.

"That's not true. I'm sure they trust you to mess things up. Hence the bridesmaid's speech."

"Can you stop being an ass, just for one moment?"

"Probably not," he said neutrally. "But I'll give it a shot."

After he realized I wasn't going to answer him, he asked, "What's on today's agenda, Princess?"

I scrambled upright, my back pressed against the headboard. "I guess I'm going to try my best to make your life a living hell and embarrass my family. You know, the usual stuff."

He reached for the blanket, tapping my knee twice. As soon as his hand met with my leg, a shot of thrill ran through me, injecting me with energy and life. It was the first time he'd touched me. *Willingly*, anyway. Gently. Not to remove me out of a place or to drag me into my room. It seemed important, and not accidental, and maybe I was crazy, but also a little intimate. I had a feeling he wanted to make me feel better and didn't know how. And Ransom *never* wanted to make anyone feel better.

"Shoot for the stars, Brat."

I arched an eyebrow. "You mean, I can actually do whatever I want today?"

"Absolutely not." His bored expression was impenetrable. "But I'm giving you a head start. For the next ten hours, you're not on a budget. You're allowed to spend your parents' money however you like. I'll deal with them. After that, you're all booked for volunteer work."

"Soup kitchen?" I asked groggily. It was celebrities' go-to thing, so I figured this was where they wanted me to go.

He shook his head. "Reservoir cleaning and recycling."

How sad is it, I thought, *that my bodyguard knows me better than my parents do.*

At first, I thought I'd hit Highland Park Village and go ham at Dior, Chanel, and Valentino. Normally, I only shopped in secondhand stores for environmental purposes, but for pissing-off-my-parents purposes, I figured it was time to renew my designer collection and donate older items to my favorite charities and thrift shops too.

As soon as Ransom and I reached the opulent shopping center, all royal arches and overflowing flower baskets, I realized no part of me wanted to shop.

That, in fact, shopping was a very depressing way to pass the time. Drawing joy from something materialistic never lasted for more than a couple hours. And…it needed to be said, most of the designer stuff was *horrendous*.

But it was much more than the act of shopping.

I was tired of the chase.

Tired of trying to fit in.

Tired of *trying*.

Designer clothes represented something I wanted to be a part of—glitz and glamour and sophistication. But deep down—or maybe not even *that* deep—I wasn't a fan of consumerism. I mean, these companies wanted us to stock up on new, expensive clothes each season, even though last season's clothes were perfectly wearable and still good to use. Overproduction resulted in waste and ecological damage. Every time I purchased a fashion item I didn't need, I put another nail into this planet's coffin.

"I don't want this," I heard myself say. I was rooted to the ground, staring back at an array of designer stores and upscale restaurants. "I don't want any of this anymore. I have enough clothes. Nice ones, too."

He stayed quiet for a moment, but I had a feeling he was relishing every word. More than that—I had a feeling he'd expected this to happen. That he somehow knew shopping wouldn't make me feel better.

"I want to go," I said.

"Where to?"

Good question. I wanted to get another tattoo. But I was still sore from yesterday, and also, I didn't have anything else I wanted engraved on my skin. My tattoos all had meaning. Maybe I could sketch something real quick? I could…but I'd run out of hotel paper. And I guessed using a pencil, rather than the unreliable hotel pen, was a better idea. But the thought of holding a pencil and paper made me feel like a poser. Some pleasures were reserved for literate people only, and this was one of them.

A flashback of a sneering Hera assaulted my memory.

"What do you need my pens for, Hallie? It's not like you're gonna write something. Give them back. I'm studying for a test. And don't ever steal from me again!"

Still…

Ransom had no idea about my…*issues*. I could draw as much as I wanted, and he wouldn't judge me.

"Can we go to…Hobby Lobby?" I turned to him. I'd never been before, but it always looked like such a wholesome store. Nothing bad ever happened in a Hobby Lobby, I bet.

His face remained unreadable, but I could tell he hadn't expected it. "Sharp turn of events."

"*Or* I could call the paps again and find a subway grate à la Marilyn Monroe so my dress flies above my underwear," I suggested sweetly. I wasn't asking to go to a nightclub, for crying out loud. *Work with me.*

"Say no more." He pulled his phone out of his pocket. "I'll find the nearest craft store."

It hadn't been the cozy adventure I'd been seeking, but we were back in the armored Ford Explorer and headed to the closest arts and crafts store in no time, where I purchased a thick sketchpad, along with a charcoal pencil set that included erasers, sharpener knives, and a double-end pencil extender.

I'd used Siri to find out what tattoo artists normally used when they sketched.

I made my way to the checkout line, before Ransom—who was suspiciously quiet, even by his standards—put his hand on my shoulder. Marking the second time today that he'd touched me, casually. And the second time I hadn't hated it.

I couldn't let myself dwell on that. It probably meant

nothing. I mean, if he liked me even a fraction, he wouldn't insist on putting me through the misery of staying in Texas, would he?

"What?" I turned around.

"While we're here…" He raised his eyebrows meaningfully.

I wasn't following. I cocked my head. "You want to hit the yarn section and learn how to knit?"

"You know me too well," he groused. "*Or* you can also buy a few drawing guides. Get the basics, you know. *Drawing for Dummies*. Set yourself up for success."

"Why would I do that?" I only doodled for myself. There was no danger in that. No potential failure. "It's just a hobby."

"It's shit you put on your body afterwards." He started striding purposefully back to the appropriate section. He jammed his hand into a fully-stocked shelf, pulling out a thick book. "*Shading, Texture, and Optical Illusions*. You wanna tell me you don't need this?" He waved the book between us.

I plucked it from his hand and flipped through the pages hurriedly, expecting lots of text. I was surprised to find none. It was all step-by-step tutorials on how to draw. With pictures. It was *amazing*. My heart picked up speed. This was the first time in years I'd felt like I could advance and educate myself through something other than vids, TED talks, and audiobooks.

You can hold a book and understand it.

"Guess it can't hurt. Do they have more like this one?" I tossed the guide into our shopping cart.

He took another one off the shelf.

Realistic Drawing Secrets.

"Hmm, I don't know about that one."

"You need to up your game." He slam-dunked it into the cart. "Another?"

"I mean, I guess. Whatever."

Soon, the cart was overflowing.

How to Draw Anime.

Artist's Guide to Realistic Animals.

How to Draw with Photorealism.

How to Draw Modern Florals.

The options were endless. I wanted to gobble everything up.

Tapping my foot against the floor while we were waiting in line for the checkout, I glanced at the time on my phone. Ransom stared, amusement dancing in his forest-green eyes.

"Did you think about what you want to do with your life yet?"

"Now's not the time," I barked at him impatiently. Must he rain on my parade, just when I was feeling a little better and participating in what he wanted? "I'll figure something out. Don't rush me."

Then—lo and behold—something amazing happened. Ransom Lockwood let loose an actual *smile*. It was small, it was hesitant, but it was there.

And it was glorious. Which made something else happen. Something—not butterflies, maybe small birds—flipped their wings in my lower belly, making my entire body tingle. We stared at each other for a beat, with intense, raw longing.

"Hello! Ready to check out?" The cashier popped the bubble we were both suspended in.

Ransom shook his head, turning to look at her, and smiled. "Absolutely."

The next week was surprisingly bearable. Possibly because my family did not summon me to any more 'casual' dinners. Everyone was in D.C., where Craig's family was from. No doubt frantic about appeasing Hera, who did not like it when life didn't go according to her detailed plan.

I tried calling my older sister and inquiring about Craig's grandfather's health—apparently, he was still hanging in there—but was sent straight to voicemail each time I did.

There was no way to admit it without sounding awful, but each time I got to her voicemail, I let out a sigh of relief. I didn't have any particular desire to speak to Hera, and I had no idea what to say about Craig's grandfather.

My time was spent volunteering at national forests and FreeTree Society (Ransom wasn't kidding, he really did sign me up for everything under the sun) and drawing nonstop.

Calluses formed on my middle finger and thumb. And yet I continued.

Even when my wrist hurt.

Even when my hands began to shake, so weak I could barely wash my hair, pick up my phone, cut my food with utensils.

Max had arrived in Dallas, armed with enough sunscreen to drown an army. He and Ransom took turns watching me. On one hand, I felt more comfortable with Max—he was chill, sweet, and never mean to me. On the other, every time Ransom was away, I was worried he was getting frisky with other women.

Why did I care? While it was true that Ransom and I were no longer at each other's throats, we were a very long way from being buddies. It was more a case of my wanting to save my energy for the battles ahead of me, with Mom, Dad, Hera, and Craig.

"So let me get this straight," Keller said. He was back in L.A. from Palm Springs, munching on a celery stick while we were on the phone. I was sketching on my pad. An elaborate tattoo of a sexy-looking Medusa, pouty and luscious, her snake hair curling over her throat, cutting off her air supply. *Beautiful Death.* "You're currently protected by two seriously hot men, and you're not getting D-ed by either of them?"

Keller didn't know that I wasn't in the business of hooking up.

"Correct."

"Okay…why?" He seemed flabbergasted.

"Because it's a bad idea."

"And since when do you shy away from those?" He laughed.

"I guess I'm trying to do better."

"By whom?" Keller demanded. "Not your vajayjay, that's for sure. The younger one seemed into you at first, right?"

"Max? Oh, I think so. He's sweet, but…I don't know, too meek, maybe? And Ransom is hot, but also a massive jerk."

"You mean, the type to release a sex tape of you two?" Keller asked dreamily. He had a thing for bastards. His ex-boyfriends were atrocious. From emotional abusers to serial cheaters, it was very easy to give up on happily-ever-after when I had a front-row seat to Keller's love life.

However, Ransom was the opposite of a man who would air out his business to the world. I wasn't worried that he'd land me in trouble. He gave me every indication he wanted to keep me away from it. He just seemed like a really bad person to put my trust in. So wildly disconnected from his soul, I wondered if he had one at all.

"Just trust me when I say they're both off-limits."

"All right, but I'm starting to worry about you, girl. I haven't seen you with any arm candy for a while."

The last man Keller had seen me with was Dash Rodgers, a Seattle Seahawks quarterback who needed a few dates in L.A. while he was negotiating a new contract. Truth was, he was desperately heartbroken from a recent breakup—his country singer fiancée had been caught cheating on him with her guitar player—and I needed a way to boost up my image to get more gigs. We both benefited from the arrangement and parted as friends. But when Keller had asked about him, I relayed my wild nights with Rodgers while he was in town, omitting what we actually did—played Monopoly and Patchwork while discussing a National Geographic documentary about whales.

"I'll get back on the horse in L.A.," I assured him.

"Just as long as you make sure the horse is well-hung."

"Keller…" I closed my eyes.

"Too much?" He laughed.

"*Way* too much."

"It sounded better in my head."

I hung up before he made a joke about giving head.

You could never be too careful.

Craig's grandfather passed away at the age of a hundred and one.

Since my parents were already in D.C., Hera demanded the funeral take place as soon as possible so that the wedding plans could continue uninterrupted.

"She's devastated," my mother felt the need to explain to me on the phone, "but she knows that's what Bill would have wanted."

Yeah. I was sure Grandpa Bill cared specifically about Hera and Craig's wedding while hospitalized with severe pneumonia as he succumbed to systematic organ failure.

"Yes. Terrible. Show must go on." I chewed on my vegetarian chow mein in my suite's room, flipping through one of my drawing books. Dallas felt much more bearable when I knew my family wasn't in town. My new, cool hobby also kept me busy.

I could hear Ransom returning from the gym, and practiced admirable self-control by not peeking outside my room to see if he was in any state of undress.

"You should probably come to the funeral." My mother sighed. "Show your support to Craig."

My blood froze in my veins. Going there…seeing everyone… seeing *him* again…

"I didn't even know Bill," I argued softly.

"Does it matter? Craig is family."

"*Your* family," I enunciated. "Not mine."

Thinking of Craig as family made me want to rip my skin off and dump it in a bonfire. Especially after I found my own rhythm, my own passion in sketching right here. I dropped my sketchbook, sitting back in my desk chair. Ransom popped his sweaty face in my door, to check that I was alive. I waved him away.

"You're coming to D.C., Hallie. I will not hear any excuses," Mom said.

"Mom—"

"Pass me to Ransom, please."

I felt like a thirteen-year-old negotiating curfew time. Groaning, I handed Ransom my phone. He stepped inside, wearing a soaked wifebeater and gray sweatpants with a promising bulge.

"Yes?" Ransom asked. "Yes," he said again. Then "When?" And finally, "She'll be there."

He hung up the phone and handed it back to me. My eyes were hot with unshed tears.

"We'll be leaving tomorrow," he announced.

I rolled the statement off my shoulders, redirecting my attention to the sketchpad in my lap. It was fine. I would just let everything fly past me. Through me, maybe. Just as long as it didn't stay *inside* me.

"Brat," he said, to draw my attention.

I picked up my sketchbook, flipping through the pages.

"*Brat.*"

Nothing. Not my name, not my problem. I'd had *enough*.

"Hallie."

I looked at him reluctantly. "Yes?"

Maybe this was the time when he grew a heart and asked me what was wrong. About my aversion to Craig. Or maybe he would talk it out with me. Try to figure out how the trip could be a little less awkward for me. "Don't forget to memorize your speech." He pointed at the pile of pages on the corner of my desk, before slamming the door and heading to the shower.

Ransom Lockwood didn't do compassion.

Chapter Eleven

Ransom

Then.

The pickpocketing turned into larceny. We ended up breaking into places, Tom, Lawrence and I. Mainly big stores and corporate chains. People who wouldn't want the hassle of pressing charges even if we got caught.

At some point, we graduated and became small-time drug dealers. Mr. Moruzzi was a prolific criminal, with many people working under him. On the surface, he was a successful businessman, with several hotdog stands across Chicago. But the amount of dirty money that passed through our hands was ridiculous.

First, we were the errand boys, fetching and picking up small parcels. Then, around junior high, we became the dealers. We never touched anything. That was Mr. Moruzzi's rule. He didn't want any druggies under his roof.

To compensate for our shitty lives, which consisted of going to school, scoring excellent grades to please CPS, then working ourselves to the bone for him (zero commission, thanks for asking), he paid us with a questionable currency—women.

Specifically, high-end prostitutes. I think he wanted to distort our view on love and marriage. There was no need for him to go the extra mile. One look at his miserable marriage to the therapist—Mrs. Moruzzi—who was hardly home, and had a lover who lived in Canada where she visited frequently, did the job.

Whenever Mrs. Moruzzi was away, he took his anger out on us. Beating was out of the question. We were all bigger and stronger than he was. Instead, he made us fight each other. For food. For money. For women.

Over the years, Lawrence, Tom, and I suffered broken ribs, cracked bones, fractured fingers, and so on, all just to survive, while Moruzzi watched on, smugly enjoying the show.

It was clear we functioned as a workforce for him. It was also clear he was never going to give us a chance to become anything more than his little pawns.

When Lawrence was seventeen and I was fifteen, he started to become antsy.

"We need an out from Moruzzi. What do we do?"

I was the first one to bring it up.

"We kill him."

Hallie

Ransom was right.

I had to get a head start on the speech if I wanted to know it by heart by the time Craig and Hera were wed.

I gathered the papers and skimmed the words, my pupils frantic, my heart pounding.

I wasn't illiterate. I knew how to read. It was just hard to make sense of the words sometimes. It took me an excruciatingly long time to read a simple paragraph. What should have been seconds, usually required minutes for me, sometimes hours, and by the time I reached the end, I oftentimes forgot the content of the text I was reading.

For instance, I would read "light" as "might" or "white" as "what" and "sound" as "ground". Words mixed together, blending into one another on the page, and I had to concentrate until my brain hurt to read one simple article.

Which was why I opted out of reading whenever possible.

Well, I didn't have the luxury of escaping reading right now.

I read out loud. It was a trick Mrs. Archibald, one of my teachers, had taught me in second grade.

"*Things will make more sense if you speak the words out loud.*"

Turned out she was right, although my parents politely asked her not to butt into their business—and my education—when she gave them a call about my struggles with reading.

Now, fourteen years after Mrs. Archibald had been let go for overstepping (I never got over the guilt, and never forgave my parents for this), I stood up and paced my hotel room, trying my hand at reading the text typed out for me, no doubt by one of my father's speechwriters.

"Dog...goom...g..." I rubbed at my forehead. Cold sweat formed over my skin. "Goo—good evening very...everything... eve...everyone." I stopped. Closed my eyes. Took a deep breath. "*Good evening, everyone.*"

One sentence. That was a start.

See? It's not so bad. Only forty more to go.

I had a decent memory. I could do it. I repeated the words out loud, inking them to my brain.

"Good evening, everyone."

"Good evening, everyone."

"Good evening, everyone."

Simple enough. Then I continued. "Lew...Let's...we...well... welc...ome? Welcome t...t...to..."

I stopped, flinging the papers onto the bed, letting out a frustrated growl. Why couldn't they record me the speech? They knew I could quickly memorize things if I could hear them. I was good at that, aural learning. I listened to things all the time. That was how I got by. But the answer was clear. My parents pretended that my problem was a figment of my imagination, not a learning disability. Like I could read just fine, but *chose* not to. Gathering the papers in a huff, I tried again. "Welcome t…to…the joint…the jet…the joining of…"

"Hera and Craig," a voice finished behind me.

I jumped, slapping a hand over my chest.

Shit, shit, shit, shit, *shit*.

Ransom was standing at the door, showered, freshly shaven, and oozing sex appeal in casual cargo pants and a black V-neck.

What must he be thinking?

That you're a dumbass or high. Exactly what he thought ten seconds ago.

He pushed off the doorjamb, advancing toward me.

"You're dyslexic?"

"Get out of my room, Random." I pushed at his chest frantically, hysterically.

Why would he say something like that?

"You are." He gathered the pages, frowning as he skimmed through them. "You can't read."

"Yes, I can."

"You can, but it's hard, and frustrating for you."

"It's fine, I'm pretty," I snorted out bitterly.

He looked up from the pages, his frown deepening. His eyes were so very green, his nose so very straight, and his mouth so very kissable. Again, I thanked my lucky stars for my shaky confidence. It didn't allow me to consider anyone romantically without chiding myself.

"Are you undiagnosed?"

"I need glasses, that's all." I knotted my arms over my chest, glaring hard at him. "I'm not dyslexic."

"Yeah, you are. Either that or you have a pervasive intellectual disability, and that can't be it. Lack of intelligence has never been your issue."

I was dizzy with the unexpected compliment. It was the first time someone had told me I was *not* an idiot. Even Keller, my best friend, never complimented me on my wits.

"Why were you never diagnosed?" Ransom pressed, a vein throbbing on the side of his forehead.

"It wasn't nece—"

"You didn't read the contract." His eyes flared. "That's why you were so clueless afterwards. You just signed it."

"Stop talking." I raised a warning finger, aiming it at him. "Just…just *stop*."

Now that we were face-to-face, it sure looked like he was angry. But it wasn't directed at me…why not? It was my failure, not his. He could read just fine.

I stomped my way to the closet and flung it open. Maybe it was time to get out on the town and grab dinner outside. I'd been cooped up inside long enough.

"No need to diagnose me. I'm just not a smart person. Is that what you want to hear? Everyone in the family made peace with it. Me included. I suffer from a lack of interest combined with an inability to do well in school." I began flinging dresses onto the bed.

Ransom got in my face, shoving himself between the closet and me. "You could have gotten a shit ton of services, tools to help you. More time for your tests, recorded textbooks, computer spell checkers, therapy. They could've found any number of ways to help you. Instead, they treated your disability as a liability to save face, instead of getting you the help you needed. *This* is why you're so mad at them."

Ransom foamed at the mouth, he was so furious. I'd never seen him so upset. I took a step back, suddenly feeling like being this man's center of attention was my own private downfall.

"I…uhm…"

Should I tell him? Should I not?

Screw it. The truth was better than all the lies I'd spewed out for years.

"You what?" he asked. "Tell me."

"When I was in second grade, my teacher, Mrs. Archibald,

told my parents I needed to get tested for dyslexia. I'd fallen behind pretty significantly, which made me drift and lose interest in class even more. My parents became really upset. Made a whole stink about how a general-ed second grade teacher didn't have the right to make such assumptions. She ended up getting fired, after Mom put pressure on the school's board. I never got tested, but…" I licked my lips, closing my eyes. That period of my life was one of the worst. Precipitating the time when I lost faith in myself. Dad was on his last year as President, and he couldn't afford the bad press. The scrutiny.

"From that moment on, teachers started helping me out with tests and assignments. And by 'helping' I mean cheating my way into decent grades. I still wasn't good, but I passed all my classes. The bigger the gap between me and my classmates became, the easier it was to believe I was just…"

"Stupid," Ransom completed for me softly.

I swallowed. "Yeah."

Now, at twenty-one, I did not consider myself high school educated. I'd missed so much material. Only in recent years, when I discovered the magic of audiobooks, did I start to catch up on subjects that had interested me. History, literature, and geography. Suddenly, I could consume books. I'd devoured all the classics. Jane Austen and Charlotte Bronte and Leo Tolstoy.

Ransom looked haunted, staring at me with eyes so deep and dark I thought I was going to drown in them.

"Your parents…" he trailed off, shaking his head. "I'm going to kill them."

Clutching his phone until I heard it crack, he stormed out of my room. I chased after him. No one was supposed to know about the Mrs. Archibald story. White-hot panic coursed through my veins. My parents would skin me alive when they found out I'd confided in him.

"Ransom, please don't tell them!" I grabbed the hem of his shirt, tugging. His phone was pressed to his ear. "They can't know that you know, I—"

But it was too late. Someone answered him on the other line.

"Mrs. Thorne? Ransom Lockwood here. Change of plans. We're not coming to D.C. In fact, it's not safe for Hallie to be anywhere but in Dallas right now. Unlike your other daughter, Hallie is famous, headline-grabbing, and a hot commodity. I don't want her star to overshadow her sister's plebeian duties. Have fun at the funeral."

He hung up.

I stared at him, shocked.

This was the first person who had truly stood up for me. Had my back more than once.

Also: *have fun at the funeral*? He was so going to hell for that one.

"I think I just fell in love with you." I stumbled back, clutching my chest, like Cupid had pierced an arrow through it.

He massaged his eye sockets, looking tired, almost deflated. "Like my day wasn't bad enough. Get dressed." He tucked his phone into his pocket, a sullen, fallen angel. "We're getting you diagnosed right now. Then I'm taking you to dinner. Vegetarian something. My treat."

Oh, my.

I'd been dyslexic less than ten minutes and I already loved every second of it.

Ransom

Well, shit.

It was official. I had a conscience.

It was wonky, out of tune, and questionable. But it was there.

Hallie Thorne was no idiot.

An extremely flawed individual? Sure.

Fucked-up? I could get behind that description.

But she had undiagnosed learning disabilities, and she walked around thinking something was wrong with *her*.

That needed to be rectified.

I didn't have long to babysit the girl, but before I left, I wanted her to know one thing.

She wasn't stupid. It wasn't her fault.

She just had a really shitty family.

Hallie

An hour later, the Explorer pulled in front of a private clinic on the outskirts of Dallas. A red-bricked, simple building surrounded by decorative plants.

"They've agreed to assess you anonymously. That means we pay a fee, and they give you a diagnosis and we fill in the paperwork with your personal data afterwards," Ransom said by way of explanation as he breezed past me, opening the door. I gingerly made my way inside, in bug sunglasses and an overkill hat.

He approached the woman behind the reception desk and talked to her quietly while I stood in the automatic doorway, looking around. I felt like I stuck out like a sore thumb, even though it was probable no one recognized me.

Why was it important for me to get diagnosed? It wasn't like I was planning to go back to school. I would never put myself through the torture.

Ransom turned around and walked over to me. He put a hand on my shoulder. I did not, in fact, detonate. But I was close. I'd never before been attracted to someone so wildly, and it scared me. Up until now, it had been really easy to pass on opportunity.

"They're going to run vision and hearing tests, and questionnaires on you. Then you'll go through a psychological assessment and they'll test your reading. You're going to be here for a while."

"What's a while?" I swallowed.

"Four, five hours."

"My parents are going to kill you if they find out." Not that I was going to tell them.

"Your parents are lucky I don't kill *them*."

A sunny, middle-aged woman in a red suit and noisy jewelry picked me up from the reception and ushered me into the depths of the building.

The first two tests—vision and hearing—were easy-peasy. The reading test, however, was a dud. I was extra slow, extra nervous, and got most of the words mixed up. By the time the psychological assessment came around, I was already exhausted.

When Ransom came back to pick me up, he held a brown bag. He shoved it in my hands as soon as I made my way to him.

"Vegan tacos with spicy cauliflower and tofu. There's some beer, too."

"You're giving a beer to an alcoholic?" I arched my eyebrows, feigning disbelief.

"We both know you're simply a lightweight. Go eat outside. I'll be there in a second."

Guess this was his version of taking me out for a meal. I would have protested if I weren't so exhausted from milking every ounce of my brain over the last four hours. I went outside, settling on a wooden bench overlooking a sad, mostly empty parking lot.

The tacos were delicious, and the beer went to my head fast.

Rather than freak out about what Ransom and the nice woman in red were currently discussing, I diverted my thoughts to exploring what I could do for a living.

Perhaps nail art. I adored nails, and it seemed like a lowkey thing to do, away from the limelight, which I started to realize I didn't actually love. Or maybe I could be a dog walker. I loved animals. I would adopt an unholy amount of dogs and cats if I could. My mother forbade it. Something about not wanting a negative headline when I moved out of the mansion and the landlord discovered my pets had destroyed his place.

I was pondering the idea of becoming a circus clown when I

felt a shadow looming over my figure from behind, blocking the sun. I whipped my head, a scowl ready on my face.

"Well?" I asked. "Is it official? Are the Guinness people coming? Am I the dumbest bitch on earth?"

He ignored my words. "Get in the car."

But when we got in the car, he remained persistently silent, and I lost my nerve to ask him what the woman had told him. If he wanted to wait to talk about it privately, it couldn't be good, right?

Listen, she said you have the intelligence of a dry erase marker, I imagined him saying in his signature, IDGAF tone.

When we got back into Dallas, I finally opened my mouth. I wanted to ask what the lady'd said, but what came out was, "I'm still hungry."

Close enough.

"Where do vegetarians eat in Texas?" he asked blandly. "This is not your natural habitat."

"There's a joint down the street." I pointed at a quaint café that looked like it had been ripped from Covent Garden, London. It had outdoor dining, bracketed by a beautiful green fence. With large display windows and dark green stucco that matched the color of Ransom's eyes. A green, ivy-ridden fence served as a barrier between the diners and the street.

"Very exposed," Ransom grumbled, dissatisfied. Still, he slipped into a parking space, unbuckling.

At the café, we were given a table right by the fence. Ransom picked up the menu and scowled. "Farm to table? Does that mean they have fried chicken?"

A teasing smile touched my lips. "No. It means they grow their vegetables and spices organically."

He closed his eyes, shaking his head. "I'm going to sue you for emotional and physical abuse after all of this is over."

I smiled, mainly because I knew he was trying to make me feel better. "Why don't you let me choose something for you?"

"Because you'll screw it up?" he volleyed back.

"Try me."

"Famous last words. Well, floor's all yours."

I ordered Baba Ghanoush with pita bread and Spanakopita for him, and zucchini cakes for myself. "And also a Greek rosé table wine," I asked the waitress, watching Ransom closely to see if he'd shut me down. A muscle didn't move in his face, and his Aviators covered his eyes, so I had no indication he was giving me a death glare, either.

"Are you not going to ask me what Barbara said?" he inquired.

"I'm guessing Barbara is the Lady in Red."

"Smart girl."

"I've a feeling you're about to deliver some news that would contradict your last statement."

I figured he'd given Barbara a fistful of cash to speed up the process of my diagnosis. Those things usually took months to get the results back.

Our waitress approached our table again, smiling nervously. She knew who we were. She presented the wine, poured us a small amount of it, and allowed us to have a taste. I swirled, sniffed, and nodded. She poured us both generous portions before leaving.

"Thanks for letting me drink." I raised my glass, chugging down half of its contents.

"My reasons are purely selfish. Perhaps you're more bearable while intoxicated."

"A guy can dream." I placed my glass down. "So what've you got for me? How dumb am I?"

"Not at all," he said, taking a sip of his wine, then scowling at it like it punched him in the crotch. I had a feeling he was more of a hard liquor man. "You passed the hearing and vision tests with flying colors. Reading and writing tests were where you struggled. Then during the psychology exam you exhibited—and this is a quote—'a higher-than-average EQ and IQ.'"

"Do you have that in English?"

"Emotional intelligence and usability slash analytical abilities. You scored high on both."

"I don't understand." The smile stretching across my face

dropped. "That…that can't be. You can't be smart and struggle to read at twenty-one."

"Yes, you can." He leaned across the table, flicking his sunglasses off. His eyes glittered with intensity. "You have a learning disability that's treatable. It's completely disconnected from your intelligence. You have a different distribution of metabolic activation than a non-dyslexic person, but that says nothing about your potential or your abilities. Dyslexic people often have advantages. For instance, you have a magnificent knack for connecting a series of mental sequencing into a coherent story. Now repeat after me—I'm not stupid."

This had to be a sadistic joke. I let out a snort. "Don't be ridiculous."

"Don't be a coward," he shot back. "*Say* it."

"No." I sat back, folding my arms over my chest. "That's embarrassing. And unnecessary."

"I'm. Not. Stupid," he repeated it louder now, drawing curious looks from people at other tables. It was unlike him to call attention to us. I looked around, my stomach cramping with anxiety. "Grow some balls, Princess."

"I reject the chauvinistic notion balls equal guts. Women are just as—"

"Spare me." He raised his palm in the air. "And just spit it out so we can get on with our lives."

"I…" I took a deep breath. "I mean, I'm not…"

"Stupid," he finished for me. "Correct. Now give me the entire sentence."

"Wait a minute." I frowned. "I thought *you* said yourself that I'm stupid."

He shook his head. "I said unbearable. Not the same thing."

"I'm not…I don't…" Tears pricked the back of my eyes.

"Goddammit, Hallie." He stood up suddenly. I did the same, out of pure instinct, my legs moving on their own accord. I had this odd, dangerous feeling that the world around us had stopped on its axis, drawing a collective breath as it watched us. We were stuck in a bubble.

And bubbles, I knew, were destined to burst.

Sunset licked the sky in brilliant blues and fierce oranges. For one, desperate, *pathetic* moment, something foreign came over me. Dark and addictive.

I felt cherished. Maybe even understood.

We were standing in front of one another, panting. The only buffer between us was a wonky table. My fingers tingled to reach across and touch him.

"Say you're not stupid." His eyes burned, consuming my soul in the process. His hands were braced over the table. "Say it to me, Hallie."

"I'm…not…" I closed my eyes and took a deep breath. "Stupid. I'm not stupid."

"*Louder.*"

"I'm not stupid!"

"Can't hear you."

"*I'm not stupid!*"

Each time I said it, another drawer in my heart unlocked. I felt a little lighter, a little better about who I was. I wanted to call my parents and say, *see? See?*

Of course, they already knew. They'd kept the truth away from me, from the world, because it embarrassed them. And the sheer discomfort it caused them was more important than my self-esteem. My self-*worth*.

And they had the audacity to tell me I wasn't trying hard enough *for them*.

My cheeks were wet and cold. I realized I was crying. Publicly.

Our waitress chose that moment to approach with our tray of food.

"Not now." Ransom lifted a hand, shooing her away. His gaze was still fixed on me. I waited for him to say something. I desperately wanted him to make the next move. Mainly because I felt there was more to this. More to us. He looked at me with new-found respect.

I could get addicted to this.

"Still want to get rid of me?" Mockery made his eyes glitter.

I shook my head, realizing this was the truth. He was horrible to me—sometimes. And overbearing—always. He was bad-mannered, and callous, but he also taught me self-worth, made me stand up for myself, and somehow, somewhere along the way started treating me as an equal.

"I…" I shifted, feeling naked and bare, my feelings raw and exposed. His eyes clung to mine, waiting for me to continue. I swallowed hard, looking down at the table. "I like you."

"You like me." A faint, ironic grin touched his beautiful lips.

I nodded.

"Look at me."

I did. He leaned forward. I did the same. We were like magnets. North and south poles. Opposites who couldn't help but attract. The impossible had become the inevitable. A kiss between us seemed unstoppable now. Urgent. A matter of life or death. His seafoam eyes drifted shut, ethereal and gray-flecked. I breathed his scent in. A mixture of leather and darkness. Destruction wrapped in sin.

He stilled, waiting for me to make the final move. To own up to the mistake that was about to happen.

The strain was excruciating. Every muscle in my body quaked. My lips hovered over his. He reached to touch my face, to guide me to his mouth.

His hand never made it to my cheek.

"Not in this lifetime, asshole." He ripped his face from mine.

I felt the blinding lights of the camera whipping at my face like a merciless belt.

The photographer—a paparazzi by his dark clothing and professional gear—lowered his camera and smiled.

"Public place, buddy. Don't hate the player, hate the game."

He realized he'd messed with the wrong man when Ransom clutched the fence separating them, hoisting himself effortlessly and jumping over to the other side. He charged after the man, who broke into a frantic run, shouldering past people blindly, clutching the camera to his chest.

The thick crowd of shoppers attempted to part in order to accommodate the chase, but the photographer was disoriented and out of shape. He flailed and fell to the ground after a few seconds. Ransom tore the camera from his hands, ripping the film out of it and dumping his equipment onto the ground.

"You can't do that!" the guy shrieked, reaching for the film. "It's private property."

"Public place." He tore the film into ribbons as he stomped back, tossing it into a trashcan without slowing down.

This was the moment our waitress mustered up the courage to tread back to our table again, holding our mostly-cold dishes, her smile hanging like a crooked picture upon her face. "Ready for your food?"

"We'll take it to-go." Ransom jumped the railing again, grabbing his keys and wallet. No sign of the charged electricity remained that had hummed between us just minutes earlier. "We're outta here."

Chapter Twelve

Hallie

"Nine Facts About Hallion's New Bodyguard!"

The next day, Keller called to let me know Ransom was officially the new Kylie Jenner bodyguard: too hot to handle and the talk of La La Land.

He went on to read every word in the article. Apparently, Hollywood was now obsessed with my close protection officer after he'd chased down a pap.

It was barely eleven in the morning in Texas, and already I had four missed calls from socialites in L.A., demanding to know if Ransom would be available to work for them in the near future.

"…worked as an offensive counterintelligence officer…" Keller read in a clandestine tone. "That means he attempted to turn enemy agents into double agents or gave them false or misleading information—isn't that hot?"

I faked a yawn. For some reason, I was embarrassed and petrified to admit I liked Ransom, even to my closest friend.

"He has a master's in mechanical engineering from MIT," Keller continued.

"What, no PhD? Can someone say *loser*?" I snorted, painting my toenails neon green, desperately trying to sound uninterested.

Ransom and I hadn't spoken to each other since that almost-kiss. He seemed to have retreated back into his hostile shell.

I heard Keller clicking on his mouse. "Says here that he's single. Twenty-nine. Has a big penthouse worth a few million in Chicago."

"How fantastically cliché."

"Says the heiress living in the L.A. mansion." Keller chuckled.

"Former First Daughter," I corrected prissily. "And for your information, I swim against the stream. I didn't go to an Ivy League school, marry a nice Jewish man, or open a charitable foundation. I'll have you know, I'm a non-conformist!"

"Yeah, yeah." It was Keller's turn to yawn. "Have you banged him yet?"

"Keller!"

"That's not a no."

"No, no, *no!*"

"How come he is still working with you? I thought you were planning to sabotage and make him quit."

"He is more hardheaded than me," I admitted.

"That's a first." There was a pause before Keller said, "You know, I think he's going to be huge in Hollywood."

"I don't think he'll be sticking around," I said, with relief. The thought of Ransom trailing behind another woman—a beautiful woman—made snakes slither in my stomach. They twisted together into a venomous ball.

We hung up. I drew myself a long, warm bath, then curled my hair and slipped into a yellow crochet-trimmed mini dress. Last night, I'd downloaded an interview with a psychologist about how to treat dyslexia to keep my mind off of Ransom. It was really inspiring, and I already had a lot of ideas on how to improve my life.

When I got back to my bedroom, a USB waited by my laptop. *Huh. That's weird.*

Certain it was from my parents, I shoved it inside and watched as a window popped open on the screen, containing an audio document titled HeraBridesmaidSpeech.mp3.

But when I double-clicked it, the low, gruff voice that filled the room was unmistakable.

Ransom.

He'd recorded the speech for me.

I closed my eyes. *Thank you.*

I slipped my earbuds in and let his voice seep into me, calm and commanding. It mortified me, how out of focus I became while listening to him. How my thighs clenched deliciously whenever his voice hit the pit of my stomach. My breathing turned heavy and ragged. Maybe it wasn't such a bad idea, that we were parting ways in just a few months.

This kind of temptation, it never had a happy ending.

After memorizing the speech, I finally made my grand appearance in the living room...only to be met with a smiling, oblivious Max. My heart dropped.

No Ransom?

Max sat on the couch, reading one of his thick sci-fi books.

"Hey, Hallie!" He stood up.

In that exact moment, I realized my fascination with Ransom had crossed the line of curiosity and turned into something bigger. Beastly and ghastly, out of control.

Possibly recognizing my distress and disorientation at seeing him and not Ransom—whom I bet was screwing another woman right now—Max suggested we go get some shopping done. My parents were still in D.C., and so was Hera.

"You must need to grab some pre-wedding items, right? Gifts and such."

I nodded faintly, my mind a million miles away. Only when we hit the shops did I remember I couldn't actually buy anything. Nor had I the desire to, for that matter.

"Max." I let out an embarrassed laugh as we slid out of the car. "I don't have a credit card. Let's turn around and go home."

Max produced a card from his pocket, wiggling his eyebrows. "For emergencies only. But putting a smile on your face qualifies as an emergency to me."

"I don't want you to get into trouble."

He was so nice, so wholesome, I hated myself for not being attracted to him. What was wrong with me? Why did I want the one man who would probably break me all over again?

"I won't get into trouble so quickly." He ducked his head, his cheeks flushing. "Ransom and Tom are notoriously hard to please. They barely hire. They wouldn't let me go so fast."

"Well, if you say so."

I made a reluctant attempt at grabbing a few pieces of fine china I thought were appropriate as a wedding gift for a young couple (Hera would *not* appreciate secondhand anything). Afterwards, Max got us iced coffees and we sat in a park and bird-watched. The day crawled to its end, each minute dragging across my nerves deliberately slow.

"Where's Ransom?" I asked when we slipped back into the Explorer.

"Hell if I know. He's a very secretive man."

"He didn't take the car," I noted.

"Not this old thing." Max took off his sunglasses, rubbing his eyes before putting them back on. "He rented a rad-ass Bugatti. You should see it, Hallie. It's a piece of heaven."

"Driven by a piece of work. What is it about smart men and dumb cars, anyway?" I wondered.

"It's an expense."

"So my father's footing the bill?"

"Pretty much."

Nice to see Ransom was using his spare time polluting the environment.

But this piece of information worked to my advantage, because when we got back to the hotel and Max parked the Explorer,

I noticed we passed a Chiron Noire—a three million dollar beast on wheels—parked at the far end of the lot.

He was here.

In my head, I'd already gone through the images of him and a leggy blonde doing all kinds of sordid acts together while Max took me on my daily walk, as if I were a Chihuahua. I was so frustrated—so incredibly furious with Ransom—that I forgot to be a good person and did something terrible to Max.

I slipped my hand in his when we entered the service elevator leading up to my suite. Max's eyes bulged out of their sockets, pinned on our entwined fingers. I bumped my shoulder to his, mustering an encouraging smile.

Max's eyes dropped to my mouth. I felt horrible for using him, and yet exhilarated at the prospect of being caught by Ransom.

"What's happening here, Hal?" Max asked softly.

"What do you want to happen?"

His throat bobbed with a swallow. "I don't know?"

The elevator dinged open. He forgot to survey the hall before we stumbled out, his focus solely on me.

We stood in front of my door. Exhilaration made my fingers shake. No excuse sufficed for what I was about to do to Max. Use him in the worst possible way. Maybe land him in trouble. But I couldn't help myself. I was so, selfishly hungry for the man on the other side of that door that I'd left my scruples like a husk of shed snakeskin back in the parking lot.

"Should we?" he wondered aloud. "I mean, I'm not supposed to—"

"We definitely should."

As soon as I rose on my toes, Max's mouth descended toward mine. His lips missed the mark, landing on the tip of my nose, before grazing over my cheek. My heart twisted in my chest when I realized this was his version of dipping his toes into the water, checking the temperature.

I'm so sorry, Max. I'll make it right. I promise.

I laced my arms around his shoulders and pulled him the

rest of the way, my lips pressing hard against his, closemouthed. Purposefully—cunningly—I bumped my arm against the surface of the suite's door, producing a soft and audible thud.

Max's mouth opened for me, searching, asking for more. Feeling like I was out of my body, out of this moment, I complied, the tip of my tongue swirling around his teasingly. Max's forehead dropped to mine and a growl came from somewhere deep in his chest, signaling his complete surrender.

As if on cue, the door flew open, and in my periphery, stood the powerhouse to all my fantasies.

The weird thing was, the kiss lasted for a few more seconds before Ransom cleared his throat. I was the first to pull away. Max was higher on desire, his descent back to reality more gradual.

Feigning surprise, I looked between my two bodyguards.

Time to save Max.

"Now, before you get your panties in a twist, it was all my idea," I squeaked, placing a protective hand over Max's arm. "I launched myself at him."

"He's a big boy. He could've fought you off," Ransom's smile, white and glorious as it was, was full of derision.

I knew I shouldn't expect hysterical tears and a tantrum, but his calmness reminded me he was the big, bad wolf and I was the naïve, red-hooded girl who would get eaten if she wasn't careful.

"Shit." Max winced, looking around us for a distraction. "Ransom, I can explain—"

"Doubt it." His boss shrugged, making himself comfortable on the threshold, not letting either of us inside.

"It's not what it looks like—"

"That's not an explanation."

"Hallie and I have been getting to know each other—" Max rubbed at the back of his neck, his ears pink.

"That's what happens when you shadow a person all day. You wanna tell me you pork all your clients?" Ransom crossed his arms flippantly.

Max looked desperate. Guilt ate at my insides like acid. I

stepped between them, tilting my chin up. "As I said, I kissed Max. It was my idea. He had nothing to do with it."

"As *I* said, I don't give two shits. You're not a part of this conversation." Ransom stared past me, at Max.

He couldn't even *look* at me. Was that good or bad? I didn't know.

There's no way of telling if he was jealous, or just pissed off because he had to deal with this complication.

"Max, go back to your room. I need to get the paperwork sorted before I sack your ass. Brat, inside." Ransom jerked his chin toward the suite. That's when I realized he hadn't called me Brat in quite a while.

Until now.

I walked inside, but not before squeezing Max's hand reassuringly. "I'm going to fix this," I whispered to him.

"No, you won't." Ransom slammed the door behind us, striding toward the floor-to-ceiling window, knotting his fingers behind his back as he looked onto the restaurant garden downstairs.

"Did you enjoy your time off?" I kicked off my wedges. I couldn't keep the venom out of my voice.

Did you have sex with someone else again?

"Not as much as you did." He walked over to a Parisian bar cart and fixed himself some whiskey, heavy on the rocks. He didn't offer me any. Our unspoken connection, that fragile bond that was created when he realized how deeply I'd been wronged by my family, had snapped like a wishbone.

"I find that hard to believe." I started unbuttoning the front buttons of my dress. He'd played this trick so many times with me, it was only fair I'd reciprocate and get undressed in front of him. But his back was to me, so he couldn't see. "Last time you took time off, a woman got compromised against the suite's window."

Ransom turned on his heel, nursing his drink, his eyes narrowed in disdain. "And *you* kissed Max because it kills you that you're not that woman."

"Nice story." I tried my hand at a calm smile.

"It's the truth, and the fact it was your doing, your fuck-up, is the only reason why I didn't fire his ass on the spot."

Ransom saw right through my charade. He knew I wanted him. Knew I was damaged just like him.

"I kissed Max because he's cute and because I wanted to have some fun."

"And yesterday?" Ransom cocked an eyebrow and referred to our almost-kiss.

Flipping my hair, I said, "No offense, Ransom, but you're too old for me."

The only thing getting old was the bullshit I was spewing at the speed of light. I was delirious with need, and nothing, and no one else could make it better but him.

He waltzed over to where I stood, my dress half undone. He smirked, crushing a perfectly transparent ice cube between his white, straight teeth.

My spine melted in that moment, it was so hot.

"What do you want, Princess?"

I blinked, considering the possibility of telling him the truth, versus feeding him another lie. I decided the truth was better. Ransom never shamed me for my truth. Not for my dyslexia, and not for my life choices.

"I want…" I craned my neck, trying to appear regal and dignified. "I want what you did to her."

It felt good to let the truth out. Even if I couldn't understand my reaction to this man.

"I want to do to you what I did to her," he surprised me by saying, his voice matter-of-fact. I allowed myself a moment of breathlessness at his words.

Yes. Finally.

"But I also don't want to mess up my life, either. Guess which option appeals to me more right now?"

"Nothing wrong with a little walk on the dark side." I mustered the courage to run my hand over his chest. He clasped my wrist, pushing it away. My back was pinned against the wall. He stood close enough for me to smell his breath, the whiskey on it, his aftershave, and that singular, sour-sweet sweat of a man.

"You're not worth it," he sneered.

"Is that why I can feel your erection digging into my thigh?" In my boldest move yet, I cupped his cock through his slacks. He was hard and terrifyingly large. I'd never touched a penis before. Willingly, anyway. I kept my hand there, even though I didn't know what to do next.

"Hallie," he warned.

"What?" My eyebrows shot to my hairline. "Nothing's happening here," I said innocently.

He studied my face. I could tell he was at war with himself.

"I don't fuck gentle," he hissed.

"No one's asking you to." I swallowed. "I want the fantasy. The degradation. I want you to break me completely, and then me to pick myself up without anyone's help."

I started rubbing at his shaft. It was clumsy—my hand was at a weird angle—but after a few seconds I felt his cock twitch in my palm in response.

"Nothing's happening here," I repeated.

"Nothing?" His silky voice caressed every inch of my body, his lips so close to mine.

"Nothing." I licked my lips, waiting for him to kiss me. I looked up, tilting my head so that our mouths were perfectly aligned.

"You want a kiss, don't you?" A mean smirk graced his lips. "I don't think so. Not after you exchanged saliva with Max."

I felt his fingers brush the inside of my thigh. My knees became weak. I opened up my limbs like a flower, inviting him to come and play. My hand rubbed his cock harder. I couldn't believe we were doing this. But then I also couldn't believe it had taken us so long.

I'd always wanted him.

From the moment I saw this stranger looming over me while I was on the balcony, sunbathing, a twisted, sick part of my brain had wanted him to pin me to the sunbed and fuck my mouth while I lay there, helpless.

"Take your tits out," he ordered dryly.

I withdrew my hand from his cock to work at the final few buttons, but he cupped my palm, keeping it pressed against his shaft.

A sardonic smirk touched his beautiful lips. "I trust you can multitask."

My left hand fumbled with the rest of the buttons of my dress, until I gave up and tore it open. My breasts spilled out. I didn't wear a bra. My boobs were always my best asset. Perky and pear-shaped, my pink nipples as small as two diamonds.

Ransom stared, taking them both in.

"And you?" I asked groggily, sounding drunk, even to my own ears. "Have you kissed someone today?"

He scooped an ice cube from his whiskey tumbler and trailed it between my tits, swirling it around one of my nipples. We both watched as it puckered, straining with sensitivity, begging to be sucked and licked.

"What am I going to do with you?" he hissed.

"Lick it better?" I smiled innocently at him.

"Only good girls get rewarded. Bad girls, however…"

He removed the ice cube from my nipple, moving it down, along my inner thigh—going up, up north. "Oh, and while we're on the subject, I don't kiss my hookups. Too many germs."

"That's not what I was asking."

"That's the answer you're getting."

"Who told you *I* want to do anything with *you* if you just had your dick in someone else?"

He gave me an awful look of indulgent compassion as if I were a stupid child. "No problem there. You're not getting dicked tonight."

His fingers and the ice cube stopped at the center of my panties. A pool of cold water formed over the fabric. I stopped rubbing him, but only because no part of me could function I was so aroused.

"Remember, Brat, nothing's happening here."

I shook my head. "Nothing," I panted. "Nothing. *Please.*"

With his expression still glacial and bored, he tucked my

panties to one side, sliding whatever was left of the ice cube—and his index finger—into me.

I let out a feral moan, chasing his touch, writhing against the wall. My virginity, at least in the technical sense, had been taken by a dildo when I was seventeen years old. And though I'd given myself many orgasms in my life, nothing had ever felt as acutely good as what he was doing to me.

"What are we doing?" His lips hovered over mine teasingly. Every time I tried to reach to kiss him, he moved away.

"Nothing." My breath picked up speed, telling him what he wanted to hear. "Nothing at all."

"Good girls get rewarded."

He added his middle finger into me, the ice dissolving inside me completely. My own juices and the cold water dripped down my legs, mixing together, traveling from my thighs to my calves.

"Ride my fingers now, Princess."

"Or what?"

Our eyes met. He searched mine relentlessly for traces of doubt. *I want the fantasy. I want you not to be considerate, or gentle.*

"Or"—his lips dragged along the side of my neck—"I'm going to throw you over my bed headfirst and fuck your ass until you bleed."

Oh. My. God.

Fear and excitement coursed through me. I pushed up and down, grinding into his body for added friction as I rode his fingers. I closed my eyes, my pleasure mixed with shame for what he was making me do. I knew he was watching, and I knew he was getting a kick out of the full control he had over me.

"Ransom…"

"No talking," he said, not moving an inch, just standing there with his fingers erect while I fucked them.

"Give me a third finger. Please."

"No."

"*Please.*" God, what was I doing? I was already regretting my behavior, and still, I continued. I picked up speed, feeling my orgasm making its way from my toes up.

"Why'd you kiss Max?" he growled.

"To piss you off!" I cried out.

"Consider this payback."

Just like that, he drew his fingers away, seconds from my orgasm. He stepped back. I slacked against the wall, my legs piling beneath me in disarray. The sweet ache of where his fingers had been still pulsated inside me. Well, now I was just *pissed*.

"Nothing happened, though, right?" He smiled pleasantly, popping the two fingers he'd used into his mouth, sucking them clean. "Hmm. Watermelon Sugar High."

"Fuck you," I moaned from my place on the floor.

He tipped his head down. "Not a fan of Harry Styles?"

"Not a fan of you!" I called out to his retreating back, watching him ambling to his room, disposing his whiskey glass on a credenza in the living room. "I'll *never* fuck an asshole like you."

He chuckled before closing the door behind him.

He knew it was a lie.

Chapter Thirteen

Ransom

Not good.

Not good at all.

Let me rephrase—*very* good. Too good. The kind of good you want to bottle up and save for a rainy day.

There was a first time for everything. Apparently, this was my first time finger-fucking my ward.

I'd never messed with a client before. Prided myself in the cool and collected way I handled my assignments, even when some of the most gorgeous, glamorous women on earth fell at my feet, begging for a joy ride.

In the end, the one who managed to get her way was the unassuming Hallie Thorne.

She was pretty enough, but nowhere near as eye-catching as many other women who'd tried—and failed—to lure me into temptation.

What made Brat ruthlessly alluring was her hostile individuality. Like a cornered, rabid animal, she fought, even without teeth and claws. She didn't give up on herself, even if, in her own eyes, she was unworthy.

It was that fine line between her defenselessness and slyness that did it for me. She was a contradiction. A tender-souled belle who didn't mind walking all over Max's future with her pointy stilettos just to make a point. An exiled Eve. A weird, mixed-breed creature.

Someone like me.

Which reminded me. I wasn't going to sack Max.

Poor asshat was a pawn in our screwed-up game. But I was going to make him sweat buckets and ensure Hallie Thorne was off-limits for him.

As for playing with America's former First Daughter's pussy juices, well, that was a one-off. I was fairly certain Brat wouldn't rat us out to her parents. Admitting she got frisky with the help would serve as more ammo against her, and they already had plenty to work with.

The next morning, I woke up knowing I had to avoid her until I got my mind straight and my cock under control. Next time I saw her, I had to sit her down and explain there would be no more *nothings* between us.

I grabbed my phone from my nightstand. The screen flashed with Tom's name.

Not in this lifetime.

Not that any part of me considered confiding in him about my transgressions last night. But Tom was usually the bearer of bad news, and I needed two cups of coffee before dealing with his ass.

I rejected the call, sat upright, and phoned Max. He answered before the dial tone started.

"Boss!" he greeted anxiously. "Listen, I haven't slept all night. I just wanted to say—"

"I don't give a crap about what you want to say." I jammed my feet into my slippers, sauntering to the closet. "Only reason your ass is not sacked and you're not on an economy flight back to Los Angeles right now is because we're overworked and understaffed. You are not to touch the ward again, Maxwell."

"I know, I know." His voice reeked of desperation. I wondered how high on the psychopath scale I'd score. I did not even feel remotely hypocritical for this transgression. "I never meant for the lines to blur this way. I was just…I mean, she was just…"

"A bag of issues and pert tits." I flung the closet open, choosing dark gray slacks and a pale blue dress shirt. "Even if she wasn't hot, it still wouldn't be okay to fondle her."

"Absolutely. You have my word. Never again." There was a pause. "I understand if you want to reassign me."

Reassigning him would be the right thing to do. But that would show Hallie that I gave a shit, that I was jealous, and that was false advertising.

"You'll take the day shift with her today," I announced, knowing damn well that Brat was going to be devastated to see Max on her case after last night. This would be the ultimate rejection. "I have business to attend to."

"In Dallas?" He sounded surprised. "Okay. You can trust me, boss. I won't let you down."

"I know you won't." I slipped a cufflink through the inside of the cuff. "Because I'll kill you if you do."

As soon as Max showed up at the suite, I slipped outside. Hallie was still asleep. I took the Bugatti and drove out to Plano, a sleepy Dallas suburb where people traded their souls for kidney-shaped pools.

The Bugatti was a spur-of-the-moment rental. A reminder that Hallie Thorne hadn't dug deep into my skin. All of her environmental work and mumbo-jumbo about global warming did my head in. I needed to remind myself that I liked fast cars, meat, and private jets.

I parked in front of a gray-stoned McMansion overlooking a golf course and a lake. Carefully trimmed shrubs and a white picket fence surrounded the property, and baby toys littered the front lawn. The whole damn nine yards.

"You son of a gun, Law." I shook my head, rounding the Bugatti and knocking on the door. A young woman with bloodshot eyes flung the door open, holding a mostly naked baby with rolls where his elbows and knees should be.

"You Ransom?" she asked, then yawned.

"To my dismay, yes."

She shoved the baby into my hands. "Lawrence is upstairs, finishing a call. You can come in. I need to jump in the shower. This little nugget just threw up all over me."

She turned around and left. I frowned at the baby, who frowned back at me. His expression said, *don't ask me. You guys are the adults here.*

"Your mother is a nutcase," I said, unsurprised. Lawrence had always had pedestrian taste when it came to the fairer sex.

I treaded inside, taking in the full bourgeois-conversion to which my good friend had succumbed.

Even though Law didn't want for himself the same lifestyle chosen by Tom and me, we remained close. He was our big brother, in all the ways that mattered, and it never occurred to me to miss out on seeing him during my time in Texas.

I crouched down to place the tiny human onto a play mat shaped like a cloud when I heard a gruff voice emerging from the marbled stairway.

"You should get one of those."

I straightened my spine. "The play mat or the baby?"

"Baby."

"Not into pets." I patted my hands clean, turning around to eyeball my friend. Lawrence was a six foot four behemoth of a man, with a bushy black beard and raven eyes to match.

He clapped my shoulder. "I see you've met Stassia and Emmanuel."

"Up close and personal." I sauntered into his trendy white kitchen, popping the fridge open. I was met with mountains of puree pouches and prepacked meals.

This was a mistake. I couldn't ask this guy for advice. He was too far gone into Family Land.

"Don't look so horrified. Beer's in the garage cooler." Lawrence closed the fridge's door in my face. "Stassia should be down any minute. We can sit there. More private."

We waited for Stassia to emerge from the quickest shower ever recorded. Once excused, we retired to the garage, where we popped beers and sat in front of a huge flat screen TV, tuning in to a baseball game.

"What brings you here?" Lawrence took a pull of his beer. "And please spare me the you-missed-me bullshit. We see each other exactly two times a year—both when I'm in Chicago for business."

Law was a sports agent and did very well for himself.

"I've got a job in your neck of the woods." I scratched my stubble.

"You travel all around the US and never made it to suburbia." Law chuckled. "Whenever you show up, it's because you wanna talk."

Other than Lawrence, I never talked to anyone about anything. Tom was great, too, but he was too geographically close to me.

Looking around, I shrugged. "Your place is depressing."

"Spill it out, then, sonny boy, and get outta here."

No point in postponing why I'd come here. I needed to get my ass kicked.

"I made a boo-boo."

"How big?"

"A wound shot?" I rubbed at my forehead, frustrated.

"Juicy." He rubbed his hands together. "I'm listening."

"I almost fucked the ward yesterday."

Lawrence's face broke into a huge grin. "That's great news, buddy."

Had he lost his grasp of the English language?

"Did you hear what I said?" I sat back, my leg jerking impatiently. "I nearly *fucked* my entire operation, and an almost-under-age girl in the process."

"It's the first time you ever lost control." Lawrence toasted the air with his beer. "She must be special."

"She's special, all right. A special kind of nightmare," I muttered.

His eyes widened with delight. He created a square with his fingers, aiming them at me. "That's a Kodak moment if I've ever seen one. Ransom Lockwood, enamored. Looks like she's giving you hell, too. I already like her."

"She's a child," I spat out, as if it was Lawrence who stuck his finger into Brat yesterday, not me.

"How young are we talking here? Twenty-five? Twenty-three?"

I averted my gaze to his parked Chevy Suburban.

"Dayum!" Lawrence cackled, enjoying the show. "Eighteen?"

"No, you gross ass. Twenty-one."

He whistled. "Rules are meant to be broken."

"So are your bones, if you keep making light of it." I peeled the label off the sweaty beer bottle, wondering if Max had adhered to my warning and kept his hands to himself today. I would tear him limb from limb if he crossed the line again.

"What's with you? It's not like you to get your panties in a twist about a woman." Law turned off the TV, swiveling toward me. "Truth is, I'm kind of relieved someone managed to penetrate the surface with you. I was starting to worry your ass would never settle down. Nothing gets to you."

"Beer does." I raised the empty bottle in my hand. "Grab me another one."

Law leaned down, seizing another beer from the cooler and hurling it my way. I caught it mid-air.

"And settling down is not an option. No woman can handle this much bullshit." I pointed at myself.

"And yet, you're here." Law quirked a brow. "If you got it all figured out, why're you asking for advice?"

"It's hard to stay away from her." I rubbed at my stubble-shadowed chin. "Her dad is the former president of the United States, and he's about to help me reel in the big fish if he's satisfied with my work. Which, my guess is he wouldn't be, if his daughter is full of my cum."

Not to mention all the other ways I wanted to play with her, now that I knew she was game.

"Business ain't everything." Law *tsked*. "You deserve happiness."

I smiled bitterly. "A good lay doesn't equal happiness."

"A good woman does."

"She's no good, and barely a woman."

"Now you're just acting like a bastard because you're angry someone managed to make you feel not-miserable for the first time in your shit-ass life."

Law's eyebrows collapsed. He looked at me so intensely, for a moment, I got ready to punch him in case he tried to hug me.

"You know it's not our fault, right? What happened with Moruzzi."

"I know that," I gritted out. I meant every word. I didn't feel regret nor shame. Whatever happened—happened. It was out of my control.

"What happened with Kozlov in L.A.... that wasn't your fault, either."

See, here, I begged to differ.

I should have never told Law about that. It was a slip of the tongue. Something I'd confessed one very drunken night.

"Whose fault was it, then?" I downed my second beer.

"Sometimes bad things happen and it's no one's fault."

"Well, part of this job is in L.A., and let's just say the Russians didn't forget about me."

"Can you blame them? You made yourself a lot of enemies before you went solo with Tom. Including our time in Chicago. We were reckless. We made a name for ourselves. You made some mistakes. One of them with a very bad person. Question is—are you ready to change, Ransom? Are you ready to grow up?"

I knew what he wanted me to say. That yes, I was ready. And yes, the string of fast cars and fast women got old. But the truth was, I was still the same asshole. Miserable and incapable of having feelings for anyone. Except for maybe an unhealthy little fascination with a woman I worked for.

"This is useless. I'm not you. I'm not Tom. I'm not built for this."

I stood up, dumping my two empty beers into a can on my way to the door. Then I stopped. Turned around, frowned, and returned to the trash, picking up both of the beer bottles.

"Where's your recycling bin?" I asked.

"In the kitchen, under the sink."

I carried the beer bottles into his house and put them in recycling on my way out.

On the drive back to Dallas, Tom called again. I couldn't put him off any longer. Especially considering he'd tried me throughout the day yesterday, too, but I'd been busy conducting job interviews with a few people who'd flown in from Austin.

I ended that day sucking Princess Thorne's pussy juices from my fingers while masturbating into the sheets like a fourteen-year-old.

"What'd you have for me?" I popped gum as I swiped the phone screen.

"I need some help," Tom used his friendly tone, which meant I wasn't going to like this.

"The app store is the blue square with the A on it." I rubbed my eyes. When he wanted something, it was usually technology related.

"Let me rephrase, I have a professional request." Tom cleared his throat. "You need to keep Miss Thorne in Texas. Or, more specifically, anywhere but in Los Angeles."

"And why's that?" I clutched the steering wheel in a death grip, asking, even though I already knew the answer.

"A little birdie told me Kozlov has a real hard-on for you and he's aware that you were working in the area."

"Remind me who said it was a good idea to send me back to Los Angeles?" My jaw ticked.

"Mine," Tom admitted. "I didn't think they'd know or care. It's been years."

I hit a traffic light. Stopped. Closed my eyes, shaking my head. Goddammit…

"Look." I was about to lie. It would be the first time I'd lied to Tom. Up until now, I only omitted the truth from him once in a while. "I've been keeping an eye. The coast is clear. Maybe your source is wrong."

What the fuck was I doing? Why was I hanging on to this assignment?

"Appreciate it," Tom said shortly. "Still, I would feel better if y'all stayed in Texas for a bit longer to throw off the scent."

"I can't tell her what to do forever."

More specifically, she now had leverage over me, and I couldn't treat her like a rag doll. The princess and I were partners in crime, and I knew she'd use what happened yesterday against me.

"Just try to stall her, all right? I'm sure they'll lose interest in a week or two." Tom sounded distracted. "Course, there's another option."

"Enlighten me."

"We can outsource this assignment. Get someone else to watch her. We might lose Thorne's support, but we'd keep her safe. It'd be better for everyone."

Not for me.

"I started the job, and I'll finish it," I bit out, hanging up the phone in his face.

Chapter Fourteen

Hallie

"Hey, you." I sat in front of the oval mirror in my suite's bedroom, applying thick, neon-blue eyeliner on my upper eyelid, pretending to be blasé.

Max's stance wilted in the mirror's reflection. He stood at the doorway, hands tucked into his front pockets, mouth screwed shut miserably. He nodded. Things had cooled off between us in recent days, our playful back and forth reduced to polite, grating conversation.

"Lucky me." I forced a smile, picking up my blush brush and stabbing it over the bronzer. "Another day without the tyrant."

"He said he'll take you to the rehearsal dinner tomorrow," Max explained, almost apologetically.

It had been almost a week since Ransom and I had done *nothing* in the suite's living room. Coincidentally, it had also been almost a week since I'd last seen him. One of the security people from the other room had picked up some of his suits and personal belongings and moved them out, while Max moved in to take over. The same person complained the footage and audio from the night Ransom had fingered me was missing. I had no doubt it was my bodyguard's doing, getting rid of the evidence.

Screw Ransom. His hot and cold games were getting old. A part of me wondered if this was another creative way to punish me for exposing a weakness of his.

Only this time, the weakness was *me*.

I dabbed my cheekbones with the brush. I'd already asked for forgiveness from Max for what I'd done that night. He'd accepted the apology, but this was all word-laundering. Something was broken between us, and we both knew it could never be repaired.

I was too occupied with Ransom. Max was focused on staying gainfully employed.

"He's real busy," Max excused his boss' behavior. "He's setting up an entire cybersecurity department, you know."

I laughed incredulously. "It's fine, Max. Seriously. I don't care."

Max studied me. "Are you okay?"

"Why wouldn't I be?" I dropped the brush, grabbing a random lipstick, squeezing it against my lips with all the grace of a hippo.

"Because your eyes are wet."

Were they? *Shit*. They were.

"Just makeup allergies," I huffed.

I was dying on the inside. The rejection was nibbling away at whatever confidence I had left. How could he do this to me?

Max stepped into my en suite bathroom, returning with a box of tissues, which made me want to cry again. He handed it to me silently.

I plucked one out, dabbing the corners of my eyes. "See? All better now."

On the seventh day after my *nothing* with Ransom, the bastard showed up in a tux at my suite's door. I opened it for him, clad in a black vintage Victorian cap-sleeved corset dress. The sleeves were white silk, and the hem of the corset was embedded with little flowers.

"Wrong room," I announced chirpily, slamming the door in his face. He slipped his shiny loafer between the door and the jamb, blocking me from closing it on him.

He shouldered past me, barely glancing at my face. He headed straight to the alcohol cart, pouring himself three fingers of whiskey.

The chutzpah of the man.

"No way I'm letting you drive under the influence." I closed the door reluctantly, wondering where Max was. Had he gone already? Without saying goodbye?

What do you expect? You used him to get back at his boss.

"We'll be driven there." Ransom downed his drink, slamming the empty glass against the cart. He checked his watch. Frowned. Then looked up, his eyes accidentally landing on my cleavage.

"What're you wearing?"

"A dress." I picked up my purse from the kitchenette counter, flinging my hair to one shoulder. "Does my skin look okay? Had to descale myself after you touched me."

"Someone doesn't handle rejection well." But his voice held no venom. He looked tired, agitated, and generally unwell.

"It would have been a rejection if you told me you weren't interested the next day." I smiled sweetly. "But what you did is called running away. I never pegged you for the hysterical type, but that's people for you. We're an unpredictable species."

Astonishingly, Ransom didn't verbally whip me for my last barb. He shook his head, grabbing his phone and wallet. "Let's get this over with."

"Finally, we're on the same page." I rolled my eyes, stomping to the door. He followed me, his tall, narrow frame shadowing mine.

The drive to my parents' mansion was silent. Mom and Dad sent out one of their drivers, which meant Ransom and I didn't have the chance to bicker loudly. Just as well. I was exhausted from overthinking what had happened between us, and wasn't looking forward to coming face-to-face with The Wicked Witch of the South and her sleek-haired fiancé.

Ten minutes before our scheduled arrival at my parents',

Ransom glanced over at me from the other side of the Escalade. "You're not to leave my sight tonight, Princess."

"Seems a bit excessive, don't you think? After going MIA for seven days."

His eyes flicked to our driver, then narrowed back at me. "Some of us have real jobs to do."

"And yours is to take care of me. If you can't handle it, hand back the monthly checks."

"Weekly," he corrected coolly. "And you were in safe hands with Max."

"They were warm, too." I let loose a malicious grin. "Not to mention...*creative*."

He crossed his legs, looking at me with easy mockery. "He didn't touch you."

"Maybe he did. Maybe he didn't. You'll never know."

"I do know, because there are cameras everywhere. Remember?"

I did now. God, I hated the man.

"Don't mistake his lapse of judgment for a trend." Ransom shook his head.

"Was that what Max and I had?" I mused. "And what would you call what *you* and I had?" I dropped my voice so we couldn't be heard. "A gap of judgment wide enough to drive a tanker through?"

"A mistake."

"If there's one mistake here, it's you."

"No doubts there. We all know the story of my origins."

"Listen here, you ass—"

He reached over, pressing his forefinger to my mouth with a dry chuckle. "What I am is irrelevant. What *you are* is what's important. And you're a client. So let's pretend that night never happened and move on. Believe it or not, I'm here to help you. Especially as it seems you lack the motivation and resources to help yourself."

I was about to bite off his finger when the Escalade pulled to a stop in front of the wrought-iron gates.

He unbuckled, sliding out of the car.

"It's showtime, Princess."

A dime was not spared on the rehearsal dinner, which consisted of the two lovebirds' families and close friends. Two hundred people in total.

Security was through the roof. Dozens of black-suited men patrolled the grounds of the mansion, with helicopters swirling low above the rooftop. Pink peonies and white roses poured out of tall antique porcelain vases, bracketing the pathway to the entrance. A wedge of golden light shining down from professional projectors made the open double doors shimmer. Ransom and I walked in to find the open-plan foyer teeming with people in suits and gowns, clutching flutes of champagne, babbling about the upcoming event.

"...heard they're going to spend 20k on fireworks alone..."

"...the invitations are apparently decked out with invisible ink and holograms to avoid wedding crashers..."

"...gown should be fantastic. The tiara is said to be on loan from the Queen of England herself. Apparently, she is an avid Julianne Thorne fan. Can you believe it?"

Plucking a glass of champagne from a wandering tray, I glided toward the inner rooms, Ransom at my heel. I brought the drink to my lips, only to have Ransom snatch it from between my fingers.

"No alcohol for you tonight."

"Tell me you're a petty baby without telling me you're a petty baby," I purred, trying not to show him how frustrated I was. I wasn't expecting a tearful reunion, but why was he so awful to me?

"Bad things happen when you drink," he reminded me.

"The worst thing that recently happened to me occurred when I was stone-cold sober."

He didn't respond. Good. I had bigger fish to fry. One of them stood at the end of the hallway, haloed by a flock of women in evening gowns.

Hera.

She looked tragically stunning. A modern-day Audrey Hepburn

in a lime dress, with a boat neckline and a hem that was *just* long enough to announce she was the star of the event. Her dark hair was pinned up, her side bangs swiped to one side neatly. She wore minimal makeup.

"Oh, yes. It's been so horrible to lose him." Hera touched a gloved hand to her chest, presumably talking about Craig's grandfather. "I kept asking—why me? Why us? It was such a difficult time for me. Still is."

Me, me, me.

Was that how I sounded? No wonder the tabloids loathed me.

Without realizing, I gravitated toward the circle of women. I felt safe, cloaked in the invisible cape of my failure to become a successful Thorne daughter. So much so, that I was genuinely surprised when my sister's eyes zeroed in on me. First, with open contempt. *How could I wear something so gauche to her rehearsal dinner?* Right before she plastered a delighted smile on her face.

"Hallie! My gosh, finally! I've missed you so." She stepped between two middle-aged ladies with too much makeup and clasped me into a special Thorne hug, where arms were involved even though bodies did not touch. I felt instantly cold. Her mouth found my ear. "Don't fuck it up for me, little sis. Please. I really want to just survive tonight. I'm exhausted."

Hera rarely showed signs of weakness, so I was actually pretty touched.

Disconnecting from me, she fluttered a hand over my arm. "Look at you! I cannot believe it's been so long."

"I can," a voice behind me said dryly. Ransom. Hera frowned at him.

"And you are?" She offered her gloved hand for him to kiss.

"Ransom Lockwood, your sister's security detail." He ignored her outreached hand, popping his ID card from the inside of his blazer.

"What a peculiar name."

"At least I'm not named after the most jealous, vengeful creature in Greek mythology," he said, low enough only for her and me to hear.

She sized him up quickly, her sharp eyes sweeping over his physique, his stony expression, the immaculate cut of his tux. The ring of women around us dissolved. People floated toward the waiters, eager to see if the hors d'oeuvres were truly gold-leafed.

Finally deciding he was not someone she wanted to cross, she turned to me. "I can't believe you missed the funeral, Hal. People talked."

"We felt strongly it wasn't safe for Miss Thorne to travel so far away," Ransom's silky voice taunted, pressing on all of Hera's sensitive points. "She's a high-profile persona."

"My sister can speak for herself." Hera reddened. "And anyway, who do you think I am?"

"A nurse, right?" he asked, knowing damn well she was a doctor, and that she would find the question insulting. "Very admirable."

Hera's eyes widened. She opened her mouth to give him a piece of her mind. I had the good sense to push myself between them. No part of me wanted to see World War III starting.

"Do you have any idea what room I could use to freshen up my makeup before we take pictures?" I asked her. Hera liked to be reminded that she knew this house much better than I did.

Reluctantly, she ripped her gaze from Ransom. She waved a hand behind her. "You can take this one. Craig is technically supposed to use it, but he's staying upstairs, in my room."

I slipped into the guestroom. Ransom shut the door behind us.

Numbly, I sat at an oak vanity desk and began brushing my hair back. The thickness in the air signaled a looming disaster. Nothing good ever happened when I was under the same roof with Hera and Craig.

Ransom pulled a book from a floating shelf, scowling. "*The Visual Display of Quantitative Information*," he read out loud. "The fun just never ends with you Thornes."

"You didn't have to be so terse with Hera." I glowered at him through the mirror, ready to pick a fight.

"No, I didn't, but it was enjoyable. She needed to be taken down a few notches."

"You baited her," I accused, stuck on a knot the brush couldn't untangle.

"She survived."

"I don't need to get into more trouble. What if she thinks you're my mouthpiece?"

"No offense, but no one in their right mind would ever think I'm the puppet and you're the monster in this relationship," he retorted smoothly. "Stop giving a shit about Hera. She doesn't extend the courtesy to you."

Sighing, I dumped the brush onto the desk, picking up a pair of scissors. I grabbed a handful of my hair, snipping the tangled part. A sudden urge to chop off all of my hair hit me. It would piss off my family so much. But as much as I wanted to hurt them, I ridiculously also wanted to be accepted by them. It was pathetic, yet the truth.

"I'm going for a quick piss. Don't go anywhere." With those romantic parting words, Ransom treaded out of the room, as darkly and quietly as he'd entered. I pressed my forehead against the cool surface of the desk. Only a few more hours to go. The wedding was tomorrow. After that, I could run back to Los Angeles. Leave the Thornes behind for a few more years.

Deciding a small nap wouldn't hurt, I closed my eyes.

The whine of the door opening announced Ransom's return. I didn't lift my head to greet him.

A glass of something—liquor, by the sharp scent of it—was set by my elbow. He hovered behind me, breathing down my neck.

"You can step back now. As much as I enjoy the creeper vibes, I'm okay," I mumbled into my arm.

A palm pressed against my shoulder. Warm and pudgy. My head immediately shot up. This wasn't Ransom's touch. Everything about Ransom was sinewy and rough.

Our eyes met in the mirror as he stood behind me.

Craig.

The man I detested more than anyone else in the entire world.

A smile stretched across his face. With a pronounced widow's peak, pale skin, golden hair, and expensive veneers, Craig screamed old money.

"Hello, Hallie. *So* good to see you." His fingers curled around my shoulder blade.

Thrown into fight-or-flight mode, I grabbed the tumbler of liquor he put next to me and turned around, tossing the content at his eyes. I missed, splashing his tux.

"You little bitch…" His hands went straight for my throat.

I flew up from the chair, making a beeline to the door. But Craig had an advantage over me—he was physically stronger, and not half as disoriented and scared. He grabbed me by the hair. My scalp burned. He shoved me against the four poster bed, trapping me with his big frame. He hiked up my dress from behind, clumsy fingers already patting their way between my legs.

I opened my mouth, letting out a desperate scream.

"I see you need a little reminder on how our get-togethers go down." Craig fisted my hair harder, burying my face into the rich wool linen, suffocating and shutting me up at the same time. Locks of coppery hair fell from my scalp, scattering on the mattress.

"Come on, now, *Hal-Pal*. It's been years, and you know I never overstep. I'll just cop a little feel. Keep you in top-notch."

His fingers patted along my inner thighs. I clutched my legs shut, bucking and escaping his touch. I couldn't breathe. The safest solution was to let Craig do his thing and get it over with. But I didn't want to be safe. I wanted to inflict pain on him. I wanted revenge. I wanted his blood.

Not today, Satan. Not today.

Craig never went all the way when he assaulted me. He never penetrated me in any way. Never kissed me, even. But he always touched where he was not supposed to. Even when I pleaded— *begged* him—not to. *Especially* when I begged him not to.

He liked tugging one off while assaulting me.

Getting off on my pain.

To him, I was the simpleminded Thorne child, the forgotten black sheep. His to play with.

His hands found the spot he was looking for, and he cupped my sex through my panties from behind, squeezing hard, letting out a satisfied groan.

"Here we are. Now let me just…do this…right quick…last time as an unmarried man…"

I heard his zipper roll down, and I screamed hard into the duvet. The pressure inside my head was so intense, I thought it'd explode. I tried to give him a roundhouse kick, but he moved away quickly. He stepped back between my legs from behind. He held my head tightly, pushing my face down onto the mattress so no one could hear me.

"Now where were we?" He chuckled.

Before I knew what was happening, Craig flew off of me. I righted myself, pushing my dress down. I caught a glimpse of the red marks his fingers left on my thighs. Ransom fisted Craig's dress shirt, slamming him against the walled mirror. The mirror broke and collapsed at their feet, the alarming noise drowned by the soft jazz music seeping from under the closed door.

"Fatal mistake." Ransom smashed Craig's head against the broken mirror. "The worst one you've made in your miserable life."

Eyes dead, jaw flexed, Ransom thrashed my sister's fiancé against the broken glass again and again.

"Wait! Wait! I can explain!" Craig cried out, trying to wriggle away from my bodyguard's grasp. He stood no chance, and he knew it.

"You can try while I smash your fucking head in, but you won't succeed." Ransom's voice was as blank as his eyes. Blood stained the shards of broken glass behind Craig's head. The glass was flat, so it didn't pierce through the skin, but my heart was still in my throat.

"Look, she's not…she is not like us, man! Her mind is…she is simple, all right?"

In response, Ransom flung Craig across the room, over the

bed. Head down, ass up, he was now in the same position I'd been in moments earlier.

Seeing him like this, at a point of such disadvantage, made me want to weep with relief.

"Let me demonstrate what it felt like for her." Ransom pushed Craig's face deep into the mattress while ripping Craig's tuxedo pants down. His boxers tangled across his ankles. From my spot in the corner of the room, I stared at his soupy skin, the way his knees bumped together in fear. He retched, collapsing forward. Then he vomited all over the bed.

"What were you going to do to her?" Ransom demanded, his hand still fisting Craig's hair. A better woman would have stopped Ransom. But I thrived on the scene, buzzing with adrenaline.

I hated Craig and couldn't help but feel triumph and relief. He was finally getting what he deserved, after all these years. All those *tears*.

Craig's muffled voice—blocked by the linen and his vomit—tried to answer the question.

Ransom tugged him up by the hair. "Repeat that."

"Nothing!" Craig cried out, tears streaming down his splotched face. "I swear!"

"Wrong answer. I'm giving you another chance, before I get creative with your punishment. Fair warning: my taste runs eclectic, and I'm a *very* adventurous man."

Craig looked delirious with pain and fear.

"What were you going to do to her?" Ransom leaned down, whispering in his ear. His fingers tightened on Craig's hair, pulling some of it out. His golden tresses fell next to my red-hot ones. Together, they looked like orange-tipped flames.

Craig closed his eyes. "I—I—I was just…I thought…I mean, I normally just…"

"He touches me and jerks off," I found my voice from my spot in the corner of the room, hugging myself protectively.

"How many times?" Ransom asked without looking at me.

"Four," I replied, including this one. The only impediment that stood between Craig and his goal was the man who was hired to protect me.

Somehow, it was not lost on me that my parents had hired Ransom.

"Hand me that hairbrush, would you, Miss Thorne?" Ransom opened his palm in my direction.

I scurried to the desk, doing as he said. Our fingers touched when I passed him the brush. The little hairs on my arms stood on end.

This wasn't going to end well, my fascination with this violent, complex man who vowed to keep me safe.

"Prepare yourself for some spanking, kiddo," Ransom announced in a talk-show host brightness. "Bite the duvet if you can't take the heat."

"The duvet is covered in vomit," Craig protested weakly.

"Your doing. *Bon appétit*."

He spanked him with the back of the brush, ten for each time he assaulted me. Forty in total. Until Craig's ass was so red, so swollen, I didn't think he could sit this month or the next. It made me feel protected and safe. Like someone had my back. And for the millionth time recently—that someone was Ransom.

Finally, Ransom let him go. Craig sagged to his knees with his pants still wrapped around his ankles, crawling toward the door. He left a trail of tears and blood.

"You'll pay for this…both of you…you won't get away with this."

Ransom yanked a tissue box from the desk, pulled one, and wiped his hands nonchalantly. "Not sure about that, buddy. If you tell anyone what happened, I'll tell everyone what *really* happened. Now, we both know Julianne and Anthony aren't Parents of the Year material when it comes to Miss Thorne, but now you've really done it. No room for error."

Craig stopped crawling. He turned around to look at us.

"They won't believe her." His eyes danced in their sockets.

"You're wrong. But even if you weren't, they'll believe *me*,"

Ransom said with confidence. "And I don't intend on keeping it in the family, either. Just think of the check I can cut with a story this juicy." Ransom let loose a low whistle, shaking his head. "You'll be making me a rich man."

I didn't think he would—selling a story to the tabloids wasn't his style—but the idea was bone-freezing. Craig must've shared the sentiment, because he rolled over the carpet, bracing himself against a wall to stand on his knees. "What do you want?"

Ransom sat down on the stool by the desk, bracing his elbows on his knees.

"You will never put a finger on this woman again."

"*Done.*" Craig's eyes singed red. He refused to look at me, focusing on Ransom only. "You think I want anything to do with her?"

"Seeing as I think very poorly of you, yes, I believe you're stupid enough to try your luck again. I'm not going to stick around forever. But I *am* going to call Miss Thorne bi-annually to ensure that you keep your promise. Consider this a lifetime warranty of mine. She was nearly assaulted while under my supervision, and now I must protect her, eternally, from the monster who tried to put his hands on her."

I could hug Ransom. I believed him. Believed he'd call. Believed he would never let a thing like that happen to me again. I also appreciated how, despite his kinks, he had such a clear sense of right and wrong, reality and fantasy.

"What else?" Craig asked, his head lolling over his chest.

"Cancel the wedding rehearsal." I found my voice. I didn't want to be here. Didn't want to pretend to be happy for this horrible couple.

He snorted. "Like I can go out there looking like *this*."

"What'll you tell people?" I directed the question at Ransom, hating myself for caring.

"He is going to tell people he had an allergic reaction, passed out, and hit the back of his head on the mirror while collapsing. We found him and alerted the staff," Ransom filled in the gaps for us.

"I'm not allergic to anything," Craig whined.

"Get creative, asshole." Ransom stood up. "Now pull your pants up and get the fuck out of here."

A moment later, the door was shut behind Craig and it was just Ransom and me again. The stench of Craig's puke engulfed the room. Ransom cracked a window open and stood next to it while I sank into the stool he'd just occupied.

"Tell me everything," he said, his voice neither soft nor heartless. "Right from the beginning."

Rehashing my weakest moments wasn't a lifelong dream of mine, but he'd just gone to bat for me, so I took a deep breath.

"The first time, I was fourteen. I was back from summer camp, only for a few days. My parents wanted to take me to the ballet with them. I preferred to stick around with Hera and Craig. See, becoming friends with my sister was an obsession for me. I wanted her to accept me. But she had other plans. She decided to go out with some friends and asked Craig to keep an eye on me…"

"I'm not staying here, Craig. But someone needs to keep an eye on Hallie, she's still young. Take a bullet for me, will ya?"

"Yeah, yeah, babe. Sure thing."

"Keep an eye on her, Craig. Fourteen is still young, all right?"

"And he took liberties," Ransom finished my sentence, piercing through the painful memory.

I nodded, licking my lips. "Craig had always been so nice and sweet to me. He helped me out with my summer homework and played ball with me in the backyard. We ordered food and played Monopoly.

"Up until then, it was all okay. Ordinary. Craig let me win, I remembered. When we were done playing, Hera still wasn't home. Craig promised he'd speak to her when she came back. Tell her to make an effort, spend more time with me. He escorted me back to my room, then told me that Hera was being really mean to him, too, sometimes. I was so mad at her for ditching me, my loyalty immediately shifted to him. I rolled with it when he dissed her. He said she was cold and unkind to him, and that she didn't even let him *kiss* her. He asked if he could touch me. Like, a simple touch.

Just touch my leg or whatever." I shook my head, remembering every moment of it, every small smile, every gesture. "I was naïve, and young, and worst of all—grateful. I said yes. I consented to it."

"You consented to nothing." Ransom closed his eyes, pressing his forehead to the side of the window. "You were fourteen, he was twenty-two. He was a manipulating piece of shit. What happened next?"

"He just touched my legs. But he touched himself, too, in the process. And that…I hadn't agreed to that. I couldn't see what he was doing. It was dark. But I knew it was wrong, and I knew we'd both get in trouble for it if people found out."

"Then what?"

"He finished, I guess." I buried my face in my hands, shaking my head. "Went to the bathroom, came back after a few minutes. I was sick with shame and worry. I told him I was gonna tell my parents. He said, 'You agreed to this. All they're going to think is that you're a slut on top of being stupid.' I believed him. At this point, I knew my parents were making excuses for me. And realistically, I wasn't going to see Craig much. I had kept hoping he and Hera would break up and I wouldn't have to deal with him again. But that wasn't how things panned out."

"And your parents never suspected?"

"My relationship with my parents is…complex. We both work hard at pretending nothing's wrong."

"You're both doing a shit job at it. What about the other times?" Ransom asked.

I rubbed at my right eyebrow. "Then it happened during a family vacation in Cabo—Craig got really drunk and knocked on my suite's door to apologize. Said it had been eating at him. When I tried to push the door closed, he barged in and did it all over again."

I heard Ransom suck in a breath, but didn't dare look at him.

"Yeah." I sighed. "That time, though, I managed to knee him in the balls. So that bought me a few years of peace and quiet."

"Third time?" he asked.

"Two years ago. Thanksgiving."

"And you never told anyone?" There was no judgment in his voice.

I swallowed the acidic saliva pooling in my mouth. "The more time that passed, the larger the secret became, and revealing it after all those years felt…weird. Like they would suspect me. Why hadn't I come to them after the first time? You always see it in comments on the internet when someone tells their abuse story. When Hera and Craig got engaged, for instance, the tabloids claimed I was extremely jealous of her. It'd have been the perfect time to come clean…if it wasn't for the terrible motive the press would have slapped on this kind of move."

"Bet you my dick Craig himself planted the idea that you were jealous," Ransom said.

I scratched my cheek. "Probably. He loves the media attention."

He raked a hand through his hair. "The first time I saw you… you thought…"

"Yeah." I stood up swiftly, collecting my purse. "I thought you came for me. I was ready to kill you if you tried something. What happened with Craig…it really screwed me up."

"Did anyone ever suspect? A friend? A teacher? A boyfriend?"

"No one." I wrinkled my nose. "All my L.A. friends, even Keller, are just skin deep. It didn't seem right. And I didn't trust anyone else. As for boyfriends…" I sucked in a breath. "I've never had one."

"Never had what?"

"A boyfriend."

Ransom gave me a GTFO look. "Bullshit."

I shrugged, smiling miserably.

"But you're not a virgin." Ransom frowned, his cheeks tinting pink. "I *know* that. I—"

"Not anatomically, no. The proud owner of my V-card is my rechargeable JoyStick. I don't have any sexual experience to speak of, other than self-pleasure." The words rushed out of me, each confession tumbling after the next. It felt good to get it off my chest, even if the person I was confiding in was my enemy.

"The first time I felt anything resembling sexual attraction to

anyone was that night, when I caught you in that dirty L.A. alley…"
I waved my purse in the air, chuckling. "Well, anyway, that was a
mistake. It's fine, though. I never needed a relationship to be satisfied sexually. I can take care of myself."

He opened his mouth, about to say something, but I couldn't
bear to listen to what it might be.

"Hey, do you think it's safe to leave?" I looked around us. "The
smell is starting to get to me."

"Hallie…" Ransom trailed off, looking miserable and disgusted
with what I'd just told him. Maybe a little bit with himself, too, for
his treatment of me. I couldn't stand it. The pity.

"Please don't be a sap." I rolled my eyes. "Can we get out of
here, or what?"

He nodded once, waltzing over to open the door for me.

Chapter Fifteen

Ransom

Then.

*L*awrence was the first to go solo.

When he turned eighteen, he got a full ride to college. We all thought Moruzzi was gonna change his tune. Sweeten up the deal for him to make him stick around in Chicago and do his biddings.

Not so. Moruzzi had decided, instead, to steal all of Lawrence's savings and told him if he moved, his life would be over.

Lawrence moved, anyway. Tom and I chipped in to help him. Together, we both had about two grand, which wasn't going to get Lawrence far, but it would buy him some time to find a job before he started his school year.

The night Lawrence left, Moruzzi drank. A lot. Mrs. Moruzzi wasn't home. She'd gone to Toronto, to spend some time with her lover. I wondered why people stayed together. Marriage looked like a terrible cage to be trapped in. I vowed to never marry.

Moruzzi decided Tom and I should fight. We had no choice, so we did. Normally, I came out on top. But this time, I saw how down and depressed Tom was about the whole thing, so I let him win.

Later that night, Tom crawled over to my bedroom to stitch me up and share a bottle of whiskey he'd stolen from Moruzzi. We did it a lot—drank his booze. Moruzzi never paid attention. He was too much of a drunkard to keep track of his liquor stash.

"We need to kill him," Tom said, after a long silence. "Or he'll kill us. I know he will. When I went to get this whiskey from his office, I saw his desk. He is trying to figure out where Law lives. I think Law's in danger."

If Tom and I killed him, we wouldn't have anywhere to go. Plus, we'd be the immediate suspects, after the police looked into it and found out what we did for him.

"We'll need to get creative first." I shook my head. "Buy time before we both turn eighteen."

For the next two years, we slowed Mr. Moruzzi down. Made him as useless, toothless, and clawless as one could be. We slipped some of the drugs he let us sell into his drinks and food when he wasn't looking, getting him unknowingly hooked. When he wanted to take a spontaneous trip to the state where Lawrence attended college, we very mistakenly loosened one of the stairs in the house, which resulted in Mr. Moruzzi breaking his leg and canceling the trip. We began messing with his sanity. Tampering with his electricity. Changing light bulbs to create different hues, different atmospheres. Cut his shoelaces shorter. Made his important documents and work things go MIA.

He became more vicious toward us. The women he'd once brought over to reward us for our good behavior were long gone. He hid food. Locked us out when we came home late. We counted down the minutes, then seconds, until it was all over.

Tom got out first. He found a good college, got a scholarship, and bailed. He asked me to come with him. Said he'd take care of me the last year before I turned eighteen. But I didn't want to slow him down.

That last year with Moruzzi was a blur. He became the meanest when we were alone. But finally, and through hard work at school, I managed to get out, too.

I remember that day. When I turned eighteen.

I didn't even bother to return home after work.

Tom picked me up. My pocket was full of money I was supposed to give Mr. Moruzzi.

"Ready to start your new life?" Tom asked. He looked good. Like he was having fun. I wanted to have fun, too. Though, I knew my upbringing had corrupted me, made me a dysfunctional person. Tom, Law, and I, we were going to make up for everything we'd lost.

I nodded. We left Chicago behind in a cloud of dust.

Craig's allergic reaction excuse sent guests into a frenzy. Nobody noticed him limping into a tinted Lexus through the back door, escorted by a group of frat boys with receding hairlines and dad bods. One of them took the driver's seat and floored it out of the estate. I slipped into one of the bathrooms to regulate my breathing and scream into the shower curtain.

Brat got hurt.

Brat got very hurt.

Brat was more than just a brat. She was a broken-winged swan. One who thought of herself as an ugly duckling.

When I got out, Hallie was standing with her family in the corner of the drawing room, assuming the role of the designated, worried sister with distinction.

"But I didn't even know he was allergic to wool," Hera sulked, while Julianne patted her shoulder and Anthony rubbed at Brat's arm. "I mean, he wears wool *all* the time. He prefers cashmere, of course—who doesn't? But…"

Unfortunately, her shit-for-brains fiancé hadn't come up with a brilliant excuse. He should have gone with something more believable. Like reptiles or pollinated fruit.

"I read somewhere that allergies can develop as you grow older," Hallie suggested helpfully, standing a bit to the side from the rest of her family.

"You read?" Hera cocked an eyebrow. "Now there's a shocker."

"Hera!" Julianne chided. "What's wrong with you? Just because you're upset doesn't mean you can pick on your sister like that."

"She's explaining allergies to a *doctor*." Hera bared her teeth. "Now get rid of the guests. I guess I wasn't destined to have a wedding rehearsal, after all." She pushed past her mother, trekking upstairs to her room, grabbing a bottle of wine from a champagne bucket on her way there.

The wedding was tomorrow, which meant that Craig somehow had to snap back into shape in that time. I'd kept that fact in mind while smashing his skull into broken glass. His face stayed pristine. Ugly as sin, but unmarred.

Julianne squeezed Hallie's arm. "Sorry about that. Hera is under a lot of stress. Give us one moment, Bunny."

She charged after her elder daughter, trying to soothe her. Anthony stayed behind, putting a hand over Hallie's shoulder.

"Why don't you stay on the ranch tonight?" He ping-ponged his gaze between us. "I know it's hectic and teeming with staff. But the wedding's tomorrow. We can go to the venue together from here. Save all of us the trouble. And we really did miss you."

"I don't have my gown with me." Hallie's hand fluttered over her midsection. She wanted to stay at the scene of the crime like I wanted to shove my dick into a meat grinder. But leaving hastily might spike her parents' suspicion. Not that I cared if that bastard, Craig, went down in flames. However, I knew Hallie didn't want people to find out about the assault, and I had to respect that.

"I'll send someone to fetch it." Anthony mustered a smile. "Whaddaya say, Sugar Pie? Make your old man happy?"

I stepped between them, noticing that Hallie felt more secure next to my body than with her own father. "We accept. Thank you for your hospitality, President Thorne."

"I'll have Annika show you to your rooms."

"Room," I corrected him coolly. Both he and Hallie eyed me curiously.

"Security here is through the roof." Anthony frowned.

"And I would really rather spend the night alone," Hallie added bitingly.

With forced patience, I said, "I don't doubt your security measures, sir. All the same, I'm the one in charge of Miss Thorne's protection. It goes without saying I'll be sleeping on the floor, if at all, while on duty."

I wasn't going to share a bed with the woman, especially after finding out just how royally I'd fucked things up by messing with her. Up until today, I had still assumed that Hallie Thorne was a reckless, overtly sexual woman who took her pleasures where she could find them. I didn't for one moment suspect what we'd done seven nights ago was anything more than an expression of curiosity.

Anthony stroked his chin, nodding. "Your jurisdiction, your rules. Annika will show you to your *room* in a bit. You all right there, Sugar Pie?" He turned to his daughter. "You look a li'l pale."

Hallie smiled sunnily. "When am I not, Pops?"

As soon as he was out of earshot, Hallie turned around, slamming her fist into my arm.

"How could you?" she whispered.

You're about to have a massive meltdown tonight after being attacked, and "I want to keep an eye on you."

"I can handle myself." She clenched her teeth.

I didn't doubt that, but I didn't want her to wander this vast, strange house all by herself, either. Couldn't chance Craig returning to seek his revenge. And some screwed-up part of me really didn't want that vicious snake, Hera, to get any alone time with her.

"As I said before, I'll take the floor."

"A place fitting for a dog."

"Exactly."

Annika materialized out of nowhere, appearing in the hallway in her pressed uniform. She gave us a bow. "Miss Thorne, your parents are beyond happy you're here. Will you be attending dinner?"

"You couldn't pay me," Hallie grunted.

"Excuse me?"

"No." Hallie cleared her throat. "I'm not hungry, I'm afraid."

"Oh. Okay."

Annika showed us to a fairly large room on the second floor. The house was mostly empty by now. All the guests had trickled out in the last hour or so, after realizing the unappeasable Hera Thorne was locked in her room, roaring at her mother.

The room was spacious and impeccably decorated. A king-sized bed with pressed Victorian linen, a few landscape paintings with heavy golden frames, two dressers laden with fresh flower vases, and a walk-in closet. The floor was carpeted—thank fuck—and there was already a stack of pillows and blankets on an antique, regency couch in the corner of the room. Since the couch stretched to about the length of my thigh, it didn't hold much promise.

"It's not too late to ask for your own room," Hallie reminded me, tucking her hands under her ass while sitting on the bed, legs dangling mid-air.

"And miss all this fun?" I looked around, finding a good spot on the floor by the windows.

"Your funeral."

"Wouldn't you wish."

"I would, actually."

A terse smile touched my lips. "That would've held more weight if you didn't cling to me every time your father was around. You trust me more than you do him."

She blew a raspberry at me childishly. "You're deranged."

Stomping to the bathroom, she returned half an hour later in an oversized gray Harvard sweatshirt, boxers, and no makeup.

I was taken aback by the sheer beauty of fresh-faced Hallie. She was stunning.

I stood by the window, watching security personnel pack their shit and retreat back into the night.

"They brought our toothbrushes and clothes from the hotel." Hallie pressed a towel to her wet hair. I could see her through the window's reflection. "It's in the grand bathroom, two doors down."

I glanced at my watch. It was ten o'clock at night.

"Will you be okay?" I asked.

"Oh, no." She rolled her eyes. "I'll collapse into a puddle of emotion and tears as soon as you walk away."

"Stay here," I said.

"Famous last words." She slid under the covers, which were tightly tucked under the mattress. "Last time you asked me to do that I was assaulted."

"Good point." I reached over to release the covers from the mattress for her. "New rule: stay here unless you feel that you're in danger, in which case come and get me."

"Better." She turned her back to me, curling into a fetal position, signaling the conversation was over.

"Hallie…" I halted, wanting to say something but knowing whatever I said was going to sound stupid.

"Please go away."

Sighing, I padded to the bathroom, grabbed a shower, shaved, and brushed my teeth. I slipped into a pair of sweatpants and a wife-beater. When I got back to the room, the lights were off. Hallie's figure rose and dipped to the rhythm of her breaths.

Rearranging the pillows on the floor, I turned my back to her, trying to get comfortable. She'd crashed. I, however, had trouble sleeping, knowing her sister's fiancé was free to roam the streets.

He wouldn't touch Hallie again, I was certain of that, but that didn't mean there wouldn't be other victims. I wanted nothing more than to throw the bastard in jail. Problem was, it wasn't in my job description, and was highly counterproductive to my main goal, which was to get the hell out of here once time was up and stay on Anthony Thorne's good side.

"Do you think I'm damaged goods?" Her voice pierced through the air.

Not so asleep, after all.

"I don't think of you as a product."

"You know what I mean." She let out a soft yawn. "Do you think I'm…broken?"

"Anyone with half a life story is broken."

"You keep dodging the question."

"No, you keep missing the point," I said calmly, shifting to turn around and look at her from across the room. Her eyes sparkled in the dark. I wasn't sure if she was crying, tired, or both.

"You have issues, yes. I don't know many people who don't. Your working assumption is that everyone else has their shit together. That's inaccurate at best and self-destructive at worst."

"I don't know many women who got themselves into the same situation I landed myself in with Craig." She picked at a fray edge of her duvet. A tear slipped down her cheek.

"You don't know many women, period," I whispered.

"What do you mean?" She sniffed.

"All your friendships are fake. You said so yourself. You surround yourself with people who hide their pain in the same way you do. You buy their act—and they buy yours."

She said nothing.

"But that's beside the point. *You* didn't insert yourself into any situation. It was all Craig. You were fourteen. Young, impressionable, and sheltered. He should be in jail right now."

"He can't go to jail."

I didn't reply. Tom would hang me by the balls if I overstepped and fucked up this post. And for good reason. I'd react the same. But the situation wasn't so simple anymore.

"Besides, if you hated rape so much—" she started.

"Stop," I cut her off. "Not the same. Not an iota of similarity. My fantasies and kinks have nothing to do with reality."

"Why do you have them, then?"

I swallowed. "Because, growing up, the way I was introduced to sex was kind of a task. That guy I told you about, Moruzzi? He made me and the other kids do bad stuff for him. And as payoff for our jobs, he'd hire prostitutes for us. The sex wasn't optional. It was mandatory. A rite of passage. For a long time, I associated sex with something I was obligated to do."

"So this is your way of taking back your sexuality." She let out a breath.

"Yes." It was the first time I admitted this to anyone.

"I get it. Then why do *I* get turned on by all this?"

I gave it some thought. "Maybe because you want to remind yourself of the important part."

"Which is?"

"That you survived."

Silence lingered before she spoke again.

"You looked like you cared about me today." She shifted under her blanket.

"Just did my job." I cleared my throat. It felt tight.

"It was your job to protect me, not to almost kill him."

"Some jobs have perks."

Another silence.

"Ransom?"

"What?"

She hesitated. I held my breath. I really shouldn't. I'd avoided her for seven days. I had no business waiting for more of her words.

"Can you…"

No.

"Maybe…"

Fuck, no.

"…hold me?"

The worst part was that I couldn't *actually* say no. I wanted to. I could not deny her anything right now.

I felt my body rising up and rounding the bed. I slipped behind Hallie, staying on the far end of the mattress. She didn't turn around. I wrapped my arms around her shoulders, leaving room for Jesus between us, and a few other biblical folks if they wanted to squeeze in.

She was shaking like a leaf. I wanted to butcher Craig until nothing was left of him but dust and those fake-ass veneered teeth.

Slowly, in hopes of calming her down without awakening my cock—which had no qualms about Hallie's distress—I began stroking her hair. It was soft and long. It smelled of coconut and flowers. Since I'd never before cuddled—I doubted I'd even said the word out loud—I went off what I saw people do in movies.

Her shakes slowly subsided.

"I want to kill him," I heard her whisper.

"I can do it for you." I was only half-joking.

"Have you ever killed someone?"

I stilled, my hand halting over the nape of her neck.

"Never mind." She burrowed deeper into me, sighing. "I don't want to know, because it's not going to matter. You're still the only one who treats me half-decently. How sad is that?"

"Very," I admitted, swallowing hard. My cock was straining against my sweatpants, hyperaware of the fact the only barrier standing between it and Hallie's ass was a flimsy pair of worn-out boxers.

"Keep holding me."

"Stop moving, then," I barked.

"Why?" Her voice dropped an octave, becoming sultry.

"Because my cock is as hard as your day has been and I would very much like for my balls not to fall off."

She wiggled that luscious butt in response. My erect cock was nestled between her ass cheeks through our clothes. I looked down under the duvet. It was the hottest shit I'd ever seen.

"Hallie." I closed my eyes, shuffling back. Half my body was hanging off of the damn mattress. I was about to fall off the bed. Still, I held her.

"Hmm?" She chased my crotch, moving her ass up and down, grinding against my cock, which needed absolutely no further encouragement to release a pearl of pre-cum which stuck to my sweatpants. My shaft swung back and forth, tapping her ass. She purred. She knew exactly what she was doing.

"Stop," I groaned, my balls tightening.

"See, I know I should." She laced one of her legs through mine, continuing to grind against me. "But you're the only man who's ever made me feel…*desire*."

"See, saying that to a Dom means whatever's happening here should end immediately, since I'm the adult in the room right now."

The words *sounded* right and *felt* right. I'd practiced the lifestyle long enough to know boundaries—mine and my partners'—and yet I couldn't fucking deny her.

She snaked a hand between us, gripping my cock through my sweatpants. "I want you, Ransom."

"I don't want to ruin you," I croaked. And I generally ruined everything I touched. Unless it was work-related.

"Ruin me anyway." Her hand slipped into my sweatpants, her thumb twirling the drop of cum on the crown of my cock, rubbing it against the sensitive part. "There's not much left to destroy as it is."

The remainder of my self-control shredded into confetti. I flipped her around so we were face-to-face. We stared at each other in the dark. I wanted to kill myself for what I was about to do.

"Kiss me," she grumbled.

Helpless, and completely fucked, I shoved my fingers into her hair, pulling her forward as my mouth crushed down on hers.

Our teeth clashed. I growled, drawing away. This was my first real kiss, at age twenty-nine, and as far as first kisses went, it was probably a lackluster one for her. Then I remembered she probably hadn't really kissed anyone, either. We were both new at this.

Hallie wouldn't let go. She tugged me closer, clasping her legs around my waist, like a human octopus, not letting me go.

She shook her head, opening her mouth against mine, the tip of her tongue searching inside, exploring, sweeping against my teeth and my tongue and the roof of my mouth.

"We aren't doing this right," I grunted. I was no expert, but I knew. She froze inside my arms. Her mouth disconnected from mine, and she pulled away, searching my eyes.

"Ransom, have you ever been—"

"*No.*"

"Okay, I won't ask."

This was painful. This was why I kept my sexual liaison on the kinky side. It was so much easier to explain why there wouldn't be kissing and cuddling.

She kissed me again, slowly now. Touching her lips to the side of my mouth. Her tongue traced my lips. Her arms wrapped around my neck. I opened my mouth. She tasted of toothpaste and something sweet and Hallie. Of her jokes and quirks and idealistic, environmental agenda.

We did that for a while. I didn't dare touch her clothes, remove anything. But I was relieved when she scooted back a little, grabbed the hem of her sweatshirt, and flung it to the floor. I kicked the blanket off of us, allowing myself to admire her tits. Her tattoos. All of her.

Take a good look and have your fill, because you're about to fuck the client and with it, your entire business plan.

My thumb traced her ink. The lotus along her midriff, the mermaid tail on her hipbone…

"Do you want to kiss me somewhere else?" Her voice sounded timid—almost childish—in my ears again. And if I wasn't too far gone, this might cause me to pull away and get my shit together.

I looked up at her, nodding. "I want to kiss you *everywhere.*"

"Please do."

I started with her neck. I licked the outline of her breasts, biting softly the part where the curve met her ribcage. It was a lovely torture. My skin felt different. More sensitive. Perhaps I was allergic to making out. Unlikely, but not out of character.

Clasping one of her nipples between my teeth, I angled my cock between her legs, finding her sleek and ready for me. I knew, as my tip nestled between her hot, wet folds, that I was making a mistake.

I knew, and still, I pressed home.

She gasped, pushing her hot mouth into my neck.

"This feels so…" she stuttered.

Please say good and not horrible, because my dick will fall off if I have to stop now.

"Yes?" I urged, moving inside her slowly, so slow it hurt. Not only because I wanted to make it good for her, but because I was pretty sure I was about to come.

"Insane!" She dropped her head to the pillow, nails digging into my waist, drawing me closer.

I swallowed her moans with demanding, deep kisses, driving

into her, spiraling with each thrust, feeling her clenching around me. I wanted her to come so badly I disgusted myself. This new version of me, the one that gave a shit, was a danger to my identity.

"Right there." Her mouth dropped into an O-shape, her eyes finding mine in the dark. I was making eye contact now while fucking. This was just great. What came next? Spooning.

You already spooned her, idiot. Pre-sex.

Her hips rolled, meeting each of my thrusts. She was good at this, I realized. A natural. One day, she was going to find someone else, hopefully someone good, who'd get to enjoy that on a daily basis.

That someone wasn't gonna be me.

Grabbing her ass, I tugged her down to the edge of the bed, sinking my feet to the floor. I couldn't stand the tenderness. The romance of it all.

Spreading her wide, I started pushing into her jerkily, the way I would if she were another faceless, highly curated Tinder hookup.

Tell me to stop. Tell me it's not good for you. Tell me I'm a bastard.

"Shit! Oh! This is so good," she cried out instead, her tits bouncing to the rhythm of my thrusts.

This was when it hit me. I wasn't wearing a condom, for the first time since I'd started having sex.

"I gotta pull out," I groaned. "We're bareback. Are you coming?"

"Gimme a few."

I drove into her harshly. "Hurry up."

As if on cue, she fell apart beneath me, her muscles squeezing my cock greedily. Her breathing became shaky. A drop of sweat rolled from my forehead, exploding inside her navel.

I pulled out, strings of my white cum ribboning over her tatted body.

This never happened. I never went off-script. Never screwed a client. Only it did happen. Was happening. Right now.

Shoving my legs into my pants, I staggered out of her room.

Now wasn't the time to start catching feelings.

Chapter Sixteen

Hallie

"**H**allie! Come here, please. They need another family photo!" My mother's overtly cheerful lilt grated from under the arched, white columns of the Art Museum of Dallas. It had been converted into a wedding venue for the day. A school trip had to be canceled to accommodate the event.

I tugged the green sage bridesmaid dress from the pebbled floor, stomping in Mom's direction. Craig had been MIA so far—an hour into the pre-wedding photos—and Hera, in her Cowen Original ivory silk asymmetric ball gown, was in advanced stages of losing her mind.

As I made my way to my parents and sister, my inner thighs still sore, my center throbbing from my encounter with Ransom last night, I heard Hera billowing into her phone: "I don't care if he's dead, Braxton! If he's not here, looking like a million bucks, in exactly twenty minutes I'm calling the whole thing off. See who's going to pay off his student debt now. The useless bastard has been freeloading for years. He's not going to make me look like an idiot."

"Ship's sailed," Ransom murmured, in his black Armani suit as I passed by him on my way to my family, his eyes stuck to his phone. My heart skipped a beat, and I whipped my head around to see if he'd make eye contact. He did.

We shared a moment. A smile. An understanding.

Yesterday was the first time I'd climaxed with a man.

The first time I'd had sex. *Real* sex.

It planted a seed of hope inside of me. That maybe I could be happy.

I slipped between my parents. Hera stood next to Dad. She flung her phone into one of the bridesmaid's hands. "Let's get this shit over with."

We were standing on the stairway leading up to the Spanish colonial revival-style museum.

Hera swung her gaze toward me. "Covering those tattoos with makeup would be too much to ask, huh?"

"Hera, *enough*," my mother chided, wrapping her fingers around my shoulder protectively.

"I don't understand what got Hera's panties in such a twist." I flipped my hair, grinning seductively to the camera as the photographer began to click away. "If aesthetics meant so much to her, she wouldn't marry a man who looks like a pug."

"You jealous bitch!"

With a savage mewl, Hera flung her bouquet, launching herself on me. Her fingers were about to encircle my neck when Ransom stepped between us, serving as a human wall. He didn't touch her, but didn't let her near me, either.

"Get out of my way!" Hera raked his chest with her French manicured nails.

"Hera, please!" Mom tugged her elder daughter's arm, trying to pull her away. Dad grabbed her other arm. They exchanged exasperated looks, dragging her down the stairs kicking and screaming.

It was nice not to be the designated troubled child for a change.

"I'll give you five." The photographer winced, stumbling back. "I know what it's like."

Did he have a narcissistic sister, too?

"You need to calm down," Mom said to Hera. "You haven't been yourself in a while. I understand the pressure, but you mustn't lash out at all of us, least of all Hallie."

"Your mother is right. We cannot afford a scene, sweetheart. These people signed an NDA, but if something leaked…" Dad added.

I continued hiding behind Ransom's back, my gaze scraping the back of his neck. Half-mooned red marks of fingernails—*my* fingernails—adorned his skin, and every fiber of my body itched to touch him again.

"Groom's here!" A douchehead in suspenders and Adrien Oxford shoes weaved through the white, round dining tables arranged around the garden, knocking over garlands and centerpieces.

Saved by the sexual abuser.

Craig trailed behind him, in a suit and over-moussed hair. Even through his thick layer of makeup, I could tell he was pale. I stiffened at the sight of him. Ransom took a step back, so we were shoulder-to-shoulder.

"Think he's mad?" I whispered.

"I think I'll grind every bone in his body into flour if he acts on it," Ransom replied.

"That's a vision."

"Just say the word, Princess." He bumped his shoulder to mine.

Sensing our presence, Craig's eyes landed on Ransom and me. His face clouded. His friend pulled him toward his awaiting bride.

"There we go, bud. One step at a time." Golden Douche grinned.

Hera tramped toward them, crashing her bouquet against the groom's chest.

"You're an hour late, moron!"

Dad grunted, rubbing his eyes. "Get me Graham on the phone. I'm going to have to make sure this doesn't get leaked to the press."

"I wasn't feeling well," Craig said cagily.

"Yeah, well, maybe you should lay off the beer every once in a while," my sister bit out.

"Get off my case, would you?" Craig flung his arms, weaving his fingers through his combed hair. "You've been on my ass for a year now. *Lose weight, whiten your teeth, smile for the cameras, clap, monkey, clap.* I can't take this anymore. I can't take *you* anymore!" He rubbed at his cheek, as if he'd been slapped. "If I'm not good enough for you, just say the word and—"

"I can't believe you have the audacity to clap back!" Hera cupped her mouth, clearly devastated.

"I can't believe it took me this long," Craig retorted.

His friend slinked toward the bar, which wasn't open yet, desperately searching for someone to serve him. I'd have almost felt sorry for Craig if I didn't hate him so fiercely.

"I hate to be the bearer of bad news." A woman in a green suit appeared from under one of the arches, clutching her iPad to her chest. "But we're on a time crunch here, and we need to wrap up the shoot in less than an hour."

"Looks like your meltdown's gonna have to wait." I pouted to Hera from the safety of being next to Ransom.

"You." Hera pointed her finger at me, while dragging her future husband toward where my parents were standing. "I'm going to make sure you pay for this. Someone call the photographer. *Now.*"

The rest of the wedding was surprisingly bearable, everything considered. Even though I didn't know anyone, people were nice to me. My parents introduced me to their friends and colleagues, proudly presenting me as their philanthropic daughter. But that could've been just to save face. *Unemployed* didn't sound quite as charming.

Whenever I felt out of place, I retreated to one of the rooms of the museum with a napkin and a pen and doodled. Doodling slowed down my heart rate. Helped my hands stop shaking. More than anything—it organized the mess in my head.

Ransom was always in my periphery, but never too close. He orbited around me, giving me space and keeping an eye on me at the same time.

After the ceremony came the unrehearsed dinner, and with

it, my speech. The couple's families sat in a row over a long, chiffon-covered table. Candlelight flickered across the garden. Hera looked regal with a crown of flowers in her hair, smiling up at me with admiring eyes. She played the part so well. Only difference was, these days I didn't envy her for it. I pitied her. Pretending full-time must be exhausting.

I stood up, clinking my fork against my champagne glass. I had not touched a drop of alcohol throughout the wedding. I was proud of myself. Drinking had been my go-to strategy to survive family functions. Today, I was oddly present. I let myself feel, even when it wasn't pleasant.

Ransom was sitting across the garden on an antique white bench, casually conversing with a man I was pretty sure was from the CIA. I still couldn't believe I'd made this man break one of his rules and have sex with me. *Kiss me*. A powerful buzz shot through me.

"Hello, all." I smiled to the audience, peppering the gesture with a little wave. "Truth is, I've had a whole speech prepared and memorized for the occasion, but of course, me being me, now that it's time to say something, I'm going to take a page out of my eyeliner's book and just wing it."

Chuckles erupted from across the table, accompanied by light claps.

I turned to look at Hera, whose tight smile collapsed like a poorly-constructed LEGO tower.

"Hera and Craig, Craig and Hera." I sighed, knowing how stressed out my sister must be. "So perfectly matched, I couldn't come up with a more fitting couple even if I tried."

So far, not even one lie, and a very minimal dose of passive-aggressiveness. I was sure the unhappy couple could read between the lines. My hand shook slightly while clasping the champagne glass when I felt Craig's eyes burning a hole through my cheek. My gaze stumbled to Ransom on instinct. He gave me a curt nod.

Continue. You are standing up for yourself. Fuck them.

"Hera is a woman of many facets. Daughter, sister, doctor,

fiancée, a philanthropist. Craig is...you know, Craig." I hitched one shoulder up. Everyone laughed, well-aware he was not as decorated and celebrated as my sister. "Some of you may wonder—how does a couple stay together for so long? Fifteen years and counting. People are dynamic. They change, evolve. Well, not these two!" I toasted the champagne glass in the air. "Craig and Hera have stayed *exactly* the same as they were when they first met. Which is why their relationship works."

Hera shifted uneasily. Craig wrapped an arm over the back of her chair, shooting my dad an unreadable glare. Maybe he hoped Dad would cut me off. Surprisingly, he didn't.

"Now, moving on to Craig, my new brother-in-law!" I said cheerfully. "Good ol' Craig. You think you know him, but trust me, this one is *full* of surprises."

Craig flashed a painful smile, nodding along, as if we were good friends. The silence blanketing the tables told me people were starting to catch up on the fact that I wasn't being necessarily straightforward. I needed to wrap this up quickly.

"When I first saw these two together, I knew, without a shadow of a doubt, that they were truly meant for each other. I believe that's still the case. Identical dreams and aspirations, not to mention moral compasses, make these two so right for one another. While it is true that I don't spend much time with them, I can honestly say, every time we are in the same room, it feels like I've never left. They sure know how to create an atmosphere."

Albeit a shitty one.

"Hera and Craig, I wish you a long, continuous marriage, full of headstrong children who mirror you in every way. To Hera and Craig, everybody." I lifted the glass in the air.

People cheered, clinked their glasses, and drank. I slanted my gaze to my sister and her husband. They both stared at me vacantly, pale and shell-shocked.

"I improvised." I smiled sweetly at them. "You don't mind now, do you?"

When the wedding was over, Ransom tucked me in one of the

limos heading back to my parents' mansion. He sat in the corner opposite from me. I raised the partition between us and the driver as soon as we slipped inside, turning to face him.

"You survived," he observed, flicking cigar ash from the dash of his blazer.

"Trust me, I'm as shocked as you are." I was so glad we were alone now. He was beginning to feel more and more like home.

"I'm not shocked. You never give yourself any credit."

"Ransom?"

"That's my name."

"I'm going to Los Angeles tomorrow," I stated, rather than asked, not leaving him much room to object.

He stared at me dispassionately, mulling this over. "Give me a few days." This time he asked, not stated.

"No." I erected my spine, taking a deep breath. "I gave you plenty of time. Los Angeles is not going to become safer in the next day or two. I find Texas triggering. I want to put some distance between myself and Hera and Craig. Surely, you can understand that."

He did. I knew he did, because he rubbed his knuckles against his sharp jaw, hissing in frustration.

"L.A.'s a den of vipers," he said quietly.

"To me, Texas is worse."

"Don't you have friends in New York?" he inquired. "Someone you could visit?"

I smiled, appreciating that he wasn't fighting me on this. "I don't have friends anywhere, remember?"

"That's not true." He pressed his lips into a hard line. "Now, you have at least one."

My heart soared in my chest. We shared conspiratorial grins. This was my chance to talk to him about what had happened between us yesterday. About our night of passion. But there was something so perfect about this moment, the tranquility of it, I didn't want to ruin it.

Tomorrow, I told myself. *Today, you faced the wedding. One battle at a time.*

"Proud of you, Princess Thorne."

"What happened to Brat?" I quirked an eyebrow.

Ransom shook his head. "Hera snatched that title five minutes into our first encounter."

I laughed, shaking my head. "*Thief.*"

Chapter Seventeen

Hallie

My parents' Ford Escape Hybrid pulled onto the tarmac of the small, private airport next to their airplane. I shuddered at the thought of the carbon footprint, but this was Ransom's ultimatum if I wanted to go back to Los Angeles.

He was adamant about not passing through LAX.

Mom got out of the passenger seat, rounding the car to hug me.

"Thanks for coming, Bunny. I know you prefer shorter visits, and I appreciate the time you've made for us." She winced. Well, at least she didn't chide me for *that* wedding speech. "You pulled through wonderfully."

"Yes, Sugar Pie. We hope you'll grace us again with your presence this Thanksgiving." Dad joined us, as Ransom pulled our suitcases out of the trunk.

No chance in hell they were seeing my face before next year.

I smiled tightly, giving them each a swift hug before inching toward the stairway of the plane. "Thanks for the hospitality. We'll…talk."

Maybe.

On the plane, it was only Ransom, one flight attendant, the pilot, and me.

"Where's Max?" I buckled my seatbelt as we got ready for takeoff.

"Already in L.A."

"How come?"

"Put him on a paid leave."

"Why?"

"He wasn't needed."

"Sounds like code for wanting the coast clear," I teased, smiling.

The flight attendant came to sit next to us, buckling in, too.

Ransom smiled warmly at me. "Get your ears checked, Princess."

I decided not to press the subject. After all, we weren't alone. Also, I didn't necessarily want to know what Ransom thought about the night we'd shared at my parents' house. A rejection would crush me. Not knowing where I stood was just as hard, but I prolonged the conversation as long as I could.

After takeoff, Ransom dedicated himself to working on his laptop. When he was done, he speared me with a glare. "Thought about what you want to do yet?"

"How do you mean?" I shifted in my seat, buying time.

Of course, I hadn't thought about it. I was terrified of my limited options, especially now that I'd been diagnosed with dyslexia.

"For a living," he clarified. "With your *life*."

"Of course, I've thought about it." I frantically searched my brain for something. I was unqualified for most jobs, so I went with an option that required very little reading and a lot of personality. "I'm thinking of becoming a medical clown."

"A medical clown?" he repeated, blinking slowly.

"Yup." I grabbed my sketchpad and some pencils. "What's wrong with that? I'll be helping people."

"It's random."

"It'll pay the bills."

"You don't give a shit about the bills."

"And you don't give a shit about me. You wanted me to get a

job, you never said I needed to become a brain surgeon. Now back off and let me live my life," I snapped.

I was hoping he would dispute that statement. A deep gap stretched between giving a shit and being in love with someone, after all. I mean, he could still care, right? Even if it was just a little bit.

Ransom exhaled, squinting at the powder blue sky we were swimming in. "Be a clown, Miss Thorne. You seem to excel in that area."

As soon as we landed, I rushed into the taxi. Ransom followed me stoically. I fell inside and tipped my head back against the leather seat, closing my eyes.

I hoped Ransom would take the passenger seat and spare me the looming humiliation of asking him about what happened between us. He'd spent last night curled on the floor as far as humanly possible from me.

Alas, I felt the seat beside me dip as he joined me in the back. My heart jackhammered. I'd waited two long days to broach the subject of us. Now we were miles away from the scene of the crime and it finally felt safe enough.

"Are we ever going to talk about it?" I blurted out.

"You becoming a medical clown?" Ransom's thumbs hovered over his phone screen. He was aggressively punching in a text message. "Gladly. You're not gonna like what I have to say, though."

I stole a look at our driver, a friendly-looking, silver-haired man in his late sixties. He was tan and wrinkled. Umm Kulthum blared out of his radio, and he had pictures of his family dangling from the rearview mirror.

Not the prototype to sell a story to the tabs.

"I'm talking about us." I dropped my voice, just in case.

"Not familiar with that term." Ransom popped his knuckles.

I felt pathetic, pressing forward when he clearly didn't want to talk about it, but knew I'd be the loser if I didn't pursue him. Ransom treated sex as an outlet, as a game. His partners changed often. Me? I needed *him*. No one else could do for me. He was sexy, but also safe. He could guide me out of my androphobia.

"I'm talking about what happened two nights ago."

He put his phone down, studying me. His eyes asked me to drop it. I held his gaze, not letting go.

"Mistakes happen." He shrugged finally. "Look at my track record."

"That was no mistake. We couldn't stop."

"Precisely," he countered. "That is the definition of an accident."

We weaved through a long traffic jam, with at least twenty more minutes until we got home. He was stuck in this conversation, whether he liked it or not.

"I have a proposition." I licked my lips.

"The answer is no."

"You haven't even heard it."

"Don't need to." He picked up his phone again. I snatched it from his hand and tucked it into my front pocket.

He arched an eyebrow. "All right. You got my attention. What is it, Princess?"

"Two nights ago…it was the first time I've been with a man. And I felt good. Secure. I even…you know." I shifted in my seat. "*Climaxed.*"

"I know." He looked pained. Like he was suffering through the conversation. I bet he was. His sexual encounters never included any sort of pillow talk.

"This is a huge win for me."

"I'm happy for you. Truly." He stared at me, waiting for the punch line.

"We can continue doing this…discreetly, until your post is up," I suggested.

He was still. So still, for a second, I wondered if he'd turned into a pillar of salt.

"Are you out of your mind?" he asked finally. "That would be a gross violation of my contract, not to mention a stain on my already filthy conscience. You're the ward. You're under my protection. What kind of scumbag would take advantage of that?"

The driver jacked up the volume of the music, signaling that he had absolutely no interest in listening to this negotiation, and that we ought to keep it down.

"Don't flatter yourself, Random. If someone is going to be taking advantage of someone here, it'd be me of you."

"You're young, vulnerable, and we're trying to get your life back on track. You have a history you should face, not bury. I don't want to make things worse for you."

"I'm of legal age, sound mind, and want to have fun for a change," I insisted.

"You need to work through what happened to you. I'm not taking any chances."

"Telling me what I need and what I don't need is chauvinistic."

"Fine. I'll rephrase—you can be with other men. But not with me."

It scissored my gut. The way he didn't trust that I was okay. I smeared a calm smile over my face, beaming through the pain.

"Thought you said I needed to stay abstinent."

If you don't crave me, at least be possessive of me.

"Change of plans. You can sleep with whomever you want." He paused, frowning down at me. "Provided fuckface doesn't mind a little audience. I'm not letting you be alone with some random."

"No one's gonna want to do that."

"No?" He made a sad face. "Too bad."

Tears pinched at the back of my nose. He was being his special brand of asshole again. The message was clear—he didn't want anything to do with me sexually. A fling was off the table. Texas was a one-off. Who knew? Maybe he wasn't into me there, either. What if he just felt bad for me because of Craig? A pity fuck. His version of a friendly pat on the back.

Yeah. That's all it was. He didn't want me to fall apart at the wedding. To be unwell when his entire job was to keep me together. He was only ever *fixing* me, not fucking me, that night.

I wanted to be sick.

"Hand me my phone back?" He opened his palm, placing it between us.

I dropped the device into his hand, looking away.

I Siri-texted Keller on my way to the house.

SOS. Need mental TLC and friendly advice. See you at my place.

By the time the taxi pulled up to my front door, Keller's cherry red Ford Mustang Shelby was already there, blocking the garage door. Keller hopped out of the car just as I materialized from the cab, wearing a neck scarf, oversized glasses, and an ironic Hawaiian shirt.

"Darling! Back from the wilderness." He kissed the air next to both my cheeks. He slid his glasses down his nose and widened his eyes to what was happening behind my shoulder, AKA the bane of my existence exiting the taxi, then pulling our suitcases out of the trunk.

"My, my. I'll have him for breakfast, lunch, dinner, and snacks."

"Just be careful not to choke," I muttered, sliding my sunglasses up to rest on my head. "He's a health hazard."

"He looks like a vice." Keller smiled to himself, hugging my shoulder. "You wanna tell me you still haven't sampled him?"

"About that." I cleared my throat. "Let's head inside. We need to talk."

"And leave him with the suitcases?" A mischievous glint zinged in Keller's eyes.

I tossed a look behind my shoulder, then gave Keller a shrug.

He winced. "Ugh. I can already tell the energy between you two is *so* not good for my skin."

Keller and I walked into my house. I grabbed a couple La Croix cans and made my way up the stairs. I locked both of us in my room before Ransom could give me the third degree about screening people before they entered the house.

"Tell me everything." Keller clapped his hands together. "Starting from the rumors your sister was a bridezilla. The tabloids are having a field day after what was leaked from the pre-wedding photo shoot. Was she that bad?"

"No," I said, crossing my legs over my bed. "She was *worse*."

Keller gasped, flinging himself next to me. "She's giving me intense Aquarius vibes. Is she an Aquarius?"

"Naturally." She was an Aries, but it was basically the same thing.

I told him about Hera's deplorable behavior, omitting the part where the groom had assaulted me. I liked Keller a lot, but I didn't fully trust him. Not with my truth, anyway. Then I told Keller about my hookup with Ransom, again neglecting all the parts that left me feeling too exposed. I didn't tell him how much it had meant to me. Falling apart in someone else's arms. Just that it happened, and that Ransom was not game for a repeat.

"But he seemed into it the night he insisted on sharing a bedroom with you." Keller munched on the tip of a tortilla chip. "Right?"

"Right." I moved uncomfortably, taking a sip of my soda. He didn't have the full context of the situation, the way Ransom had also saved me from Craig's abusive hands, so he didn't get the whole picture. "But I think it was just a moment of weakness on his part. We were at my parents', and everything just…simmered."

"Once a weakness, always a weakness." Keller shook his head. "All he needs is a little push in the right direction. Who wouldn't want to do you? I mean, *I* would. You're super hot."

I smiled, reaching to squeeze his hand. "How are things at Main Squeeze?"

"Oh. Fine. You know. The holiday season is upon us, so I'm waiting for people to gain weight so they'll start their crash diets." He hopped off of my bed, sauntering to my window to light up his joint. "That's what I'm capitalizing on. Other people's misery. Making a living is such a tedious job, Hal, let me tell you."

I leaned back on my satin pillow, braiding a lock of my hair absentmindedly. "You can always take a break if it's too much."

"And who'd run Main Squeeze?" Keller perched his ass on the windowsill, pushing the rolled cigarette between his lips.

"I don't know, hire a manager?"

Keller smiled lovingly at me. "Oh, Hal-Pal, I do love you."

Maybe he did, but he also patronized me constantly, and I didn't know why. Keller couldn't possibly run an actual business by himself, right? That was a thing only grownups did.

"Hey, Hal." Keller frowned, looking out my window as he lit up his joint. In front of him sprawled the stunning view of the Hollywood Hills and my neighbors' Olympic pool. "There's a strange car sitting in the back of your neighbors' driveway."

"Strange how?" I yawned.

"Strange…like, there's a person in the passenger's seat taking photos of *me* through the window."

I jumped out of bed, charging toward the window. Shoving Keller aside, I saw a huge, black Escalade parked in front of my neighbors' garage. A man was sitting in the passenger seat, taking pictures of my window, his face hidden by the huge smartphone he was holding.

My nostrils flared.

"Can you see his license plate?" I tugged my phone out of my pocket, taking pictures of the guy, just in case. Where was Ransom? How did he not see this?

"Nope." Keller frowned, grabbing his phone. "Let me go to the spare bedroom and see if I can take a picture of it from a better angle."

"Thanks."

While Keller tried to get the license plate, I ran toward Ransom's room. He wasn't there. I heard the water running in the bathroom next to it. So this was why he hadn't seen that car. I pounded on the door, my lungs scorching with fear.

Who were these people?

What did they want?

Was this why Ransom didn't want us to go back to Los Angeles? But it made no sense. I'd never had anyone follow me before.

The bathroom door swung open. Ransom was standing there, condensation rolling off of his glistening, muscular chest and shoulders. He had a small towel wrapped around his waist.

"Sweet Jesus," I heard Keller groan behind my back. "The man is unreal."

"What is it?" Ransom demanded, ignoring Keller.

"There's a suspicious car parked right in front of my bedroom window. And some jackass inside it took pictures of me just now."

He shouldered past me without another word.

Flying down the stairs, nearly buck naked.

Chapter Eighteen

Ransom

I jumped into the stupid Hipmobile, hitting the accelerator and rounding Hallie's mansion. The plan was to block the assholes from leaving the neighbors' driveway. Too late. The perp was already flooring it down the street, careening toward the main gates. I followed them, naked, soap bubbles still sliding down my wet skin.

The Russians showed up as soon as Hallie and I hit California ground, making their intentions clear. They hadn't forgotten about me, what I did, or where I was.

I was hedging my bets on the front gate being closed. I'd hopefully be able to corner them, beat the crap out of them, and find out where Kozlov was. I wanted to get real nice and personal with him and settle our beef once and for all.

The Escalade zinged past the manicured lawns and excessive Spanish Villas, careening downhill before the gate came into view. Unfortunately, it was wide open. Some YouTube star who lived in the neighborhood snailed his way inside in his H1 Hummer.

The Russians laced through the open wrought iron gate and out of the neighborhood. Still on their heels, I slammed my bare foot over the accelerator.

I flicked my phone and called Max.

"Boss?" he answered immediately.

"You need to get to Hallie's house right now and keep an eye on her."

"What's happening? Is she okay?" He sounded worried, and that made me feel...no, fuck that. It didn't make me feel. Because I didn't *feel*. But I wondered why the hell he cared about a woman who used him to get to me.

"She's fine. Someone followed us home from the airport and I'm chasing their asses down. I don't want her alone."

I didn't want her with *him*, either. But life was about compromise.

"Who could it be? Didn't we run a background check on her before starting the post?"

Well, Max, this actually has nothing to do with her and everything to do with me, not that you're paid to butt into my shit.

"Not sure yet," I said through gritted teeth.

"I'll be there in fifteen minutes."

"*Armed.*"

"Of course!" Max said. "I—"

I killed the call. My eyes were still zeroed in on the Escalade. The license plate was covered in reflective tape, probably to shake off speed cameras. I could make out some of the numbers, but not all of them.

The two-way road from Hallie's neighborhood snaked along a mountain. The entire right-hand side was a cliff, bracketed by a low guardrail. The Escalade zigzagged dangerously between the two lanes, trying to throw me off. No cars came from the opposite direction. But when one did appear from the side of the mountain, I floored it and got as close to the Escalade as I could, nearly kissing its bumper. They were trying to lose me. Well, motherfuckers worked really hard to get to me, the least I could do was grace them with my presence.

The driver swirled to the opposite lane again, trying to make the driver of a passing Prius divert their car into my lane and collide with the Nissan.

The Prius grazed me on the left side and I felt the car almost tipping onto the guardrail. I broke left, trying not to lose the Escalade, which was picking up speed, capitalizing on the fact I needed to regain my balance.

The Prius pulled to the right uphill. I could tell the driver was shaken, but uninjured.

The Escalade and I were heading to a multi-lane intersection forking north, south, and east. The Escalade shot through traffic, slipping in and out of the lanes. People honked. Some pulled to the side, not taking any chances. Ten seconds later, the light turned green and the intersection flooded in a river of cars coming from all directions. The Escalade disappeared between them.

"*Fuck*." I punched the car horn, producing a deafening sound.

It was done. I couldn't find them. 1-0 to the home team. This was my cue to tell Tom he was right. The Russians were in the picture. I should bow out and let someone else take care of the Thorne Princess. It was the right thing to do. Shit, it was the *smart* thing to do. And all my excuses for staying were dumb at best and pathetic at worst.

I needed to think.

Lurching the Nissan LEAF into reverse, I made an illegal U-turn and darted back to Hallie's neighborhood. By the time I arrived, Max was already there. He sat with Hallie and Keller in the kitchen.

It looked like they were having some sort of vegan DoorDash feast. Keller was in the middle of telling them about his non-conflict, organic, sustainable Brazilian farm where he sourced most of the fruits and vegetables for his juices. It sounded like the least cost-efficient business plan I'd ever heard of.

Max just kept muttering, "Wow," while sipping on his green smoothie.

"Can I just say," Keller lifted his head from his green bowl, his gaze zeroing in on my crotch, "you look delectable in your birthday suit."

I looked down. The towel was still wrapped around my waist,

but my cock was swinging about under it, like a limp third leg. I glanced at Hallie coolly to see if she shared his fascination. She busied herself trying to spear a cherry tomato onto her fork.

"I'm going to head out for a few hours." I directed this at Max, the only person in the room who didn't want to ride my cock.

Max nodded. "Let me know if you need me to stay overnight."

A part of me longed to put him in way of temptation. If he fucked her, I could fire him, could bail on this post, and go back to my ordinary life.

"I'll let you know."

I went upstairs and dressed in a pair of dark cigar pants, leather sneakers, and a black tee. I grabbed my wallet and phone and made my way downstairs.

I opted for Hallie's BMW Hydrogen 7. The Nissan LEAF was banged up due to my brush with the Russians.

I drove down to the nearest bar. A black-bricked low building with a pink neon sign stared back at me. *Cocks and Tails*. Los Angeles was not known for its subtlety. I wanted to be found by Kozlov. Wanted them to corner me.

Pushing the wooden, round-topped door, I shoved past a mass of sweaty, half-naked people dancing to the tune of a truly horrible remix of "In a Manner of Speaking" by Nouvelle Vague. I was about to turn around and head out—this was a mistake, I didn't need a beer, I needed to make shit right—when I noticed a smaller, separate room for bar-goers. I waltzed inside. The space was dark, gloomy, with high stools and soft erotic paintings. The array of people at the bar sat either in couples or alone, squinting at their smartphones to see where their Tinder date was.

What the hell. One drink wouldn't hurt.

I slid onto a stool and rapped the bar.

"Jameson, neat."

"Coming right up," a barkeep with a blunt haircut and facial piercings squeaked.

As if on cue, a woman of the *Desperate Housewives* variety—tall, leggy, blonde, with enough makeup to paint a house, slipped onto the seat next to me. She wore a hot pink blazer, matching shorts, and white kitten heels.

"According to the women's magazine I read today as I waited for my dentist appointment, men who order Jameson know what they're doing." She signaled the bartender with her hand.

"White Russian for me." Then, turning toward me, the woman—twenty-nine? Thirty?—grinned seductively. "What does my drink order say about me?"

"That you've never worked in a bar before, so you are under the misguided assumption the milk in the fridge hasn't expired," I deadpanned.

She let loose a throaty laugh, caressing her throat. "Maybe I'm optimistic."

"Isn't optimistic the PC word for delusional?" What the hell was wrong with me? Did I want to bed this woman, or get kneed in the balls by her?

She laughed again, undeterred. "I like a guy who is quick-witted."

"And I like to work for my sexual conquests. Care to at least pretend to make it hard for me?"

I could practically envision Hallie giving me her *holy shitballs, you're tragic* face.

The bartender returned with both our drinks. I noticed the leggy blonde sniffing her black-on-white cocktail before taking a sip. I glanced around me, hoping to see suspicious people who might look like they'd followed me. This time, I *wanted* to be caught.

"Sorry to disappoint, but I think the milk is in its prime." She shot me a sidelong smirk. "And for the record, so am I."

I offered her a curt nod. It was becoming extremely difficult to repel her. Maybe I was better off just fucking her and telling Hallie. One of us needed to screw up to stop our oversight from happening again. And I could always count on myself to let people down.

"Are you always this forward?" I asked.

"Only when I want something real bad."

Smirking, I said, "That can't be a total stranger you just met at the bar. So why don't you tell me why you're here?"

"Damn. Maybe you're as good as they say you are." The woman pivoted on her stool, angling her entire body toward me. "Let's cut to the chase."

Glancing down to her impractical heels, I *tsked*. "If you want to continue being at a point of disadvantage."

"I know who you are." She placed her hand between us on the bar.

Was she working for Kozlov? Or was she FBI? She looked too refined for the former and too dumb for the latter.

"You do?" I took a sip of my drink. "Enlighten me, then."

"You're Ransom Lockwood of Lockwood and Whitfield Protection Group. A security company based in Chicago. You currently work with Hallie Thorne, daughter of President Anthony Thorne. And you're an impossible man to hire, which makes me wonder if there's an interesting backstory behind why you chose to protect the First Daughter." She raised her glass in a toast, downing it in its entirety.

I motioned for the barkeep to get her a refill.

Expressionless, I turned back to her, not confirming nor denying her words. "Where are you going with this?"

"Where do you want me to go with it?" she purred.

Far the fuck away from me.

I just came here to get cornered by the Bratva, lady.

I shrugged. "You're the one who's here with an agenda and my unauthorized Wikipedia page."

"What did you come here for?" She rested her chin on top of her knuckles.

"A quick fuck," I was half-lying, half warming up to the idea.

I needed to get Hallie out of my system, out of my head, out of my life. This woman seemed like an unlikely candidate, now that she knew who I was. No matter. Plenty more fishnet stockings in the sea.

"What if you could get out of here with a satisfying fuck *and* five hundred thousand dollars richer?" She played with the edge of her blazer, exposing slivers of her skin. Of her boring, smooth, unmarked body.

Stop thinking about Hallie. She is not an option.

The bartender reappeared with the second White Russian for the woman, while I still nursed my first Jameson.

"I'd say you are full of bullshit," I stated.

"Well, that's because you're a skeptic. But I'm about to change that." She offered me her hand. "I'm Anna."

I stood up, plucking out my wallet and throwing a wad of cash onto the bar. "And I'm out of here."

"Wait!" She reached for the hem of my shirt, balling it. "Don't you want to hear my offer?"

"For sex and half a mill?" I arched an eyebrow. "It's either a pyramid scheme or a job. I'm not interested in either."

"As I said, you're a skeptic, and I'm about to change that." She smoothed a hand over my torso. "Sit down."

I did, but only because the thought of going back to Hallie's place and watching her ignore me was strangely unbearable.

"You have three minutes," I announced.

"I don't think so. Finish your drink and get another one. I want us to be on an even field when we have this conversation." She gestured with her chin to my Jameson.

"You're not in a position to negotiate," I reminded her.

"Sure I am." She raised my glass, putting it to my lips. "I offer money, sex, and power. The most sought-after things in the universe. Now, bottoms up."

Taking another sip, I studied her again. She was good-looking, in an obvious L.A. way. Inflated breasts, lips, and not a wrinkle to be found. She'd probably be good in bed. Women of her range had read all the books and owned the award-winning sex toys.

"What do you want?" I asked bluntly.

"Hallie 'Hallion' Thorne's head on a platter." She licked her lips, her eyes boring into mine with manic intensity. "I want to know everything about President Thorne's wild child. All the dirty deets.

The interesting secrets. Why she's alone here? Why she dropped out of college? What it's like in her big, lonely mansion?"

I thought about Hallie's dyslexia. Sexual abuse. Fucked-up family life and insecurities. The Thornes were hiding so much. Instead of giving her the support she needed, in case of making her an advocate, lifting her up to the position she deserved, they tucked her away, then were surprised when she became bitter and uncooperative.

"Who do you work for?" I asked.

"*Yellow Vault*."

Yellow Vault was one of the worst tabloids out there. Their headlines rarely had anything to do with reality. Whenever I passed by a stack of the wasted paper in a bodega or kiosk while grabbing a coffee, I wondered who was soulless and corrupt enough to come up with these headlines.

PRINCE FREDERIK'S SEX DWARF EATEN BY GIRAFFE.

THE POPE'S DEADLY PARTY BINGE.

PREGNANT BY THE SAME MAN! CAN THESE TWO ACTRESSES SURVIVE THE SHAME?

"Let me get this straight." I leaned against the bar. "You think I'll break my NDA and ruin my good name for a chance to earn ten percent of my annual salary and the opportunity to tit-fuck a pair of plastic jugs?"

Anna pushed my fresh drink toward me along the bar, her face impassive. "I think you're interested. I've made it this far with you, haven't I? Drink up."

Amused that she thought such an obvious ploy could work on me, I smirked. "If I have another drink, so should you."

"Deal." She ordered shots. "And back to our conversation—I don't know why you're contemplating taking my offer, but I can tell you are. Might not be the money. And the sex is definitely just a small perk. But whatever's making you want to go for it—listen to that voice. You're nothing in the Thorne operation. Just another service provider. And this article will be risk-free, I guarantee. You'll be an anonymous source. I can sign whatever your lawyer sends my way."

If Hallie found out I'd sold her secrets, I wouldn't have to keep away. She'd make sure she had nothing to do with me all on her own. The idea wasn't completely bad.

Anna and I downed more shots.

She put her hand on my shoulder, letting out a little excited gasp. "Wow. Someone's been working out."

"There are rules if you want to have sex," I said, ignoring her observation. "Non-negotiable, just like my terms for this deal."

"Let's hear 'em out."

She waved to the bartender, ordering more shots.

That's when I realized I knew Anna.

Up close and personal.

And that she recognized me, too.

Three hours later, I tripped out of a taxi, stumbling my way to Hallie's front door. I couldn't take the car. I couldn't even *walk* to the car. What I could do was recognize I'd made a terrible mistake, and that I was going to regret it.

After two unsuccessful attempts to punch the security code at the door later, the massive piece of wood swung open on its own accord. Max stood on the other side, looking sleepy, still in his day clothes.

What time was it? I glanced down at my watch. Four in the morning. Great.

"Everything okay, boss?" Max asked, stepping sideways to allow me entrance. I zigzagged to the kitchen, the room around me spinning. I didn't drink much. At least, not *that* much. Which led me to believe the ever-resourceful Anna had spiked one of my shots after she'd realized I recognized her, probably while I was busy checking my phone for texts from a certain Hallion.

I pulled a cabinet open, took out a glass, and poured myself tap water, gulping it in one go.

"Fine. Get the fuck out of here."

"You sure?" Max shifted in his spot, barefoot. "You don't look like…hmm…"

"Like what?" I demanded.

"Like you're in a state to protect someone else."

"Well, I am. And you're no longer needed. Get out."

"Ransom—"

"*Out!*"

He moved around the house silently. He took his bag and put his jacket on. On his way out the door, he rapped the doorframe, letting out a sigh. "I'll be around if you need me."

"Around where? A park bench?" I spat out.

He shook his head and exited the house.

I dragged myself up the stairs, pushing through not to stop by her door. I got into the bathroom, brushed my teeth, got out of my whiskey-soaked shirt, and walked out.

I needed to at least check on her to make sure she was alive. Or that's what I told myself. It was my professional duty, if nothing else.

I strolled over to her door and pushed it lightly. The silhouette of her back rising and falling was breathtaking. She wore a crème, sleeveless shirt, her ruby hair pooling over her pillow.

I was weak.

So weak.

Weak when I stepped into her room, shutting the door behind me quietly.

Weak when I told myself that it was better to sleep with her, just in case.

Weak when I slipped into her bed.

Weak when I circled my arms around her and tried to pretend tonight had never happened.

She stirred inside my arms, kicking the blanket off. She smelled of vanilla and fruity smoothies and like a broken princess, and I couldn't take it anymore. The perfect combination of sweet and tragic.

Pressing my nose against the back of her neck, I told myself that it was okay. I'd been drugged. I was allowed a misstep.

My lips found the hollow part between her neck and shoulder. I sucked on it softly. She let out a soft moan.

"Should I stop?" I croaked, my tongue moving along her salty skin.

"Not yet," she breathed out, flipping from her side to her back. I caught her mouth with mine, kissing her slow and deep, awakening her as softly as I could. My cock was throbbing in my cigar pants.

My lips dragged along her skin, drinking her in, while my fingers fumbled with her boy shorts. I loved that she didn't wear sexy, skimpy clothes to bed. That she didn't try to impress.

I dipped my index finger into her. She was soaking wet and warm, so warm. My free hand went to unbuckle myself. She reached for my palm, stopping me mid-move.

"Not so fast."

Pulling away, I stared down at her, searching her eyes in the dark. I was panting like a chased animal and hoped she didn't smell the alcohol on my breath, or the woman's perfume clinging to my clothes.

You're a bastard for doing this to her. Especially now. Especially after all this.

"Tell me how it works, then," I whispered.

She placed her hand over my heart. It was beating like crazy. I hated that she had this effect on me. Hated that she knew it, too.

"Eat me out, and then maybe—*maybe*—I'll fuck you."

She had the audacity to yawn in my face, smiling sleepily up at me afterwards, as if to say, *Whatcha gonna do about that, cowboy?*

I'd never gone down on a woman before. I knew a true take-it-or-leave-it offer when I saw one. Hallie would kick me out if I wouldn't do as she wished.

I reached down, biting her chin softly. "Anyone ever told you you're a brat?"

"Yes, and often." She pushed my head down her body, spreading her legs, her shorts still intact. I tugged the fabric between her legs to one side, licking my lips. My cock was so engorged I wondered if I had blood circulation coming to my brain at all. Leaning down, I kissed her slit. The warmth of my lips found the heat of her center. She moaned, surprising me again by peering between her legs curiously, watching me.

I started French-kissing her pussy. Dragging my tongue in and out of her. She tasted good. Earthy and sweet. My new favorite dessert.

Pushing her wider using my fingers, I dug deeper with my tongue. Her hand found my hair. She pulled at it, tilting my face up to watch her.

Fuck, she was hot when she was being a controlling bitch.

"Suck my clit," she demanded.

"Ask nicely."

"Suck my clit, or I'm kicking you out." She awarded me with a winning smile in the dark.

I needed no further instructions and dug right in, sucking on the small bud while finger-fucking her. As much as I enjoyed it—and I did enjoy it—I waited for the moment she'd come, pull me up, and let me in. I needed to be inside her. To erase the day from my memory. But I also recognized what she was doing here. Taking control. Just the way I did when I played my little fantasy games.

"More fingers." She flung one of her legs over my shoulder.

I complied.

"I'm coming."

"Yes," I breathed, picking up the pace. "Shit, yes."

She fell apart, her muscles clenching around my fingers. A rush of warmth traveled through her. She shuddered violently, and I wondered what brand of stupid idiot I was to think only women enjoyed giving oral sex. This was officially the best thing since sliced bread.

I pulled away, quickly unbuckling my belt.

With the room around me still spinning, I felt the tip of Hallie's leg as she pushed me off the mattress, her foot pressed against my chest. I lost my balance and fell flat on my ass at the foot of her bed.

"What the hell?" I inquired from my new position on the floor.

"The hell, is you've been an asshole to me all day. A mistake, my ass, Random. We're going to have sex on the reg. Now that you've given me what I wanted, I'm ready to go back to sleep. Make sure you close the door on your way out."

She offered me another yawn, turning around to her original position, on her side, hair flung against her pillow.

Chapter Nineteen

Hallie

The weeks after Ransom stumbled into my room in the middle of the night smelling like a low-end brothel passed in fake domestic bliss.

Max was MIA, due to Ransom never leaving my side. Day and night, he followed me everywhere. To my stupid Hollywood premieres, tacky friends' birthday bashes, and even to my Pilates and smoothie dates with Keller.

The day after he ate me out, I slept late, went down to the kitchen in my sunglasses, and demanded he give my credit card back.

"You want in my bed, you'll need to give me equal rights."

To my surprise, he didn't argue. He didn't try to sleep with me again, either.

…until three days later, when I dragged him with me to a secondhand shop and tried on a fabulous Balenciaga mini dress.

"Random, could you help me zip it up?" I purred from the changing room.

He joined me inside, slipping the zipper up my back silently. I turned toward him, smirking. "How do I look?"

"Good enough to eat," he said dejectedly, turning around, about to leave.

"Then do."

He pinned me to the floor-to-ceiling mirror and fucked me mercilessly, playing out our fantasies while I tried to kick him off, our moans muffled by the hot, dirty kiss we shared the entire time, until he came inside me.

That had been one of the many times we had sex. Each time he had sex with me, he hated himself for it, and I knew it. It didn't sit well with me. But I couldn't help it. I became so addicted to him, I couldn't stop.

One day, we took the car and drove out to Runyon Canyon, and he ended up bending me over the trunk of the car and taking me from behind.

Another time, he snuck into my room in the middle of the night.

I couldn't decide if he felt guilty for doing something unprofessional, doing it with a twenty-one-year-old, or because my background made him wonder if I was somehow punishing myself by sleeping with him.

Either way, I was enjoying not only his body, but also his attention.

Ransom protected me fiercely. Much more than before. Sometimes—oftentimes, actually—I wondered if there was more to his behavior. Why he flung himself in front of me whenever someone rushed toward me to ask for a photograph or an autograph. Why he now patrolled the house three times before he went to bed every night. Why he insisted on armoring my car. But Ransom didn't give me anything. Even when I tried to pry information about who those people were who'd taken pictures of me the other day with Keller.

"You've nothing to worry about," he'd evaded the question. "As long as I'm here, they won't get to you."

"And after you're gone?"

"They won't bother you. Trust me."

That wasn't a satisfying explanation to say the least, but it was all I had to work with.

My parents still tried to call and arrange for me to come home. I rarely picked up, and when I did, I told them I was busy trying to find an interesting college program. It wasn't a lie. Not entirely. I had looked into programs, but mainly for sketching and painting.

Hera and Craig went on their two-week honeymoon to Montenegro. Neither of them tried to contact me, and I fooled myself into believing I could probably avoid them for a few more years.

All I had to do was make sure that next time we were in the same zip code, I had a bodyguard with me. Just in case Craig sought revenge.

Ransom stopped bothering me about what I wanted to do with my life. Or at least, he stopped pestering me about it. He still brought the subject up, but never pressed.

The only issue that *did* give us a constant reason to argue was him asking me again and again to see a therapist about what happened with Craig, and the dyslexia.

Each conversation went the same way.

"Do *you* have a therapist, Random?"

"No."

"Why's that?"

"I'm beyond repair."

"And I could be easily mended?"

"You show promise. Potential. A *soul*. Things I don't possess."

"I'll go to therapy if you go to therapy."

This was the part he'd usually give me an *are-you-insane?* look. The part where I smiled back in triumph. "There you have it."

Life was good. Suspiciously good, actually. I should have known it would come to an end. Specifically, in the form of my family.

Three weeks after Ransom and I got back from Texas, I woke up to a string of text messages from Keller.

Keller: <<<Link>>> *The Thornes Like You've Never Seen Them Before! Anthony, Julianne, Hera, and Craig discuss Love, Marriage, and Loyalty!*

Keller: <<<Voice>>> **Pass the puke bucket. Hera is trying SO hard. And she looks terrible in this shoot!**

Keller: <<<Voice>>> **Why aren't you there, by the way? Looks like a whole family ordeal.**

I clicked on the link, my heart jackhammering in my chest. Ransom lay beside me, snoring softly. He didn't always sleep in my bed, but recently, he'd done it more and more.

I saw an array of photos of my parents, Hera and Craig standing in my parents' vast garden. Dogs included. Everybody smiling into the camera. One big, happy family.

Punching Ransom in the arm, I shoved my phone in his face. I couldn't read fast enough—if at all—in my current state.

He stirred awake, not looking to be in any particular hurry to know why I'd assaulted him. He leaned back against the bedframe, plucking the phone from between my fingers.

"Jesus Christ, Craig's isn't the first face I want to see when I wake up," he mumbled, digging the base of his palm into his eye socket.

"Read it," I ordered, folding my arms over my chest.

He shot me an unsure look. "What the hell for?"

"I'm going to have a shitty day either way. At least let me know why I'm bummed."

With a sigh, he began reading.

"*...Julianne, 55, cannot stop gushing about the new addition to the family. 'Craig's everything we've ever wanted in a son. He is loyal, loving, steadfast, and puts his family above all else. Watching him grow alongside Hera into this courageous, virtuous man has been very inspiring.'*"

"*While Anthony, 60, insists: 'Everything Hera has ever achieved was on her own merit. She is the most hardworking, compassionate,*" *loving human being I've ever met. Fathering her has been by far my favorite, most honorable role.'"*

"...President Thorne insists that, despite his daughter Hallie not being present for the shoot or the interview, things have never been better. 'The truth is, there will always be rumors, but that's just what they are. Rumors. Hallie adores her new brother-in-law and has never been closer to Hera. They're truly two peas in a pod.'"

"This, on the heels of Miss Thorne delivering a less than favorable speech in her duty as maid of honor, makes people wonder..."

"Stop!" I ripped my phone from his hand, flinging it across the floor. It skidded until it hit the wall. I jumped out of the bed, pacing back and forth, feeling sick to my stomach. "This is such undiluted horse crap."

Ransom stayed in my bed, eyeing me through calculating eyes. No matter how many times we'd had sex, how many nights we shared, every time I saw myself through his eyes, I shuddered. He treated me clinically. Like his unfinished, messy job.

"You're upset."

"No shit I'm upset!" I flung my arms in the air. "I'm officially no longer a member of the Thorne family, according to this article."

"Does it bother you?" he asked.

"No!"

"Yes, it does. I suggest you do something about it." He reached for the nightstand, unhooking his phone from its charger.

"And give them the satisfaction of knowing I've read it?" I let out a huff.

His eyes were dead on his screen as he scrolled. "The entire world has read it. It's on every media outlet out there. Even videos, pictures, and snippets on the news."

This wasn't just spitting in my face. It was throwing an entire bucket of saliva.

I stopped pacing, turning to him. "What do you think I should do?"

"Get on a goddamn plane and give them a piece of your mind.

Confront them. About everything. Craig. Your undiagnosed dyslexia. Their poor treatment of you," he said, straight-faced.

I faltered. "But what if—"

"Every worst-case scenario has already happened," he cut me off, flinging the blanket and collecting his phone, wallet, and gun, which was always within reach. "They made this asshole your brother-in-law, they deprived you of context, opportunity, and better life conditions. They treat you like a second-class citizen. I fail to see how this could get any harder for you, Princess."

He was right, and I knew it. More than that, I felt ready for a showdown with my family. I didn't know what it was. Maybe the constant realizations with which I'd been bombarded. My learning disabilities. My newfound talent at sketching. Overcoming my aversion to sex. And, yes, maybe even coming to terms with the fact I didn't have any real friends, any real family, and despite all that, I'd still managed to survive.

I nodded curtly. "Pack up, Random. We're going to Texas."

Other than almost slapping Ransom when he inquired whether I wanted to channel my wrath into angry, exploratory hate sex, the plane ride to Dallas went without a hitch. A car was waiting for us at the airport. We didn't have any luggage.

Throughout the car ride, I could tell Ransom was relieved we weren't in Los Angeles. His shoulders were lax, and his jaw wasn't tense for the first time in weeks.

I didn't have time or the desire to ask him about it. I was solely focused on ripping my family a new one. The audacity of these people killed me.

As soon as the car pulled up to my parents' gate, I stormed out, Ransom following closely behind me.

"Excuse me, Miss Thorne, but I don't believe your parents are expect—" Daphne in the eternal business casual blazer confronted me when I got to their door. I shouldered past her, going straight up the stairs to my father's office. What was she going to do, arrest me for visiting my family? Nah. Doing so would create horrible headlines for the precious Thorne family.

I took the stairs two at a time, whirling past housekeepers and administrative staff. When I reached Dad's double doors, I didn't bother knocking. I swanned right inside.

Dad was sitting in his office with a few suited men in their forties and fifties. One of them I recognized as Wolfe Keaton, a dashing Chicago-based senator. By the air of self-importance and cigar stench in the room, I could tell the rest were also politicians. *Good*. This deserved an audience.

He looked up, his eyes flaring in shock at the sight of me. Pushing himself back in his seat, I held up a hand to stop him.

"No. Don't stand. That'd give you an advantage over me when I run after I finish my speech."

I had no doubt at all he'd want to wring my neck once I was done with him.

"What's going on, Sugar Pie?" he asked, still sprawled in his chair. He couldn't afford to look flustered.

"Such a great question." I leaned a shoulder over the door, sighing. "What *is* wrong? I guess a better question would be what is *right* in my life. And the answer is—not a whole bunch. I have you to thank for that."

The three men in the room exchanged looks. They knew they shouldn't be present for this type of conversation. Mr. Keaton stood up, buttoning his suit blazer.

"Well, Tony, it's been a pleasure, as always…"

"Do stay." I pushed off the doorframe, striding deeper into the room. "I think you'll get a nice, intimate glimpse into your good friend's family life."

"Hallie." Dad frowned, tucking his cigar into an ashtray. "I don't like the theatrics. Say what you came here to say."

"I saw the article." I was in front of his desk now. I slammed the glossy, high-brow magazine onto the desk. I thought buying it at the airport was a nice touch. "Really moving, this picture of familial bliss."

"Hey." He darted up to his feet. "We called you countless times. We tried to get you to join us. You were unreachable."

"And you couldn't get through to me via my ever-present body-guard, whom you appointed to shadow me despite my objections?"

"We were worried for your safety. You were out and about, not being careful…" He shook his head, as if ridding himself of this horrific image.

"Oh, yeah." I rolled my eyes, plucking his cigar from the ash-tray and pushing it into my mouth. I hated the taste. Still, I puffed on it, just for effect. "Nothing says *I worry about my daughter* more than hiding her learning disabilities from her!" I pounded my open palm against his desk. He didn't wince. No. Dad was made of sturdier stuff. We held each other's gazes. Suddenly, I didn't give one damn if he cut my finances off. It was worth it. Getting answers was worth it.

"As much as we appreciate the show—and I do have a soft spot for theatrics—we should be going." Keaton gave a careless toss of his wrist. "Gentlemen, follow me. Tony, best of luck with…*this*."

They walked out, passing by Ransom, who stayed at the door. My attention was solely on Dad.

"Hallie…" He winced.

"Why didn't you tell me I was dyslexic?" I hissed. "That was neglectful, careless, and above all—cruel. I thought I was simple. Stupid. Disposable. You locked me in a golden cage and kept me a secret from the world."

"Oh, Sugar Pie…" He shook his head, at a loss for words. I had him on that, and he knew it.

"Don't *Sugar Pie* me. You did everything in your power to hide my so-called 'secret'. Even at the price of making me feel like a complete idiot. Then you froze me out of the family—"

"Now, that didn't happen!" he thundered. "*You* were the one who pulled back. You were the one who kept on wanting to go out of state for school. You were the one who made up reasons not to join us for holidays and vacations. You did everything you could to show us that you were unhappy with us. That we did a terrible job with you."

"You did." I went over to the window and flicked the cigar out onto Mom's precious rosebushes. It felt good to inflict a little destruction on the people I felt so bitter and angry toward.

"We wanted to protect you." My father rushed behind me, trying to clasp my shoulders. I shrugged him off. "Believe it or not, it wasn't to hurt you. We *love* you. We wanted to spare you the headache. And we thought that we could. With our connections and our pull. The world was at our feet and we thought we could shield you from all the things wrong with it. We didn't want you to carry the stigma. Didn't want you to be singled out. So we downplayed it."

"There's no shame in dyslexia." I twisted around, facing him. "You took an innocent learning disability and made it into a liability. You *broke* me."

He closed his eyes, taking a deep breath. I could tell he was devastated—my father never showed signs of emotion, and this, for him, was a lot. I relished his pain.

"Hallie—"

"Admit it," I cut him off. "I'm invisible. I'm not in this house, not in these rooms, not in your soul, in your *veins*. You try, but I can see your heart's not in it. Know how I know?"

He blinked, staring at me, bracing himself for the blow. I smiled.

"I know because you refused to read the writing on the wall."

"How do you mean?" The wariness in his expression told me he knew a blow was coming his way.

"Craig," I choked out his name, taking a step back from Dad. "Craig has been sexually abusing me. For years."

The world spun out of focus as my father, for the first time since I was born, broke down in tears. He turned around, giving me his back to ensure I couldn't see them. Pressed his face to the wall, his shoulders quaking uncontrollably.

"No," I heard a gasp coming from the door. "No, no, no."

Mom stood there, in her cashmere suit, her fingers fluttering over her lips. She stared at me, awe-struck. "Hallie, tell me this is not true."

For some reason, I never thought they'd believe me if I came forward. Never thought they would take me seriously. I guess they didn't think I was as much of an airhead as they'd made me peg myself to be.

"I'm not telling you anything." Coldly, I gave her my back, picking one of the random whiskey glasses on the desk and tossing it down. "You're hardly my mother. Save for giving birth to me, you've been pretty absent from my life."

"Of course, I'm your mother!" Mom choked out. "Tony, do something."

Through the reflection of the spotless window, I could see her collapsing onto the floor, bracing herself by one of the walls.

"If this is true…" Dad stalked toward me, his face red and angry. "If he really hurt you—"

"Oh God, Dad, not this." I plopped down on his chair, crossing my ankles on his desk. "The *if* part is so unnecessary and insulting. Especially since, as I recall, you ran for re-election on the promise of not silencing women, their experiences, or their struggles."

"I'm not doubting you." He went down on one knee, trying to catch my gaze unsuccessfully. "I'm trying to understand…trying to digest what's happening here…"

"Don't bother." I waved him off. "No words can suffice for what I've been through. The experience is awash in shame, pain, and regret. You were right to do the article without me. I'm really not a part of this family anymore. Mr. Lockwood?" I called out, glancing at the door.

Ransom appeared like a demon summoned, hands behind his back.

"Miss Thorne?"

"Our next stop is my sister's apartment in downtown Dallas. Could you ensure the car's ready?"

"Absolutely," he said readily, the glint in his eyes telling me he was proud.

Then it happened. Out of all the moments, of all the days, of all the times we'd spent together.

Like a punch to the gut came the awful, tragic realization that I was in love with Ransom Lockwood.

Orphaned. Soulless. Heartless. And broken to a fault.

In love with his good parts as well as the bad ones. The ugly parts and those so beautiful it made it impossible for me to think about him and breathe at the same time.

I was in love with how he made me feel, with whom he made me become. Once he left, he was going to take my heart with him, and I could do nothing about it.

In a daze, I stood, making my way to the door. My parents tried to stop me. My mother flung herself in front of the door, crying desperately for me to stay. I sidestepped her, feeling at ease about what had happened with my parents and completely pan-icked about being in love with Ransom.

"We're making a stop at a police station first."

Ransom delivered the news with the quiet finality of a man who knew he would not be met with resistance. No turning back from this one. My actions at my parents' house couldn't be undone. I didn't *want* them to be undone. Craig had committed atrocious acts against me, and he deserved to pay for it.

"It's going to be embarrassing." I nibbled on my thumbnail, looking out the window.

"It's going to be empowering," Ransom retorted.

A thought occurred to me. One I must've shoved to the back of my mind while confronting my parents, who, by the way, were blowing up my phone and going straight to voicemail.

Turning sharply to my bodyguard, I said, "They can terminate your contract at any time. I basically spat in their faces and told them, not in so many words, that their assistance and financial support is unappreciated."

I couldn't imagine how I'd manage to survive without my parents' help, but I knew it was time to remove myself from under their wing.

"They can't." Ransom punched something into his phone.

"How do you know?"

"I write my own contracts. No exit clause."

"They might fire you just to spite me and keep you on their payroll."

"You think very lowly of your family." His eyes shifted from his screen, scanning me intently. "Besides," he smiled, "they still think you hate me, remember? No way they'll let you be rid of me now."

Disappointment crashed into me, and I realized foolishly that I'd expected him to tell me he'd stay, even if they fired him.

The car slowed to a stop by a curb. Ransom tucked his phone into his pocket. "We're here."

Filing a complaint against Craig was relatively painless, everything considered. I recited the incidents coldly, in what almost felt like an out-of-body experience.

The two officers who took my statement allowed Ransom to be in the room, and asked their questions gently, giving me time to sort out the thoughts in my head.

When I walked out of the police station an hour later, I had fifteen missed calls from Mom, twenty from Dad, and dozens of unread messages.

Ransom and I slipped into the car. I rubbed at my temples, feeling the beginning of a headache. "I don't even know where my sister lives."

She'd never invited me over, never made the faintest effort to get to know me.

"I have it," Ransom said.

"I wonder what life is going to be like after you," I blurted out. "After you're gone."

He flashed me a smile. "Same as before, but with a lot more googling."

Hera and Craig lived in an aquarium-like skyscraper downtown. All azure glass and high ceilings. The type with twenty-four-hour concierge, gym, spa, gourmet restaurant, and business center. Before we got there, Ransom asked the driver to stop by a small flower shop and purchased a big bouquet.

I stared at him, puzzled. "Looking to make a move, now that she'll most likely be single?" I arched an eyebrow.

The only reason I believed Hera would be single was because there was no way she'd put up with the embarrassment of standing by Craig's side if this went to trial.

"You know me too well," Ransom said flatly.

When we entered Hera and Craig's building, Ransom's game became clear to me. He approached the uniformed concierge, holding the bouquet.

"Hello, I'm Ransom Lockwood, and this is Miss Hallie Thorne, Hera Thorne's sister. We're here on a social call, but would like to keep it a surprise from the newlywed couple."

The man, in his mid-fifties, eyed the flowers with a smile. "Of course. Unfortunately, it goes against our policy. What apartment shall I ring?"

"Six-two-four," Ransom said easily. "But preferably, you'd let us pass. See, we've arranged a surprise for the couple. I'm sure they'd appreciate the full impact of it if we arrive unannounced."

The man looked torn. On one hand, there was a protocol. On the other, Ransom was incredibly convincing, and the flowers were gorgeous.

Finally, he groaned, "All right."

And so we slipped into the elevator to the sixth floor, heading toward Hera and Craig's apartment.

"A surprise, huh?" I stared up at the mirrored ceiling of the elevator.

"No lies there," Ransom muttered.

"What if Craig tries to attack me?" I sucked in a quick breath.

"Then he'll meet his premature and extremely painful death in my hands."

The elevator slid open. We both walked out.

My legs were shaking, my palms sweaty, but astonishingly, no part of me wanted to turn around and run away. I wanted to see this through.

When I reached Hera and Craig's door, I raised my fist and rapped four times. The door swung open immediately, as if someone were already expecting us on the other side.

Hera. Sweaty and gaunt-looking, probably after a spin class. Her Alo Yoga attire clung to her boney figure. Her hair was a mess. Her mouth was twisted in a bitter smile.

"Came for your victory dance?" She bared her teeth.

"Is that what you think this is?" I narrowed my eyes at her.

How delusional could a person be to think any part of this was fun for me? Mom and Dad were clueless. But Hera? She was disgusting.

Hera leaned a hip against the door, taking a sip of her bottled water. "Well, my husband is currently being taken into custody on attempted rape allegations, and I'm here barricaded in my apartment waiting for Mom and Dad to send their PR staff to clean up this mess, so, yeah. I think you're having a great day. Finally, good, respectful Hera messed up and Hallion comes out on top."

Craig was in custody? Already? That was fast. And also weird. Maybe I wasn't the first one who'd complained? Maybe there were others?

"You're insane." My fingers twitched, begging to grab her and shake her. "And think very highly of yourself."

"No, *you* are jealous." She stabbed my chest with her finger. "And you're also out of here."

She tried to slam the door in my face. Ransom reached a flattened palm against it, pushing it all the way open and sauntering inside with little effort. I followed him. I wasn't going to leave until I told her my side of the story. Not because I cared about her opinion—but because she deserved to be tormented by the truth. It wasn't about hurting her—it was about standing up for myself.

"You're trespassing!" Hera exclaimed.

"Indeed." Ransom headed for the kitchen, opening the fridge casually, fixing himself a lemonade. "Even still, my guess is you're not going to call the police and report your sister's visit right now. You know, considering the circumstances."

She stared at him with eyes full of fire and wrath. I stepped into her line of vision, snapping my fingers in her face.

"Focus," I ordered.

"On what?" she cried out. "It's obvious to all, Craig didn't do it. It's just a lie you made. I know about your little fling when you were in college. He told me! He may be a cheat, but he is not that kind of person. He—"

"He first molested me when I was fourteen," I started, undeterred. Her mouth fell open.

"*What*?"

"And it went on for years. As recent as a few weeks ago, the day of your wedding rehearsal and the mysterious allergy. But I'm guessing you were onto him one of the later times he did it, and he told you I seduced him, right? That I wanted it. That I *asked* for it, even. Which is why you hate me so much these days."

It all started to make sense to me now. Her behavior toward me. Toward Craig. She thought we were lovers.

Her face contorted in recognition. As if everything finally made sense now. Something else lurked behind her blue eyes. A vacant, hollow sadness I'd never seen before.

Transfixed on me, she collapsed on the arm of the sofa for support. "I...I...I didn't...I never thought..."

"And you never asked," I said pointedly.

"You're right." Her eyes filled with tears. "I just accepted his version, swallowed my pride, and moved on, thinking you must hate me so much to do this to me and my relationship. Please tell me everything, Hallie. Please."

And so I did. I didn't miss one detail, from the first time to the last one, just three weeks ago. The way I tried to fight him off. To stop him. How I'd changed, little by little, after each attack. Craig took pieces of my soul, until nothing was left. Until I became the plastic shell she'd seen plastered on Hollywood tabloids, flashing her nipple to the entire world.

Because I knew what I was.

Damaged goods.

"But why didn't you tell me?" Hera flew up from the couch, walking over to her floor-to-ceiling window. She wasn't crying anymore, but she looked wrecked.

"I wanted to." I watched her back. "So many times. But each time I tried to speak to you, you were busy, or dismissive, or not available for me. You wanted nothing to do with me. I knew where I stood with you. You were ashamed of my dyslexia, with my lack of academic achievement. You didn't want my averageness to rub off on you. You liked being completely separate entities. I never measured up to you. You were the shining star who burned everything in her path, and I was lost in your shadow."

She turned around to me, wrapping her arms around herself. "How could I have missed this?"

"Easily," I said tiredly. "Craig only showed one side of himself to you."

She shook her head. "He had anger issues. I mean, *does*. He still has them. He broke one of Mom's vases when we had a fight a while back. Another time, he kicked a friend of mine out of our apartment because she teased him about his SAT score. He's been in therapy for a while now. Two, three years maybe? I thought he was doing better. I never imagined his hotheadedness could translate into…"

"Sexual violence?" I completed for her.

"Yes."

Tears engulfed her eyes. She tried to fight them. After all, she was Hera, the wife of Zeus, the queen of all gods. Utterly untouchable.

"All this time, I stayed with him because I didn't want to

cause a headline. The public really loved that Craig and I were high school sweethearts, so I tried to push through with the relationship." She sniffed. "So you didn't make it all up to get back at me for that article?"

I closed my eyes, taking a breath. "Hera, I'm sorry to disappoint, but even though I'm not happy with the way my life has gone, I never wanted to be you. No offense, but it looks like you're leading a pretty miserable life. You don't give yourself any breathing room. You work yourself to the bone, exhaust your body with punishing workouts, and you always do whatever people expect of you, without any consideration for what *you* want. I don't actually think you're even in love with Craig. I've seen you two together. It looks more like an arrangement of convenience than anything else. You want to be this perfect creature, but Hera…" I opened my eyes, smiling sadly. "The person you're trying to be doesn't exist. You're killing yourself trying to become her."

Her tears fell freely now, covering her cheeks. She collapsed on the floor. Her forehead touched the cool marble. Her back quivered with sobs.

"I made a horrible mistake marrying him."

"I'm sorry," I whispered.

I didn't fail to notice how Hera was still focused on *her* life, *her* decisions, *her* mistakes, *her* heartache. Even though I was the one with the trauma. The one who'd been wronged. I supposed sympathy was too much to ask. Especially considering we were all on the brink of a national scandal.

As if reading my thoughts, she tilted her head and stared at me. "Your life's going to change forever, too, you know." She used the couch's back to try to steady herself before standing upright. "As soon as the news breaks, everyone will know. Are you ready for that?"

"Ready? No." I smiled, turning around and ambling to the door. "Prepared? Yes."

The drive to the airport passed in contemplative silence.

Scrolling through names of L.A. based therapists on my phone, I clicked on the pictures of ones who looked friendly. All women. I couldn't see myself pouring my heart out to a man after everything I'd been through.

Ransom looked grim and deep in thought. I was amazed he didn't use the time to work on his phone.

"You sick or something?" I took a break from my therapist shopping.

He glanced at me, still a million miles away. "No."

"You seem distracted."

"Just thinking."

"What about?"

His eyes clung to mine, the answer inside them. He was hiding something. I understood, I'd lived my life cloaked in secrets, too. Something deep and dark and dangerous.

"I'm trying to think how to put it into words."

"You're scaring me."

"Focus on finding a therapist, Hallie. You'll need one."

He twisted his head back, watching as cars swished by. I lowered my gaze back to my phone, my eyes landing on a fifty-something woman in a funky emerald blazer and a welcoming smile. She had the Rachel haircut—totally nineties—her hair as flame-red as mine.

Ilona Queen, PsyD
Licensed Clinical Psychologist
Alcohol addiction, substance abuse, eating disorder, trauma, PTSD, and relationship issues.

I clicked on the *Book a Consultation* button and held my breath. Maybe this was the beginning of the end.

And the end of thinking I couldn't rewrite my beginning.

Chapter Twenty

Ransom

Then.

As it turned out, we didn't even have to kill Mr. Moruzzi.

The work of saints was often done through others. In our case—Mrs. Moruzzi.

Apparently, Mr. Moruzzi was sitting on quite a hefty sum of life insurance. Don't ask me why that dumb fuck thought it would be a good idea to have a good insurance policy when everyone in his life wanted to see him dead.

On the news, we heard it was an accident. A terrible human error. The loving couple simply went hunting together, as they often did (according to the reporters, not to reality, which was more like Mrs. Moruzzi couldn't fucking stand her husband or the filthy orphans he brought home to work for him).

One shot to the head. It actually pierced all the way through and hit the deer, too. The deer survived. Mr. Moruzzi—not so much.

Mrs. Moruzzi did everything right. She called the cops immediately. Told them her version of things. The Moruzzis were a well-off couple from the nice part of Chicago, who'd adopted three sons, all of whom were in college. No one would ever suspect homicide.

Mrs. Moruzzi was off the hook.
And so was I, or at least I'd thought.
Because a few years later, I did take a life.
The most precious life there was.
A life never meant to be taken.

"I think I found a really good therapist."

Hallie sat in front of me on the plane. She angled her phone better, showing me a picture of a woman who looked like an older version of herself. "I still don't know how I'll afford her, seeing as I'm putting scissors to my parents' credit card as soon as I get back to Los Angeles, but I'm thinking Keller might let me work at Main Squeeze."

Staring into her blue eyes, all I could think about was how much I didn't want her in Los Angeles. How much more affordable it would be for her to move elsewhere and start over. And, naturally, how it would make my life as her bodyguard.

"How will you make rent?"

Her face fell. She hadn't thought of that. "I guess…I won't? I'll have to find something smaller. A studio, maybe. Would you mind very much moving into a studio apartment?"

I wouldn't mind sharing a tuna can with this woman, but that wasn't the issue.

"Los Angeles is expensive." I tried another angle. "And unsafe."

"Okay, Sherlock." She quirked an eyebrow, sitting back as the plane took off. "What's your point? You know I'm not moving to Texas."

"Texas and California aren't the only states in the federation."

"You think I should move somewhere I don't know?"

"I think you should start fresh." I reframed it. "Go somewhere where rent is cheap, where the paparazzi won't hound you." *Or any Bratva members.*

She mulled it over, munching on her lower lip. In my defense, moving her elsewhere wouldn't only benefit me. She didn't need all the paps swarming around her when shit hit the fan and news started breaking about Craig.

"I guess...Minnesota is beautiful this time of the year." She looked mystified by the idea of taking a new path, maybe a new identity.

I nodded encouragingly.

Hallie shook her head, suddenly frowning. "No, I can't do that. I can't just up and leave. It would send the wrong message. Like I'm running away."

"You can't stay in Los Angeles," I said impatiently, thinking about Kozlov, about stupid Anna, about all the complications.

"Of course, I can." She smiled. "And if I run into financial issues, at least I'll have—"

"Your life's in danger," I cut her off, tired of orbiting around the same issue.

She blinked, staring at me wide-eyed, as if I'd slapped her. "My life's in danger?" she repeated, dumbfounded. "How? Why? Craig?"

Digging my fingers into my eye sockets, I let out a shaky breath.

"Nothing to do with him. You've been in danger for months," I said. "Ever since I came into your life, to be exact."

"Tell me everything." Her tone was cold, unyielding. She was already a different woman from the one who'd tried to stab me with a soda bottle. She was made of sturdier stuff. And I wondered if she knew it.

"Back when I worked in domestic counter-terrorism, my job was to take down the L.A. Bratva. The Russian mafia operation had gained power quickly and taken control of the streets, especially around Hidden Hills, Westlake Village, and downtown. The illegal gambling and money laundering were bothersome, but not a deal breaker. Human and arms trafficking was where the government drew the line, and it was becoming clear we had a problem on our hands. The year I stepped into the role, thirty-three innocent people were killed by them."

Her head hung down in sorrow, but she didn't say anything, which allowed me to finish.

"The ringleader was a guy named Vasily Kozlov. A nasty son of a bitch with an impressive track record for taking the lives of those who crossed him. The mission was to get our hands on him, dead or alive. Breathing was always preferable, but it wasn't necessary."

This was the part I dreaded. I took a deep breath. I hadn't re-hashed that day since the moment I'd handed in my resignation and given the agency an on-record statement of what happened. Law knew most of it. Tom, only some.

"One day, we got word of a meeting. Illegal weapons were being exchanged between the Bratva and some NorCal MC club. The hot tip we'd received disclosed the exchange of two hundred 9mms and an array of rifles. The meeting took place in the back of a Georgian restaurant. We raided the joint."

I stopped and closed my eyes, letting my head drop between my shoulders. I had no clue why I was telling her this. I could've given her the short version. The one that wouldn't paint me as a monster.

But she deserved to know the whole truth.

That I was, in fact, a monster. And monsters could only thrive in the dark. Far away from her and everything she represented.

"Tell me," she croaked, reaching to touch my hand. "Show me your vulnerabilities. You've already seen so many of mine."

"It was a back-alley raid. We kicked down the exit door. But it was a setup. Kozlov wanted the people on the case—*us*—slaughtered. We were met with DIY smoke bombs that made it impossible to breathe, let alone see. But I was a stubborn bastard and I just took it as an invitation to hand in Kozlov's head on a silver platter. I pushed forward with two of my colleagues, barreling through the narrow, dark corridor. I could hear people running, screaming in Russian. Guess they'd thought we'd retreat once we were met with the smoke bombs. Suddenly, I found myself in a room with about a dozen men. One of them was Kozlov."

I was physically sick with the memory of what happened next.

No part of me wanted to continue this story. I slammed my eyes shut.

"He raised his hand and pointed it toward me. I thought he had a gun. Thought he was going to kill me."

Silence.

"What did you do?"

"I fired three shots," I croaked. "Straight up the middle."

I felt my heartbeat in my throat when my lips parted again to finish my story. "Hallie…"

"Yes?"

"He was holding his baby. His two-year-old son. It was his version of a white flag."

The memory crashed into me all at once.

The crying I'd heard only in retrospect.

The gasps.

The gurgles.

The silence.

The blood. The blood. The blood.

I'd killed a baby. An innocent child. A pure soul, who'd found himself in an unfortunate circumstance.

With the remainder of my energy, I said, "Kozlov survived. The bullets never passed through his son's body. That toddler was his human shield. I resigned and moved back to Chicago. I knew Kozlov had vowed to avenge his son's death—and honestly, I couldn't blame him for that part—but also knew that for him, stepping onto Chicago territory was an issue. Different Bratvas, different jurisdictions. He couldn't just barge into Chicago and shed blood."

"But in Los Angeles, he can," Hallie finished for me.

I nodded. "And he knows I'm with you, which makes you a target, too."

"Have you ever spoken to anyone about what happened?"

Shaking my head, I let out a soft chuckle. "Who would I talk to? My friend, Law, knows some of the story, but he has his own shit to take care of. Family. A job. He doesn't have time to be my therapist.

Tom's great, but he is one of Moruzzi's children. Tom wouldn't see it as a big deal. We've both done some pretty fucked-up shit."

"You must have more people who care about you."

"Must I, now?" I gave her a crooked grin.

"Ransom…" She unbuckled her safety belt, shooting to her feet and stepping toward me. She perched her ass on my lap, tucking her chin over the top of my head as she hugged me. "I hate that you've been through all this, but I also loathe that you've only told me about it right now. That was really stupid."

"I'm well aware." My arms circled her waist, an instinct more than anything else. I didn't speak.

"Look at me now." She grabbed my face, angling it so our eyes met. "You're not a monster."

I smiled grimly. "Spare me the *Days of Our Lives* moment. I am, and I've learned to live with it."

"You're *not* a monster," she repeated. "You made a mistake. A horrible, innocent mistake. No part of you wanted to kill that child. None."

I closed my eyes, envisioning the little pudgy thing. I didn't know how much of it was true and how much was my imagination. The round cheeks. The pillowy rolls on his legs.

"You're not a monster," she repeated, louder this time. "You, Ransom Lockwood, will never, ever, ever convince me that you're a monster."

It undid me. My face felt hot and wet. Was I…was I crying? What the *fuck*? I never cried. I doubted I'd cried even as an infant, since the day I was left on that church's steps.

"They slaughtered my former boss, Ian Holmes. Buried him in his backyard. Kozlov killed a lot of people, Hallie. And none of them deserved it. He needs to be stopped, and it ruins me to know I'm not the man to stop him."

"It's not your job to save the world." She stroked my cheeks, and at that moment, for a brief second, I believed her.

"Don't fight the emotions you're experiencing. Feel them." She kissed my temple, the crown of my head, the tip of my nose. "You've been through horrible trauma. You're allowed to break. Breaking can be good. It gives you the opportunity to reassemble yourself from scratch."

I looked up at her, catching her lips with mine. It was going to be torture to say goodbye to this woman.

But I was going to do it anyway, when our six months were up.

She deserved much more than I had to give.

We held hands on the drive back to her place, marking the first time I'd held hands with a woman instead of holding someone's hands above their head. I didn't hate it. Maybe Hallie was right. Perhaps I, The Robot, could let myself feel every once in a while.

"I think I'll look at places outside of Los Angeles," Hallie said as we neared her neighborhood.

"Thank you," I said quietly, knowing it was because of me. Because of my bullshit, my sins, my mistakes.

"What about Dennis and Ethel?" She sniffed.

I stared at her blankly. Who the fuck were they, her chia pets?

"My driver and his wife," she explained. "I won't be able to afford Dennis' services anymore. They need the income."

She cared about others. Deeply. It was hard to remember why I'd ever thought she was a shallow little tart.

"Do you have any idea how old Dennis is?"

She shook her head. I did. I knew. Because I'd had every part of her life examined to a T before I flew to Los Angeles.

"He's sixty-eight."

"Okay…"

"He doesn't want to work anymore. He wants to retire."

Anthony Thorne told me as much on our phone call prior to my taking the job.

"He does?" She winced. "But then… why did he stay?"

"Because of you. He loves you like a granddaughter. I sent him on vacation not as punishment, but because he was exhausted. You were out and about all hours of the night. He couldn't keep up—he's not a teenager."

"How had I not noticed that?" she murmured. "I've been a terrible brat."

"Not so terrible. But a brat, indeed." I squeezed her hand.

The driver slowed as he approached her neighborhood. Hallie entered the code to open up the gate. It had been a short trip, but it sure packed one hell of a punch.

"That's weird." Hallie looked outside the passenger window, craning her neck slightly. "There's a car I don't know parked outside my house."

My skin prickled with awareness. If it was who I thought it was, he was about to enter a world of pain.

The driver stopped a few feet from a red Jaguar convertible.

"Don't kill the engine," I instructed, flinging open my side of the door. "Hallie, stay here and don't get out until I tell you to. Call the police if need be—but do. Not. Leave."

I got out, slamming the door behind me and walking over to the car, one hand over the gun tucked into my waistband. The car didn't scream mafia, but maybe it was just a clever disguise.

The door to the Jaguar opened and out slipped Anna.

Let's-fuck-and-ruin-Hallie-Thorne-Anna.

The good news was that Hallie's life wasn't in danger.

The bad news was that mine was, if Hallie ever came face-to-face with the woman.

Anna tossed her bombshell hair to one shoulder, leaning over to kiss both my cheeks.

"Ransom, darling, I've missed you."

"Can't say the feeling's mutual." I pulled away, giving her a once-over. What was she doing here?

"I thought you'd call me." She gave me a seductive smile.

"Here. Get yourself some better instincts." I pulled my wallet, tugging out a fifty-dollar bill.

She folded her arms over her chest, refusing to touch the money.

I sighed. "How can I help you, Anna?"

"Well, as you know, we have unfinished business to attend to."

"Everything's quite finished," I supplied. "You shouldn't have come here."

How'd she get the address? Stupid question. She worked for a tabloid. Most of her paparazzi colleagues could point her in the right direction with their eyes closed.

"I need a scoop."

"You need a career change," I countered. "As I said before, I'm not giving you jack shit on my client."

She smoothed my shirt, grinning up at me.

"Oh, come on, big guy. I have an even better offer on the table. My boss just green-lit it. Aren't you at least a bit curious to hear what we're willing to offer for an exclusive story?"

"Ransom?" I heard a voice from my right. *Hallie.*

She stepped out of the car, waving the driver goodbye. She must've figured Anna posed no danger. That's where she was wrong.

Anna straightened her back, letting loose a smile.

"Oh, hi, Hallie Thorne. You don't know me, but I—"

"I know you." Hallie stopped in front of both of us, and I didn't like it, how Anna and I looked like a unit together, opposite her. "You wrote a scathing piece about me after my nip slip. Your picture's right next to your column."

It was the first time I hurt for someone else, and it was a massive pain in the neck. The empathy sliced through me like a knife. It was almost hard to breathe.

"Great memory!" Anna cooed. "Maybe you weren't as drugged up as I thought you were."

"Please don't let the truth about me mess up with your narrative." Hallie smiled coldly. "To you, I'll always be a fuck-up. Now, what are you doing at my house?"

"Ransom and I are old friends."

"Is that so?" Hallie's eyes darted to me in question. I gave a curt nod.

"Ransom, would you like to take our conversation somewhere private?" Anna ignored Hallie's presence, smiling at me.

"You can say whatever you have to say right here."

"You sure about that?" Anna's eyes warned me that I wasn't going to like the next part.

I did not negotiate with terrorists.

"Positive."

"Well, I was just wondering when we're going to hook up…" She gave a meaningful beat, studying Hallie with zeal. "*Again.*"

Hallie froze in her spot. Her face betrayed nothing. But I saw it. The disappointment. It hadn't appeared when I'd told her I'd killed an innocent child. But it was there now, written all over her face.

Both were mistakes on my end. But only one was in my control.

"Now would seem like a very good time for you two to talk." Hallie recovered quickly, bumping past my shoulder on her way to her door. "Seeing as I have some things to do."

The door slammed behind her before I could explain.

"You idiot." I turned to Anna, rage bubbling in my bloodstream. "What did you do that for?"

"It was the truth, wasn't it?" Anna asked defiantly.

"A very selective truth," I spat out. "You knew damn well my chances of ever touching you again with a ten-foot pole were zero on a good day, and most of my days are bad."

"Still." Anna opened the door to her Jaguar, slipping inside. "It was worth it. Because now I know without a doubt you're porking the client, and that's one hell of a juicy headline. Thanks, pal."

I pushed the door open, expecting carnage. At the very least, a heavy piece of furniture thrown in my direction.

Instead, I found a human-sized lump on the couch, lying in front of a turned-off TV. She didn't move until I closed the door, making myself known.

She sat upright, wiping her face on her sleeve.

"I can explain," I said, not because that's what men usually said, but because I really, honestly could. There was a good explanation to all of this.

Hallie stood up, making her way upstairs. I followed her, jarred by her lack of response. For the first time in my life, I didn't know what to do.

"Is it weird that I don't want you to?" she finally said. "I kind of feel like this is a golden opportunity to cut the cord. It should've happened long ago. In fact, I can't believe we've made it this far."

Was she talking about my post as her bodyguard or about fucking each other's brains out? Either way, I didn't like the implication. I wasn't done with her. Not by a long mile.

She pushed the door to her room open, stepping into her walk-in closet. There, she grabbed out a couple large suitcases, flung them open, and began throwing clothes into them.

"Are you leaving?" I placed an elbow on her wall.

"Eventually." She tossed a few gowns into the open jaws of her suitcase. "Once I figure out where I'm going."

"I'm coming with you."

"No need." She flung more shirts into a suitcase, still not looking at me. "I'm sure my parents won't mind you quitting the job at this point. Or, if you still want Dad's connections, just stay here and we'll pretend you're still protecting me. It'd throw the Russians off my scent, anyway."

She wasn't wrong.

And still. *And still.*

"You think I'd stay without you?" Why did it sound so hideous, the idea of being without her? "Is that how you know me?"

Still packing, she said, "I don't know the first thing about you. That's the problem."

"Of course, you know me."

Or at least, she knew me more than everyone else.

She turned around to face me, clutching a skirt between her fingers. "Fine. You're right. I do know you. Which is why I know you'll listen to me this time. I want you to leave. I need to think. I need to be by myself. We've been stuck together for weeks now. Or is it months? How long has it been?" She let out a brittle chuckle. "Everything's been a blur since you stormed into my world. I don't remember my life without you. Which scares me. I want you to respect my boundaries for once and leave. Don't call Max, either. I want to be alone."

"You can't—"

"You saw firsthand how everybody I know let me down," she cut me off, her eyes pink, her chin wobbly. "Please. You fucked up. You fucked *her*. For once in your life, do something altruistic. Let me go."

"Hallie…"

Nothing else came out. She was right. Nobody respected her wishes. And if I chose not to leave her, I'd be doing the same. But how could I walk away when I knew she could be in danger?

"Leave," she said quietly. "For me," she added. "For us."

I closed my eyes.

I wanted to explain so badly. But she asked me not to. And I couldn't be one of those people who didn't give two shits about what she wanted. She deserved better.

"Four hours," I heard myself say, each word tasting like metal in my mouth. "I'm giving you four hours to cool down. Because you're right. I do respect your wishes, and if I could take things back…" I faltered. "I would take back our entire beginning. Re-do it."

She pushed me out of her walk-in closet, closing the door behind her back with a soft click.

Chapter Twenty-One

Hallie

The green phone symbol on my iPhone was adorned with a red ninety-nine missed calls circle.

Mom.

Dad.

Texas Landline.

I tucked the phone back into my pocket, continuing to pack. I didn't know where I was going; I just knew I had to leave. This life I lived wasn't mine. Every minute I shared with Ransom was making it harder for me to say goodbye to him. And I was going to have to say goodbye to him. Soon.

By the time he got back, he wouldn't find me here.

I glanced at the clock on my nightstand. It said three in the afternoon. Two out of my four Ransom-less hours had passed. I was almost finished packing. I was proud of myself for not crying. I wanted so badly to sob into my pillow. Ransom sleeping with this horrible woman was the last straw in a disastrous month.

Terrible, and yet so predictable. You knew he was a soulless man.

What stopped me from hating him all the way was the revelation of what he'd been through years ago. That boy. I knew he carried it in his heart every day, the burden of his sin making it hard for him to breathe.

He was wrong. He wasn't a lost cause. He did have a soul. Maybe even a good one. But he buried it so deep inside, I'd come to terms with the fact I couldn't pull it from the ruins of his tragedies. Only he could do that for himself.

Turned out the old cliché was right all along—only we had the power to better ourselves.

I heard the door whining open downstairs. My jaw clenched.

"I thought we agreed on four hours, Random," I lamented, loudly enough for him to hear.

Footsteps pounded up the stairway. One...*two* pairs.

Why were there two pairs? Who was he with?

My heart rattled against my ribcage.

I let go of the clothes I was holding and crawled under my bed. It was my safest bet. The only escape route from my bedroom was the balcony, and last time the Russians paid us a visit, they parked directly in front of it.

The footsteps grew closer, louder. I sucked in a breath, lowering my head to try to peek through the curtain of linen hiding me from view.

I saw two pairs of smart shoes. They entered my room with purpose, speaking briskly between themselves in Russian.

Shit, shit, shit.

One waltzed into my closet, kicking the half-full suitcases aside. The other approached my window, probably to see if I jumped through it.

Window Guy told Closet Guy something in Russian. They both laughed. They walked out of my room, filing in and out of rooms on the second floor. They knew I was here somewhere. They'd heard me.

I contemplated trying to take out my phone and call Ransom, but decided against it. My phone was a mini, so small I'd tucked it inside my waistline. It could easily slip and make noise.

Closet Guy trudged outside my home gym, growling. He and

the other man met in the hallway again. Their hushed voices didn't sound so smug now. My heart beat so hard I was surprised they didn't hear it.

Were they going to leave? Ransom was their main objective. He clearly wasn't here. No way he could hide under any piece of furniture. He was massive.

One of them began making his way downstairs. I drew in a lungful of air. *Almost out of the woods.* Then the other pair of shoes turned in my direction, swiftly lurching forward.

No. No. No. No.

The feet disappeared in my periphery. I couldn't follow his location without shifting around and making a noise. Everything was quiet. I didn't dare to breathe. Suddenly, a pair of hands grabbed my ankles from behind and dragged me out from under my bed. My fingers automatically clawed onto the rug.

I jerked forward, bumping my head against the bedframe in the process.

Kicking his hands off in an attempt to fight back, I started screaming. The man flipped me onto my back, grunted in annoyance, and pressed his palm over my mouth. My teeth dug into his skin. The metallic tang of blood exploded in my mouth. He didn't relent. In fact, he laughed.

Laughed and laughed and laughed.

He's not Craig. He's not going to hurt you like that. Pull yourself together.

The man's face came into focus, as I blinked the white dots of adrenaline away. Even without ever meeting him, I knew it was Kozlov himself. His face was scarred in deep, purposeful slashes. Knife wounds. His eyes were very small and very black. Two raisins full of hatred.

With a swift bark in Russian, he made the person next to him pull me up to my feet. The man patted me down for devices and weapons. Dizzy on my feet, I prayed he wouldn't find my phone. Halting on my pockets, the man took a step back and shook his head.

I let out a ragged exhale. He'd missed it.

Glancing around the room, I tried to look for something to attack the two men with. Kozlov's assistant, in the meantime, brought together both my arms behind my back and bound them with thick black tape. I wanted to throw up. I'd never felt so helpless in my life.

You had to send your bodyguard away, didn't you? All because you were jealous and petty and childish.

Although, it was also true that he brought trouble right to my doorstep, and if I made it out of this alive, I should destroy his career, for that alone, as punishment.

Kozlov turned on his heel and made his way down the stairs. This was my chance to try to take down his assistant. The man shoved me from behind toward the stairs. I complied, hoping he'd loosen his guard on me. But when we got to the edge of the stairs, I managed to slam my body into his, pushing him down. He gripped the bannister quickly with one hand, using his spare to sink his fingers into my hair. He tugged violently, lurching me toward his mouth. My scalp burned.

"Behave, little girl," he commanded in a thick accent. And I didn't know why, but hearing him speak in English made everything so much more real and frightening.

Chances were high, I wasn't getting out of this alive.

On our journey downstairs, I noticed all of my Nest cameras had been covered. Kozlov had cased the house beforehand, probably when Ransom and I were in Texas. Otherwise, he wouldn't be familiar with their locations.

"I don't know where he is," I groaned when I noticed Kozlov standing by the door, waiting for his soldier and me. "I'll be no help."

Kozlov smiled serenely, half-patting half-slapping my cheek. "He'll come for you. You mean something to him."

Jesus. How closely did they follow us?

Black cloth wrapped around my eyes from behind, secured firmly in a double knot. I was shoved outside, into a car—not a spacious one by the feel of it—where I sat quietly while three voices conversed in Russian.

Sorting hysterically through my jumbled thoughts, I tried figuring out what they wanted from me. I was obviously a means to an end. Something to lure Ransom into their territory. Then again, I doubted they'd spare my life if things went sideways.

The drive was excruciatingly slow, but I didn't know if it was because they'd taken me far, or on account of my nerves being shot.

When the car finally came to a stop, I didn't know whether to feel relief or renewed fear. The door to the back seat flung open. The person who sat next to me got out first, pulling me along. Since I sat in the middle, I felt the person behind me poking my back, egging me on.

"Where are you taking me?" I hiccupped. "I'm President Thorne's daughter. If you think you'll get away with this, you've got another thing coming."

Even to myself, I sounded like a weak side character in a slasher film, destined to die quickly and painfully to move the plot along.

I heard Kozlov chuckling near me. "Relax."

"Are you serious right now? You want me to *relax*?"

He didn't answer.

We went up a flight of stairs. Each step I took felt like I was nearing a death sentence.

The place smelled weird. A mixture of dust, food, and old wool. I wondered where we were. How close we were to civilization.

"When will you take my blindfold off?" I tried to keep my voice calm. Keep the conversation going. Remind them that I was human, and innocent.

"Soon." Kozlov sounded almost cheery.

"You don't expect him to come here, do you?" I asked. "He doesn't know where this place is."

"I don't," he confirmed. "I plan on dangling you in front of him somewhere else. Once I decide on the details."

"And if he doesn't take the bait?" My voice echoed in an empty, dank room. A shove to my shoulder made my ass meet a hard wooden chair. Someone behind me untied my blindfold.

Kozlov stood in front of me, chuckling as he opened his arms. "Then I suppose the bait would become useless to us."

No need to tie me down. I was in no danger of escaping. A big, bald man stood by the door of the small back office. Kozlov was right in front of me, holding a gun, and his assistant was sitting behind a desk, awaiting instructions.

The phone tucked in my waistband burned my skin, demanding to be used. I could ask to go to the bathroom and see if I had service. Whatever I chose to do, it needed to be done before my battery died.

Kozlov strode toward me, tugging at his dress pants before crouching slightly to bring himself to my eye level. "Miss Thorne, here is what's going to happen. I'm going to ask you questions about your employee, and you are going to answer them truthfully. If you don't, you will be thrashed. If you refuse to cooperate, you will be thrashed. If you lie, you will be thrashed. Am I understood?"

I nodded. Though, shockingly, I had no desire to share anything about Ransom with him.

It made no sense at all. The man had brought this disastrous situation upon me singlehandedly. I should be singing about him, volunteering any piece of information I had.

Kozlov grabbed a chair and positioned it in front of me. He sank into it.

"One—where does Lockwood keep his weapon?"

That was an easy one. I didn't even need to lie. I had no idea. I shook my head. "Don't know."

"Miss Thorne." Kozlov smiled regretfully, as if he was on my side. The good cop. "I really wouldn't like to hurt you more than absolutely necessary. Answer my question."

"I would love to," I said, my eyes leveled with his. "But I don't know the answer to your question. Not sure if you noticed, but he's a pretty secretive guy."

The whip came from behind. At some point, his assistant

must've stood up and taken off his belt. My back was protected by the chair, mostly, but it licked the nape of my neck, burning like a thousand fires.

I let out a soft moan, but didn't cry. I couldn't let them win. These people, who trafficked women in and out of the country. Who murdered, and raped, and put weapons into the hands of criminals.

"Question number two," Kozlov announced, standing up and waltzing the room nonchalantly. "Are you fucking him?"

"How is that your business?" I thundered.

"Everything he does is my business," he said quietly. "He killed my son."

"It was an accident!" I blurted out. I knew it was the wrong thing to say before I even finished the sentence. Knew it, because even as I heard it, I realized how miserable it sounded to the ears of the father of that baby.

All Kozlov did was look past me, give a little nod, and turn around, his back to me. I sucked in a breath, bracing myself for what I knew was about to come.

The belt hit my shoulder first.

Then the back of my head.

Then the back of my knees.

I choked on my screams, swallowed down my tears, and refused to break down. My head hung limply on my chest. I was sweating buckets. I couldn't take it anymore. But I couldn't tell them anything about Ransom, either.

I found out I was a loyal, trustworthy person…only to waste those traits on a screwed-up man who had no feelings and twice as many issues as me. Typical.

"Now let's try again, Miss Thorne. And this time, with a little more cooperation…"

In the corner of my eye, I saw Kozlov advancing toward me. My whole body flinched. He raised his hand, no doubt with intentions to hit me. I sucked in a breath.

"Stop."

The voice was deadly calm. My heart stumbled all over the

place, ping-ponging inside me. I looked to the door at the same time Kozlov did. Ransom stood inside it with his arm wrapped around the bodyguard's throat, his gun to his temple.

I wanted to cry out in relief, but my throat was choked with sobs.

Kozlov turned fully toward him, looking amused more than scared.

"How did you find us?" he inquired, almost politely.

"My client carries a mini iPhone, and I track her whereabouts constantly."

Kozlov's gaze flew to his assistant, who recoiled beside me, knowing he would pay dearly for the mistake.

The Bratva soldier was completely still in Ransom's headlock, aware that my bodyguard had no qualms about putting a bullet in his head if the situation demanded.

"What's the plan?" Kozlov smiled. "Finish the job you started with Yefim and kill all of us?"

Yefim. The boy's name was Yefim. I saw Ransom's jaw harden, his nostrils flaring. He knew that. Of course he knew that. I bet he relived that moment every hour of his life.

Kozlov's assistant pulled a gun from his waistband, pointing it at Ransom.

Fuck. Could my life get any messier with this man around? And to think this all started with a *nip slip*.

"Because," Kozlov smiled indulgently, "if you kill me, it looks like you'll be killed, too."

"Nice deductive abilities." Ransom shoved the bodyguard forward, treading deeper into the room. "I have no immediate plans to kill any of you, as tempting as it is."

"Right," Kozlov said. "So how do you see this playing out?"

"Simply." Ransom let loose one of his signature, devil-may-care smiles. "This restaurant is crowned with an entire SWAT team, twenty LAPD cops for backup, a helicopter, the DA, and an unholy amount of security vehicles. You killed an FBI agent, dipshit. You can surrender yourself quietly—my least favorite option—or you could go out in a blaze of glory and let me kill you. This, I like better, since I'd get to make it slow and painful, for how you treated Miss Thorne."

It never occurred to me, until he said it, that I looked like a mess. But I'd been roughed up by Kozlov and his assistant, and I'm sure all those thrashes had left marks.

"If we both go down, I would have no regrets," Kozlov said quietly. "You killed my son."

"I hate myself every day for it." For the first time since I'd met him, Ransom's voice broke. "I think about that boy more than I think about the parents who left me. More than I think about my own goddamn life. But I had no idea. None at all. You put him right in front of me. In harm's way. What kind of bastard father does that?"

"So...you should be forgiven?" Kozlov huffed, looking resigned. His shoulders drooped, and he seemed fed up and tired all of a sudden.

Both men looked broken.

"No," Ransom said. "You should trust in my pain. Because I feel it. Every. Single. Fucking. Day."

Behind Ransom's back, SWAT team members gathered. Ransom let go of the bodyguard, pushing him forward. He staggered toward Kozlov.

"Game over, Kozlov. Either you come out of here like a dog or in a body bag."

"Was all this planned?" Kozlov demanded. "Did you want me to kidnap her?"

The mere suggestion made my blood turn to lava. It was possible. Totally possible. Which made me furious.

Ransom shook his head. "I would never do that to her."

"I don't believe you have any limits," said Kozlov.

And, sadly, I shared the sentiment.

Kozlov closed his eyes. All he did to show his submission was a curt, barely-there nod to his bodyguard and soldier in the room.

Ransom stepped aside. The SWAT team stalked in, handcuffing

Kozlov and his crew. My eyes followed the men who'd kidnapped me. I was afraid if I blinked, they'd be on top of me again, wrestling me to the floor, hitting me.

"You're safe now." His voice seeped into my ear, so close his hot breath caressed the side of my neck.

"You tracked my phone," I said tonelessly.

I shouldn't be surprised. I was, and always would be, just another job for Ransom. Perhaps one with perks, but ultimately, I was a notch on his belt.

"I couldn't chance you getting hurt." He worked quickly to untie my hands from behind.

I turned to look at him. The anger made my eyes burn. I was shaking with rage.

"I'm officially relieving you of your duties, Mr. Lockwood."

All around us, feds and SWAT team members were unplugging computers, confiscating documents, tearing down the room.

He searched my face, his own expression rigid and defiant.

"Look, you didn't give me time to explain." He helped me stand up, taking special care not to touch me where I'd been whipped. "This shit with Anna…yes, I did sleep with her. But it happened in college. She found me at a hole-in-the-wall a few weeks ago. Tracked me down and tried rekindling something in exchange for information about you. I cut her off. We had a few drinks. She spiked one of mine, I think. Then I stumbled out and caught a cab, cursing at her the entire time. I didn't touch her. I swear."

Raising a hand to stop him, I shook my head. "You think I care about you and her?"

He blinked, confused. "Yes?"

Throwing my head back, I let out a laugh.

"Oh, Ransom, you really do think you're God's gift to women. I couldn't give two shits about what you did with Anna."

That wasn't exactly the truth, but I had more pressing matters to tend to.

"I care that you had me tracked without telling me. I care that you put my life in danger. That you *knew* people were after you, that I could get hurt, and still, you put yourself first. I wanted to run away from you in the four hours you gave me to 'self-reflect.'" I said the last words with air quotes. "You're not only a terrible human, you're also a terrible bodyg—sorry, *close protection officer.*" I rolled my eyes, on a roll now, thinking about all the different ways he was cruel and callous to me. I couldn't let myself stop now. Or cave in. Allow him to stay. He had to go. He *had* to. For the safety of my heart. "You're just awful all around. It's true, what Dorothy Parker once said. Beauty is skin deep, but ugly goes clean to the bone."

It killed me to say all of this to him. Especially after he'd confided in me about what he'd done to Kozlov's son. But I couldn't allow for mercy to have a place in my heart. He was going to destroy me if he stayed. I had to make him leave.

I snatched my arm away from him, realizing that he'd tried to touch me during my little speech.

"You don't know what you're saying," he said levelly. "You've just been through one heck of an ordeal. You need to give a brief statement, and then we'll get you home."

I stepped back from him, putting more room between us. "Let's get it over with."

I woke up with a start.

My head throbbed. The yolky slivers of the setting sun seeped through my bedroom window, warming my skin.

My body hurt. My head hurt. Everything hurt.

Blinking away sleep, I angled my face toward the clock on my nightstand. Seven o'clock in the evening. My guess was I'd slept through most of yesterday and was waking up to a new day.

Next to the clock was a pack of Tylenol—the extra strength ones—a bottle of water, and what looked like a doctor's prescription. My phone was there, too.

Reaching for it, I felt my back muscles straining, my neck screaming in pain where I'd been beaten. The skin was going to peel off soon, I knew without even looking. I was going to feel the aftershocks of what happened to me for weeks to come.

Grabbing my phone, I sifted through the last calls. Mom. Dad. Hera—that was a new one. Keller called a few times, and so did NeNe and Tara. I couldn't imagine myself relaying everything that had happened to me in the last forty-eight hours to anyone, if that's what they were calling about.

Had news leaked yet?

About the kidnap? About Craig and sexual assault charges? About Ransom and me, via Anna?

Only one way to find out.

Unplastering myself from the bed, I dragged myself into the shower. At first, I turned the water too hot. Then, realizing my mistake, how wounded and raw my skin felt, I quickly twisted the shower diverter, opting for ice-cold water. It was a quick affair, followed by patting myself dry carefully. Putting a robe on was too painful. I walked over to my bathroom mirror and lifted my hair up, inspecting the back of my neck and shoulders. The welts looked angry, purple, and deep. Tears filled my eyes.

He could've prevented this.

He could've given the job to Max.

His grandiose, self-centered, Napoleon complex wouldn't allow him not to finish something he'd started.

Well, he'd finished me, all right. I had nothing left to give.

And yet, for the first time in my life, I knew what I should do with terrifying clarity.

After lathering my back and neck with aloe, I slipped into my most comfortable pair of pajamas and popped two Tylenol. I made my way downstairs. Ransom sat on my couch, going through his iPad, laptop, and phone simultaneously.

Yup. News broke, all right. The dirty laundry had been aired.

He stood when I appeared in the stairway, as if summoned by a queen.

"Your parents came by earlier."

I smiled noncommittally. "Of course, they did. Word must've gotten out that I'd been kidnapped."

"It's all in the news," Ransom confirmed, looking awkward for once in his life. "The Bratva, the arrests, Craig was taken into custody. All of it."

Papa Thorne simply couldn't stomach passing on the photo-op. And if he couldn't get a picture of him hugging his Sugar Pie, then at the very least, paparazzi snaps of him and Mom embracing one another as they landed in Los Angeles, braving the tarmac winds on their way to their private car.

"I've no plans to see them."

"Figured." Ransom licked his lips. "I told Anthony it wasn't a good time."

"I also don't think it's good for me to see *you*," I finished.

He arched an eyebrow. "If this is about the Anna article, no one's buying it. All your friends have denied it publicly. Keller. Tara. The other one with the weird name."

One less shit storm to worry about, but I knew it didn't make any difference.

I pushed off the bannister. "Sit down."

He did. I took the seat as far away from him as possible, knowing how hard it was going to be. If too much of his scent met my nose, if too much of his green eyes touched my soul, I'd cave and let him stay. I'd crack and settle. I'd take a temporary arrangement, even though I wanted happily-ever-after.

Worse still, even if Ransom wanted something serious with me, he was right. I had too many obstacles to overcome. I needed to face the Craig trial alone. I needed to get a job alone. I needed to go through therapy—alone.

"Ransom," I said, businesslike. "The way I see it, you have two choices. Either you leave here now without putting up a fight, and I don't make the fact your recklessness almost made me lose my life a public matter." My assertiveness surprised me. So did the serenity in my voice. "I will not involve Tom, or the police, or my parents. I will not tarnish The Robot's pristine reputation."

"Are you threatening me?" His voice was ice-cold.

I shook my head. "Just stating the chain of events, as they will happen, if you don't evacuate this house yourself. Because the second choice—if you stay…"

I didn't have to finish the sentence.

He knew I meant business, because he sucked in his cheeks, fighting to keep calm.

"What about your safety?"

"I'm safe enough," I insisted. "You were never supposed to keep me from harm's way. You were supposed to babysit me and scare the living crap out of me from making mistakes. Now that Kozlov is locked up, along with the top men in his organization, and you will no longer be here in Los Angeles, the Bratva won't have a reason to get anywhere near me."

"What about my babysitting duties?" he spat out.

"I don't need a babysitter anymore."

"Your father will not consent to this." Ransom stood up, puffing his chest. One last-ditch effort to assert his power over me. I stood right along with him, taking a few steps forward.

Toe-to-toe.

Nose-to-nose.

Our heartbeats, however, were out of whack. Mine was racing, trying to claw its way out of my chest. Ransom's, as always, was slow and steady.

He was who he was. A dark horse who'd made it against all odds—without pedigree, without a name, and without a soul. He wasn't malicious, no. Simply careless. And I could no longer afford to surround myself with people who didn't care about me.

"You'll convince him." I tipped my chin up.

"You're making a mistake." Ransom caught the tip of my chin between his fingers. I swatted his hand away.

"Stop telling me what I'm feeling, what I'm thinking, what I'm doing. Stop gaslighting me. Just leave. Right now. And never contact me again."

"Do you truly mean it?"

I closed my eyes, the pain too much to bear. "*Truly.*"

And I knew in that moment he'd never contact me again. That he was too proud, too fucked-up, to ever concede. Bow down. Show weakness.

I forced my body to step back, feeling like my legs were made out of concrete. Turning away from him, giving him my back, was the hardest thing I'd had to do.

He was, after all, my protector.

The man who taught me so much about myself.

The man who made me laugh.

Who made me live again.

Who made love to me, when I'd thought I would perish under the touch of another.

"Princess." His voice made me stop at the foot of the curved stairway. I didn't turn around. Didn't trust myself enough. "I'm really proud of you."

"I know."

"You're doing the right thing."

"I know that, too."

He'd wanted to say something else. I could feel it. But in the end, all I heard was the soft click of my door as it shut.

For the first time ever, I allowed myself to let go, collapse on the stairs, sobbing into my arms, letting my whole body break, and not just my heart.

Chapter Twenty-Two

Ransom

"**Y**ou goddamn idiot."

Tom plastered his forehead to the cool steel of our agency's door, closing his eyes. His breathing was labored, and he looked ready to kill someone.

Me. I was that someone. And I deserved a good beating for what I'd done.

Leaning against my desk with my arms crossed, I let him blow off some steam.

"You put your client at risk, let her out of your sight, *and* kept the entire mess from me. I can't believe you."

He pushed off of the door, pivoting into the common area of the agency. He kicked a trashcan. It rolled along the floor, spitting crumpled papers and chewed gum.

With calm I didn't feel, I noted, "You were the genius who insisted I take the job."

"I didn't know your beef with the Russians was an ongoing matter!" Tom threw his arms up in the air, shouting.

"Neither did I," I flat-out lied.

"And now she *fired* you."

That one sliced through my chest like a rusty knife.

"We've decided it was best if we parted ways. She won't say a word to her father about it. He'll think it was just the mafia being the mafia. She's high profile, loaded, sought-after—"

"Something's not making sense here." He raised his hand, stopping me midsentence.

I arched an eyebrow. "Oh?"

"You've never kept shit like this from me. Ever." Tom stalked toward me, his eyes zinging with determination. "You're not giving me the whole story. Why did you keep it to yourself? Why didn't you tell me about the Russians right away?"

Because I couldn't stay away from a certain Thorne Princess.

"I can handle my own problems."

"*Bullshit!*" He slammed his palms against my chest, pushing me. The desk scraped behind me. "Give me the missing piece."

"There's no missing piece."

"I'll go and ask Miss Thorne herself. She'll answer, too. That girl couldn't lie if her life depended on it," Tom warned.

He wasn't wrong. Hallie was pure as fresh-fallen snow. Still, what were the chances he'd hurl his ass all the way to California just to ask her? I stared at him flatly, calling his bluff.

Tom waltzed over to our secretary's desk, ripping a Post-it note from a pile and scribbling something, slapping it against her screen.

Get me on a flight to L.A. Today.

—T

He picked up the phone and made a call.

"What're you doing?" I asked tersely. I didn't have patience for this shit. I was tired, agitated, and above all, still digesting the fact that Hallie had thrown me out of her life.

"Calling Holmes' daughter. At the funeral—which you bailed on, by the fucking way—I promised I'd give her a call if I'm in Cali again. She wants to talk about her dad."

The asshole meant business. He was going to jet to California and hear from my former employee how I'd fucked her.

It was time to face the music, even if it sounded like a cat in heat.

"I fucked her," I spat out finally.

Tom froze, his phone still pinned to his ear. I heard a few, faint *hellos* from the other line. Slowly—very fucking slowly—he lowered his phone, killed the call, and tucked it into the inner pocket of his blazer.

"You *fucked* the ward?"

Hearing the words flung back at me, they sounded all wrong. I waved my hand dismissively.

"It was more of an affair."

"You don't do affairs. You do contracts and NDAs and rape fantasies. All the sordid shit."

"People change."

"People—yes. Not you." His hands quivered with anger and he balled them into fists by his sides. He snarled, animal-like, making his way to me.

I stood straighter, my muscles tensing in case we had to rough it out. Wouldn't be the first time. We were forced to do this a lot as kids. Solve our disagreements with our fists.

"Are you insinuating I'm incapable of developing feelings?" I drawled.

"I'm not insinuating, it's a proven fact. I'd put money on it."

But he wouldn't win. Not this time. Because I did, in fact, have feelings. Lots of them. I felt angry and out of place. Confused, too. It was the first time a woman had kicked me out of her bed—out of her place. A woman who, specifically, I wasn't done with.

No matter. It was supposed to be good that Hallie and I were now on opposite sides of the continent. Nothing would've come out of our little fling.

So why did I feel like such a goddamn mess?

Realizing Tom was waiting for an answer, I finally said, "Look, it doesn't even matter. Whatever happened, happened, and it's behind us now. Anthony will never know. She'd never tell him. Schedule a call with McAfee. I'll explain the Russian kidnap blunder. If anything, it's a good thing." I pushed Tom out of my personal space, striding toward the wall-to-wall window overlooking Chicago's skyline and The Loop.

"Good?" he snorted out behind me. "Walk me through your logic, Lockwood."

I reached for the bottle of cognac in the Ralph Lauren liquor cabinet, pouring myself a generous drink. "The fact of the matter is, she was kidnapped, and it took me less than two hours to find her and save her. In the process, I also got Kozlov and company locked up. Two birds, one stone. McAfee will be impressed by that."

"Will he also be impressed with you getting fired?"

I took a swig of my drink, rolling it in my mouth. "No one has to know I was terminated. As far as McAfee is concerned, we shifted things around. I decided to go back to the main office now that the threat's been removed, and we assigned someone else to the job."

"There's no one else on the job," Tom pointed out.

I turned to give him one of my special, *you-don't-fucking-say* looks.

"I hadn't noticed," I deadpanned.

"Asshole." Tom clenched his teeth. "Fine. But only if we get Max back on the job. I don't want to lie."

I shook my head. "There's zero chance of Hallie letting any of us near her ever again."

And rightly so. I'd fucked up royally with her. I was lucky I didn't have a lawsuit the size of Belgium waiting for me right now.

"No bodyguard—no McAfee." Tom crossed his arms over his chest.

"Are you kidding me?" I snarled. "You *promised*. That was the only reason I went out there in the first place."

He raised his palms up. "Let's settle. We'll put surveillance on her without telling her, to make sure she doesn't run into any trouble. Put our minds at ease, and we don't have to ask her for favors. I understand how tricky it might be, to ask her for a solid considering your…*indiscretion*."

Perfect solution. One that would put my mind at ease, too.

Yet, I couldn't fucking do it. Couldn't bring myself to go against Hallie's specific request not to be followed, just to save my own ass. I didn't care to think about what it meant. I just knew I couldn't do this to her.

"No." I hung my head down.

"No?" Tom echoed, raising an eyebrow.

"No," I said. "I can't have her followed. She said it's over. We need to respect that."

"Since when do you *respect* other people's rules?" Tom spat out. "Who even are you?"

Both were good questions, and I didn't have an answer for either of them. All I knew was I wanted this conversation over. I walked over to my office, retrieving my wallet, keys, and laptop before walking out the door.

"Secure the meeting with McAfee. I want to talk to Thorne and have him introduce us to whoever we need in D.C."

I dipped out of the office, slamming the door behind me.

That night, I stumbled into a bar near my apartment and drank myself half to death.

I showed up at work the next morning, after a CrossFit session, showered, dapper, and ready to conquer the world. Pressing hard on all work-related issues, I convinced myself that diligence was all it took. Twenty-four hours to get Hallie Thorne out of my system. Just like a bad stomach bug.

She was no longer my job, my problem, or a part of my life.

The plan went well until the clock hit seven and everyone left the office for home. I went straight to the bar. *Again.*

Other people—normal people—had someone waiting for them at home. A spouse, a girlfriend, a kid, a goddamn pet. For the first time in my life, there was someone I actually wanted to see, and I couldn't. The only time I didn't want solitude, I had been forced to have it.

The next day was the same. I functioned. I attended meetings. I assigned agents to cases. I briefed. I courted. I even got McAfee on the phone and, as expected, he seemed pleased with how I'd handled the Hallie Thorne kidnapping case. A case that was now appearing less on newspaper headlines and popping up more on pages four and five, right next to the grocery coupons and adult incontinence diaper ads.

After all, she was fine.

I was fine.

So fine, in fact, that I decided to visit the bar again after my conversation with McAfee, to celebrate. McAfee had promised to connect me with Thorne's former security firm to talk about potential clients for my cybersecurity venture.

One week turned into two.

Two into three.

Before I knew it, I'd clocked in a whole month.

At some point around the two-week mark, I stopped hitting the bars and started hitting the liquor store. No point in shooting the shit with bartenders or sidestepping horny housewives looking for dirty fucks while I got good and hammered.

One day, I looked at the calendar and realized I'd drunk myself numb for thirty days straight. I briefly considered throwing my own ass into rehab for a spell. But that would be the smart thing to do. The *right* thing to do.

I went cold turkey instead.

I threw all the bottles of whiskey and cognac into the trash. Doubled-down on the CrossFit. Cleaned up my act.

Sober, with a new haircut, and frequenting Tom's Brady Bunch home for goddamn family dinners, I finally made it.

I stopped thinking about Hallie.

I stopped thinking about the day she told me to go fuck myself.

And started living my life.

It was really that simple.

See, asshole? You can do anything you put your mind to. You are, after all, Ransom Lockwood.

Chapter Twenty-Three

Hallie

"Are we ever going to talk about him?" Keller peered at me from behind his kitchen wall, munching on a green nacho chip. Kale, probably.

"Who?" I didn't look up from where I was sketching on the couch. Also known as my new bed for the past month, ever since I'd moved in after I kicked Ransom out, and never bothered to open any of the envelopes my parents sent containing new credit cards.

"Voldemort."

"We do not speak his name." I shuddered.

"Ransom, then."

"Not talking about him, either."

I was drawing a wounded heart strung together like a corset. The heart was melting, leaking from between the threads. I bit down my lower lip to suppress a moan of pain. His name alone made me want to cry.

"Oh, honey, it's okay to not be okay." Keller sat on the arm of the couch, stroking my hair.

"No, it's not." I stood up, waltzing over to my suitcase at the corner of his living room, flipping it open. In it, I'd stowed an envelope full of cash. Cash I'd saved from years ago. Dad always said it was good to have cash handy, and he wasn't wrong. I needed it for when I paid for my occupational therapy as well as tutoring to help me manage my learning disabilities and dyslexia. Then there was Ilona. She didn't come cheap, either.

I slipped the money out of the envelope, counting silently. Only a grand left there. Nothing more. *Shit*.

"I can lend you some money," Keller's voice offered from his spot on the couch.

"I don't want your money; I want you to give me a job."

I flipped the suitcase shut, stood up, and walked over to the kitchen to get a glass of water. We'd had this conversation countless times before. I was desperate to get a job at Main Squeeze. But Keller kept suggesting he should just give me money until I got back on my feet again. I couldn't accept his offer. I didn't want to be indebted to him—to anyone—and I didn't know when my financial situation would improve.

Keller followed me to his kitchen. He had a one-bedroom apartment in West Hollywood. It was tiny, but impeccably designed. Gray upholstered sectionals and recliners made out of fine leather, Persian-style tufted rugs, faux fur throws, and abstract paintings he'd gotten for dirt cheap in Downtown L.A. on the Art Walk.

I filled myself a glass of tap water before turning around and leaning against his all-white kitchen counter.

"Honey, you know I would. In a heartbeat." Keller squeezed my arms, his face full of remorse.

"What's stopping you, then?" I demanded. "Why wouldn't you give me a chance?"

"Well, it's not a game, working for Main Squeeze." He pretzeled uncomfortably, rubbing the back of his neck. "You'll have to wake up early for shifts, cut all the fruit and veggies at five in the morning…deal with *impossible* customers."

"And you don't trust me to do a good job?" I arched an eyebrow, feeling my eyelid twitch in annoyance.

He squirmed. "You've never held a job in your life, Hal."

"There's a first time for everything."

"True." He sighed, looking tortured. "But Main Squeeze is a really huge deal to me. It's my bread and butter, and I cannot afford any hiccups. I don't think you understand." He closed his mouth, shaking his head. "Honey, I really *don't* take a dime from my father. If this goes to hell, I won't be able to pay my mortgage on this place. I won't be able to pay the lease on my car. I don't have a plan B. *Or* a plan C. It's all I have. This small juicery. My dad is a deadbeat rock star who is in love with himself, his cocaine, and whatever girl is currently sucking his dick—not sure who it is this month, but she's bound to be younger than me. I don't have anything to fall back on. Mommy and Daddy Thorne won't bail me out. And I love you!" he exclaimed passionately. "But..."

"But you can't count on me," I finished softly.

I got it. I truly did. Keller knew me before I'd made the change. Before I realized life wasn't a rollercoaster of designer bags and mistakes. He knew me as the girl with the driver, with the credit cards, with the house that didn't match her nonexistent salary. He loved me for who I was. A hang-out buddy. A girl who was quick-witted and always fun to be around. But he wouldn't necessarily trust me with his livelihood.

And...I couldn't fault him for it.

I'd given him no reason whatsoever to believe I understood and could participate in the real world. So far.

Nodding weakly, I turned around and rinsed the glass I'd used, putting it on the dish rack. "I gotta go."

"Oh, honey, don't be like that! I don't have anything until two o'clock. We can binge-watch *Selling Sunset* and eat those organic coconut-date thingies from Whole Foods that look healthy but are actually hella calorie-dense."

Giving him a tight smile, I grabbed the hem of his shirt and pulled him into a squeeze.

"You're fine, Keller. I'm not mad. You're letting me stay here rent-free until I figure my shit out. You owe me nothing. Please don't feel like you do."

He pulled away from me, his whole body jerking. "Who are you and what did you do with my petty, albeit adorable, friend?"

I shrugged. "Maybe I grew up."

His face eased. "Yeah. I'm starting to suspect maybe you have."

Armed with my JanSport backpack (admittedly, it was so much more practical than any designer bag I owned), I made my way to Dennis' first. This past month, I'd made it a point to visit him and his wife once a week. Sometimes I brought snacks and coffee. But this last time, I was short on cash. Maybe after I managed to sell my old designer items to consignment stores.

Ethel opened the door for me, all smiles. "If it isn't my favorite girl!"

After weeding out their garden and staying for a cup of coffee ("*Doing something for others will make your soul feel good,*" Ilona told me), I bid them farewell.

"Where are you headed?" Dennis asked.

"Sunset Boulevard."

"That's miles away!" he thundered dramatically. "Let me drive you."

I laughed, shaking my head. "No chance in hell."

"And what about on earth?" he sassed. God, I loved his dad jokes. I was so glad to have him back in my life, even if not as my driver.

"Not here, either." I paused, frowning as I thought about it. "You know, Dennis, I loved that we were a team for so long. You were my favorite part about Los Angeles. Still are."

But not for long. He and Ethel were heading back to the East Coast soon, to reunite with their family in Maryland.

"But is it weird that I love taking the bus? There's something really great about just sitting in front of a window, watching the city zip by, with your headphones and just…disappearing for a little bit."

Dennis' mouth widened into a satisfied smile. His eyes shone.

"Yes." He clucked his tongue. "I feel the same way every time I read a book. Goodbye, Hallie."

I saluted him, winking at Ethel. "Until next week, folks."

I arrived at Misfits and Shadows, my favorite tattoo shop, half an hour early.

This was a first for me. I was usually in the habit of being late for everything. It made me feel important, sought-after. Not anymore. I was now thriving on being organized, calculated, and always on time.

In one of our bi-weekly sessions, Ilona pointed out that perhaps I was feeling so down about myself because I never gave myself a chance to succeed.

"Always late, never prepared. It's almost like you want to fail, Hallie, so you can prove to yourself that yes, you are, in fact, all those things you believe people think about you."

Misfits and Shadows was as wacky and colorful as the rest of Sunset Boulevard. The building itself was all black. Instead of a sign, there was purple and pink graffiti with the joint's name, decorated with three-dimensional skulls and roses. The artists here were the best. Back in my heyday, when I had very little to do with my time, I would spend hours sitting here, planning my next design with them.

I stared at the name of the tattoo shop, took a deep breath, and turned around promptly, walking in the other direction.

I couldn't do it.

I couldn't handle failing.

It was horrible, and cowardly, and stupid, but it was the honest truth.

Hearing the word 'no' was going to undo me.

My phone rang in my pocket. I tugged it out, punching a placebo button on the light to cross the street.

Mom

It wasn't the first time she'd called this week.

It wasn't going to be the last time, either.

I should feel bad, but I didn't. It was complicated. Ilona assured me that it was okay to take some time, step away from the situation, and examine my feelings before I faced my family.

Weirdly enough, I didn't feel the dread and embarrassment that usually accompanied a call from my mother. Just a dull ache in my chest—an ache that burned a little hotter, a little deeper at the thought of giving up on the opportunity to try to make something of myself.

Not answering Mom was a choice I could undo.

Not showing up to my first intern interview would be something I'd definitely regret.

I pivoted, stomping my way back to the tattoo shop with purpose. I was still fifteen minutes early. I pushed the glass door, tornadoing to the reception counter before self-doubt weighted down my legs again. The place was packed, as usual. Misfits and Shadows didn't accept walk-ins, and it wasn't hard to see why. They were the busiest parlor in Los Angeles.

"Hallie!" Meadow, the receptionist with the Chelsea haircut, three lip rings, and an abundance of green eyeliner greeted me. "You're here. Want something to drink while I get Grady?"

Grady was the big boss. The owner. The guy who inked all the famous people in town. He hadn't been accepting new clients in a decade or so. I'd managed to squeeze in with him only twice, when he was in a good mood and had last-minute cancellations.

A ball of anxiety lodged in my throat. I swallowed hard, pushing through it.

"If you don't advance yourself—who will?"—Ilona.

"Water would be great." *With a side of Xanax.*

"Sure. Have a seat."

I did, tucking myself between an excited couple who came to get matching tattoos and a large biker who kept fingering a tattoo on his arm he was obviously re-doing. I hugged my backpack to my chest, reminding myself that this place was like home. I'd been here dozens of times before. Knew who each of the four stations in the studio belonged to. Recognized the red vinyl chairs each artist had—and remembered that Grady's had a huge rip in it.

If he said no—I would be all right.

If things are not failing, you're not innovative enough. Elon Musk's words, not mine.

Meadow returned with a glass of water. A few moments later, Grady appeared—a scrawny, thoroughly-tatted, aging rock star type of a man who enjoyed muscle shirts and collecting pencils from all over the world.

"Hal. Good to see you." He stopped in front of me.

I stood up, slinging my backpack over my shoulder, feeling like a kid. I reached to shake his hand. "Thanks for having me."

"My pleasure. Let's talk in my office."

His office was at the back, and totally isolated, which was a relief, because I didn't want an audience. The minute I sat down in front of him, he laced his fingers together, sitting back.

"Why do you want to become a tattoo artist?"

"Because it's my passion. It's what I think about every morning and every night. Because I want to change lives. I want to help people hide their scars. Enhance their personalities. Their beauty. Who they are. Because the more time I spend on this earth, the more I believe that self-expression is one of the most important gifts we owe to ourselves. And because..." I took a deep breath, bracing myself, preparing to say something positive about myself for the first time. "Because I think I can be damn amazing at it with the right guidance. And I think you're the best in the business."

By Grady's slight smile, I could tell he was satisfied with the answer.

"You've been a longtime client," he pointed out.

I nodded. "As I said, you are my first choice. My *only* choice right now, to be honest, for an apprenticeship."

"I've never taken a client on as an intern before. It's a demanding apprenticeship," Grady warned. He pushed open his desk drawer, pulling a pile of pencils out and beginning to sharpen them.

"We're talking two years of no salary at all. I know your background and know you have means—"

"Actually, I don't," I cut him off. "But that doesn't matter. I'm okay with a long internship. I have a lot of stuff in storage I can sell to pull me through. And I'm getting a part-time job in a few days."

If someone would give me a chance.

"You'd start from the bottom up if I were to take you on," he continued. "Taking out the trash, setting up and breaking down stations, going on coffee runs, and covering for Meadow whenever she bails on work, which is every time she breaks up with a boyfriend, *which* is every other month."

I had long-suspected Grady was in love with Meadow, just by silently observing the two of them over the years.

I smiled. "I can do that. No problem."

"The first thing you'll do, approximately six months after you become the shop's designated errand girl, is mix ink. I won't let you touch live skin before the one-year mark."

"Sounds fair."

"You'll do about a hundred and fifty tattoos for free—and you'll have to find volunteers if you get accepted."

"I have a large net and larger contact list. I can make it happen," I said with confidence that—surprisingly—I was beginning to feel.

"And you'll pay for the ink."

It sounded like Grady was trying to scare me off the job. Maybe, like Keller, he thought I couldn't do it.

But I just kept on nodding, keeping my smile intact, even when my hope began crumbling. "It doesn't matter what you hit me with, Grady, I promise you. I want this more than anything else. I'll prove myself to you."

"All right." He sighed, dropping the pencil he'd sharpened into the drawer and picking another one. "Let's see what you've got."

With trembling fingers, I produced my sketch pad from my backpack, silently handing it to him. An arrow of excuses was at the tip of my tongue, tight-stringed and ready to be fired.

These are just early sketches.

Flip to the end and see how much progress I've made.
If it's not enough, I can take night classes.

But I didn't say anything. I waited patiently as he flipped through the pages, observing my sketches intently. The shackle-mouthed angel with the broken wings, the devil who laughed menacingly, the hearts in cages, and portraits of animals and dragons and warriors.

He stopped when he got to the sketch of a girl who looked a lot like me, wearing a crown of thorns. He drew a long breath, stealing all the oxygen in the room. My muscles stiffened as I awaited his verdict.

"Is this you?" he asked quietly.

The face of the girl—me—was out of proportion. It was one of my earliest pieces. I think I'd drawn it the first time Ransom and I were in Texas.

"Yeah," I said, resisting the urge to explain I could now render a human face a lot better.

"It's full of pain."

My eyes dragged up to meet his. "Aren't we all?"

A smile tugged at his lips. "When can you start?"

Chapter Twenty-Four

Hallie

Three months later.

Y ou are getting up there and opening this lock, Hallie Thorne.
   I gave myself a pep talk, swinging the entrance door to
   my Westwood building.

Perhaps an apartment was a big name for what I was renting.
The property was a two-story house that had been converted into
four studio apartments—two on the first floor and two on the second. Details were dicey regarding the legality of this arrangement,
but it was a safe enough neighborhood, and the rent was dirt cheap.

Leaning my secondhand bike against the wall in the dank hallway, I looked to the carpeted stairway leading up to my apartment
with a sigh.

"The lock is not going to give you trouble," I repeated sternly
to myself, aloud this time.

Yes, it will. It always did. It took me twenty minutes to open
my apartment every day. But I wasn't in a position to bargain with
my landlord, and living with Keller was something we were both
growing to hate. I did not approve of his random hookups that

never called and always grabbed the last La Croix can from the fridge before they slipped out.

He, on the other hand, was tired of someone occupying his living room and using all the hot water in the shower.

Stomping my way up, I brushed my fingers over the walls. My finger pads were so calloused, so worn-out from work, feeling any pressure against them felt good. My phone danced in my pocket, signaling a text message, and for the thousandth time, I took it out, hoping I might be seeing Ransom's name.

Keller: Hey honey, good news. Derryck from the café across the street needs his place cleaned three times a week. Should I give him your number? X

I typed a quick *yup* and continued my journey upstairs.

For a while, I saw Ransom everywhere. At the discount supermarket I frequented. At the bike shop. At the movie theater, whenever I went with Keller, and even at the tattoo parlor where I interned.

Since I hadn't been able to find any part-time job—Keller's guess was that every time people saw my name on a résumé they assumed it was a prank—I had to resort to cleaning Main Squeeze and the joint next to it, a dispensary called High Fashion, every night. It paid the bills—sort of. And maybe it was the weed fumes, but I could swear I'd seen Ransom there, too.

But in the last few days, the situation had improved. I would find myself not thinking about him for an entire hour, sometimes even two. When my head hit the pillow, exhaustion won the war against heartbreak, and I was able to sleep instead of obsess over him—what was he doing? Who was he with? Did he think about me, too?

It was true, what they said. A life of hard work kept you out of trouble…and away from sin.

After all, I'd done the right thing. Ransom had never really cared about me. That was why he found it so easy to stay away.

When I reached the top of the stairs, I was so exhausted from my shift at the tattoo shop that I collapsed onto my door with a groan. Only, my body wasn't met with a mass of hard wood. I fell on something softer…and definitely curvier.

"Bunny, you look like hell!" my mother greeted me in her signature, Julianne Thorne way.

Pulling back, I stumbled until my back hit the opposite wall, blinking. I was immediately alert. In front of me stood Dad, Hera, and Mom. No bodyguards. No security detail. For a moment, I was tempted to bark at them to go back to Texas. But then I remembered something Ilona had told me last week.

"You can't stay away from your family forever. Even though they're imperfect, and your feelings are valid, they still love you and care deeply about you in their own way. Don't give up on them before you try to turn your relationship around."

"W—what are you doing here?" I wrestled the words out of my mouth. Barely.

"It's time we talk," my father said, softly but sternly. It was his no-nonsense tone, and I hadn't heard it in so long. I'd missed it, I realized foolishly. I missed his tough love. I missed his any-kind-of-love.

"We haven't talked since that awful day when you came to Texas for a few hours. Since…" Mom drew a shaky breath, stopping midsentence.

Since I made it clear I did not consider them family after overlooking Craig's behavior toward me.

But I'd made some progress since. I'd realized that maybe they weren't the ones I should be angry at for that particular offense. They had their faults—they tampered with my life, with my decisions, with my well-being, and clipped my wings, putting me in a nice, golden cage. But as Ilona pointed out in one of our many sessions, they were not maliciously abusive, even if abuse did occur. And Craig's assaults happened discreetly enough not to provoke any suspicion from them.

I swung my gaze to Hera, popping an eyebrow. "Where's your husband?"

I already knew the answer. For once in my life, I was the snarky sister.

Hera pursed her lips, looking down. "He's living at his parents' now. He posted bail shortly after he got arrested."

"Probably the first time he had to feel any sort of discomfort in his life."

"Are you going ahead with the trial?" my sister asked.

Smiling demurely, I said, "Contrary to popular belief, I always finish what I start."

"We're getting a divorce," Hera blurted out.

"Of course." I remained unaffected. "It's bad publicity to stay with him after what happened. Lots of headlines."

"Is that what you think?" Hera's mouth hung open.

I shrugged.

"Look, Hallie, we would love to talk to you inside, in privacy." This was Dad, looking so lost, so out of his natural habitat, a pang of sorrow actually prickled at my skin. I'd never seen him so out of sorts.

I didn't think my apartment had enough space for all of us, but I shoved my key into the lock anyway. I started messing with it when it got stuck. With a huff, I explained, "It's a tricky one."

Dad stepped into my personal space, taking over, holding the handle and the key. "The secret is you have to pull the handle toward you as you shove the key as deep as you can before turning." He pushed the door open effortlessly.

With a skeptical frown, I asked, "How did you know that?"

"I worked for a locksmith all summer, every summer when I was a teenager."

"I had no idea."

"That's because I hardly ever spoke to you girls about anything of importance. I'd like to change that. Now, come."

We all filed into my living room. I didn't make any apologies for the size of my apartment or the state of it. Or the fact the couch looked like it had seen better days—in the nineties.

Mom and Hera sat on my tiny couch, while Dad took the only stool by the breakfast nook. I landed on my twin-sized bed.

Dad looked between Hera and Mom. I always felt like they were a team, independent from me in every way, shape, and form. It seemed that way now, too. Like they spoke a secret language through their eyes alone.

"I'll start," Dad said decisively, when both Mom and Hera looked away, embarrassed. "The entire family owes you an apology, Hallie. And I think the right time to give you that apology was the day you came to Texas to tell us about Craig. We were so shell-shocked, so angry—at him, at ourselves—that the tragedy was clouded by rage. By the time we got our heads straight, digested everything that was said, that was *done*, you refused to take any of our calls. Ransom advised us to stay away—"

At the mention of his name, my heart gave a leap. But my face did not twitch. "And, well, we gave you some space. We kept calling, but we didn't barge in. Until it became apparent that you wanted nothing to do with us—probably for good. Am I right here, Sugar Pie? Do you not want anything to do with us?"

Yes. No. Maybe?

"It's complicated," I said finally. "Your presence here doesn't only remind me of what happened with Craig and went undetected. For me, you symbolize my loss of independence. Or my never really gaining it in the first place. All the lies, the cover-ups about my dyslexia…the way you substitute your love and affection for me with mansions and designer bags…I'm mad at you. I'm angry at *myself* for letting it happen. And I'm not finished being angry."

"Fair." Dad rubbed his jaw. "We're not going to push you to do anything you're not ready for. But we have some things to say before we leave here. First of all, I'd like to apologize. This is a blanket statement, Hallie, so listen carefully. I apologize for not being present when I should have. For making the wrong decisions when you were too young to make them for yourself. For hurting you in my bid to protect you. For drowning you in material things instead of attention. For being absent, and focused on myself, on my career, when life began to unravel for you. For letting it spin out of control the way it did. Most of all," he sucked in a breath, his lower lip quivering slightly, "I apologize for not being the father you deserved."

You could've heard a pin drop. The place was so small our knees touched together. It was ridiculous to see all these powerful people sitting in a nine hundred dollar a month studio.

"My turn." Mom wiped the corner of her eye, an embarrassed chuckle on her lips. "I would like to apologize, too. I suspect my role has played a big part in how you're feeling right now. I'd been... so obsessed with my place in this world, with my title, with what I wanted to achieve, that I completely neglected you. Both of you." She looked at Hera, too.

"Only with Hera, it was...different. She stayed close. She didn't want to live far away. She sought my attention and advice actively, so it was easier to form a closer relationship with her. I foolishly believed if I gave you your space, you'd come to me eventually. That we would have a relationship. A part of me even resented you—my own daughter—for your lack of interest in me and my accomplishments. Instead of trying to figure out a way to you, I was waiting for you to find a way to me. I am so sorry. I never meant to cause you harm. I genuinely believed putting you through some tests that would label you a certain way would harm your self-esteem, not elevate it. I trusted in my way with such conviction, I couldn't imagine, for a moment, a scenario where I could be wrong. I am so sorry, Hallie. If you just give me the chance, I know I can make the situation better. For both of us. Start over fresh."

Again, I said nothing. It was a lot to process. My gaze was pinned on Hera. She was the only one who hadn't said anything. A part of me didn't think she would. Hallmark movies aside, people didn't usually have epiphanies. Light bulb moments or defining points where they suddenly knew what to say and what to do. And recognizing your own errors was especially hard.

Cautiously, Hera opened her mouth. But instead of an apology, something else entirely came out.

"I hate my life."

The words rang around the room, seeping into the walls.

"I've always hated my life," she said, sitting a little straighter. "I've taken the opposite path from you, Hallie. You were always about making your own mark in the world, living your life as you saw fit, exploring who you are. I only wanted to be a part of the Thorne legacy. I wanted to become someone Mom and Dad would be proud of. But on my way to it, I forgot to figure out who I really was."

She didn't look at any of us but continued talking as if in some sort of a trance.

"I went to med school because it looked great on paper. I dated Craig because the story was amazing—childhood sweethearts, ski vacations together from age nine. I stuck around Mom and Dad, even though I missed the East Coast every day. I wanted to be the perfect one. The *good* one. And I paid a terrible price for it. But I think, out of all the damage I've done…" She licked her lips, her eyes glittering unshed tears. "The most awful was that somewhere along the way, I became a horrible person. A person who didn't care about anything but her image. A monster that fed on its own misery. I'm really sorry, Hallie. You didn't deserve this. Not the bad treatment, or my doubt, or my attitude. I'd been horrible to you in the past, for no other reason than wanting to be the best and hating the competition. I'm sorry. I'm sorry I let my insecurities ruin everything."

This was the time to say something important and profound. But I couldn't find the words. So…I said nothing.

We sat there in silence for a few minutes. I used the time to get used to their presence.

Hera spoke first, wiping at her wet eyes.

"Gosh, this is awkward. Let's grab something to eat. I didn't eat any of the private plane food. It looked like it had sat in the fridge for years."

It put a smile on my face, despite my best efforts.

"Bunny, do you know a place?" Mom asked.

"Well, yes, but it's vegetarian."

"All the better." Dad stood up. "Getting tired of all that red meat."

I took them to an Indian restaurant, where I ate my weight in Chole, rice, and baked samosas. I enjoyed the food so much I wanted to weep. I hadn't eaten out in weeks. Maybe months. Fine dining had become a luxury I couldn't afford.

My family must've picked up on the rabid animal vibes, because my dad patted the corners of his mouth clean, pretending like it wasn't a huge deal that he was here, in this little neighborhood restaurant with no less than three secret service agents watching us.

"You know, you can always get an allowance from us. It doesn't have to be an extravagant one."

"No, thank you." I set my fork down onto the table, too full to breathe. "I won't take your money, but..." I glanced between the three members of my truly screwed-up family. "I'll share your company. Maybe. Baby steps and all."

Hera smiled. "Baby steps."

"So..." Dad cleared his throat. "Are we going to talk about the kidnapping scare?"

Eh. I hadn't discussed it with anyone, other than the police for a statement and some follow-up questions. Weirdly—or maybe not so weirdly—I wasn't even worried about being a target. Traumatized—yes. It was pretty horrible to go through all that. But not scared. I knew the incident had nothing to do with me and everything to do with Ransom. And besides, everyone who took part in the kidnapping operation was locked up and awaiting trial on hefty charges. I heard the DA was stitching up an airtight case against Kozlov.

"It was barely two hours," I minimized.

"Still," Dad said. "I cannot imagine what you went through in those hours."

"It wasn't the highlight of my life. No." I became cagey and uncooperative. I knew where the conversation was going.

"Ransom saved the day," Mom stated. I didn't reply. "Yet...you decided it was best you part ways with him. How come?"

"It was more of a mutual decision," I lied, searching desperately for the waiter so I could signal for the check. "He wanted to go back to Chicago, and this happened on the heels of everything with you guys, and I just…I wanted to be alone. Completely alone. And the only reason I'd ever agreed to have him babysit me in the first place was because I depended on your money. Which is not the case anymore."

It was also one of the reasons why I would never take a dime from them again. The feeling attached to it made my skin crawl.

Mom nodded. "You seemed to have gotten along fine."

Hera tried to catch my gaze. I stared at the ceiling. I didn't want to think about him. His name alone did awful, delicious things to my stomach, even now. I hated how I missed him. Missed him despite everything.

"I rolled with the punches," I said finally.

"I met with him the other day," Dad said conversationally. I felt his gaze on my face, and I couldn't help it. I broke down and peered at him, every cell in my body thirsty to hear more.

"Oh, yeah?"

He nodded. "He is opening a cybersecurity department. I promised I'd help him."

"I hope he's doing well," I said cautiously. I meant every word of it. I did hope he was well. Even if it was without me.

"He's a hard guy to read."

"Hmm."

"He asked about you." Dad picked up his glass. Swirled the imported beer inside it. My heart raced dangerously.

"Yeah?" My voice was high-pitched. Different.

"I told him I had no idea. That you cut us all off."

"And how did he respond?" I no longer tried to feign indifference.

Dad stared ahead, pinning me with a look. "He looked *proud*."

"You had something special with this man, didn't you?" Mom sniffed.

"Oh, Mom, shut up. This is so over the line!" I cupped my face, channeling the bratty teenager I never had the chance to be.

"I'm not saying it was romantic!" Mom screeched. "Just that you seemed to deeply care for each other. I remember him being very protective of you."

"Uh, *duh*! He was my bodyguard. Can we talk about something else?"

"Yes!" Hera announced with a flourish. "Let's talk about how I want a divorce party! One with a funny cake and empowering movies and cocktails! Cocktails with sugar in them! I want to go wild."

I laughed.

For the first time, I felt like I had a family.

A dysfunctional, weird family.

But a family, nonetheless.

Chapter Twenty-Five

Ransom

Three months later.

"What I'm hearing is, we will be your first stab at campus security." Dax Gorsuch, the insufferable human answer for a fart, AKA the provost of Clarence University, Chicago, sat in front of me in my boardroom. He looked so full of himself, as if all I'd need was a pin to make him burst and bleed liquid ego.

I felt Tom's eyes land on me. I was the one who handled potential clients. Tom wasn't good at public speaking. Or, you know, at speaking in general, for that fucking matter.

"No." Tom cleared his throat finally, when he realized I wasn't going to say anything. "That's incorrect, sir. We actually have extensive experience with securing large events and parties. We are experts at access control, security assessment, systems monitoring, and preventive hallway and parking lot intervention."

"It's going to be bad." Gorsuch stroked his wobbly chin, drumming his fingers on my custom oval wooden table, leaving marks. "We're bringing in this whacky, extremist political news personality. He'll bring his own security, but we're already seeing demonstrations on campus. It'll get violent. One hundred percent. And I really don't want a lawsuit on my hands."

The words went in one ear and right out the other. I couldn't give two shits about this lecture at Clarence University. All I could think about—all I'd *been* thinking about—in the past seven months was Hallie Fucking Thorne.

Her scent.

Her smile.

Her ink.

The goddamn doodles she left everywhere. I was a man possessed, and I couldn't have a straight thought without her tainting it. She haunted me during the day and came to me at night. I couldn't escape her. And I wanted to. Fuck, I wanted to forget about her.

That was what she wanted. She told me to stay away. So I did.

Through the fog in my head, I could hear Tom stuttering a lackluster answer to Gorsuch.

"…train our bodyguards to make the safest decision at any given time. We've dealt with many situations where high-profile media personalities were under threat in the past. Isn't that right, *Ransom*?"

My name was more spat than said. I shot him a sidelong glance. If looks could kill, I'd be slumped on my crème leather upholstery chair, suffering eighteen gunshot wounds.

I finally ripped myself out of my haze and pinned Gorsuch with a vicious glare.

"Look, you're here, which means that you've pretty much already decided who you're going with. Rightly so. We're the best in Chicago, and we have federal contracts to testify to that fact. We're not going to sit here and list the reasons why you should hire us. Now, here's the part where you want to call us out on our hubris. That's fine. Take your business elsewhere. Just put aside the money for the lawyers, settlement fees, and mediation for when something happens on campus and dozens of lawsuits get shoved up your ass." I buttoned my blazer with one hand, to the stunned face of the provost. "Have a nice day." I walked out.

"Excuse him. He's…uhm, clinically insane." Tom darted up behind me, following me out of the boardroom.

The gray hallway closed in on us. Had it always been this fucking narrow and dim? Not that I was missing Los Angeles and its traffic, pollution, and plastic people, but Chicago could be miserable sometimes.

"What the fuck is wrong with you?" Tom whisper-shouted under his breath.

I waved him off, not breaking my stride to my office. "It's a small job, and he's making you sweat for it. Fuck it."

"A job is a job," Tom insisted.

"No," I explained with patronizing patience. "A job is a contract between two parties, based on mutual respect. I'm not kissing anyone's ass."

"You've never kissed ass." Tom jumped before me, blocking my way to my door. We both knew I could punch him square in the face and get to my destination. But the truth was, work could wait. I'd done nothing *but* work for the past seven months.

"What's eating you, Ransom?" His eyes searched mine frantically.

"Nothing."

"You haven't been yourself."

"*Myself* is a total pain in the ass, and that's exactly what I am right now."

She's twenty-one. Twenty. One. What is it about her that made her impossible to forget?

"Look…" He sighed. "You're giving me unhinged vibes, and seeing as you're my business partner, it makes me feel some kinda way. Come over to dinner tonight? Lisa would really like to see you. The kids miss you, too."

Biggest load of horse shit I'd ever heard, but my social calendar was wide open. Plus, seeing Lisa and the kids might wrestle me into something resembling chivalrous. Or at least not total dipshit behavior. Gorsuch trailed out of the boardroom, shoving a bunch of papers in Tom's chest on his way out.

"Don't fuck it up," he muttered.

I arched an eyebrow to Tom. "See?"

Tom shook his head, looking exhausted. "Just be at my place at six. Look presentable. Oh, and don't drink!"

"I haven't drunk in months."

"Yup." Tom retreated, walking backward to his office as he watched me. "I'm well aware, assface. You've been insufferable to a fault."

One kid sat in my lap, and another on my shoulders as I tried watching a football game in Tom's living room.

"Have they always been this heavy? This needy?" I asked as a tiny finger found its way into my nostril, its owner giggling in delight.

Lisa stared at me levelly from the recliner. "Ransom, they're five."

At six, I was already an expert pickpocket who stole to ensure my belly was full, and fought tooth and nail for my spot on a grubby cot. I had no idea how normal kids behaved at that age.

"Uncle Rand-son, do monthsters exist?"

"Uncle Rand-son, who is stronger, Thor or Spiderman?"

"Monsters don't exist, unless you count politicians and lawyers. Thor is a hammer-wielding god, and Spiderman is a teenager wearing a latex suit, so you do the math. Also, tell your mommy to bring me a beer."

"Tell your uncle to get his own," Lisa said sunnily.

I shook the children off of me and stood up, walking to Tom and Lisa's kitchen. Food was going to be ready in ten minutes, which meant I needed to endure the excruciating punishment of small talk until then. I didn't feel like eating. I didn't feel like being entertained. All I wanted to do was go home and conduct one of my weekly online searches on Hallie. Searches that were becoming more and more frustrating, seeing as she had disappeared from the face of the earth, or at least the reach of the internet. No movie premieres, no parties, no paparazzi pictures at The Ivy.

Naturally, I could get her ass tailed and find out whatever I wanted to know about her. But it was such a dick move—such an obsessive stalker vibe—I couldn't bring myself to do it.

I flung the fridge open, taking out three beers for Lisa, Tom, and me. I popped the caps with my thumb. They slam-dunked straight into the sink. Pivoting, I was about to make my way back to the living room when I found Lisa standing in front of me. She stared at me primly, her hands pinned to her waist.

"What's going on with you?"

"Nothing." I frowned, sidestepping her. "Mind your business."

"It's hard when you're making it impossible for my husband to handle his work professionally. You're not all in, are you?" She followed my steps, staying closely behind.

Snorting out, I said, "That's a bit fucking extravagant, sweetheart. I clock in about three times the amount of hours your husband does."

"You're distracted, agitated, and you're not bringing your A-game," she continued, undeterred. Goddamn Lisa and her BA in psychology. "Stop. Turn around. Help me set the table," she commanded.

I halted, glancing at the dinner table. "It's already set."

"Help me get the roast out of the oven, then."

I took a swig of my beer, setting all three on the table before making my way back to the kitchen. "You're a pain in the ass, Lisa."

"Sure. But you can't afford to be picky with your friends, so just roll with it." She hopped onto the counter, watching as I served my hostess her dinner at her table.

"The lasagna and casserole are in the other two ovens," she sing-songed.

"Yeah, Roger that."

"So…" Her eyes were on me the entire time. I grabbed the kitchen towels and started setting the table with food. "I think I know what'll make you feel better."

"Doubt it," I grumbled, setting the roast down onto the table. "You'd have to shut up and leave me be, and I've a feeling I'm not that lucky."

"I have someone to set you up with," she said.

"No, thanks."

"She's brilliant!" Lisa exclaimed. "Funny, smart, beautiful..."

She's not Hallie, I finished for her in my head. It was impossible to move on.

"I'm not in the market for that," I snarled, returning to grab the lasagna and casserole.

"Why, is there someone else you're interested in?" she cooed.

"No," I hissed.

Lisa dangled her legs over the counter, hands tucked under her ass. She was glowing, and I hated it. "I think there is."

"Dinner's served," I ignored her. "Call the parasites you refer to as family."

"Just go to L.A., Ransom. If you love her so much. It's obvious that you do."

"I don't know what you're talking about." I jammed the carving fork and knife into the roast, carving it like it was the face of someone I hated.

"This isn't something you're going to get over." She hopped off the counter, making her way to me. "You've obviously never been in love before."

She touched my shoulder. I jerked away on contact, turning to growl in her face. "I'm not in love with anyone, and even if I was— which I'm not—she doesn't want to see me. She made it abundantly clear. I'm an asshole, and a bastard, but I'm not so selfish as to shit all over her valid request. Happy now?"

By the size of Lisa's eyes—two fat moons glowing back at me—I knew I looked like I needed to calm the fuck down. And if that wasn't a telltale sign, then the fact that Tom appeared in my periphery, his stance inviting trouble, was.

"Immensely!" Lisa flung her arms over my shoulders in a hug. I froze, still holding the knife and carving fork. What the fuck was happening? I wanted it to un-happen. I didn't want to be touched by anyone. Well, not *anyone*. But not her. "Finally, you feel something, Ransom. This is huge."

"This is stupid." I pulled back, face thundering. "Nothing about this is okay. I have a weird obsession with a woman I used to work for. A woman who is eight years my junior."

"You're in love."

"This isn't what love looks like," I spat out.

"It's *exactly* what love looks like," Tom interjected from his spot by the table. "Go to Los Angeles, you prick."

"She doesn't want to see me."

"She said that seven months ago," Tom pointed out.

"She also doesn't have the memory of a goldfish," I countered. "She meant it then. She means it now."

"Ransom—go!" Now it was Lisa's turn.

"I don't want to bother her."

"You won't be," Tom assured me.

"How do you—"

"Oh, for God's sake!" Lisa threw her hands in the air. "Because I talk to her, okay? I talk to her on the phone about twice a month, and she is still crazy about you. She hates you for what you did, for how you treated her, for a lot of things, but she is still very much into you. So, for the love of God, please, *please*, Ransom, just go to Los Angeles and man-up. The ship's sailed. You're never going to be able to un-feel again. Not once you've gained feelings. They won't go away. Now that you know what it's like to feel—make sure you both feel *good*."

She was going to strangle me.

First and foremost, for grabbing a private plane from Chicago to Los Angeles.

A billionaire client had owed me a favor and he agreed to lend me the plane if I paid for the pilot and fuel.

Second, because I was showing up at her doorstep.

While it was entirely possible that Hallie still thought about me occasionally like Lisa said—she was a sentimental creature—she also nearly pushed me off a fucking cliff the last time we saw each other.

But at the end of the day, Lisa was right. I had to at least try to plead my case.

There was only one tiny problem—I had no goddamn idea where she lived these days, and very little time to conduct my research. I boarded the plane just two hours after my conversation with Lisa and Tom.

My first call was to Keller. He seemed to be her good friend, and I still had his contact from when I worked for her.

"Hola?" he chirped into the phone.

I sat back on the plush white recliner on the plane. "Keller, it's Ransom."

There was a pause before he said, "The fuck?"

"Hallie's former bodyguard."

"I know who you are. My memory is *impeccable*. Do you know how much gingko I consume? The levels of flavonoids and terpendois in my body are insane."

Was he even speaking in English?

"What do you want?" Keller asked.

Obviously, Hallie had not sung my praises to her best friend after our showdown.

"I'll be in the area in a couple of hours and I'd like to meet Miss Thorne. Can you tell me her new address?"

"No, I cannot," he said resolutely. "You can call her and ask for yourself."

"We both know the answer will be no." I wondered what inspired me to have this conversation on the phone and not face-to-face. Keller had a weakness for aesthetically pleasing people. "And I want to talk to her."

"And I want to romance Neil Patrick Harris. But guess what?

He's already taken. And I'm not a homewrecker. Oh, and I'm pretty sure he lives in Sherman Oaks, where the traffic is *insane*."

This man was entirely too much. How Hallie suffered through a conversation with him was a mystery.

"Keller." I used my most menacing tone. "She'd want to hear what I have to say."

"Sure about that, honey?" he asked sweetly. "Great. Then call her and ask for her address. Buh-bye!"

He hung up the phone. I looked at the device with a scowl, then dialed Max. He answered immediately. I didn't even care that he was filling a post in Russia and was in a different time zone.

"Max."

"What's up, boss?"

"I need Hallie Thorne's new address." This was also going to give me a good indication as to whether the two kept in touch or not.

There was a beat of silence before he said, "Boss...I have no idea. I tried to call her a few times after what happened. She never picked up and I didn't want to get in trouble."

Fuck.

"Is there anything—" he started, but I hung up on his face, dialing the next number.

NeNe, her friend—she hadn't heard from her in months.

Dennis, her former driver—he told me to go fuck myself, not in so many words, for hurting his Hallie.

It became clear to me that I had to do what I very much dreaded. I dialed the number, shifting uneasily in my seat.

Love, my ass. Love is supposed to be fun and cozy. I've seen movies. This is fatal attraction bullshit.

The line went alive with a soft click.

"Lockwood? Is everything okay?"

I had the former president of the United States on the line. All because I wanted to talk to a *girl*. Fuck my life sideways. If this plane crashed in a few minutes, I would not be missed.

"President Thorne. Yes. Nothing to worry about," I said coolly, hoping I sounded less deranged than my actions right now. "I called to check in."

"So early in the morning?" He chuckled. "I don't think so, and I'm a busy man, so you better spit it out, son."

This. Was. Painful.

"I'm on my way to Los Angeles and I wanted to have a word with your daughter. I'm finding it hard to reach her." *Mainly because I don't have the balls to call her and get her voicemail.* "I was wondering if you'd be able to give me her address, sir."

"Her address?" he repeated, recovering from his shock quickly. "I don't think so, Ransom. I just won her trust back. Barely. I'm not going to break it."

Something interesting happened to me in that moment. I felt genuine relief. Not because he wouldn't cooperate—fuck that, it was another setback I didn't need—but because I liked to hear that Hallie was reconnecting with her family.

I had to get off the phone and start making my connections in Los Angeles work.

"All right," I said, powering up my laptop as we spoke. "Have a—"

"That's it?" Thorne asked, sounding almost offended.

"Huh?"

"You're just going to take no for an answer?"

I arched my eyebrows, wondering if the fucker was having a stroke.

"I've never been accused of being a gentleman, but even my ass was taught no means no."

"'No' always means open to negotiations," Thorne replied. "'Get the fuck out' means no. That's the rule."

I sat back, stroking my bottom lip. "All right. Let's negotiate."

"Where are you right now?" he asked.

"A private plane. Geographically speaking, we're above Colorado. Just passed Boulder."

"She is not going to like the private plane angle."

"In this case, what she doesn't know can't hurt us?"

"Fair enough. What are your intentions with my daughter?"

Fuck her into the next decade?

Beg for her forgiveness?

Ask her out on a date?

I had no game plan. No strategy. I was playing it by ear, and I loathed every minute of it.

"Just talk," I said through a tight jaw.

"Don't lie to me."

Fair enough. "I would like to explain myself and my actions. We parted ways not on the best terms, and I feel that there's room for an apology on my end."

"Getting warmer." Thorne chuckled, and I heard him lighting up a cigar. "Try again."

"What do you want me to say?" I roared, losing it. "That I can't stop thinking about her? That I'm obsessed with her? That I want to be next to her all the time? That I know she's too good for me, too young for me, too *everything* for me, and still don't give a damn?"

Tell me you're a goddamn psycho without telling me you're a goddamn psycho, Hallie giggles in my head.

But Thorne just chuckled some more, sounding thoroughly amused.

"Yes. I would love to hear all those things. I happen to think my daughter is a fantastic catch and share the sentiment that she is too good for you." He paused. "And too young for you, too."

I groaned, "Let's cut to the chase."

"That's no way to talk to your president," he mused.

"You're no longer my president."

"I'll throw you a bone."

"Make sure there's some meat on it." I bared my teeth.

"I won't give you her address, but I can tell you where she works."

She *worked*? I would've fallen flat on my ass if I wasn't seated.

"Hit me with it."

"Misfits and Shadows."

"Please tell me it's not a sex dungeon," I grumbled, already typing out the name on my laptop.

Thorne roared out a laugh. "Who knew you could crack a joke, Lockwood? No. It's a tattoo shop."

"Will she be working today?"

"I'm her father, not her secretary."

"Thanks for the clarification. The pencil skirt threw me off."

He laughed again. "Go get her, son."

"I intend to, sir."

Chapter Twenty-Six

Ransom

It was pissing rain by the time I landed in Los Angeles. I couldn't remember the last time it had rained in this godforsaken hellhole. But of course, for me, it did.

A taxi was waiting outside the small airport. I slipped inside, giving the man behind the wheel the Misfits and Shadows address.

Hallie seemed to have found her path, her independence, and a way back to her family. I was happy for her, but also worried. Worried I had nothing to offer her anymore. She was done.

She'd pulled through. She didn't need me anymore.

The taxi pulled up at the Sunset Boulevard joint. I got out, feeling like an idiot without an umbrella. It was still pissing wet, the rain falling from fat gray clouds like needles.

I jogged my way to the front door, pushing it open and shaking raindrops off myself like a dog. A girl with an array of piercings and tattoos at the counter stared at me blankly.

"Do you have an appointment?"

Glancing around me, I noticed the place was jam-packed.

"No." I approached her, dumping my paws onto the counter between us. "I'm not here to get a tattoo."

"Oh." She yawned. "No soliciting, bro."

"I'm here for Hallie Thorne."

"And you are?" She cocked her head sideways.

Her nightmare.

"Her...friend." Overstatement of the fucking century.

"Your name?"

"Ransom."

"Cool name."

I smiled cordially. "Can you tell her I'm here?"

"Oh, yeah. She isn't here, Ransom."

Now she was telling me this?

"When will she be here?"

She shrugged, pushing her bottom lip out. "No clue."

I looked around me, calculating my next move. The place was crowded, the humidity rising.

"Will she be here today at all?" I tried again.

"Oh, yeah!" she said brightly, smiling up at me. "For sure, for sure. I just don't know when she'll be in."

"I'll wait, then." I turned around to look for a seat, but there weren't any available.

"That's a good idea, but you'll have to do it outside. Company rules."

"Company?" I whirled around to sneer at her. "It's a goddamn tattoo parlor, not JPMorgan."

"Yeah, well, my boss doesn't allow loitering. You'll have to wait outside."

"It's raining sheets." I gestured to the window, in case she hadn't noticed.

"Sorry, dude."

Karma was in the mood to fuck me real slow to candlelight today. I trudged outside, slamming the door on my way out. There was no knowing when Hallie would be here, and I didn't want to scare her off by calling and asking.

To make matters worse, I couldn't wait nearby. All the bars and restaurants around were still closed—it was too early—and there wasn't a Starbucks in sight.

Pathetically, I found myself standing and waiting in the rain. I had no idea when she'd show up. *If* she'd show up. I just knew I had to try. I couldn't continue existing meaninglessly. It was excruciating.

I also hadn't fucked anyone in over seven months, and was pretty sure my balls were about to fall off.

I paced the street, back and forth. A new feeling I had yet to experience trickled into me as the hours ticked by: doubt.

It's been too long.

It's too soon to start trying.

She's moved on.

This was unchartered territory for me, as I was usually sure of everything I did, down to my meals for the next month or two.

By hour four, I started getting really pissed off. The idiot kid at the reception must've been wrong. It was close to late afternoon and still no Hallie.

I marched back into the parlor, slapping my palms over her counter again. This time, I created two small ponds of water. I was soaking wet, to the fucking bone.

"When's she coming?" I demanded.

The girl looked up from her iPad, completely unfazed. "Who?"

What a moron…

"Hallie," I said through gritted teeth. "Hallie Thorne."

"Oh." She clapped her hands together. "Yeah, she's been here for a while now, came in through the employee entrance."

Back. Fucking. Door. Of course.

My eyes traveled up. I spotted her behind a dividing wall. She stood there, her scarlet hair swirled into a half-assed bun, sweeping the floor in simple denim and a bodysuit that highlighted her curves—and tattoos.

I wanted to hug her. I wanted to kiss her. I wanted to—

"Sir? Sir? You're dripping all over the floor. And you look… kind of blue? Purple? Are you okay?"

Was I okay? I couldn't feel my toes or fingers, and my right ear was numb. Otherwise I was fine.

"Hallie!" I called out. The place was still packed, and I looked less than the dashing prince she deserved. She looked up and stopped whistling to the song playing in the background.

Her entire expression melted. I couldn't tell what she was feeling. Was she happy? Sad? Annoyed to see me?

"What are you doing here?" She narrowed her eyes.

Shit. Annoyed, then.

"We need to talk."

She leaned the broom against a wall and walked over to the reception desk. I was aware of the intrigued audience following our interaction.

"No, we don't." She leaned one hip against the counter.

The need to touch her charred my fingertips.

"Hallie—"

"I told you not to contact me." Her face was still, but her voice quivered. It surprised me that she looked exactly as I remembered her. And yet, I couldn't stop looking. Couldn't get enough. Nothing made any sense.

"You've said a lot of things I don't think you meant," I said softly. "You said you were a failure, and that was bullshit. That you were stupid—you are the smartest person I know. You said no one wants you."

"That one's still true." She spread her arms in the air, smiling winningly.

"Someone does want you."

An exasperated laugh rose from the bottom of her belly. "Right." And then. "Who?"

"*Me*."

I stared at her expectantly. The entire parlor was doing the same. She looked at me blankly, waiting for more. I took a deep breath.

"Look, I stayed away, but it's been miserable for me. I missed you so much." The words clogged my throat. "Actually, I think I missed you even before I knew you ever existed. But now that we've met, it's become impossible to move on. I tried to go back to my old life. To be The Robot again. I can't. I'm not a robot. I haven't been that robot for a long time now. Because of you. You have to believe me, I didn't stay away because it was easy. I did it because I thought I was doing right by you."

"So what brings you here?" she taunted, but her eyes were shining, her shoulders slumped. "You decided you no longer care about doing what's right by me?"

"No," I groaned. Everything was freezing in my body, and I suspected I was spiking a fever. "I realized it was all bullshit. That we both needed to see each other, at least one more time, to see if we could make it work."

"We can't make it work," Hallie said with conviction. "You put yourself before me. I could have been killed. And by the way, you're blue."

Ignoring the last part, I said, "I knew nothing would happen to you."

"How?"

"Because I was fucking crazy about you!" I threw my arms in the air, frustrated. "I didn't leave you out of my sight for one second. The only time you were not right next to me was the time they took you, and even then, as soon as I realized something was amiss, I ripped this fucking city to shreds in order to find you."

She opened her mouth, about to say something, then clapped it shut.

"I think you should go," she said finally.

"Hallie—"

"You said we needed to see each other one more time to find out if it could work. You got your answer. It can't. I want you to leave." Tears made her eyes shine. "Respect my wishes and leave."

I wanted to die a million times over.

But I couldn't say no to her.

I turned around and began making my way outside. I didn't have a plan or another destination in mind. At some point, I was going to strangle my best friend's wife for misleading me, but other than that, no goal.

I walked out to the rain. My feet and clothes were heavy. The street was empty, save for a few cars sailing by and an out-of-service traffic light that signaled the beginning of a brewing storm.

About to round a corner, I heaved myself forward. Behind me I heard the echo of a voice. I needed to get to the hospital. Something wasn't right.

"Wait! Stop!"

Hallie's voice rang in my ears. It sounded like it was coming from the inside of my body. Shit. I was hallucinating. I needed to hail a taxi and hurl myself into the ER.

I stopped walking, calling a taxi on my phone. The app was down. *Figures.*

Something tackled into me from behind. I lurched forward, almost falling straight into traffic. A desperate hand tugged me back to safety, pulling me with it back to the curb.

"I called you! Didn't you hear me?"

I blinked to get the person who spoke to me into focus. It was Hallie. Definitely Hallie. Her face animated and annoyed. *Beautiful.* And I'd lost her.

"I didn't hear," I said quietly.

Rain was pouring down on both of us with no shelter in sight. I was sure I looked pathetic. But for some reason, it didn't bother me so much.

"Did you really mean what you said?" she panted, out of breath. "About wanting me?"

"All I want is you," I admitted. "Trust me, I tried to substitute you with alcohol, training, work—"

"Women?" She cut into my words.

I shook my head. "I can't even smell another woman without wanting her to be you."

She laughed, and through her laugh, I saw some tears, too. "My little robot."

"What do *you* want?" I asked. "Tell me. Because it seems like you've turned your entire life around in seven months. You have your own place, you work, you took control of your life. I trust this

Hallie to make a good decision about her life. And I'm not sure if that leaves me in or out of it."

"You're in." She grabbed the hem of my shirt, jerking me close.

"I'm an asshole," I warned, in case she wasn't paying attention.

"But you're *my* asshole. And I love you."

"I—"

I was going to tell her I loved her, too. But passing out on top of her seemed like a more appropriate plan, so I did just that.

I woke up two hours later with a drip infused into my vein in a pale blue hospital room.

Hallie sat by my side. Her forehead was scrunched in worry.

"You were saying?" She lifted an eyebrow, all sass. "We were kind of in the middle of a conversation when you decided to be all dramatic."

I laughed, which turned into a vicious cough. My ribs felt like they were about to break.

"I was saying that I love you. I have for a while now. I just didn't own it."

"And now you do?" She pressed her cheek on the back of my hand, looking up at me with those angel eyes.

"Now I am."

"I'm staying in Los Angeles, you know," she said, after a pause.

I nodded. "We'll work around that. You don't have to change anything for me. Now, tell me something interesting to distract me from feeling like I got hit by every truck on the West Coast."

"Anything interesting?" She *hmmed*.

"Yeah. Anything. Surprise me."

She pulled her phone out of her green peacoat and typed something out. I watched, fascinated. She hadn't been able to do that just a few months ago. She was obviously working hard. Her fingers shook, but she smiled. Instinctively, I reached to grab her free hand.

"Ah, here's a good one." She shot me an embarrassed smile.

"Humans tend to fall in love with people who have a different immune system from theirs, but have similar lung volume, ear lobe length, and metabolic rate."

I blinked, watching her. "That is the least romantic thing I've ever heard." She giggled.

"And yet, the fact that you've read this makes me want to kiss the shit out of you and finish what we started on the sidewalk."

"So, do."

And I did.

Epilogue

Hallie

One year later.

"I hate this place," Ransom greets me merrily as I slip into our little Prius.

I snap the safety belt, waving goodbye to Meadow, who is just closing up Misfits and Shadows, and Grady, who watches her doing so longingly.

The night is dark, but Sunset Boulevard dazzles brightly. Twinkling lights stretch their limbs along the boulevard as more businesses open up their gates, turning on their neon signs. The moon hangs high and silvery, a perfect crescent, dangling like an earring.

"You don't have to suffer it for very long." I pat his thigh.

Ransom leans in to kiss the side of my neck, his lips brushing their way to mine. He kisses me long and hard, his tongue prodding my lips open, seeking access. I clutch the side of his jaw, deepening our kiss, running out of breath and inhibitions.

This is how we do things, every time he lands in Los Angeles from Chicago, or I go to visit him. We claw at each other like tomorrow never comes.

Like the next time is just a maybe.

Because it is.

Nothing is guaranteed in life.

We learned this the hard way.

When he pulls away, he tucks a lock of my hair behind my ear. "I'll be suffering long enough. The last thing I want is to go to Texas and play happy family with your sister."

I make a face, pushing at his chest as he revs the car to life. "Not nice. She's been trying extra hard."

"The tagline for her life."

The car lurches its way toward LAX, where we'll be boarding a plane to Texas. Hera is getting married...*again*. This time to a very nice medical technician named Jeff. He coaches the local T-ball team and wants three kids and always asks the elderly ladies for a dance at functions.

In short—he is good. And real.

Craig is currently in prison, serving three years. It might not sound like much, but I know that no matter what, his life, as he knew it, is ruined. He got stripped of everything he cared about, and for me, that's enough.

"You're thinking about how nice Jeff is again," Ransom murmurs, looking about ready to punch a wall.

"The devil called. He wants his attitude back." I laugh.

"Tell him he should know better than to ask a bastard like me for anything. I'm keeping it."

Despite the traffic, we get to LAX in time. We park in the long-term parking lot and check our bags and ourselves into the next flight to Dallas. We hold hands. We grin at each other. We're the couple I used to look at from across the street and loathe, because they looked so wholesome.

"Are you having second thoughts?" he asks. I know he means about moving to Chicago.

"Not really." I scrunch my nose. "I know you can't move your business elsewhere. I can. Art doesn't have an address. Its home is in our souls."

Ever since his cybersecurity department opened, it blew up. Ransom travels a lot, but his hub remains in Chicago.

"That is the most Hallie statement I've ever heard." He smiles.

He squeezes my hand, bringing it over to his mouth, brushing his lips against the back of it.

"You'd have done the same for me," I say, knowing it's the truth.

"In a heartbeat."

A make-out session on the terminal seats and a coffee later, we board the plane. I no longer travel to Texas with lead in the pit of my stomach. I feel good. Light, even. I have my own room in my parents' house. And Mom makes it a point to free up time for me whenever I'm there to go shopping, eat, or just head out for a nice stroll. It's still not the kind of relationship I'd dreamed of when I lay in a strange bed in a foreign country, in boarding school accommodations that didn't belong to me. But it's a start.

After takeoff, Ransom turns around and gives me that smirk. The one that turns my bones marshmallow-soft. It's infectious, and I find myself smiling back. We still power-struggle. We still push each other to the edge, challenge one another every step of the way. But the game has become so much more fun, now that I know that his love is unconditional.

"Care to join the Mile High Club?" He quirks a thick eyebrow.

I tap my lips, pretending to think about it. "Was it Groucho Marx who said he wouldn't want to be accepted to any club that's willing to have him?"

It's a midnight flight. The few people in business class are fast asleep.

"Did he say that? Well, I don't trust people with moustaches," Ransom deadpans.

I let out a soft laugh. "What a thing to say."

"It's scientific." He frowns, dead serious. "There's a reason why no president after Grover Cleveland had a moustache. They were advised against it. Not just bad associations, but bad character traits."

I'm grinning, delighted to be basking in his attention, in his passion once again. We see each other every two weeks, but lately, it hasn't been enough.

"I'll go first, and you wait a few minutes." I bite down on my lower lip. "And...Ran?"

He stares at me.

"Let's pretend like I don't want it."

He gives me a nod. I stand up, slipping into the narrow passageway and making my way to the lavatory. Before I even click the door shut, he is behind me, blocking my path to close it.

"You're playing dirty, Mr. Lockwood."

"Well, Miss Thorne, it's the only way I know how to play."

Ransom

It is a tediously boring ceremony.

With all the staples of a boring couple: swan-shaped ice statues, white peonies, and one malnourished, anxious bride. The upside—and there is, indeed, only one positive to the event—is the fact that it will be over soon.

My girlfriend—the bridesmaid—is currently skipping between people, the social butterfly that she is, accepting compliments about her breathtaking beauty. I lounge back in my seat and watch her thrive. It's a peculiar feeling, to care for someone else. But I don't hate the helplessness that comes with feeling this way toward someone anymore.

Anthony plops down in a chair beside me with a long-suffering sigh, a cigar tucked in the side of his mouth. He claps my shoulder. "She's happy."

"The one who is getting hitched, or the one who is about to?" I drawl.

He chuckles. "Easy there, tiger. Hallie hasn't said yes yet."

Because I haven't asked her. But I will, tomorrow. When we go back to Chicago and I show her the place I rented for her. A tattoo parlor in The Loop. Somewhere she can flourish and do her own thing. No better place to go down on one knee than in her own kingdom.

"She will," I say with confidence.

"Probably." He withdraws the cigar from his lips, sending a plume of smoke skyward. "She is crazy about you."

As if sensing the conversation is about her, my girlfriend twists her head, peeks at us from behind her shoulder, and gives us that big Hallie beam that makes constellations light up in the sky.

"I will make you a very miserable man if you hurt her, son."

"Sir." A smile tugs at my lips. "If I ever hurt her, she'd hurt me back twice as hard. That's why I'm marrying her."

Hallie turns away, just as Anthony swivels toward me. He fingers the hem of my blazer, where my skin meets the fabric. "What's that?"

Before I can answer, he pulls the blazer up, just enough to make the sliver of ink peeking from my tux reveal itself into a full-blown sleeve.

"She needed one hundred and fifty tattoos under her belt for her internship," I say.

"And you decided *all* of them would be done on you?" Anthony chuckles.

"Not all." I smirk. "But most."

Over a short period of time, Hallie has used me as her personal canvas. She carved my past, my present, and my future onto my skin. Faces and quotes and people who meant something to me over the years.

"She marked you." Anthony gives me an appeasing once-over, like he is finally sold on me. About to make an offer on a horse.

I sit back and watch the love of my life as she becomes an integral part of her family.

"She didn't need any ink to do that."

BIG BELLS AND BEAUTIFUL BALLROOMS: HALLION IS GETTING MARRIED!

By Anna Brooks, *Yellow Vault* contributor

Hallie Thorne has given her image a makeover... and that includes a sexy, high-profiled bodyguard of a boyfriend. Or should we call him now...her fiancé?!

You heard it here first, Vaulters. Our dear socialite, our favorite party girl, is tying the knot! Check out this exclusive photo of Hallie and her beau, Ransom Lockwood, sharing an ice cream and a pretty hot and heavy kiss in downtown Chicago. Why, we never thought we'd see the day. One thing is for sure—if this girl could find her happy ending, then my dear Vaulters, I can assure you—so can you!

The End.

Acknowledgements

This is the first book of mine which is also available for sale in Comic Sans, a dyslexia-friendlier font. If you have dyslexia or a learning disorder and would like to purchase a copy of my book in paperback in this font, please visit www.authorljshen.com and use Contact Us for more information.

With this out of the way, I would like to thank the numerous people who made this book possible. First and foremost, my editors, Mara White, Tamara Mataya, Sarah Plocher and Paige Smith. Thank you for your guidance, patience, and attention to detail. I strive to become a better writer because of you.

To my sensitivity reader and kinkster reader, who wished not to be named, for your honesty, time, and sense of humor. You made the bad parts bearable.

And to Stacey Blake for the awesome formatting and Lena Yang for the stunning cover. You. Rock. So. Hard.

To Tijuana Turner, my marketing manager extraordinaire, not just for this book, but for being there the entire year I was down for the count, caring for two wee babies and their unimpressed big brother. Thank you for holding the torch.

Same goes to Vanessa Villegas, Marta Bor, Ratula Roy, Amy Halter, Sarah Plocher, Yamina Kirky, Jan Cassi, and Pang Theo. A million thank yous for everything.

Catherine Anderson and Jenn Watson from Social Butterfly PR—thank you for all you do for me, day in and day out. I am forever grateful.

And to my agent, Kimberly Brower, for all the support and dedication. I truly appreciate all you do for me.

Last but not least, to the bloggers, readers, TikTokers, librarians, and bookshop employees who read, recommend, and talk about my books. I couldn't have done it without you.

All my love,

LJ Shen

Stay Connected

Contact L.J. Shen on Social Media

Facebook: facebook.com/authorljshen

Instagram: Instagram.com/authorljshen

TikTok: tiktok.com/@authorljshen

Website: authorljshen.com

Curious about Wolfe Keaton? A sneak peek to my arranged marriage, mafia romance—*The Kiss Thief*:

PROLOGUE

What sucked the most was that I, Francesca Rossi, had my entire future locked inside an unremarkable old wooden box.

Since the day I'd been made aware of it—at six years old—I knew that whatever waited for me inside was going to either kill or save me. So it was no wonder that yesterday at dawn, when the sun kissed the sky, I decided to rush fate and open it.

I wasn't supposed to know where my mother kept the key.

I wasn't supposed to know where my father kept the box.

But the thing about sitting at home all day and grooming yourself to death so you could meet your parents' next-to-impossible standards? You have time—in spades.

"Hold still, Francesca, or I'll prick you with the needle," Veronica whined underneath me.

My eyes ran across the yellow note for the hundredth time as my mother's stylist helped me get into my dress as if I was an invalid. I inked the words to memory, locking them in a drawer in my brain no one else had access to.

Excitement blasted through my veins like a jazzy tune, my eyes zinging with determination in the mirror in front of me. I folded the piece of paper with shaky fingers and shoved it into the cleavage under my unlaced corset.

I started pacing in the room again, too animated to stand still, making Mama's hairdresser and stylist bark at me as they chased me around the dressing room comically.

I am Groucho Marx in Duck Soup. *Catch me if you can.*

Veronica tugged at the end of my corset, pulling me back to the mirror as if I were on a leash.

"Hey, ouch." I winced.

"Stand still, I said!"

It was not uncommon for my parents' employees to treat me like a glorified, well-bred poodle. Not that it mattered. I was going to kiss Angelo Bandini tonight. More specifically—I was going to let *him* kiss *me*.

I'd be lying if I said I hadn't thought about kissing Angelo every night since I returned a year ago from the Swiss boarding school my parents threw me in. At nineteen, Arthur and Sofia Rossi had officially decided to introduce me to the Chicagoan society and let me have my pick of a future husband from the hundreds of eligible Italian-American men who were affiliated with The Outfit. Tonight was going to kick-start a chain of events and social calls, but I already knew whom I wanted to marry.

Papa and Mama had informed me that college wasn't in the cards for me. I needed to attend to the task of finding the perfect husband, seeing as I was an only child and the sole heir to the Rossi businesses. Being the first woman in my family to ever earn a degree had been a dream of mine, but I was nowhere near dumb enough to defy them. Our maid, Clara, often said, "You don't need to meet a husband, Frankie. You need to meet your parents' expectations."

She wasn't wrong. I was born into a gilded cage. It was spacious, but locked, nonetheless. Trying to escape it was risking death. I didn't like being a prisoner, but I imagined I'd like it much less than being six feet under. And so I'd never even dared to peek through the bars of my prison and see what was on the other side.

My father, Arthur Rossi, was the head of The Outfit.

The title sounded painfully merciless for a man who'd braided my hair, taught me how to play the piano, and even shed a fierce tear at my London recital when I played the piano in front of an audience of thousands.

Angelo—you guessed it—was the perfect husband in the eyes of my parents. Attractive, well-heeled, and thoroughly moneyed. His family owned every second building on University Village, and most of the properties were used by my father for his many illicit projects.

I'd known Angelo since birth. We watched each other grow the way flowers blossom. Slowly, yet fast at the same time. During luxurious summer vacations and under the strict supervision of our relatives, Made Men—men who had been formally induced as full members of the mafia—and bodyguards.

Angelo had four siblings, two dogs, and a smile that would melt the Italian ice cream in your palm. His father ran the accounting firm that worked with my family, and we both took the same annual Sicilian vacations in Syracuse.

Over the years, I'd watched as Angelo's soft blond curls darkened and were tamed with a trim. How his glittering, ocean-blue eyes became less playful and broodier, hardened by the things his father no doubt had shown and taught him. How his voice had deepened, his Italian accent sharpened, and he began to fill his slender boy-frame with muscles and height and confidence. He became more mysterious and less impulsive, spoke less often, but when he did, his words liquefied my insides.

Falling in love was so tragic. No wonder it made people so sad.

And while I looked at Angelo as if he could melt ice cream, I wasn't the only girl who melted from his constant frown whenever he looked at me.

It made me sick to think that when I went back to my all-girls' Catholic school, he'd gone back to Chicago to hang out and talk and *kiss* other girls. But he'd always made me feel like I was The Girl. He sneaked flowers into my hair, let me sip some of his wine when no one was looking, and laughed with his eyes whenever I spoke. When his younger brothers taunted me, he flicked their ears and warned them off. And every summer, he found a way to steal a moment with me and kiss the tip of my nose.

"Francesca Rossi, you're even prettier than you were last summer."

"You always say that."

"And I always mean it. I'm not in the habit of wasting words."

"Tell me something important, then."

"You, my goddess, will one day be my wife."

I tended to every memory from each summer like it was a sacred garden, guarded it with fenced affection, and watered it until it grew to a fairy-tale-like recollection.

More than anything, I remembered how, each summer, I'd hold my breath until he snuck into my room, or the shop I'd visit, or the tree I'd read a book under. How he began to prolong our "moments" as the years ticked by and we entered adolescence, watching me with open amusement as I tried—and failed—to act like one of the boys when I was so painfully and brutally a girl.

I tucked the note deeper into my bra just as Veronica dug her meaty fingers into my ivory flesh, gathering the corset behind me from both ends and tightening it around my waist.

"To be nineteen and gorgeous again," she bellowed rather dramatically. The silky cream strings strained against one another, and I gasped. Only the royal crust of the Italian Outfit still used stylists and maids to get ready for an event. But as far as my parents were concerned—we were the Windsors. "Remember the days, Alma?"

The hairdresser snorted, pinning my bangs sideways as she completed my wavy chignon updo. "Honey, get off your high horse. You were pretty like a Hallmark card when you were nineteen. Francesca, here, is *The Creation of Adam*. Not the same league. Not even the same ball game."

I felt my skin flare with embarrassment. I had a sense that people enjoyed what they saw when they looked at me, but I was mortified by the idea of beauty. It was powerful yet slippery. A beautifully wrapped gift I was bound to lose one day. I didn't want to open it or ravish in its perks. It would only make parting ways with it more difficult.

The only person I wanted to notice my appearance tonight at the Art Institute of Chicago masquerade was Angelo. The theme of the gala was Gods and Goddesses through the Greek and Roman mythologies. I knew most women would show up as Aphrodite or Venus. Maybe Hera or Rhea, if originality struck them. Not me. I was Nemesis, the goddess of retribution. Angelo had always called me a deity, and tonight, I was going to justify my pet name by showing up as the most powerful goddess of them all.

It may have been silly in the 21st century to want to get married at nineteen in an arranged marriage, but in The Outfit, we all bowed to tradition. Ours happened to belong firmly in the 1800s.

"What was in the note?" Veronica clipped a set of velvety black wings to my back after sliding my dress over my body. It was a strapless gown the color of the clear summer sky with magnificent organza blue scallops. The tulle trailed two feet behind me, pooling like an ocean at my maids' feet. "You know, the one you stuck in your corset for safekeeping." She snickered, sliding golden feather-wing earrings into my ears.

"That"—I smiled dramatically, meeting her gaze in the mirror in front of us, my hand fluttering over my chest where the note rested—"is the beginning of the rest of my life."

CHAPTER ONE

Francesca

"I didn't know Venus had wings."

Angelo kissed the back of my hand at the doors to the Art Institute of Chicago. My heart sank before I pushed the silly disappointment aside. He was only baiting me. Besides, he looked so dazzlingly handsome in his tux tonight, I could forgive any mistake he made, short of coldhearted murder.

The men, unlike the women at the gala, wore a uniform of tuxedos and demi-masks. Angelo complemented his suit with a golden-leafed Venetian masquerade mask that took over most of his face. Our parents exchanged pleasantries while we stood in front of each other, drinking in every freckle and inch of flesh on one another. I didn't explain my Nemesis costume to him. We'd have time—an entire lifetime—to discuss mythology. I just needed to make sure that tonight we'd have another fleeting summer moment. Only this time, when he kissed my nose, I'd look up and lock our lips, and fate, together.

I am Cupid, shooting an arrow of love straight into Angelo's heart.

"You look more beautiful than the last time I saw you." Angelo clutched the fabric of his suit over where his heart beat, feigning surrender. Everyone around us had gone quiet, and I noticed our fathers staring at one another conspiratorially.

Two powerful, wealthy Italian-American families with strong mutual ties.

Don Vito Corleone would be proud.

"You saw me a week ago at Gianna's wedding." I fought the urge to lick my lips as Angelo stared me straight in the eyes.

"Weddings suit you, but having you all to myself suits you more," he said simply, throwing my heart into fifth gear, before twisting toward my father. "Mr. Rossi, may I escort your daughter to the table?"

My father clasped my shoulder from behind. I was only vaguely aware of his presence as a thick fog of euphoria engulfed me. "Keep your hands where I can see them."

"Always, sir."

Angelo and I entwined our arms together as one of the dozens of waiters showed us to our seats at the table clothed in gold and graced with fine black china. Angelo leaned and whispered in my ear, "Or at least until you're officially mine."

The Rossis and Bandinis had been placed a few seats away from each other—much to my disappointment, but not to my surprise. My father was always at the heart of every party and paid a pretty penny to have the best seats everywhere he went. Across from me, the governor of Illinois, Preston Bishop, and his wife fretted over the wine list. Next to them was a man I didn't know. He wore a simple all-black demi-mask and a tux that must've cost a fortune by its rich fabric and impeccable cut. He was seated next to a boisterous blonde in a white French tulle camisole gown. One of dozens of Venuses who arrived in the same number.

The man looked bored to death, swirling the whiskey in his glass as he ignored the beautiful woman by his side. When she tried to lean in and speak to him, he turned the other way and checked his phone, before completely losing interest in all things combined and staring at the wall behind me.

A pang of sorrow sliced through me. She deserved better than what he was offering. Better than a cold, foreboding man who sent chills down your spine without even looking at you.

I bet he could keep ice cream chilled for days on end.

"You and Angelo seem to be taken with one another," Papa remarked conversationally, glancing at my elbows, which were propped on the table. I withdrew them immediately, smiling politely.

"He's nice." I'd say 'super nice', but my father absolutely detested modern slang.

"He fits the puzzle," Papa snipped. "He asked if he could take you out next week, and I said yes. With Mario's supervision, of course."

Of course. Mario was one of Dad's dozens of musclemen. He had the shape and IQ of a brick. I had a feeling Papa wasn't going to let me sneak anywhere he couldn't see me tonight, precisely because he knew Angelo and I got along a little too well. Papa was overall supportive, but he wanted things to be done a certain way. A way most people my age would find backward or maybe even borderline barbaric. I wasn't stupid. I knew I was digging myself a hole by not fighting for my right for education and gainful employment. I knew that *I* should be the one to decide whom I wanted to marry.

But I also knew that it was his way or the highway. Breaking free came with the price of leaving my family behind—and my family was my entire world.

Other than tradition, The Chicagoan Outfit was vastly different from the version they portrayed in the movies. No gritty alleyways, slimy drug addicts, and bloody combats with the law. Nowadays, it was all about money laundering, acquisition, and recycling. My father openly courted the police, mingled with top-tier politicians, and even helped the FBI nail high-profile suspects.

In fact, that was precisely why we were here tonight. Papa had agreed to donate a staggering amount of money to a new charity foundation designed to help at-risk youth acquire a higher education.

Oh, irony, my loyal friend.

I sipped champagne and stared across the table at Angelo, making conversation with a girl named Emily whose father owned the biggest baseball stadium in Illinois. Angelo told her he was about to enroll into a master's program at Northwestern, while simultaneously joining his father's accounting firm. The truth was, he was going to launder money for my father and serve The Outfit until the rest of his days. I was getting lost in their conversation when Governor Bishop turned his attention to me.

"And what about you, Little Rossi? Are you attending college?"

Everyone around us was conversing and laughing, other than the man in front of me. He still ignored his date in favor of downing his drink and disregarding his phone, which flashed with a hundred messages a minute. Now that he looked at me, he also looked *through* me. I vaguely wondered how old he was. He looked older than me, but not quite Papa's age.

"Me?" I smiled courteously, my spine stiffening. I smoothed my napkin over my lap. My manners were flawless, and I was well versed in mindless conversations. I'd learned Latin, etiquette, and general knowledge at school. I could entertain anyone, from world leaders to a piece of chewed gum. "Oh, I just graduated a year ago. I'm now working toward expanding my social repertoire and forming connections here in Chicago."

"In other words, you neither work nor study," the man in front of me commented flatly, knocking his drink back and shooting my father a vicious grin. I felt my ears pinking as I blinked at my father for help. He mustn't have heard because he seemed to let the remark brush him by.

"Jesus Christ," the blond woman next to the rude man growled, reddening. He waved her off.

"We're among friends. No one would leak this."

Leak this? Who the hell was he?

I perked up, taking a sip of my drink. "There are other things I do, of course."

"Do share," he taunted in mock fascination. Our side of the

table fell silent. It was a grim kind of silence. The type that hinted a cringeworthy moment was upon us.

"I love charities…"

"That's not an actual activity. What do you *do?*"

Verbs, Francesca. Think verbs.

"I ride horses and enjoy gardening. I play the piano. I…ah, shop for all the things I need." I was making it worse, and I knew it. But he wouldn't let me divert the conversation elsewhere, and no one else stepped in to my rescue.

"Those are hobbies and luxuries. What's your contribution to society, Miss Rossi, other than supporting the US economy by buying enough clothes to cover North America?"

Utensils cluttered on fine china. A woman gasped. The leftovers of chatter stopped completely.

"That's enough," my father hissed, his voice frosty, his eyes dead. I flinched, but the man in the mask remained composed, straight-spined and, if anything, gaily amused at the turn the conversation had taken.

"I tend to agree, Arthur. I think I've learned everything there is to know about your daughter. And in a minute, no less."

"Have you forgotten your political and public duties at home, along with your manners?" my father remarked, forever well mannered.

The man grinned wolfishly. "On the contrary, Mr. Rossi. I think I remember them quite clearly, much to your future disappointment."

Preston Bishop and his wife extinguished the social disaster by asking me more questions about my upbringing in Europe, my recitals, and what I wanted to study (botany, though I wasn't stupid enough to point out that college was not in my cards). My parents smiled at my flawless conduct, and even the woman next to the rude stranger tentatively joined the conversation, talking about her European trip during her gap year. She was a journalist and had traveled all over the world. But no matter how nice everyone was, I couldn't shake the terrible humiliation I'd suffered under the sharp tongue of her date, who—by the way—got back to staring at the bottom of his freshly poured tumbler with an expression that oozed boredom.

I contemplated telling him he didn't need another drink but professional help could work wonders.

After dinner came the dancing. Each woman in attendance had a dance card filled with names of those who made an undisclosed bid. All the profits went to charity.

I went to check my card on the long table containing the names of the women who'd attended. My heart beat faster as I scanned it, spotting Angelo's name. My exhilaration was quickly replaced with dread when I realized my card was full to the brim with Italian-sounding names, much longer than the others scattered around it, and I would likely spend the rest of the night dancing until my feet were numb. Sneaking a kiss with Angelo was going to be tricky.

My first dance was with a federal judge. Then a raging Italian-American playboy from New York, who told me he'd come here just to see if the rumors about my looks were true. He kissed the hem of my skirt like a medieval duke before his friends dragged his drunken butt back to their table. *Please don't ask my father for a date*, I groaned inwardly. He seemed like the kind of rich tool who'd make my life some variation of *The Godfather*. The third was Governor Bishop, and the fourth was Angelo. It was a relatively short waltz, but I tried not to let it dampen my mood.

"There she is." Angelo's face lit up when he approached me and the governor for our dance.

Chandeliers seeped from the ceiling, and the marble floor sang with the clinking heels of the dancers. Angelo dipped his head to mine, taking my hand in his, and placing his other hand on my waist.

"You look beautiful. Even more so than two hours ago," he breathed, sending warm air to my face. Tiny, velvety butterfly wings tickled at my heart.

"Good to know, because I can't breathe in this thing." I laughed, my eyes wildly searching his. I knew he couldn't kiss me now, and a dash of panic washed over the butterflies, drowning them in dread. What if we couldn't catch each other at all? Then the note would be useless.

This wooden box will save me or kill me.

"I'd love to give you mouth-to-mouth whenever you're out of breath." He skimmed my face, his throat bobbing with a swallow. "But I would start with a simple date next week, if you are interested."

"I'm interested," I said much too quickly. He laughed, his forehead falling to mine.

"Would you like to know when?"

"When we're going out?" I asked dumbly.

"That, too. Friday, by the way. But I meant when was the point in which I knew you were going to be my wife?" he asked without missing a beat. I could barely bring myself to nod. I wanted to cry. I felt his hand tightening around my waist and realized I was losing my balance.

"It was the summer you turned sixteen. I was twenty. Cradle snatcher." He laughed. "We arrived at our Sicilian cabin late. I was rolling my suitcase by the river next to our adjoined cabins when I spotted you threading flowers into a crown on the dock. You were smiling at the flowers, so pretty and elusive, and I didn't want to break the spell by talking to you. Then the wind swiped the flowers everywhere. You didn't even hesitate. You jumped headfirst into the river and retrieved every single flower that had drifted from the crown, even though you knew it wouldn't survive. Why did you do that?"

"It was my mother's birthday," I admitted. "Failure was not an option. The birthday crown turned out pretty, by the way."

My eyes drifted to the useless space between our chests.

"Failure is not an option," Angelo repeated thoughtfully.

"You kissed my nose in the restroom of that restaurant that day," I pointed out.

"I remember."

"Are you going to steal a nose-kiss tonight?" I asked.

"I would never steal from you, Frankie. I'd buy my kiss from you at full price, down to the penny," he sparred good-naturedly, winking at me, "but I'm afraid that between your shockingly full card and my obligations to mingle with every Made Man who was lucky enough to snatch an invitation to this thing, a raincheck may be required. Don't worry, I've already told Mario I'd tip him generously for taking his time fetching our car from the valet on Friday."

The trickle of panic was now a full-blown downpour of terror. If he wasn't going to kiss me tonight, the note's prediction would go to waste.

"Please?" I tried to smile brighter, masking my terror with eagerness. "My legs could use the break."

He bit his fist and laughed. "So many sexual innuendos, Francesca."

I didn't know if I wanted to cry with despair or scream with frustration. Probably both. The song hadn't ended yet, and we were still swaying in each other's arms, lulled inside a dark spell, when I felt a firm, strong hand plastered on the bare part of my upper back.

"I believe it's my turn." I heard the low voice booming behind me. I turned around with a scowl to find the rude man in the black demi-mask staring back at me.

He was tall—six-foot-three or four—with tousled ink-black hair smoothed back to tantalizing perfection. His sinewy, hard physique was slim yet broad. His eyes were pebble gray, slanted, and menacing, and his too-square jaw framed his bowed lips perfectly, giving his otherwise too-handsome appearance a gritty edge. A scornful, impersonal smirk graced his lips and I wanted to slap it off his face. He was obviously still amused with what he thought was a bunch of nonsense I spat out at the dinner table. And we clearly had an audience as I noticed half the room was now glaring at us with open interest. The women looked at him like hungry sharks in a fishbowl. The men had half-curved grins of hilarity.

"Mind your hands," Angelo snarled when the song changed, and he could no longer keep me in his arms.

"Mind your business," the man deadpanned.

"Are you sure you're on my card?" I turned to the man with a polite yet distant smile. I was still disoriented from the exchange with Angelo when the stranger pulled me against his hard body and pressed a possessive hand lower than socially acceptable on my back, a second from groping my butt.

"Answer me," I hissed.

"My bid on your card was the highest," he replied dryly.

"The bids are anonymous. You don't know how much other people have paid," I kept my lips pursed to keep myself from yelling.

"I know it's nowhere near the realm of what this dance is worth."

Un-freaking-believable.

We began to waltz around the room as other couples were not only spinning and mingling but also stealing envious glances at us. Naked, raw ogles that told me that whomever the blonde he'd come to the masquerade with was, she wasn't his wife. And that I might have been all the rage in The Outfit, but the rude man was in high demand, too.

I was stiff and cold in his arms, but he didn't seem to notice—or mind. He knew how to waltz better than most men, but he was technical, and lacked warmth and Angelo's playfulness.

"Nemesis." He took me by surprise, his rapacious gaze stripping me bare. "Distributing glee and dealing misery. Seems at odds with the submissive girl who entertained Bishop and his horsey wife at the table."

I choked on my own saliva. Did he just call the governor's wife horsey? And *me* submissive? I looked away, ignoring the addictive scent of his cologne, and the way his marble body felt against mine.

"Nemesis is my spirit animal. She was the one to lure Narcissus to a pool where he saw his own reflection and died of vanity. Pride is a terrible illness." I flashed him a taunting smirk.

"Some of us could use catching it." He bared his straight white teeth.

"Arrogance is a disease. Compassion is the cure. Most gods didn't like Nemesis, but that's because she had a backbone."

"Do you?" He arched a dark eyebrow.

"Do I…?" I blinked, the courteous grin on my face crumpling. He was even ruder when we were alone.

"Have a backbone," he provided. He stared at me so boldly and intimately, it felt like he breathed fire into my soul. I wanted to step out of his touch and jump into a pool full of ice.

"Of course, I do," I responded, my spine stiffening. "What's with the manners? Were you raised by wild coyotes?"

"Give me an example," he said, ignoring my quip. I was beginning to draw away from him, but he jerked me back into his arms. The glitzy ballroom distorted into a backdrop, and even though I was starting to notice that the man behind the demi-mask was unusually beautiful, the ugliness of his behavior was the only thing that stood out.

I am a warrior and a lady…and a sane person who can deal with this horrid man.

"I really like Angelo Bandini." I dropped my voice, slicing my gaze from his eyes and toward the table where Angelo's family had been seated. My father was sitting a few seats away, staring at us coldly, surrounded by Made Men who chatted away.

"And see, in my family, we have a tradition dating back ten generations. Prior to her wedding, a Rossi bride is to open a wooden chest—carved and made by a witch who lived in my ancestors' Italian village—and read three notes written to her by the last Rossi girl to marry. It's kind of a good luck charm mixed with a talisman and a bit of fortunetelling. I stole the chest tonight and opened one of the notes, all so I could rush fate. It said that tonight I was going to be kissed by the love of my life, and well…" I drew my lower lip into my mouth and sucked it, peering under my eyelashes at Angelo's empty seat. The man stared at me stoically, as though I was a foreign film he couldn't understand. "I'm going to kiss him tonight."

"That's your backbone?"

"When I have an ambition, I go for it."

A conceited frown crinkled his mask, as if to say I was a

complete and utter moron. I looked him straight in the eye. My father taught me that the best way to deal with men like him was to confront, not run. Because, this man? He'd chase.

Yes, I believe in that tradition.

No, I don't care what you think.

Then it occurred to me that over the course of the evening, I'd offered him my entire life story and didn't even ask for his name. I didn't want to know, but etiquette demanded that I at least pretend.

"I forgot to ask who you are."

"That's because you didn't care," he quipped.

He regarded me with the same taciturnity. It was an oxymoron of fierce boredom. I said nothing because it was true.

"Senator Wolfe Keaton." The words rolled off his tongue sharply.

"Aren't you a little young to be a senator?" I complimented him on principal to see if I could defrost the thick layer of asshole he'd built around himself. Some people just needed a tight hug. Around the neck. Wait, I was actually thinking about choking him. Not the same thing.

"Thirty. Celebrated in September. Got elected this November."

"Congratulations." *I couldn't care less.* "You must be thrilled."

"Over the goddamn moon." He drew me even closer, pulling my body flush against his.

"Can I ask you a personal question?" I cleared my throat.

"Only if I can do the same," he shot.

I considered it.

"You can."

He dipped his chin down, giving me permission to continue.

"Why did you ask to dance with me, not to mention paid good money for the dubious pleasure, if you obviously think everything I stand for is shallow and distasteful?"

For the first time tonight, something that resembled a smile crossed his face. It looked unnatural, almost illusory. I decided he was not in the habit of laughing often. Or at all.

"I wanted to see for myself if the rumors about your beauty were true."

That again. I resisted the urge to stomp on his foot. Men were such simple creatures. But, I reminded myself, Angelo thought I was pretty even *before*. When I still had braces, a blanket of freckles covering my nose and cheeks, and unruly, mousy-brown hair I had yet to learn how to tame.

"My turn," he said, without voicing his verdict on my looks. "Have you picked out names for your children with your Bangini yet?"

It was an odd question, one that was no doubt designed to make fun of me. I wanted to turn around and walk away from him right there and then. But the music was fading, and it was stupid to throw in the towel on an encounter that would end shortly. Besides, everything that came out of my mouth seemed to bother him. Why ruin a perfect strike?

"*Bandini.* And yes, I have, as a matter of fact. Christian, Joshua, and Emmaline."

Okay, I might've picked the sexes, too. That was what happened when you had too much time on your hands.

Now the stranger in the demi-mask was grinning fully, and if my anger didn't make it feel as though pure venom ran through my veins, I could appreciate his commercial-worthy dental hygiene. Instead of bowing his head and kissing my hand, as the brochure for the masquerade had indicated was compulsory, he took a step back and saluted me in mockery. "Thank you, Francesca Rossi."

"For the dance?"

"For the insight."

The night became progressively worse after the cursed dance with Senator Keaton. Angelo was sitting at a table with a group of men, locked in a heated argument, as I was tossed from one pair of arms to the other, mingling and smiling and losing my hope and sanity, one song at a time. I couldn't believe the absurdity of my situation. I stole my mother's wooden box—the one and only thing I'd ever stolen—to read my note and get the courage to show Angelo how I felt. If he wasn't going to kiss me tonight—if *no one* was going to kiss me tonight—did that mean I was doomed to live a loveless life?

Three hours into the masquerade, I managed to slip out the entrance of the museum and stood on the wide concrete steps, breathing in the crisp spring night. My last dance had to leave early. Thankfully, his wife had gone into labor.

I hugged my own arms, braving the Chicago wind and laughing sadly at nothing in particular. One yellow cab zipped by the tall buildings, and a couple huddled together were zigzagging giddily to their destination.

Click.

It sounded like someone shut down the universe. The lampposts along the street turned off unexpectedly, and all the light faded from view.

It was morbidly beautiful; the only light visible was the shimmering lonely crescent above my head. I felt an arm wrap around my waist from behind. The touch was confident and strong, curving around my body like the man it belonged to had studied it for a while.

For years.

I turned around. Angelo's gold and black masquerade mask stared back at me. All the air left my lungs, my body turning into goo, slacking in his arms with relief.

"You came," I whispered.

His thumb brushed my cheeks. A soft, wordless nod.

Yes.

He leaned down and pressed his lips to mine. My heart squealed inside my chest.

Shut the front door. This is happening.

I grabbed the edges of his suit, pulling him closer. I'd imagined our kiss countless times before, but I'd never expected it to feel like this. Like home. Like oxygen. Like forever. His full lips fluttered over mine, sending hot air into my mouth, and he explored, and nipped, and bit my lower lip before claiming my mouth with his, slanting his head sideways and dipping down for a ferocious caress.

He opened his mouth, his tongue peeking out and swiping mine. I returned the favor. He drew me close, devouring me slowly and passionately, pressing his hand to the small of my back and groaning into my mouth like I was water in the desert. I moaned into his lips and licked every corner of his mouth with zero expertise, feeling embarrassed, aroused, and more importantly, free.

Free. In his arms. Was there anything more liberating than feeling loved?

I swayed in the security of his arms, kissing him for a good three minutes before my senses crawled back into my foggy brain. He tasted of whiskey and not the wine Angelo had been drinking all night. He was significantly taller than me—taller than Angelo—even if not by much. Then his aftershave drifted into my nose, and I remembered the icy pebble eyes, raw power, and dark sensuality that licked flames of anger inside my guts. I took a slow breath and felt the burn inside me.

No.

I tore my lips from his and stumbled back, tripping over a stair. He grabbed my wrist and yanked me back to prevent my fall but made no effort to resume our kiss.

"You!" I cried out, my voice shaking. With perfect timing, the streetlamps came back to life, illuminating the sharp curves of his face.

Angelo had soft curves over a defined jaw. This man was all harsh streaks and cut edges. He looked nothing like my crush, even with a demi-mask on.

How did he do that? *Why* did he do that? Tears pooled in my eyes, but I held them back. I didn't want to give this complete stranger the satisfaction of seeing me crumple.

"How dare you," I said quietly, biting my cheeks until the taste of warm blood filled my mouth to keep from screaming.

He took a step back, sliding Angelo's mask off—God knows how he got his hands on it—and tossing it on the stairs like it was contaminated. His unmasked face was unveiled like a piece of art.

Brutal and intimidating, it demanded my attention. I took a step sideways, putting more space between us.

"How? Easily." He was so dismissive; he was flirting with open disdain. "A smart girl, however, would have asked for the *why*."

"The why?" I scoffed, refusing to let the last five minutes register. I'd been kissed by someone else. Angelo—according to my family tradition—was not going to be the love of my life. This jerk, however…

Now it was his turn to take a step sideways. His broad back had been blocking the entrance to the museum, so I failed to see who was standing there, his shoulders slack, his mouth agape, his face gloriously unmasked, drinking in the scene.

Angelo took one look at my swollen lips, turned around, and stalked back in with Emily running after him.

The Wolfe was no longer in sheep's clothing as he made his way up the stairs, giving me his back. When he reached the doors, his date poured out as if on cue. Wolfe took her arm in his and led her downstairs, not sparing me a look as I wilted on the cement stairs. I could hear his date murmuring something, his dry response to her, and her laughter ringing in the air like a wind chime.

When the door to their limo slammed shut, my lips stung so bad I had to touch them to make sure he didn't set them on fire. The power outage wasn't coincidental. He did it.

He took the power. *My* power.

I yanked the note out of my corset and threw it against the stair, stomping over it like a tantrum-prone kid.

Wolfe Keaton was a kiss thief.

He just wanted a decent book to read ...

Not too much to ask, is it? It was in 1935 when Allen Lane, Managing Director of Bodley Head Publishers, stood on a platform at Exeter railway station looking for something good to read on his journey back to London. His choice was limited to popular magazines and poor-quality paperbacks – the same choice faced every day by the vast majority of readers, few of whom could afford hardbacks. Lane's disappointment and subsequent anger at the range of books generally available led him to found a company – and change the world.

'We believed in the existence in this country of a vast reading public for intelligent books at a low price, and staked everything on it'
Sir Allen Lane, 1902–1970, founder of Penguin Books

The quality paperback had arrived – and not just in bookshops. Lane was adamant that his Penguins should appear in chain stores and tobacconists, and should cost no more than a packet of cigarettes.

Reading habits (and cigarette prices) have changed since 1935, but Penguin still believes in publishing the best books for everybody to enjoy. We still believe that good design costs no more than bad design, and we still believe that quality books published passionately and responsibly make the world a better place.

So wherever you see the little bird – whether it's on a piece of prize-winning literary fiction or a celebrity autobiography, political tour de force or historical masterpiece, a serial-killer thriller, reference book, world classic or a piece of pure escapism – you can bet that it represents the very best that the genre has to offer.

Whatever you like to read – trust Penguin.